PRAISE FOR

Sweet Nothings

"Sparkling, witty, and poignant.
Sweet Nothings is absolutely delicious!"

—Jane Porter, author of *The Good Daughter*

PRAISE FOR

Something New

"She writes with sparkle and humor."

—Sally Koslow

"A breezy read."

—*Publishers Weekly*

sweet nothings

Janis Thomas

BERKLEY BOOKS, NEW YORK

THE BERKLEY PUBLISHING GROUP
Published by the Penguin Group
Penguin Group (USA) Inc.
375 Hudson Street, New York, New York 10014, USA

USA | Canada | UK | Ireland | Australia | New Zealand | India | South Africa | China

Penguin Books Ltd., Registered Offices: 80 Strand, London WC2R 0RL, England
For more information about the Penguin Group, visit penguin.com.

This book is an original publication of The Berkley Publishing Group.

Library of Congress Cataloging-in-Publication Data

Thomas, Janis.
Sweet Nothings / Janis Thomas.
pages cm
ISBN 978-0-425-26482-9
1. Marital conflict—Fiction.   2. Adultery—Fiction.   3. Life change events—Fiction.
4. Domestic Fiction.   I. Title.
PS3620.H62796S93   2013
813'.6—dc23   2013003091

PUBLISHING HISTORY
Berkley trade paperback edition: July 2013

PRINTED IN THE UNITED STATES OF AMERICA

10 9 8 7 6 5 4 3 2 1

Cover design by Lesley Worrell
Book design by Laura K. Corless

In loving memory of Elena "Miss Elle" Parrino
Beautiful cakes, beautiful heart.

ACKNOWLEDGMENTS

Like my character Ruby, I have been making cakes for almost twenty-five years, but unlike her, I have never done so on a professional level. It's hard work and the hours are long. My hat is off to those who devote their lives to making beautiful, edible creations that bring so much joy to others.

As a writer, I have been blessed with amazing individuals who believe in me, support me, and make my writing better. Wendy Sherman, my incredible agent, has impeccable taste in all things (including restaurants) and I am honored that she represents me. I couldn't ask for a better champion. Thanks also to Jackie Cantor, my editor at Berkley Books. Her thoughtful insights are invaluable, her suggestions are always right on the mark, and her kindness and compassion on a personal level are a blessing to me. (Can't wait for the sushi education to continue!) Thank you, Kim Perel at Wendy Sherman Associates, and Amanda Ng and the rest of the staff at Berkley Books for bringing *Sweet Nothings* to life.

I am grateful for my family, the wacky, wonderful and strong-willed group of people I have been fortunate enough to be around my entire life. Thanks to my parents, Sharon and Lenerd, for always encouraging my creative pursuits even if they both secretly thought I should go to law school; to my siblings, Mark, Craig, and Sharilyn for their love and support and for allowing me to annoy them from the time I was born; to Jacqueline, my niece, for loving me despite the fact that I wear sneakers and rarely pluck my eyebrows; to my aunt Hilary for the way we can laugh for fifteen minutes over a single word (Special!); to Larry, for reading my books even though he doesn't like to admit it. To Brian, HaiQi, my aunts, uncles, cousins, nieces, nephews, and in-laws . . . I love you all!

Thanks to the family I've chosen: Linda Beth Coler-Fields, who likes New York in June and has been known to cause trouble in the sewers; Penny Thiedemann, whose Penny-thoughts are legendary; Jordan "Uncle J-man" Fields, who gives the best hugs ever; Stefanie Morse, whose friendship hasn't changed despite the years. Thanks to Lisa Tsuda and her exceptionally keen eye. Thanks to the Southern California Writers Conference and to all my fellow writers who plant themselves in front of the computer on a daily basis in the hopes of creating stories that will sweep readers away. Thanks to all the Hawes Moms, who are inspirations to me on a daily basis. And again, to the Friends of Fiction and Sometimes Non Book Club.

And, as always, thanks to Alex for his love and devotion to our family, and for biting his tongue (most of the time) about my less-than-spectacular housekeeping skills. And to my children, A.J. and Elle, who constantly amaze me. I pray that I am the mom you both deserve.

1

The Soufflé Collapses

My forty-fourth birthday is in less than three months. I haven't given it much thought up until now. But I just decided that for the first time in twenty years, I won't be making my birthday cake. This is a little gift I'm giving myself, like the Franklin Covey day planner I paid way too much for, or the black truffle oil I couldn't steer my shopping cart away from, or the gloriously slutty, lace push-up bra I bought after a root canal when I was still a bit loopy from the nitrous oxide. But I definitely think I deserve this gift. In fact, I am going to need to give myself a slew of gifts in the near future. Because at this moment my husband of eighteen years is leaving me for another woman.

Walter—that's my husband—is currently circling the cooktop island of our kitchen like a hamster on a horizontal Habitrail wheel. He is talking, probably saying something important, but I'm having difficulty concentrating on his words because I'm fixated on the chartreuse polo shirt he's wearing. I know for a fact that I didn't buy this shirt for him. It looks terrible against his pale skin, making him look like he has an incurable disease (don't I *wish* just about now). And along with the shirt, his hair has been gelled and carefully tousled in an attempt at casual chic. And because I'm certain that Walter has never even heard the term "casual chic," I can only assume the trendy hairdo and the green shirt have been foisted upon him by his new—God help me—amour.

"You want me to be happy, right?" he asks, and I think, *Is this a trick question?*

"I, uh . . ." I clear my throat, hoping to dislodge my heart, or whichever organ has wedged itself into my esophagus. "I thought we were happy, Walter," I manage to say.

"Ha!" he cries, pumping a fist into the air as though he just got a difficult answer correct on *Jeopardy!* "You *thought* we were happy. That's just it. *You* thought we were happy. *I* thought we were happy. Everyone thought we were happy."

"And we're not?"

He stops in his tracks, much to my relief, since watching him go around and around is making me nauseous. Perhaps his telling me he's leaving has something to do with my roiling insides, but I can focus on him more easily when he's standing in one place.

"Not what?" he asks.

"What?"

He looks bewildered for a moment. "And we're not what?"

I squint at him, suddenly confused myself. "Happy?" I offer.

"Right!" he exclaims, relieved. "We're not. Happy."

"Okay," I concede, although with little enthusiasm.

"See? You agree with me!" he says triumphantly. "I knew you weren't happy!"

I resist the urge to slap a palm against my forehead. "Walter, this is *your* show. I'm just a spectator."

"Ha!" Again with the "ha!" One more and I am going to smack him. He's got it coming, dropping this bomb on me at six forty-five on a Saturday morning. At least he didn't have to wake me to give me the news. I was already in the kitchen, testing out a new recipe for a white chocolate soufflé with raspberry Grand Marnier sauce. I was just about to pull the large ramekin out of the oven when he swooped in and completely blindsided me with his announcement. Needless to say, I was so flabbergasted by his revelation that I let the oven door slam shut, which knocked the life—and air—out of my beautiful soufflé. Its deflated corpse now decorates my granite counter.

"This is exactly the problem!" he says, jabbing a finger in my general direction. "If you weren't happy all this time, why didn't you say anything?"

"I didn't know I wasn't happy, Walter." Okay, maybe this is just a teensy bit of a lie. But honestly, after eighteen years of marriage, you don't wake up every morning singing "I've Got the World on a String." It's more like "What's It All About, Alfie?"—substituting your husband's name for the Alfie part, although "What's It All About, Walter?" doesn't have quite the same ring to it. My life, up until seventeen minutes ago, was just fine, thank you very much. Not a roller-coaster kind of life, or a leaping out of an airplane kind of existence, but a nice, calm, dependable carousel, with pretty horses and an amiable melody coming from the calliope and a few flashing lights to give the illusion of excitement every now and then.

"Oh, you knew, all right, Ruby. You've known all along! You don't even wear a wedding ring, for God's sake!"

He's right. I haven't since I opened the bakery. A ring is a liability when my hands are in dough half the day. I bring it out for special occasions, although I can't quite remember the last time I wore it. "You know the reason for that, Walter," I say.

"Yes, I do. What I don't know is why you married me in the first place!"

"Because I love you?" I offer.

To which he responds with—you guessed it—"Ha!"

That's it! In a fit of fury I rush at him, snarling, fists flailing, and proceed to use him as a human punching bag for the next ten minutes, hitting him with all of my strength and pent-up aggression until he is nothing more than a shell of broken bones on my kitchen floor.

Okay, not really. But I do heave a sigh. A really *violent* sigh.

"I don't think you ever truly loved me, Ruby. Maybe you thought you did. Maybe I thought I loved you." His words have the impact of a sucker punch to the stomach and I am at a loss for a reply. "I just didn't know the difference between what you and I had and the real thing. But I do now."

"With *her*?" I ask because I can't help myself.

"I'm forty-seven years old, Ruby. Two and a half years from fifty. I don't have time to pussyfoot around. I have an opportunity to be with someone who is . . . who could very well be my . . . my . . ."

Don't say it, Walter. Please don't say it.

". . . soul mate."

You said it! Well, fuck! Excuse the expression.

"I never meant for it to happen. I swear. I fought it, out of respect for you."

"How chivalrous of you."

"Out of respect for *us,* okay? I pretended that it was nothing. That I was projecting. That I was having a midlife crisis. But I can't play this game anymore. I want to be with Cheryl and she wants to be with me."

Cheryl? "Cheryl? The blonde in accounting?"

Walter swallows, his Adam's apple bobbing up and down. He nods wordlessly.

I gape at Walter, incredulous. Not because I know Cheryl or because she's been a guest in my home for holiday parties or the occasional dinner or because she took my family out on her father's yacht last summer. But because she is not the twentysomething, perky-breasted, clueless bimbo I pictured my husband leaving me for. Cheryl's forty, if she's a day. She has to dye her hair just like I do, and take women's over-forty vitamins, just like me, and probably has a drawer full of plastic-surgery brochures just like mine. And unless she was lured by the classy UV-coated tri-fold from Dr. "Firming" Phil Feinstein and recently bought herself a tummy tuck and some lipo, I'm fairly certain she outweighs me by at least ten pounds.

He's leaving me for Cheryl?

Of course, she does dress better than I do, with her designer business suits and complementary accessories, and her hair is always perfectly coiffed, her makeup in place even at four in the afternoon. I glance down at my apron and my pink pajama bottoms covered with smiley frogs and lily pads and my clenched hands that are flaking with dry skin from washing twenty-five pans a day, and my ragged fingernails that I keep extremely short so that batter and dough can't get underneath and cause a fungus. I think of Cheryl's long, acrylic, French-tipped nails and try to make myself feel better by telling myself that women with perfect fingernails cannot possibly make white chocolate soufflés with raspberry Grand Marnier sauce. I glance at the counter and the ramekin I filled about forty minutes ago and I think, *Well, neither can I.*

"She makes me happy, Rube."

I want to scream and shriek and hurl various culinary objects at my husband. The KitchenAid mixer we got for our fifteenth anniversary, perhaps, or one of the copper pots hanging above the stove, or better yet, the very sharp knife I use for dicing and mincing. In my mind's eye, I see myself grab the knife from the block, take aim, and chuck it at Walter with the skill of Lara Croft. I witness his subsequent muted "ugh" and the look of surprise on his face as he realizes there is a very long blade piercing his heart; see him drop to the floor like a sack of cheating, wife-abandoning potatoes. But again, it's only a fantasy, because in reality how would I get the blood out of the grout? Besides, with my luck, Walter wouldn't die but would "partially" recover, and when the cops hauled me off to prison for attempted murder, who would end up raising my children? *Cheryl.* That's who.

Wait a minute. He can't be serious. I mean, honestly, he cannot be serious!

"You can't be serious, Walter," I say calmly.

His face twists into a grimace. "And why not? Because it's not *like* me? Because I'm so damn predictable? Because I always do the right thing?"

I fumble with the tie on my apron, contemplating how to answer him in a way that won't sound hostile or condescending. "Well, uh, yes."

"Ha!" he fires back, and this time I just shrug. "That's it, Ruby! I'm not that person anymore. Maybe I never was. Maybe I've felt my whole life like breaking out of the chains that imprisoned me, but I never had the guts or the opportunity or the support of someone who wanted me to!"

He squints at me as though I am the warden of the prison that has been his life. In all fairness, I probably have been. From the moment we met twenty years ago, I placed Walter in a category: the nice-simple-reliable-normal-sane-and-wonderfully-comfortable category. How *shameful* of me.

"But Cheryl wants me to be who I am, to do the things I've always wanted to do, like go on safari and swim with dolphins and bungee jump."

"Since when do you want to bungee jump?"

"I don't!" he cries. "But if I ever want to, Cheryl will support me and encourage me, not tell me to make sure my life insurance policy is paid up."

"But you're afraid of heights, Walter."

"The point is, I'm a different person with her. I'm the man I always wanted to be. If that's wrong, so be it. I never imagined I could feel this way. And I'm not giving it up, no matter the consequences."

I stand by the sink in stunned silence, praying that the sudden burning of my cheeks is not due to an oncoming hot flash. Bad enough my husband is casting me aside for free-spirited-patron-saint-of-the-rebirthed-middle-aged-man Cheryl. All I need right now is to be consumed with a dizzying hormonal firestorm and the accompanying racehorse sweats. I swipe my fingers across my forehead and am relieved when they come away dry.

Stay calm, Ruby, I tell myself. *Treat this like a recipe. What ingredients do you need to save a marriage?*

My eyes slide to the spice rack at the back of the counter. To buy some time, I grab the rack and pull it toward me, then empty the various bottles out onto the granite.

"What are you doing?" Walter asks.

"Organizing the spice rack," I say evenly.

"Now?" His voice is incredulous. "Right this minute? While I'm leaving you?"

Allspice, basil, bay leaves, cardamom, cinnamon, cumin, dill, fennel seed, ginger . . . I really need a separate rack for herbs . . .

"You organized that last week!" he says accusingly.

I set the ginger down and turn to face him. "I get it, Walter. You want more out of your life." I swallow. "Out of your *love* life. But this isn't just about you and me. It's about our family. You know? Our kids. What about them?"

As if on cue, my fourteen-year-old son, Kevin, staggers into the kitchen and makes his way to the refrigerator like a zombie in a horror movie, utterly unaware that his father and I are present. If I didn't know my son better, I would think he's been on an all-night bender. But this is simply the way he greets each day, sliding into consciousness with the reluctance of a vampire being coaxed into the sun.

Walter glances at Kevin wordlessly as he opens the fridge and retrieves a carton of milk. After pouring some into a glass without spilling a drop, which is a miracle in my opinion since his eyes are currently closed, Kevin turns and leans against the counter.

"Mornin'," he mumbles. His sandy-blond hair is in need of a trim, with various strands sticking straight out from his head like clumpy antennae. He downs the milk, stifles a burp, then pulls his eyes halfway open and squints at me. "Whazzup?"

"Your father is leaving," I tell him in a hoarse whisper.

Kevin nods toward his father. "Bye." He sets the glass down, ambles to the den, and plops down onto the couch. Thirty seconds later, I hear him start to snore.

I envy my son the ease with which he can slip into slumber. At this moment I would give anything to be able to climb under my covers and sleep for about four months. But sleep has never been a friend to me, and I'm certain it would elude me now more than ever, snickering at me as I tossed and turned and prayed for the blissful ignorance of its embrace.

I see Walter glance at his watch. "I have to go," he says simply.

"Early date?" I ask, and although I am trying for snide, my words sound needy and pathetic to my own ears.

Walter takes a deep breath and straightens to his full height of five seven and a half. He looks me in the eye and says, "I'm sorry, Ruby."

You will be! I want to yell at him, using a very theatrical, B-movie-bad-guy kind of voice, but my lips remain closed. He lingers for a few seconds, as if waiting for me to say something, then drops his head and moves toward the hallway. He disappears around the corner, and a moment later, I hear the front door open and close.

I glance at the clock on the microwave and see that it is 7:17. I can feel my heartbeat in my throat, pumping at double speed, and now the sweating—or what I lovingly refer to as High Tide—begins, beads of perspiration popping out first on my forehead, then a millisecond later on my upper lip.

Oh God, a hot flash.

I have only recently started experiencing this fabulous symptom of middle age, and I'm never prepared for it. But there's no avoiding this one. The wave will wash down my entire body, all the way to my toenails, and if you think that toenails do not sweat, you have obviously never been perimenopausal. Turning toward the sink, I grasp the counter and gaze out at the blazing summer morning. On the other side of my window, in the beautiful garden that Enrique and his cousins lovingly tend to every Wednesday, birds are singing their lilting morning melodies, squirrels are scampering up trees and over fences, and the neighbors' cat is lolling about on our lawn. It's *Wild Kingdom* out there. But the pastoral scene does nothing to calm me down or cool my innards.

I open the tap and make a cup of my hands, then splash water on my face, over and over again, as I feel the perspiration trickle down the middle of my back, down and through my butt crack (wonderful!), on the backs of my knees, my feet, and—yes—my toenails. And as I unsuccessfully try to cool myself down, one thought careens through my head: *Walter left me for Cheryl.*

I just cannot wrap my mind around this, can't make sense of the last thirty minutes. Disbelieving, disillusion-provoked rage boils up inside of me. *I'll kill him. I'll kill her. I'll kill them both! No, death would be too kind. I'll kill his shrink! And her . . . her . . .* manicurist!

"Mom?"

I quickly shut off the water, along with my emotions, and turn to see Kevin standing in the breakfast nook with his arms crossed over his chest, stifling a yawn.

"Hi, honey," I say, infusing my voice with false cheer and pasting on a smile that probably makes me look like the Crypt Keeper. At least the inferno that was charbroiling me from the inside has ratcheted down a notch. But my stomach feels as though I was a recent guest on *Fear Factor.* I try not to think about horse intestines and maggots and duck eggs with the little chicks still inside. "You're up early."

"Yeah," he agrees. "Luke's picking me up at eight. Big swell from Hurricane Emily last week."

I nod, although I don't see how one can use the words "swell" and "hurricane" in the same sentence. You gotta love surfers.

"Does the beach cleanup start today?" Kevin and his friends have undertaken a two-week initiative to remove all trash from the Pelican Point shoreline. I am impressed by their commitment and relieved that my son has an ecological conscience at such an early age. Plus, it keeps him occupied and off drugs, hallelujah.

"Nah. That starts Monday. Just riding the waves this morning. But the hurricane is going to bring in a lot of shi— stuff with it, so we're going to have our hands full." He stops talking and gazes at me. "Are you okay, Mom? You look kind of like you're going to hurl."

I am not going to hurl. I am not going to hurl. What idiot came up with the expression "hurl" anyway?

"I'm fine, Kev. No hurling happening around here."

Kevin looks past me at the ceramic-encased hockey puck on the counter. "Is that breakfast?"

"Uh, no," I say. That's when tears threaten, and as I attempt to keep myself together for the sake of my son, I realize that life is a lot like soufflés. You gather your ingredients, the scant flour that somehow holds the delicate batter together and the flavorings that you carefully add—too little and there will be no taste, too much and your resulting product will be cloying—then you patiently beat your egg whites to shiny peaks, lightly fold everything together, and put your ramekin in the oven. And even when you get that far and you've done everything just so, the tiniest mistake— like slamming the oven door, for example, or laying the ramekin down on the counter a touch too hard, or cursing at just above the proper decibel level—and that soufflé will drop and shrivel like an erection in an ice bath.

So, too, have I gathered the ingredients of my life and carefully flavored them, patiently beat my whites, and lovingly folded together all the elements of my existence. Put my proverbial batter into the appropriately prepared ramekin and gently placed my world into the oven. And yet I must have done something wrong, made some false move or ignored an important step in the recipe, because my life has suddenly collapsed around me into a charred, inedible ruin.

"I think I'll just have some cereal," Kevin states, absently scratching his underarm.

I nod mutely, then race out of the kitchen, past the corkboard overflowing with notes from Walter, invitations addressed to *Mr. and Mrs. McMillan,* and a coupon for a vitamin supplement that ensures prostate health, and rush to the downstairs bathroom where I *hurl* to within an inch of my life.

2

Tapioca Pudding

For as long as I've been baking, which is so many years now that I can refer to this block of time not only in decades, but as a fraction of a *century,* I've had a tendency to compare people with desserts.

Walter—if I may use my very recently estranged husband as an example—always seemed like shortbread to me. A simple cookie. A reliable cookie. Ordinary yet hardy. Made from three universally loved ingredients. The kind of cookie you can bring to any occasion and everyone will eat one and like it, although they probably won't remark upon it later, because it's not a triple fudge brownie. I realize this comparison might sound unflattering, but honestly, I *love* shortbread.

My son, Kevin, is a white-chocolate-macadamia-nut cookie. A little nutty but always sweet, and always a delight. My daughter, Colleen, who I have not yet seen this morning because, at sixteen, she is a great believer in beauty sleep, is definitely a seven-layer-dream-bar kind of girl. She can be any or all layers at a time: the crumbly, sandy crust, the salty nuts, the bittersweet chocolate chips, the sharp, dry shredded coconut, and/or the gooey condensed milk. I love my daughter desperately, but often I have no idea which layer she is going to be, and have to tailor my words and actions accordingly.

My best friend and business partner, Isabelle, is definitely crème brûlée. Hard, tough exterior, but crack through it and she is a creamy, rich, and generous soul. When I was younger, my mother always brought to mind a puff-pastry fruit tart, with all the many dimensions and textures that lie on top of a delicate yet sturdy crust. These days, I think of her as a linzer torte, but I'll get to that later. If I dislike a person on sight, I immediately categorize him or her as a fruitcake, because . . . well . . . *gag* me.

I have never assigned a particular dessert to myself, and I would like to think it's because I am an ever-changing entity. Some days, I'm a chocolate-chip cookie. Other days, I'm a rum-soaked raisin-oatmeal bar with maple drizzle. Occasionally, when I'm experiencing the Bloat and find myself crying at car commercials, I am a cream puff. But on this morning, there is no doubt as to what dessert I embody. Tapioca pudding, without question. I am a runny, lumpy, dribbling, snotty mess, and no amount of cinnamon or vanilla is going to save me.

On the heels of the hurling episode, during which I expelled the entire contents of my stomach, as well as possibly a kidney or two, I claimed a case of twenty-four-hour bubonic plague to Kevin and retreated to my bedroom. I made myself guzzle two glasses of water because dehydration wreaks havoc on my middle-aged skin. Then, just to really punish myself, I perused Walter's side of the closet and his chest of drawers, both of which are slightly less full than they were last night. Conspicuously missing are two Samsonite suitcases and his shaving kit. All in all, he has not removed much from his now-former home, but considering the Chartreuse Shirt, I can deduce that he has a whole stash of unflatteringly colored ensembles elsewhere (read: at *Cheryl's*).

After staring at the empty shelf in the medicine cabinet for a moment longer than any sane person would do, I climbed into my bed and tucked myself under the down comforter, even though it's the middle of June. A small mountain of used Kleenex has sprouted up from Walter's pillow, and I clutch the tissue box to me like a blankie. Ordinarily, I am not prone to self-indulgent crying jags; I pride myself on my ability to keep my emotions in check, to disguise my anger or sadness or rage with an unwavering, well-practiced smile. But under the circumstances, I am willing to forgive myself for this uncharacteristic display of grief. It's only right that I allow myself some wallow time. And since Kevin has gone surfing and Colleen is still sleeping and Walter is off with *Cheryl,* there is no one to witness my moment—or moments—of weakness.

I stare across the room at the TV, which is on but set on mute, a reminder that my husband was in this room less than an hour ago. Walter habitually turns on the television in the morning, reaching for the bedside remote before he is fully conscious. He switches the channel to CNN, scoots to the edge of the bed, and stares at the screen for five minutes before shutting off the sound and going about his morning ablutions. Right now CNN is showing footage of the aftermath of Hurricane Emily: decimated houses, cars being washed down flooded streets, a dog barking from a rooftop, children weeping. As I gaze at the images, a part of me feels ashamed for my self-pity. These people's lives have been utterly destroyed. They will never be the same. I might never be the same, but at least my home is intact, my car is safely in the garage, and I don't even have a dog, let alone one trapped on the roof.

I manage to put a halt to the geysers that are my tear ducts and take a few slow breaths. Okay, so I am not the only wife to be left for another woman. It happens all the time, right? It happened to Lydia Markham just last year. Lydia chose to deal with her abandonment by eating. And eating. And eating. She ate everything in sight for six months; anything edible went into her mouth, including her beloved Persian's Purina Cat Chow when she'd emptied the entire fridge and pantry and could find nothing else to stuff into her face. She gained a hundred pounds in half a year, then proceeded to get a spot as a contestant on *The Biggest Loser*, where she lost all the weight, won the grand prize, fell in love with the second-place winner, and got a book deal. So she's not doing too badly. And, of course, Phil Markham had had the decency to leave Lydia for his twenty-two-year-old perky-breasted secretary.

But me? I've been left for middle-aged *Cheryl*. How am I going to explain that? My humiliation inspires another three minutes of blubbering and I pull the comforter up over my head so as not to see the devastation of Emily, which I know is a lot worse than the devastation of Walter, but it doesn't feel that way right now. It feels like my entire world has blown apart. The life I so carefully carved out for myself, with patience and persistence and compromises, has been yanked out from under me. I am careening down a bottomless crevasse that has opened up beneath my bed and I am flailing to find purchase along the rocky—

Rocky-Road Milk-Chocolate S'More Squares!

My defense mechanism suddenly kicks in and I am grateful.

Freshly baked graham crackers with a hint of molasses, cut small . . .

When I am overloaded by emotions or otherwise cannot deal with life, my subconscious steps in and takes over, propelling me into a state of dessert mania, which is a lot more pleasant than thinking about spousal abandonment. New ideas for recipes fill my head, some good and some absolutely dreadful, but they leave no room for contemplation of anything not sweet-related. I call them my stressipes. I know that this reflex is purely denial and avoidance, but it's much cheaper than Xanax, and I've come up with a few bestsellers for the bakery as a result. I always write down the recipes that work, and someday I hope to fill a cookbook with them, though I know I'll have to come up with a different title. "Stressipes" sounds, well, stressful.

Homemade marshmallow cream and roasted almonds sandwiched between bite-size graham-cracker squares, enrobed with Callebaut milk chocolate.

As I envision the small delectable squares, how I will garnish them (with shaved dark chocolate for contrast) and the way I'll display them in the bakery (in the prized real estate that is reserved for our weekly specials—top shelf, center), Walter and this disastrous morning are momentarily forgotten. But my brief mental sojourn doesn't last. Because suddenly I realize that I am starting to suffocate from the thousands of goose feathers lying on top of my face.

I reach up, grab the comforter and pull it down to my waist, suck in a huge gulp of air, then jerk with surprise. My daughter is standing right next to the bed, staring down at me with a mixture of confusion and adolescent pique.

"Hi, honey!" I manage as I wiggle myself into a sitting position.

"What are you doing, Mom?" she asks suspiciously, her furrowed brow in direct contrast with her fresh-faced youth. At sixteen, Colleen is a beauty, having bypassed that awkward teen stage and moved directly into precollegiate perfection. Her skin is china-doll smooth and pale with a smattering of freckles across the bridge of her nose, her eyes are crystal blue, and her hair is a long silky blond that would do any shampoo commercial proud.

"I'm, uh, thinking about a new recipe," I say brightly. *Well? It's true.*

"In bed?" She narrows her eyes at me.

I shrug and try on a smile. "Sometimes I do my best thinking in bed."

"O-kay," she says, then glances at the pile of tissues beside me. Her gaze moves back to my face and I feel her scrutinize my features. "Your eyes are red."

"Allergies," I state without hesitation. The last thing I want to do is tell my daughter that her father left me—*and* her *and* her brother—at 7:17 on the first Saturday of summer vacation for a fortysomething, Prada-wearing, yacht-owning, blond accountant named *Cheryl*. I can't bear to see the look of heartbreak on her face. Colleen thinks Walter is *wonderful,* still calls him Daddy. I don't have the strength to shatter her illusions of a superhero dad (I'll call him Chartreuse-Man) or deal with her questions about whether he still loves her or bear her subsequent ranting about how it must be *my* fault. I know I'll have to endure all of these things at some point. But what if Walter decides at three thirty this afternoon that he made a huge mistake and wants to come home? I'll have given my children seven hours of sheer torture over nothing. I tell myself that it's probably better to wait awhile, just to make sure the whole thing sticks. Like for five or six years.

"Where's Daddy?" she asks, casually turning away from me to inspect her reflection in the mirror. Although it's only nine o'clock, Colleen is showered, dressed, and perfectly coiffed, her hair swept back in a loose clip and a mere kiss of makeup on her face. She wears a stonewashed denim skirt that stops midway down her tanned thighs, a peachy-pink halter top over her budding chest, and a pair of wedge sandals, which reveal toenails decorated with daisies. Ah, to be sixteen again.

"Golf," I reply without thinking, then catch a glimpse of Walter's golf bag through the open closet door, only two feet from Colleen and directly in her line of vision should she take her eyes off her own image. "Uh, Rolf!" I stammer. "*Rolf.* Rolf Bachman's in town. They're having breakfast." I silently thank God that Walter has a colleague whose name rhymes with golf.

"Ugh," she says frowning. "He's icky."

"Why do you say that?"

"The way he talks," Colleen explains as she adjusts the dangle on one of her earrings. "He spits!"

Rolf Bachman is one of the nicest men on the planet, but I admit, his Hungarian accent makes the saliva jet from his mouth like a Waterpik set to high. He is, however, aware of this fact and always has a handkerchief ready for any verbal emergencies.

"What are you doing today?" I ask, purposely redirecting the conversation away from the bald-faced lie I just told her.

"The Queen Team is setting up today," she informs me. "They finally gave us our room."

Colleen has a job with the local rec center to help run a summer program called Little Princesses. Girls aged four to eight are taught manners, poise, style, and grace. My daughter possesses all of these qualities and is taking her duties very seriously. She even went so far as to sacrifice her precious magazine collection, cutting out page after page from *Vogue, Glamour,* and *Mademoiselle* to create a humongous collage for the rec room wall. And although I have serious qualms about little girls being introduced to Kate Moss and Calvin Klein at such an early age, Colleen is excited about it and I know the program will give her something to focus on for the next three months.

"And tonight Rachael and Zoe are coming over, remember?" She turns to face me. "You and Daddy are still going to that party?"

Party? *Oh, crap.* The Josefsbergs' twenty-fifth wedding anniversary. Of course. I was at the bakery till eleven last night, putting the finishing touches on their enormous chocolate chiffon cake. But with all the excitement of the morning, it slipped my mind.

"I'm not sure, honey," I say, my voice somewhat strangled.

"Oh my God!" she cries. "You said you were going!"

I realize that the idea of Colleen and her girlfriends doing their nails and curling their hair and discussing *boys* in front of Walter and me would be like me having sex in front of my own parents.

"You, like, *have* to go!"

Sex. My brain seizes upon that one little word. *Sex. Sex sex sex sexsexsexsex.* While Colleen wrings her hands in dismay, I try to think of the last time I *had* sex. This is June. I stare past my daughter at the wall of my bedroom, sifting through my short-term memory for the occasion. When that doesn't work, I turn to my long-term memory. January? December? *Oh God. November? Wait!* I know I've had sex in the last year, *haven't I?*

"I already told Rachael and Zoe we'd have the house to ourselves."

"Your brother will be here," I absently remind her, still pondering the "How long has Ruby been celibate?" question.

"Kevin doesn't count," she says. "He'll just be in his room listening to Coldplay and searching the Net for extreme surf videos."

If I am honest with myself, lately . . . uh, recently . . .

okay, for a long while I haven't really been in the mood for sex. And neither has Walter. But I assumed it was just a phase we were going through, one we would joke about later, like "Remember that year when we had absolutely no desire to touch each other? Ha ha ha. That was hilarious! Ha ha ha. Come on, let's go boink!"

Then this morning I found out that Walter *has* been in the mood for sex, just not with me.

"Are you all right, Mom? You look like you're going to barf."

Argh! Barf. Doesn't anyone use the word "vomit" anymore?

"No, sweetie, I'm fine," I assure her.

It should come as no surprise that the moment my daughter leaves the room, I race into my master bathroom and *barf* up the precious water I forced myself to drink, and possibly my pancreas along with it.

3

Spilled (Sweetened Condensed) Milk

Saturday is one of my two days off from the Muffin Top, so when I walk through the front door, dressed in my usual uniform of jeans and T-shirt, I am greeted by the cacophony of jangling bells and a hearty "Why the hell are *you* here?" I swallow back my comment—*Because I* own *the place!*—and make my way to the display case to check on the inventory of baked goods.

"Good morning, Marcy," I say pleasantly as the young woman moves toward me with a tray of chocolate croissants in her hand. Marcy is our only full-time employee and also our *best* employee. She has no life to speak of, so she is always available to open or close, or do both if necessary. She can make lemon poppy-seed muffins that melt in your mouth and inspire acid flashbacks for a month. And aside from the fact that her hair is a different primary or secondary color every month, and she has a skeleton tattoo on her wrist which she covers with a Hello Kitty Band-Aid, and her nose and eyebrow are pierced, she is all of the things you want your staff to be: trustworthy, smart, friendly, and clean. Also, she never complains when her paycheck is a few days late due to the fact that we had to use her wages to pay the electricity bill. ("No electrici-tee, no cook-ee, no job-ee for Mar-cee," she always jokes.)

Marcy is also a wee bit wack-ee. If I had to assign a dessert to her, it would be a walnut date bar. Very nutty, a little fruity, and something that most people think they won't like, but—once they take a bite—realize is wonderful.

"Seriously, Ruby-doobie-doo. It's your day off. What are you doing here?"

I suddenly feel like Richard Gere in *An Officer and a Gentleman,* although with far less ripped abs. *I got nowhere else to go!* I want to cry. This is not entirely true. I could go to Albertsons, where they are having a two-for-one sale on Stoli, or I could go to CVS and buy a bottle of sleeping pills, or I could go to Guy's Gun Shop down the street and get myself a sleek little .22, you know, not to commit murder or anything, but just for the mere satisfaction of scaring the crap out of Walter when I point it at his man parts.

But ultimately, the only place that offers me solace, other than my home, which up until three hours ago was always a safe haven for me, is my little bakery in downtown Pelican Point. The shop is small but cozy with an exhibition kitchen, a display case that runs almost the entire length of the room, and a small alcove with five bistro tables for the occasional customer who wants to eat in. The far wall boasts our logo, a bevy of muffin tops cascading down a chocolate waterfall, which I designed and one of Kevin's talented friends painted for us.

I always wanted to own a bakery, ever since my mom taught me how to bake a cake. I wouldn't call this a dream because I didn't have dreams. I had goals, realistic, achievable goals—still do—and this was one of them. And it's just as I planned, right down to the plum-colored napkins. Well, except for the booming business part. I thought we'd have lines out the door, and not because I was being unrealistic, but because our baked goods are fantastic and our shop is warm and inviting. And the first year we did fine, got good reviews, and did some cakes for town functions. But sales have been flagging for the last six months. Not catastrophically, but enough to concern me. I can't bear to imagine the Muffin Top closing, especially now, especially this morning.

I shove the thought away and feel my shoulders loosen as soon as I step into the kitchen. The air is scented with molten chocolate and blueberries, and my empty stomach reacts with a strident rumble. I am not hungry, unfortunately. I am too afraid of *hurling* or *barfing* up anything I put in my mouth, but the delectable aroma in the Muffin Top is like a much-needed balm for my fractured psyche. As I scan the room, I take a few deep breaths, in, out, in, out. My personal life has turned upside down, but here in my bakery, I am in control, I have power. It might only be power over flour and sugar and butter, but I'll take it where I can get it.

A young college-aged man sits at one of the tables in the alcove staring vacantly at the screen of his laptop, the crumbly remains of a blueberry muffin on a plate beside him. Otherwise, the bakery is deserted. The morning rush—which is actually more of a trickle—is over, and for this I am thankful. The fewer people I come in contact with today, the better. I can hide my grief and angst with the best of them, as I did with my children earlier, but it's damn exhausting.

"Are you okay, Ruby?" Marcy asks me. "You look a little pale."

Perhaps because I have vomited up all of my inner organs? "I'm fine!" I say, hoping I sound more cheerful than manic. "My stomach is a little upset, that's all." Am I the queen of understatement, or what? "How are things going here?"

"Pretty good morning, abso-tively, poso-lutely!" Marcy singsongs. "Sold out of the Cream Cheese Surprises."

"Nice," I say, nodding. I slowly walk along the display case, checking the trays. We keep things simple at the Muffin Top, selling only muffins (duh), cupcakes, and cakes, although we have a great variety of each. We branch out with our weekly specials, which are mostly made from my stressipes—the ones that *work*. Occasionally Izzy brings in a recipe (usually from a crazy relative, sometimes from the Internet, always completely off-the-wall) and forces me to produce and sell the item, like the Cherry Chili Bomb Tarts sitting, unsold, in the display case, which look a bit like something you might see on *CSI* but which Isabelle insisted on trying because the recipe was handed down from her *abuela* one week before she died. The staff and I refer to these offerings as Izzy's Inedibles, although only behind her back, lest we provoke her fiery Latina rage. Isabelle runs the business side of the bakery; finances and marketing and the like, and she rarely intrudes upon my domain, the *baking*. (The only item of hers that ever sold out was a chipotle mole brownie bar that Izzy insisted on making herself and which allegedly contained a hallucinogenic Mexican spice.) The Muffin Top has the capacity—and the ingredients—to make pies, cookies, brownies, and most other desserts, but we do so only for special events or upon request.

Marcy makes a show of wiping down the service counter, all the while surreptitiously peering at me. When I finish my perusal, I grab a clean apron from the metal shelving unit and casually inspect the contents of our three convection ovens. In one, three blueberry crumb cakes are turning golden—Mrs. Kleinfeld's standing Saturday order. In the next, giant balls of dough are morphing into four-inch circles of heaven—our weekly special, double fudge chunk cookies, a stressipe that came to me last week when I couldn't get my minivan started. In the third oven, our signature caramel toffee cupcakes bubble merrily.

"Where's Izzy?" I inquire, wishing my stomach weren't still flip-flopping from this morning's intestinal fireworks.

"Bank," Marcy says. "Tucking our *dinero* safely away." She brings her hand to a halt midwipe and squints at me. "Uh, Ruby Tuesday, seriously. What are you doing here? You know we can handle it without you, right?"

"Of course," I assure her. "I just . . ." *Just, what?* I ask myself. Just couldn't stand moping around my house gazing at all of the framed photographs of a smiling, happy family, a smiling, happy *couple,* as I did for a full hour after Colleen left? Just couldn't bear another moment alone with my thoughts, pondering the shape of my life without Walter there to round it out? Just couldn't deal with the reality of what's happened to me?

I can't finish the sentence, and as it turns out, I don't have to. Because at that moment the door slams open, and my best friend, Isabelle, whirls into the bakery, eyes wild and breathing like a marathon runner on mile twenty-five.

"Walter left you for another woman? That son of a bitch! I'll kill him!"

"You can't kill him," I say calmly, leaning back in my chair. Isabelle and I have repaired to our cramped office behind the kitchen. Our communal desk is covered with paperwork, supply catalogs, and recipes, and I absently glance at a picture of a slab of dark chocolate from a new purveyor.

"Don't tell me you haven't thought about it."

"Murder is illegal."

"So what? You think I care about laws at a time like

this?" Isabelle paces the faux-Oriental rug with such venom I fear she might dig a trench in it. "I can do time!" she announces confidently. And knowing my friend, she probably could. At five eleven and a hundred and sixty pounds, with her shiny black mane that falls halfway down her back and a takes-no-crap attitude, she might become the Queen of Cell Block A. " 'Course, we could do it and hide the body, make sure nobody ever found out."

"They always find out."

"Not in my neighborhood, *chica.*" Usually, Isabelle speaks with very little trace of an accent, but when she's angry or upset, she'll bring out the barrio. I find it amusing most of the time, but at this moment, the single word *"chica"* gives me pause.

"I'm not a *chica,* Izzy. I'm a *mujer.* I'm a *vieja mujer* whose husband left her for another *vieja mujer.*"

She stops pacing long enough to smile at me with her perfect white teeth. "See that? You got the sex right on the adjectives. You can't be too bad off, now, can you?"

A question occurs to me and I look up at her. "How did you find out? It just happened."

The color rises on her coffee-with-cream cheeks. "I called him."

"When?"

"Fifteen minutes ago! I had to discuss a few things with him."

I gape at Isabelle. Because there is absolutely no reason why she would be talking to Walter on a Saturday morning. "Like what?"

"Oh, for God's sake! Your birthday? Eighty-eight days from now? I thought Walter and I could throw you a surprise party or something."

I let out a breath and shake my head. "I'm turning

forty-four, Iz. It's not a big enough birthday for a surprise party."

"Exactly!" she cries. "You definitely would have been surprised! And he starts telling me that it's 'unlikely' that he will be helping to celebrate your birthday and that 'under no ill-begotten circumstances' would he be taking part in any 'planning thereof.' What does that even mean? 'Planning thereof'?"

I shrug. "You know Walter."

"I thought I did," she retorts. "But he's gone and gotten body-snatched. Seriously! He starts going on about how he met someone and then he gets all googly-voiced. *Walter— googly-voiced!* Saying how she makes him feel *whole* again! What kind of *Jerry Maguire* bullshit is that anyway? I mean, for God's sake—" She stops abruptly. "Oh, Ruby. I'm sorry. Me and my big mouth. You don't need to hear all this."

"It's okay," I assure her, taking solace in the fact that there is nothing left in my system to throw up. "He told me the same thing this morning. That *Cheryl* is his soul mate."

"His *what*? Oh, *Dios mío*. That *pendejo* jerk-off!"

You said it, sister.

We are both silent for a moment. Then Izzy starts in again. "What kind of a name is *Cheryl* anyway?" She resumes pacing. "He can't leave you for a *Cheryl*!"

"You'd prefer Susan or Lisbeth or Sharon?" I offer.

"I'm telling you, Ruby, this is not Walter! He's got his meds all screwed up, that's what it is. You wait and see. He's going to wake up tomorrow morning and realize what a big mistake he made and he's gonna come crawling back to you, begging your forgiveness. Just see if he doesn't."

I know Isabelle is saying what she thinks I want to hear. And maybe she even believes her own words. After all, the scenario she's describing happens regularly with middle-aged men. The grass they thought was greener turns out to have just as many weeds and worms as the one they've grown tired of mowing. But I have a sneaking suspicion that Walter will be much happier with his new lawn. I know *Cheryl*. She is definitely a Kentucky bluegrass kind of gal. Whereas I more closely resemble crabgrass.

"What are you thinking about?" Izzy asks me.

"Grass," I say plainly.

"Don't you worry about it. I'll get you some from my cousin Julio and you can smoke yourself into a coma. That's what I'd do."

"No, Izzy, don't get me pot. Please." The last time I got stoned—with Izzy, of course—I ended up staring at a brick wall for three hours trying to find patterns in the cement grout. And then I proceeded to lay waste to an entire box of Mallomars, a bag of pork rinds, and a platter of some kind of Mexican delicacy that I cannot pronounce, which more than slightly resembled baby poop.

Clearly, marijuana and I are *not* BFFs.

"You're right," Izzy agrees, probably remembering the same night. "You should stick with Valium."

"I don't want Valium," I say, picking at one of the silkscreened muffin tops on my apron. "But there is something you can do for me."

"Anything, Ruby. You just name it and Izzy will make it done. Especially if you're asking me to have Mama put a curse on Walter. You know her magic. She could make all of his hair fall out. Everywhere on his body, that *chingado*!"

"Izzy, relax!" I rub my face, attempting to mash my features into a look of complacency. "I don't want Mama to put a curse on Walter." *Yet*. "I just need you to take the anniversary cake to the Josefsberg party tonight."

Isabelle looks at me as though I'd just asked her to dig up

her dead grandmother. Simply put, my friend has an irratio-nal fear of carrying, delivering, touching, or otherwise be-ing in close proximity to any of my edible theme cakes as a result of an unfortunate encounter she had with the Pelican Point pier cake I made for the mayor's luncheon last fall. Let's just say a large, brazen, Latina tsunami struck, deci-mating the pier and the surrounding graham-cracker-and-white-chocolate shoreline. (The mayor had to settle for a triple-decker Winky the Clown Cake, and if you knew Mayor Todd McPhereson, you would understand the irony.)

"But, I . . ." she stutters. "But, you . . ." She clears her throat. "I thought you were going to the party, you know, as a guest."

"Yes," I say evenly. "I *was* going. I was going with my *husband*." I feel anger stirring up inside of me, but I deter-minedly tamp it down. "But now my husband is with *Cheryl*. He's probably taking *her* to the party."

"He wouldn't!" Izzy practically shrieks. "Walter's not going to take that *puta* anywhere. He can't. 'Cause if he does, everyone will know what a cocksucking lowlife he is. Leaving *you*! The perfect wife. The perfect mom. He's gonna have to move to another state, 'cause no one around here is going to have anything to do with him. No, Ruby. He isn't taking her to the party. He's hiding her under a rock. Trust me on—"

I raise my hand to interrupt her. "I do trust you, Izzy. But I am not going to the party alone. If you don't want to take the cake, fine. I'll get Marcy to do it."

"But you've got to go!" she insists. "If you cancel now, they'll know something's up. You know the gossip in this town. Like when Bobby showed up at that fund-raiser with a black eye. Even though he swore he whacked himself with his own tennis racquet, everyone assumed the worst. And the next day, three people at the firm gave him brochures on spousal-abuse support groups! And the cops drove by our house five times a day for three weeks! Assholes!"

I do remember the incident she's referring to—how people gave Izzy the fish eye when they came into the Muffin Top. I had defended my friend vehemently—not because I don't think Isabelle is capable of violence, but because I know that *she* knows how to cause bodily harm without leaving a mark (learned, I assume, from her uncle Gustavo, who, as local legend has it, was an underling in the Mexican Mafia before immigrating to the States, where he now runs a fertilizer supply store). But despite my protestations, everyone believed that Izzy was a husband beater until Bobby played in an exhibition tennis match with the town council, during which he tripped over his own sneakers, fell headfirst into the net pole, and ended up in the ER.

"Plus," she continues, "the Muffin Top really needs the publicity right now. We don't do something drastic, and we're going to have to have a serious conversation. This party's a big deal—the Josefsbergs are big shots, there'll probably be pictures in *Orange Coast* magazine. Adelle gets her picture in that rag every goddamned week and look at *her* business."

Adelle's Bakery is our biggest competition in Pelican Point, although I wouldn't say we're exactly in the same league. For example, Adelle's marketing budget is bigger than our net yearly sales. Adelle herself is a brash, brazen redhead who once streaked through city hall wearing fake double-E breasts—on the *outside* of her shirt. The next day, she sold a record number of baked goods, especially the cupcakes decorated to look like boobs.

"Look," Izzy says, perching her considerable butt on the edge of the desk. "You go. You deliver the cake. You make

up some lame excuse about Walter being sick or having a
mild case of brain damage. You drink a couple of glasses of
wine, mingle for five minutes, get your picture taken with
your masterpiece, then you get the hell out of there. Easy as
cake."

"Pie," I correct her.

"What?"

"Easy as pie."

"Yeah, whatever."

4

Egg (Wash) on Your Face

The Josefsbergs' soiree starts at six thirty. I glance at my cell phone on the bathroom counter. All day I've been waiting for it to ring, praying it will ring, hoping it will ring, checking it every few minutes in case I accidentally shut off the sound—and no, Walter hasn't called. According to the LCD display, I have one hour to make myself presentable and get back to the bakery, and another half hour to transport the cake to my friends' palatial beachside estate. As I gaze at my reflection, I realize that one hour just isn't going to cut it. *Four* hours, a bucket of Spackle, and some spray paint, maybe.

I am not suddenly feeling old, which I assume is how certain women feel when their husbands leave them for young nubile girls with nary a line on their peaches-and-cream faces and tummies they can proudly, nakedly flaunt to the world, navel rings included. But *my* husband left me for another fortysomething, so the age thing doesn't come into play. My features are all familiar to me—my blue eyes, my high cheekbones (thanks, Mom), and full lips (thanks, Dad)—they're all just where I left them. My body is the same, too—not fat, not thin, just an average size eight that I manage to keep fit with my rigorous baking schedule. And despite the fact that I wear little makeup and froggy pajamas, I know that, for my age, I am an attractive woman, in an earthy kind of way.

But now, as I study my own image and I allow my expression to relax, stripping away the forced composure I work so hard to maintain, I see how the corners of my mouth automatically pull down in a frown. My eyes, with the crow's-feet firmly etched beside them from years of painting on a smile in the face of adversity, look weary. My shoulder-blade-length hair, which I color every three months with Natural Instincts and usually just sweep back into a ponytail anyway, looks flat and lifeless. There are dark circles the size of ten-pound bags of flour under my eyes and my complexion is sallow.

I realize that this didn't just happen. Someone didn't take a giant ice cream spoon and scoop the life out of me this morning. This isn't the result of Walter's departure or my vomiting escapades, although those certainly didn't help. This has been happening for a while now and I just didn't notice.

If I am completely honest with myself, I have to admit that I look . . . unhappy.

Oh, crap. Walter was right.

I hear the doorbell echo through the house, signaling the arrival of my daughter's friends. I'm glad that Colleen has a distraction for the evening. It will keep her from pondering her father's absence. Normally, she scrutinizes things from every angle (which is why her eyebrows are tweezed to perfection). But earlier, when she asked again where Walter was, and I quickly told her that he was at an emergency work conference, she was so distracted by preparations for her sleepover that she merely responded with a nod.

My son is far easier to deceive—God, what a thing for a mother to say! Perhaps because he is a surfer, Kevin is generally a laid-back, go-with-the-flow kind of guy. A naked octogenarian gymnast with body paint and no earlobes could somersault into our living room and Kevin would casually offer him a soda. He didn't even mention his dad, and I felt such a pang of guilt over my lie of omission that I allowed him to have his friend Luke over and even gave them money for pizza. Of course, Colleen was furious, so I also had to extract a promise—a double-Dutch-hand-on-the-heart-oath-to-the-bodhisattva—that the boys would in no way annoy, tease, or torture the girls (like during a sleepover a few years back, when Kevin and his cronies stole the girls' padded bras from their belongings, soaked them in water, and stuck them in the freezer).

I glance at my cell again. A quarter of an hour has passed and I'm no closer to being ready than I was when I stepped in front of the mirror. Hurriedly, I reach into the drawer for some lipstick. Although I've accepted the fact that no amount of makeup will mask the withered, scooped-out quality I am currently sporting, I've also relaxed my standards a bit. My goal is to appear as though I actually have a pulse. Not very lofty, I admit, but at least it's doable.

The Josefsbergs live in the priciest neighborhood in Pelican Point—the Cove. If you've got two million dollars lying around, you could buy yourself about ten square feet of oceanfront property. Ted Josefsberg was a mild-mannered mortgage broker when he bought ten thousand shares of a little-known cellular company called T-Mobile. Now he golfs, sails his yacht around the world, and finances his wife's annual personal improvements (read: plastic surgery).

As I pull into the circular driveway of their faux-Italian villa, a young kid—yes, he's probably in college, but after a woman turns forty everyone she sees looks like a kid—appears beside my minivan, eyeing me dubiously. I roll down my window and smile.

"I'm delivering the cake," I say. He nods and makes a point of *not* opening my door for me. I open it myself, then step down out of the van and try to surreptitiously yank my dress down over my butt.

"So, you, like, want me to keep your, uh, car here, right?"

"No," I reply calmly. "I'm also a guest."

"Um, okay," the kid says, climbing behind the wheel. I have no doubt that he plans to park my car as far away from the house as possible—like, say, Siberia—lest it be seen by one of the other more-classy-car-driving guests.

I pop the hatch on the van, gaze down at the anniversary cake, and heave a sigh of relief. Although I take great pains to make sure my cakes are structurally sound, and I secure them in the back of the van as best I can, I am never certain how much damage will occur during the ride. Southern California roads are less than spectacular, with their uneven rutted pavements and numerous potholes that give me a heart attack every time I drive over one. There have been times when I've had to rebuild an entire cake in the back of the minivan with the custom repair kit I always bring. But tonight, nothing is amiss—no cracked fondant, no broken appliqués—and I feel a flash of pride as I carefully withdraw my masterpiece.

Because this is the Josefsbergs' silver anniversary, I was instructed by Miriam to create something that not only went over the top, but also represented their twenty-five years of marital bliss. (Excuse me while I just step aside and gag. Okay, better.) And so I built a castle of flour, sugar, butter, white chocolate, and fondant, with silver-painted turrets, a shimmering moat, and flags in the colors of their wedding:

lilac and baby blue. When I finished it last night, I named it, as I always name my creations, *The Fortress of Love*. But tonight, after the whole Walter debacle, I have decided to rename it *The Grand Illusion*.

Anyway, it is gorgeous, and I know that Miriam is going to pee in her pants over it—although not literally, as she confided in me many years ago that she practices her Kegel exercises four times a day and has done so since she turned thirty.

As soon as I am clear of the minivan, the valet stomps on the gas and careens around the circular driveway toward the street with the hatch gaping open. Luckily, I stowed my repair kit in the foot bay of the passenger seat and not in the back, otherwise Birdsong Lane would now be strewn with assorted decorating paraphernalia.

Hauling the fifty-pound cake, I head for the front door. Because I can't possibly bear the weight of my burden with only one hand, I am reduced to knocking on the door by way of kicking it with my three-year-old estate-sale Louboutin pumps. Within five seconds, I am greeted by a server wearing a uniform of black dress, frilly white apron, ruffled black serving hat, and a name tag that reads *Christy*. Her expression is one of submissive deference until she spots the cake.

"Ah," she says, visibly relaxing. "Come on in, hon. I'll show you where it goes."

She steps aside to let me enter, then leads me across the polished marble foyer, down the long hallway, and into the great room.

All of the furniture has been removed to accommodate a dozen round tables for guests and a smaller rectangular table for the happy couple. An abundance of lilac, silver, and light blue balloons float in the air, halfway between the floor and the vaulted ceiling, and I wonder just how the party planner accomplished their exact placement, helium being so darn fussy and all. Several servers scurry about, placing glassware and utensils, refolding napkins, and rearranging floral centerpieces.

No other guests are present, as I assume they have all been ushered to the back garden for the cocktail hour. Christy gestures toward a lone bistro table in the corner, covered with lilac linens and sprinkled with baby-blue hyacinth petals. I eagerly make my way to it and set the cake down, then stand back to take in the effect.

"It's just amazing!" Christy exclaims, then she looks at me expectantly. "I assume the Josefsbergs have settled with you already? Or will you be billing them?"

"Um, actually, it's my gift to them," I tell her. "I'm a guest." Although I can't prove this because my invitation is in my purse in the minivan, which I assume is now parked somewhere in the Outer Banks.

"Of course!" Christy says, looking at me as if for the first time and taking in my simple yet elegant black dress, my slightly careless—though I prefer the term "carefree"—chignon, and my sparkly party earrings. Her manner once again changes almost imperceptibly. "Let me show you to the garden . . . *ma'am*."

Just then, the doorbell rings and the girl's eyes dart nervously toward the foyer.

"I can show myself to the garden," I assure her. She nods her thanks and hurries off.

I stand for a moment, unmoving. I've been so focused on getting the castle cake here in one piece that for an entire half hour I'd forgotten my troubles. But as I gaze around the room at all of the festive decorations, my situation slams into me with renewed force. I am here alone. Walter is off with *Cheryl*. I've been cheated on. I've been deserted. I am never going to celebrate my own twenty-fifth anniversary. Oh God, what am I doing here?

If ever there were a chance to escape, now is the time. I could lie in wait in the alcove by the foyer until Christy passes by with the new arrivals, slip out the front door, walk three miles to my car, and speed off into the night and no one would be the wiser.

But Miriam is a good friend and has been for fifteen years. And despite their wealth, the house, the yacht, their six cars, the servants, and Miriam's annual nip/tuck sessions, the Josefsbergs have remained surprisingly down-to-earth. Ted still coaches Little League even though their boys are in college, and Miriam volunteers at the Pelican Point Library twice a week.

No, I have to stay. I owe it to them to celebrate their marriage, even if mine has imploded like a supernova. Besides, no one knows about Walter and me. It'll be fine. I'll follow Izzy's instructions, make excuses for Walter, sample the wine and the sumptuous food, and duck out before the dancing. No problem. Easy as cake.

Throwing my shoulders back and plastering on a smile, I head down the long hallway toward the patio.

The garden and grounds have been transformed into a sparkling wonderland, with strings of twinkling lights everywhere and glowing silver stars hanging from tree branches and bushes. Two full-service bars are positioned on either side of the patio and throngs of guests mill about between them. In the low light of dusk, I can barely make out the beach and the Pacific Ocean just beyond the Josefsbergs' property, and the sound of the surf is muted by soft jazz, the cascading water of several fountains, and the chatter and laughter of people taking advantage of free booze.

At the open French doors, I scan the crowd, and for a split second I am seized with dread at the possibility of Walter being here. I see the Levinsons and the Gaineses, the Pearsons and the Hammonds. Michael and Michele Franklin are perched by the infinity pool having what looks like a serious discussion. Jerry Meyers and Frank Holcomb are huddled together conversing intently while their wives, Liv and Lucille, gaze at each other with bored expressions. There is no sign of Walter, thank God. I spot Miriam holding court next to one of the bars, looking stunning in a shimmery silver-blue sheath, her blond hair flowing freely about her shoulders, holding a martini glass. I have long thought of Miriam as a chocolate-mousse parfait, tall and slender and elegant with layers that are both complex and light as air. She is talking candidly to another couple, gesturing with her free hand, pointing to her brow, her eyes, and her mouth, and I can only guess that she is regaling them with the tale of her latest Juvéderm injections.

I take a deep breath and step outside, purposefully heading for my friend. But something odd happens as I weave past the other guests. When they catch sight of me, each of them abruptly moves out of my way, and I suddenly feel like Moses parting the Red Sea. I lock eyes with Liv Meyers, but as I lift my hand to wave at her, she quickly turns away. I tell myself that she probably didn't see me, but the same thing happens with Lucille Holcomb, only she doesn't just turn away, she visibly flinches. A niggling sliver of unease creeps up my spine as I continue forward. Michele Franklin nearly falls into the infinity pool when I pass, and when she sees me, Claire Gaines almost chokes on a goat-cheese canapé, spluttering and coughing and grabbing on to Jack Gaines's arm for support.

As sweat trickles down my back and dampens my armpits, I suddenly recall one of the most humiliating things that ever happened to me. I was in Manhattan, staying with a friend while taking an extension course at Hunter College. It was late fall and the weather was cool but not yet cold. I had plans to meet my friend and her coworkers for drinks after my class, so I was dressed for a night out—tight Lycra skirt, formfitting black top, nude panty hose, and, as was my preference at the time due to (forgive my candor) a propensity toward yeast infections, no underwear. Plus, my backpack, which was a necessary if unfashionable addition to my ensemble.

As I walked down the street using my best New York stride, I started hearing hoots and hollers behind me. Because I was not a stranger to catcalls from lascivious construction workers (those were the days) and I knew better than to egg them on, I summarily ignored all of the urgent pleas for my attention. By the time I reached Lexington Avenue, I had begun to notice a slight draft on my derriere. I casually glanced in the window of a darkened storefront, and when I saw my reflection, I nearly fainted from embarrassment, right there on the corner of Sixty-third Street. My urgent pace had caused my Lycra skirt to creep up, and it was now bunched up under my backpack, exposing my almost-naked ass to the world at large. And I had been walking this way for God knows how many blocks.

I am experiencing a similar rush of humiliation at this moment, although I'm certain my dress is in place *and* I'm wearing underwear.

They know, they know, they know. Blood rushes through

my brain with deafening force and my heart starts to slam against my ribs. *You're imagining things,* I tell myself sternly. *You're projecting. Nobody knows. How could they?*

"Oh my God, Ruby!" Miriam cries, coming at me like a freight train. "What are you doing here?"

"I, uh . . ." My horror increases exponentially as the conversations around me drop to hushed whispers. "I brought the cake."

"Oh my. I just figured you'd have one of your staff bring it." She ushers me over toward the infinity pool and drapes an arm around my shoulder. Her contact-lens-enhanced eyes are full of sympathy. "Are you okay? Do you need anything? Do you have a good lawyer?"

I am so flabbergasted, I cannot form words. Miriam nods quickly, knowingly. "I'll get you David Greenberg's number. Norma Devane used him and he's fantastic. Jewish, you know." She says this last in a low, conspiratorial tone, as if she herself doesn't celebrate Passover, which I know for a fact she does, having attended her last three seders.

"But, I . . ." I look around and see that all of the guests are glancing nervously in our direction.

They know.

"I don't understand." My voice is a thin squeak. "How did you find out? How did *everyone* find out? What did Walter do? Take out a radio spot?"

Miriam squeezes my shoulder and lowers her head. "Worse, honey. He posted it on Facebook."

I am a pariah. I am a leper. I am an open, oozing, puckering cold sore. Worse, I am a laughingstock. Of course, I am also, at this moment, on a mission to get blindingly drunk.

After Miriam's (gulp) Facebook revelation, I made a desperate attempt at a swift getaway so that I could go home and spend the remainder of the evening contemplating suicide. But Miriam was having none of it. She immediately took me under her protective wing, practically catapulted me to the nearest bar, and ordered me a double SKYY martini with extra olives.

"You can't just cower and hide, Ruby," she'd whispered to me. "If you do, he wins. You have to hold your head high and show the world—and Walter—that you're fine. Absolutely and utterly *all right*!" Then she'd broken into a painful rendition of that Kenny Loggins song from *Caddyshack*. "And if anyone looks at you funny, you just tell them—politely—to go fuck themselves." Actually, quite a few guests were looking at us *funny* right then, but I'm sure it had as much to do with hearing Miriam belt out "I'm all right / Don't nobody worry about me" in her thin, warbling soprano as it did with my personal humiliation.

I am now seated at a ten-top in the far corner of the great room, about as far from the table of honor as you can get and still be inside the house. You know, *that* table. The one reserved for recent abandonees, illegitimate relatives, and those people who were invited, but the hosts—if pressed—would admit they didn't really want them to show up. The man to my left sits militarily straight and gazes at his water glass with a look of consternation. Back when I was alive and noticed such things, I would have called him attractive. Wavy, sandy-blond hair interspersed with a touch of gray, strong chin, and green eyes. But the way he's looking at his water makes me wonder about his mental state. The seat beside him is filled with a balding, portly fellow who wears a polka-dot bow tie and clacks his utensils against his flatware à la Ringo Starr. Across the table sits an elderly couple inspecting the breadbasket and a pair of androgynous teenagers busily typing into their iPhones. Three of the ten seats are empty.

I'm chasing the martini with a glass of cold Chablis and am in a bit of a haze, have almost forgotten that—oh God! My husband posted his affair and subsequent abandonment on Facebook. Facebook!

The man next to me jerks in his seat and the elderly man and woman across the table give me sharp looks of disdain. I realize that I have exclaimed out loud.

"Sorry," I say, then proceed to burp. Loudly. I press my hand to my mouth and mumble "Excuse me" through my fingers.

"It's the Chablis," the man to my left says, tearing his eyes away from his water. "It used to make my wife hiccup uncontrollably."

"Your wife?" I ask, for lack of anything else to say. "Is she, uh, here?"

"She died," he says abruptly. "Of a horrible, fatal, disfiguring disease that dragged on for months and months, leaving her a shriveled unrecognizable husk."

Shocked by his revelation, I reflexively reach out and place my hand on his. "I'm so sorry!" I stammer. "That's terrible."

He glances at my hand, then lifts his gaze to my face. Suddenly the corners of his mouth pull up into a grin. "Actually, I just wanted to try saying that out loud. To see if it felt better than the truth."

My jaw drops and I quickly yank my hand back. "And the truth is . . . ?"

His grin instantly morphs into a frown. "She left me . . . for . . . another woman."

I blow out a breath and tsk because I know how he feels. Clearly, this guy is a nut job, but I understand why he lied about his wife. Far better to be widowed than abandoned. If only Walter had dropped dead, I would be the recipient of compassion and sympathy rather than sideways looks of pity and disdain. "Ah," I say with a nod. And before I can stop myself, I ask, "Did she post it on Facebook?"

He squints at me as if I'm mocking him, then relaxes back into his chair. "No. She tweeted it."

"Social media," I say, raising my Chablis in a toast.

He picks up his water and clinks it against my wineglass. "It'll fuck you every time."

I take a long swallow of my wine, absently wondering how I'll be able to avoid a DUI on the way home, then set my glass down and grab a roll from the basket in front of me.

"I'm Jacob Salt, by the way."

"I'm Ruby Pepper," I reply. I start to giggle and then I burp. Again. "Sorry. Kidding." Well? It serves him right for telling me his wife died horribly. "I'm Ruby McMillan."

His brow furrows. "Ruby McMillan? Why does that name sound familiar?"

I shrug, then tear apart the roll, covertly studying Jacob Salt with my peripheral vision. He really is very handsome, despite the fact that he's a lunatic.

"I own the Muffin Top," I offer. "Well, co-own. I did the cake."

"You made that? It's amazing!" He stares at me openly, reverently, and I feel warmth spread through me, which is either the result of his green-eyed gaze or just the Chablis mixing with the vodka and thundering through my veins. I quickly stuff a piece of roll into my mouth in a latent attempt to soak up some alcohol.

"Look," Jacob says, "I'm sorry about the whole dead wife thing. It's just . . . I'm new in town and, well, you know how it is. So many questions. Everyone wants to know about the new single guy."

"Especially the divorced women," I mumble around the wad of bread in my mouth. *You're going to be one of those divorced women.* Oh, crap! Divorced. Me! I suddenly pray that I'll choke to death on the roll. But unfortunately, I swallow my mouthful without incident. "So how do you know Miriam and Ted?"

"Oh, I've known Ted for years."

A server appears and sets two plates in front of us and my stomach turns over at the sight of the rare slab of prime rib, vegetables, and potatoes au gratin. Ordinarily, I love a nice, juicy, tender cut of beef, but tonight the thought of chewing on a piece of meat makes me seriously queasy. I push my fork around my plate for the sake of appearances but don't bother to pick up my knife.

"We worked together," Jacob continues, cutting into his prime rib with gusto. "At Franchise Funding. Before Ted went and hit the stock-market lotto. I ran the San Francisco office."

"Franchise holds the note on our mortgage," I say, mounding some potatoes onto the side of my plate like Richard Dreyfuss in *Close Encounters of the Third Kind.* "Ted set it up for us back in the day. We got handed over to Elaine Singer when he retired. She's out on maternity leave right now, isn't she?"

"Mmm," he murmurs, and I can't tell whether he's saying yes or commenting on the perfectly cooked meat. From the satisfied look on his face, I'd say it's the latter. "Apparently, it's permanent. Elaine's not coming back. That's why they brought me down here. To take over her accounts. I put in for the transfer, needed a change of scenery." He chuckles sheepishly. "I mean, it's been eighteen months since Kristen, well, you know, found herself. And I've moved on. But it's hard to be constantly bombarded with the memories. Places you've frequented as a couple, things you've done."

Wow. I hadn't thought of that. I still have such fun to look forward to.

"Plus, all the gays in San Fran," he adds. "Don't get me wrong. I'm all for gays. I love gays!"

The volume and force of his words reach the far side of the table and I see the elderly woman flinch then start to choke on her prime rib. I consider going over to her to offer the Heimlich maneuver, but the CPR class I took was more than a decade ago, and because of my lack of practice during the interim, I would probably just break a few of her ribs. The woman's husband pats her on the back ineffectually as she coughs and splutters, her eyes bulging from their sockets. The teenagers do not even look up from their iPhones. Jacob doesn't seem to notice either, just spears an asparagus and waves it around madly.

"I do! Gays are wonderful. But it got to the point where every time I saw a rainbow flag I wanted to hang myself!"

I watch as the elderly woman spews a half-chewed chunk of beef onto the table. It bounces off her champagne flute and lands next to the butter ramekin. Quick as lightning, she reaches out and stabs it with her fork, then pops it back into her mouth. I suppress a shudder, remembering how my great-aunt Ethel would always say, "Waste not, want not."

Jacob has stopped talking and I turn toward him to find him staring at me with a frown.

"McMillan?" he says, and I nod. "Ruby and *Walter* Mc-Millan?"

I nod again, trying to smile, but the expression on his face is filling me with dread.

"26735 Cherry Lane?" His frown becomes a grimace.

"That's us." I feel my smile cracking as my pulse starts to race. "We tried to find a Peach Lane or a Blueberry Lane because I really hate cherry pie. Not that I don't make a great one, mind you. I do, with a dash of almond extract to enhance the cherry filling!" Oh God. I can't seem to stop the stream of nonsense pouring from my mouth. "But I definitely prefer peach pie. Or blueberry. We saw a house on Strawberry Fields Drive, but Walter hates the Beatles, and anyway, it only had one bathroom and absolutely no closet space to speak of."

Jacob has resumed his scrutiny of his water glass. Suddenly stone-cold sober, I grab my Chablis and down it in one gulp.

"Mr. Salt? Jacob?" My voice comes out a hoarse whisper as I set my empty glass down. "What is it?"

He remains silent and refuses to look at me.

"Please. Tell me."

Without raising his eyes, he says, "You should probably speak with your husband."

I stare at the side of his head, at his longish salt-and-pepper sideburns and nicely shaped earlobes and his square jaw, which is clenched tight as a drum. I take a deep breath, trying desperately to stay calm.

"Um, well, Mr. Salt, you see, I can't *speak with my husband.* Because he's not here. He's with *Cheryl,* the wonder accountant." My voice rises, but my tone is singsong, which makes me sound more than a little manic. "Of course, you don't know this because you are not one of his three thousand four hundred and eighty-five Facebook friends. But if you send him a friend request, I'm sure he'll confirm you, and then you can get your own personal play-by-play of how he's sticking it to his soon-to-be ex-wife while he, uh, *sticks it to Cheryl.*"

I glance around to find that every single person at my table—including the two teens—looks as though a pterodactyl just laid an egg on the centerpiece. I smile brightly at them. "What? I'm fine. Mr. Salt and I are having a friendly little discussion. Not to worry."

Just then, a server wanders over to check our plates and Jacob grasps her arm. "I'll have a Dewar's, neat."

"Mr. Salt."

He finally looks at me, his face a study of forced ambivalence. He clears his throat once, twice, three times for good measure. "Your mortgage is in arrears," he says calmly. "I have spoken with your, uh, Mr. McMillan, and he claims that he is in the process of filing for bankruptcy and has no intention of bringing your mortgage current. I am afraid that you are scheduled for foreclosure."

At the word "foreclosure," I bolt to my feet, banging against the table with my hip and causing Jacob Salt's precious water glass to crash against his plate, the water flooding his meal and cascading over the table and into his lap. The synapses in my brain have apparently gone on strike because all I can manage to say is "Eeeyak!" The sounds of the party around me—laughter, music, forks clinking against porcelain—are muted, muffled, as though I am hearing them from somewhere underwater. As calmly as possible—which is not very, considering that I am shaking like a meth addict in withdrawal—I sidestep around my chair and stumble to the hallway. My heels clack against the marble floor as I race for the foyer, fumble with the front doorknob, and burst out into the night air.

The valet leans against a column smoking a cigarette. When he sees me, he quickly flicks his butt onto the manicured lawn.

"Chrysler minivan," I announce breathlessly.

"Are you okay, ma'am?" he asks nervously. I want to deck him.

"Fine," I answer automatically. "Yup. That's me. Fine. Right as rain. Couldn't be better. Just get me my car, okay?"

He nods, slowly backing away from me. "It'll be a few minutes." He turns and trots off down the driveway.

I stand frozen for a moment, my eyes darting back and forth between the valet's retreating form and the bed of perennials to my left. On legs that feel like lead, I stagger over to the flower bed, bend over, and proceed to shower the lovely pink-and-white impatiens with white wine, vodka, and part of a sourdough roll.

Half an hour later, I sit cross-legged on my bed and stare at the screen of my laptop, plagued with disbelief, my misery like a living thing. Not only has Walter cheated on me with his colleague, deserted my children and me, and announced it on the most widely used social networking site in the world . . . not only has he stopped paying the mortgage, thereby starting foreclosure proceedings on *my* house, but now I discover he has perpetrated the ultimate assault on my dignity.

He has dumped me as a Facebook friend.

My humiliation is complete.

5

Hush Puppies and Linzer Torte

"Where's Daddy?"

Those are the first two words I hear on Sunday morning and I am not remotely prepared for them. I've deluded myself into thinking I'd have more time, foolishly assumed that my kids' friends would still be here when I arose, distracting Colleen and Kevin with their presence. But unfortunately for me, Rachael and Zoe and little Luke Tucker have already headed home to get ready for church. (Why, oh, why couldn't my kids be friends with heathens?)

"Mom?"

Colleen is standing by the counter, waiting for her sprouted-wheat bagel to toast, at which point she will apply exactly one tablespoon of butter and one tablespoon of honey from the jar on the counter. Kevin sits at the table, shoveling Lucky Charms into his mouth, which I find suspicious since I have never bought that particular brand of cereal in my life.

"Where's Daddy?" Again, the question. Again, I ignore it. I shuffle to the coffeemaker in the corner of the kitchen. Out of habit, I dump enough grounds into the filter for a full pot, then, realizing, pour half of them back into the canister. I feel my children's eyes boring into the back of my head—well, Colleen's eyes anyhow; Kevin doesn't have the talent for steely-eyed gazes. I know they are both waiting for me to say something, to offer up some kind of explanation as to why their father is conspicuously absent on a Sunday morning—a time Walter always referred to as "Sacred Family Time" (so noted in his BlackBerry calendar). But I'll be damned if I am going to get into the whole sordid affair (pun intended) before I am sufficiently caffeinated.

"Why didn't Daddy come home last night?" Colleen asks as her bagel pops up.

I watch as the precious dark brown liquid begins to drip drip drip through the filter and I think, *Please hurry.*

"How do you know he didn't come home?" My eyes are glued to the carafe, willing the coffee to brew faster.

"The bathroom light was still on when I got up this morning."

Damn, damn, and double damn! I forgot about the light. Ever since my kids understood the concept of electricity—or, at least, the concept of light switches—they have left the bathroom light on at bedtime. When they were young, they did so to ward off werewolves and vampires and the rabid raccoon they were convinced lived in the pantry. Now they do so out of habit. And every night, Walter makes his rounds, checks locks, sets the alarm, makes sure I haven't left anything in the oven, and rounds up any and all abandoned dishes and glassware. And always, *always,* turns off the bathroom light. ("Electricity isn't free, Ruby." Chuckle chuckle.)

"Mom, where's Daddy?" Colleen's voice holds an accusatory edge, and I realize that I can no longer avoid the issue, much as I'd like to. I turn and meet my daughter's eyes.

Okay. How do I handle this? What do I say? *Just tell them the truth, Ruby. Don't sugarcoat it. Just be honest and give it to them straight. They can handle it.*

"Your father was abducted by aliens."

Kevin snorts with laughter, but Colleen just glares at me. "Mom!"

"Well? It could happen. Remember that guy in Utah who disappeared for two weeks and then popped back into his living room right in the middle of *Survivor* with needle marks all over his body—"

"Mom!"

"Okay. The truth is . . ." God, help me, please. "Your father was run over by a gas tanker and he's in a coma at Mercy General."

"Mobil or Chevron?" Kevin asks between bites.

"Kevin!" Colleen snaps at her brother, then plants her hands on her hips and faces me. "If you don't tell me what's going on right now, I am never speaking to you again!"

I've heard this threat before—the longest Colleen ever lasted was three days, and she only gave in because her hair was starting to fall out from a diet of Multi Grain Cheerios and canned asparagus. But the look of sheer desperation on her face draws me up short.

"All right," I say, putting my palms up in defeat. "Here it is. Your father has left."

Silence descends upon the kitchen; the only sound is the gurgling of my precious French roast. Colleen's eyes are laserlike upon me, and I can see the wheels turning in her brain.

"That's it? End of story?"

I force myself to take a breath. "Well, I don't see how the particulars make much difference. But if you must know, your father has fallen in love with someone else."

"What?" Colleen shrieks.

"Gross," Kevin mutters.

"Her name is Cheryl and she works with your dad at the paper company."

"The blonde with the big . . . teeth?" Kevin asks, and I nod. "You know, Col. The one with the boat."

"Yacht," I correct archly.

"Are we gonna have to call her Mommy?"

"Kevin!" Colleen's eyes are wide and unblinking. "This is a nightmare! This is a complete nightmare! Why are you just standing there like everything's okay?"

"Yeah, Mom," Kevin agrees mildly. "Shouldn't you be having a nervous breakdown or something?"

"Oh, I fully intend to," I assure him. "Right after I have a cup of coffee."

"How can you be joking about this? This is so not funny!"

Colleen whirls around and stomps to the phone on the far counter, grabs the receiver, and starts dialing madly. I decide not to mention that I've already tried calling Walter—thirteen times on the way home from the Josefsberg party, and another seven times during the night as I lay awake staring at the ceiling. But he did not pick up and has not responded to any of my messages, which went from calm and collected to calm and hostile. I'm also leaving out the whole mortgage/foreclosure issue because the kids have enough to process without having to witness something they've never seen before—a completely hysterical mother. I need to remain levelheaded for their benefit. I can cry and moan and *hurl* on my own time.

"Maybe you ought to call him from your cell phone, honey," I suggest. "So he'll know it's you."

Colleen merely glares at me. "Hi, Daddy. It's Colleen." For a brief second I think Walter has actually answered and I feel my hopes rise. But then I see tears spill onto Colleen's cheeks as she continues uninterrupted. "Please call me when you get this, okay? Mom just told us what's going on."

Hiccup. Sniff. "Please, Daddy. Call me. I really want to talk to you."

She sets the phone down and turns to glower at me, her lower lip doing the samba, her previously perfect eye makeup oozing down her cheeks. "How could you let this happen?" she cries. "Why didn't you stop him?"

"I tried," I tell her, then I wonder. *Did I? Did I* really *try?* But what more could I have done? Gotten down on my knees and begged him to stay? What a fine image for Walter to take with him—a middle-aged, hollowed-out shell of a woman crawling on the floor, pleading with him not to leave. That wouldn't have kept him here. That would have made him *run*.

"I think your father has been unhappy for a while now. And I also think that the only reason he stayed for as long as he did was because of you two."

My words ring false to my own ears, but I understand that my children need to hear this. How can I possibly explain Walter's flagrant disregard for them yesterday morning? This is not their fault, and I refuse to shatter them further by revealing what a complete bastard their father is. Even if I desperately want to. Even if he is.

I heave a sigh, then grab for the half-full—or half-empty, depending on how you look at life—carafe from the coffee-maker and pour some coffee into my waiting mug.

"Look," I say in as casual a tone as I can muster. "I'm going out to see your grandma today. Either of you want to come?" Neither one answers. "Okay. I'll go by myself this time."

"How can you act like nothing's wrong? Like everything's just fine and dandy?"

If only Colleen knew how I'd thrown up half my body weight yesterday, or that I'd spent the entire night alternating between gut-wrenching sobs and body-quaking fear. Or that I have absolutely no idea what the hell I am going to do now.

"It's not fine and dandy," I say evenly. "Not even remotely."

I gaze at Colleen's and Kevin's crestfallen faces and feel a fresh dose of resentment. Yesterday, Walter was Superhero Dad to them. Today, he is Captain Megajerk. I love my kids fiercely. But I cannot shield them from their pain. When they were little, and something bad or frightening or sad happened, I would gather them up and herd them to my bedroom and the three of us would snuggle and tickle and pillow-fight in the "big bed" until they felt better. Then we would all march downstairs and bake something sweet. But they are grown now, teenagers. They are old enough to grasp what is happening, to understand the ramifications of Walter's selfishness. I am no longer able to soothe them with snuggles or tickles or pillow fights. It occurs to me now that I have lost my superpowers, too.

Maple pecan cookies with toasted oats and toffee chips . . .

Well, maybe not *all* of my superpowers.

"How about we make some cookies?"

Mom is having one of her good days today, and for this I am thankful, but also concerned about how she will take my news, or whether I should tell her at all. When I find her on the patio of Casitas en la Mesa, which overlooks the Pacific Ocean, she is seated under an umbrella at one of the garden tables. She stares out at the rolling green grounds of the senior living residence, singing "The Lonely Goatherd" in her soft, lilting soprano. Her eyes are bright, and the corners of her mouth are pulled upward like two happy commas punctuating her song.

"Hi, Mom," I say, walking toward her with a tray of cookies in hand. As usual, she doesn't respond, just continues the chorus, stretching her voice up to the high notes. *Yodelay-eee. Yodelay-ee-ee. Yodelay-eee. Yodelay-eeeeeee.*

I wait a few seconds to see whether she is done or is about to head into verse number two. She looks well, but then, she always does. At seventy-three, Estelle Simmons is heartbreakingly beautiful. Her silver hair is cut short to accentuate high cheekbones and almond-shaped eyes the color of the sea. The lines on her face are not nearly as deep as they should be for her age, though she has never had a face-lift or any other kind of work. I wonder if this is because her mind has released her from the stress and worries that plague most of us and, in turn, cause us to set our mouths grimly, to frown excessively and furrow our brows in anger. She does none of these things anymore, merely smiles or grins, or gazes vacantly into faces she no longer recognizes. I have seen other Alzheimer patients struggle against their disease, their pain etched into their faces as they violently dig into their ailing minds for answers that will never come. But my mother seems to have accepted her lot gracefully, and this is a relief to me. She may not know me, or anyone else; she may not be able to tell you what day it is or the name of our president. But I know that she passes her days in a detached contentment that I almost envy. *Almost.*

She turns to me now, her expression open and expectant, as though I am a friend, long-forgotten but still welcome.

"I just love that song, don't you?"

I nod. "You sing it beautifully."

"I remember when we performed it with marionettes, in the great room of the estate. That was something, I tell you."

For reasons unbeknownst to her doctors, my mother believes that she is Maria von Trapp from *The Sound of Music*. I can think of no other character, either real or fictitious, that I would want my mother to believe she is. Without the Nazis, of course.

I pull out the chair beside her and sit down, place the cookies on the table in front of me, then fold my hands together as though I am about to say grace.

"I'm sorry, dear. I've forgotten your name." This is the catchphrase my mother has adopted, as if to guard against the truth, as if to say, *It's only your name I can't remember, not the rest of my life.*

"My name is Ruby," I tell her, as I always do.

Her eyes light up. "Ah, Ruby. Like Ruby Keeler! Very popular when I was young. She'd already left show business by the time I came to America. So talented, though."

Actually, I'd been named for Ruby Keeler, back when my mom had dreamed that her baby girl would sing and dance with her namesake's flair. Unfortunately, I cannot carry a tune in a mixing bowl, never could. And as for my ill-fated tap-dancing lessons, I'd rather not get into it.

"It's lovely to see you," she says, and for a split second I allow myself the fantasy that she knows me and who I am to her. I feel my chest swell, but just as quickly deflate when she adds, "You remind me of my daughter Brigitta."

Tears threaten, and I swallow hard, hoping to force down the lump that has risen in my throat. Mom places her hand on mine, a motherly gesture, warm and sincere and comforting. I notice, not for the first time, how her veins show through her papery skin.

"A lovely girl, Brigitta."

Some days I remind her of Liesl, other days of Marta. Gretl, once, when an infected bug bite in the middle of my part line forced me to wear my hair in two ponytails. At least she has never compared me with Kurt or Friedrich.

"Quite a bookworm, too," she adds. "But so serious. Always so serious." She reaches up and places her fingertips on my forehead, then proceeds to smooth away my frown with her gentle touch. "What's wrong, dear? You look troubled."

"Oh, Mom." I try to keep my voice even. I don't want to upset her, to shatter her tranquility even if it is only an illusion born of a troubled mind. But I would give anything if I could have my mother back for ten minutes, five, even. A mere sixty seconds. If I could lay out all of my problems at her feet and receive her maternal wisdom. Feel her arms around me, whispering in my ear: *You'll be all right, Ruby. Everything will be fine.*

"Don't fret, dear," she says, sliding her hand across my temple and down my cheek until she is cupping my face. "Everything will be fine."

I take a sharp breath, then search my mother's eyes for the barest hint of recognition. I've thought, many times, that I've seen it, but in my heart I know that it's just wishful thinking on my part, my desperate hope being projected onto my mother's face. She doesn't know me anymore, and she never will. Although this is not new information, it once again fills me with grief, and tears burst through the weakened dam of my will and spill down my cheeks, wetting my mother's fingers. I let them flow freely now, and I realize that my mother is the only person with whom I feel comfortable crying. And I understand why. Because an hour from now, my tears will be forgotten.

She pats my cheek and smiles sympathetically. "There, there. Let it out now."

And I do, with abandon, shucking my usual stoicism in favor of releasing my pent-up emotions. And my mother, as kind to strangers in the present as ever she was in her life—and for all intents and purposes, I *am* a stranger to her—returns her hand to my hand and waits patiently while I weep. I think of Walter and the safe and comfortable life we built for ourselves and our children, a haven in a chaotic world. Passionless, certainly, lacking in spontaneity, and bereft of surprises. But a life I could count on, take for granted, point to without regrets, and proclaim loudly that I had created it and it was mine. And now that very life has been yanked out from under me like a favorite rug whose weave has come unraveled without my noticing.

As the wretched tears continue to flow, the rational part of my brain understands that these are tears born of my own guilt. Because I know that I am to blame for what has happened. Yes, I've been a true and faithful wife to Walter—the only time I even considered cheating on him was when George Clooney came to town to film a scene for one of his movies, and even then I only got within fifty yards of him. And though I did give Walter the best years of my life, as the cliché goes, I realize that I never gave Walter the one thing he wanted from me most. My heart.

The thing is, I never believed in fairy tales and all of the malarkey fed to young girls by Walt Disney's band of pied pipers. Prince Charming was a two-dimensional animated character, but did not exist in 3- (or 4-) D. Of course, I giggled and gossiped and ogled the water-polo players in high school along with my friends, and faked crushes on Shaun Cassidy and Leif Garrett (really, why?) and Christopher Atkins. But inside, I knew the Cinderella story was just that. A story. I'd seen firsthand through my parents that "happily ever after" was just an overused phrase.

My father had been my mother's Prince Charming—she said so herself—handsome and beguiling, and he'd given her the full-court press, nearly overwhelming her with his pursuit. She told me once that being the focus of my dad's attention was like being at the center of the universe—which was a very powerful feeling for a girl from Des Moines, no matter how beautiful or vivacious she herself had been. And she'd fallen for him, hard and fast, had tied a ribbon around her heart, and presented it to him on a crystal platter.

But the sparks faded quickly, and my father's true colors bled through, breaking my mother's gifted heart over and over again. She'd been stoic, never letting on that his "working late" bothered her, or that his sudden "business trips" caused her pain, or that his perpetual dissatisfaction with her cooking/housework/child rearing upset her in the least. But I'd seen the weariness in her eyes, the way her shoulders slumped whenever he called to say he was stuck late at the office, heard her muffled crying late in the night.

So I'd rejected all the trappings of romance. My parents jokingly dubbed me Rational Ruby at an early age, and I embraced my moniker, wore it like a badge of honor. My friends would lose their minds over various men, and I would watch from the periphery, smiling smugly, knowing that I would never fall to such depths of despair as they did when a relationship crashed and burned. Of course, conversely, I would never be lifted to such heights of ecstasy, but that was fine by me. Ecstasy withdrawal isn't pretty.

And then I'd met Walter, sensible, agreeable Walter. I allowed him into my life, allowed myself to love him. But it was never an all-consuming, fiery, passionate, I-cannot-exist-without-you, you-complete-me kind of love. It was a calm and content kind of love. And I admit I was arrogant. I witnessed so many of my friends—especially the ones who'd had stars in their eyes—get knocked down by reality, some of them divorcing before the ink on their marriage licenses dried. I congratulated myself, for even though, to them, I had settled for Walter, I'd been right. My marriage, based on reality and practicality, was still going strong.

The problem between us was that Walter believed in true love. He believed in soul mates, too, and made the monumental error of miscasting me as his. I have always thought that one plus one makes *two,* whereas Walter believes that the "right one" plus the "right one" equals one *squared. One to the infinite power of love.* He actually said that to me on our wedding day, and I laughed at him as though it were the funniest joke in the world. And I remember the hurt in his eyes, which I pretended not to see as I flagged down one of the servers for another glass of champagne.

His leaving, I understand now, was inevitable. Because he believes in soul mates, and I don't. He believes in true love and I believe in recipes. And now he has found his soul mate, his true love. *Cheryl.* And I am left in ruins.

"I'm getting divorced, Mom," I mumble, choking a bit on the D-word.

"You know, we didn't get divorced in my day," she says. "It just wasn't done." She smiles wistfully. "Of course, I would never have divorced the Captain. He was so handsome and commanding. He was my Prince Charming!"

As I wipe the last of the tears from my face with my sleeve, I absently wonder how my dad—gone for two years now—would feel about being replaced by the image of Christopher Plummer.

"I might lose my house, too," I say miserably. "The kids and I are going to end up in a shack."

"The estate had one hundred and twelve rooms. Ah, it was lovely. But when we escaped to Switzerland, we had to live in a pied-à-terre with only seven rooms! And do you know what? We were just fine. We made the best of it."

Mom slowly withdraws her hand and sits up straight in her seat. She grins at me, her eyes twinkling with glee. "Do you know what we should do?"

I sniffle and do my best to smile back at her. "What?" I ask.

"We should do what I always do when my children are upset. We should sing 'My Favorite Things'!"

I sigh and take one final swipe at my eyes. "That's a great idea, Mom," I agree. "You start."

6

Croquembouche

If Studio 54 had been an upscale food market in suburbia circa 2012, it would be Bridges. All that's missing from the place is a disco ball. The store, which is situated at the northern tip of Pelican Point, is the go-to place for the local moms to see and be seen, and it's usually so busy on Sunday nights that you'd think they were serving two-for-one Cosmopolitans. (In fact, the wine bar in the back corner past the produce is the hot spot, as the market gives out free samples of whatever vintage is currently on sale.) Pelican Point husbands are under the impression that their wives are dutifully gathering the weekly groceries for the house, when, in reality, the women are getting tipsy on as many two-ounce tasters as they can consume in their allotted shopping time, trading diet tips, discussing errant offspring behavior, and exhibiting the results of their latest plastic-surgery adventures.

I am more of an Albertsons/Trader Joe's/Target kind of gal. Since I resent paying fourteen dollars for a single peach and I have no collagen injections to display, I am an unsuitable patron for this particular establishment. But Bridges is on the way from Casitas en la Mesa, and I'm already late getting back to the kids, who I fear might be devising ways to get their father to come home, à la *The Parent Trap* (even though they are neither twin girls nor eight years old). So I have decided to stop into the chichi market for the few items I need.

Mistake.

As I push the cart through stands of fruit so perfect it looks like wax, I catch sight of the crowd of moms gathered at the wine bar. Gina McGee, former PTA president, is having a quasi-serious discussion with Stacey Leach, current PTA president. They are both wearing plum-colored sweatsuits that probably cost more than my entire wardrobe. CeeCee Braddock-Jones is admiring a diamond pendant draped around Holly Morgan's neck while politely sipping Merlot from a shot-glass-size plastic cup. Deanne Fields holds a cup of wine in each hand, one white, one red, and she alternately sips each while nodding at Laura Newman, who is reading aloud from a small pamphlet.

This group makes up a small part of the Pelican Point ladies with whom I have socialized since my kids started preschool. I think of them as croquembouche, because each one is like a perfect little honey-glazed, custard-filled cream puff, but when stacked together, they make an impressive and formidable structure.

I grab a couple of bananas that are a glowing sun yellow from stem to heel—Bridges bananas wouldn't dare have spots of brown on them—and set them in my cart, then push toward the Granny Smiths. I've had an apple cobbler recipe bouncing around in my head for a couple of weeks, and it doesn't hurt to stack the culinary deck in my favor by purchasing the best damn apples in the world. I walk past baskets of golf-ball-size strawberries and blackberries that appear to be on steroids, and just as I reach the cherimoyas, I glance over at the wine bar to find six pairs of eyes trained upon me. The women's expressions range from ambivalence to disdain to evil glee.

Gina slowly turns away, touching Stacey on the sleeve of her distressed velour jacket. Deanne quickly guzzles both of her shots of wine, then makes a show of grabbing Laura's pamphlet and burying her nose in it. Holly raises her hand to her lips, ostensibly in an effort to hide her smirk, but I don't doubt that she uses her *left* hand on purpose in order to exhibit her fourteen-thousand-carat wedding ring.

Ah, I think. *More of Walter's Facebook friends.* Well, maybe *they* aren't, but their husbands definitely are. After last night and this morning, I realize what a small town I live in. I know everyone. Either through my children's school— like these women—or Walter's work or the bakery or the freaking community center. Oh, why couldn't I live in a huge thriving metropolis with millions of people who don't meet each other's eyes when they walk down the street and have no idea to whom they've been living next door for the last twenty years?

In a town like Pelican Point, you learn things about people that you almost wish you didn't. For example, in '09, Gina's husband patted a coworker's bottom and evaded a sexual harassment charge by donating a monstrous sum to the sheriff's department. Deanne's daughter, Francine, a schoolmate of Colleen's, has been in rehab twice. Stacey's son, Marco, wears thick black eyeliner, mascara, and lipstick to school, which the principal allows only because it's MAC, and the boy has taken to picketing for the right to try out for the girls' cheerleading squad. Laura herself was caught shoplifting a three-dollar bracelet from Odd Lots last year and had to act as crossing guard for six months as penance. And Holly's oldest daughter, Rea, also a classmate of Colleen's, was chosen as a homecoming princess, a rare honor for a junior, but rumor has it that she was given the tiara because she performed oral sex on half the football team. (Talk about TMI!)

This treasure trove of dirt used to make me feel almost superior. I would, once again, congratulate myself on my perfect life and my perfect family. *At least I don't have* their *problems,* I'd think. But that was yesterday. Today is another day. A day when I realize that these women, with their cross-dressing/alcoholic/hooker-in-training offspring, their derelict husbands, and their kleptomaniac tendencies, have it great compared to me.

I swallow hard, knowing I have to make a choice. I can bypass them without a word. Or I can attempt small talk with women who actually look alive—as opposed to how I look, which, after my crying jag with my mom and the lack of food in my system, makes me a perfect candidate for a guest spot on *The Walking Dead.*

"Hi, Ruby." CeeCee Braddock-Jones. The only one of the bunch who has the decency to smile warmly at me. I'll have to bake her some muffins.

"Hi, CeeCee." I give a halfhearted wave as I make my way to the wine bar. "Hi, ladies."

I think of the hundreds of hours I've spent with each of these women, on the school grounds waiting for pickup, on the soccer and baseball fields pretending to be watching the games, at interminable PTA meetings and depressingly dry church socials and mandatory town fund-raisers and weekly street fairs. I have never felt uncomfortable around them, always felt a part of the group, bonded through our mutual state of housewife/mother-dom. But oddly, in the space of twenty seconds, on the short journey from the produce section to the wine bar, I realize that overnight I have been ostracized. I am no longer one of them.

"How are you holding up?" CeeCee asks softly.

I take a breath, knowing that my practiced smile is at odds with the bags under my eyes. "Well, you know. I think I'm still trying to process it. It just happened yesterday."

"Oh!" Deanne exclaims, directing her words to the others rather than to me. "When Mack ran off, the first twenty-four hours felt like three weeks!"

Mack being her German-shepherd–border-collie mix.

"Yes, well . . ." I can't think of a response other than *Are you drunk or just an idiot?* Both, I think.

There is an awkward silence, during which I irrationally pray that Bridges was built over a dormant volcano that will suddenly become *un*-dormant and blow the seven of us into the stratosphere on the heels of angry molten lava.

"It gets easier," offers Laura. Laura's first husband was caught stealing from the pensions of his coworkers in order to fund a sex-change operation and currently resides in Joliet with a cell mate named Bubba. But that happened twenty years ago. It didn't take long for the twenty-two-year-old former Miss Redondo Beach to snap up hubby number two: macho, football-stat-quoting Jack Newman.

"Oh, sure. Give it time." This comes from Stacey Leach, who still has not looked me in the eye.

"Maybe he'll come to his senses," CeeCee says. "Sometimes men just need to pretend they're in control. I bet he'll come crawling back to you before you know it."

"Don't be ridiculous," Holly snaps, still grinning like an executioner who really likes his job. "Didn't you see Walter's latest post? He is *so* not going back."

"Holly!" CeeCee cries. "You know I don't do Facebook!"

The five women look at CeeCee in horror. Not only is she *not* on Facebook, but she has the guts to say so out loud. I, however, am more concerned about Walter's alleged "latest post."

"What, exactly, did Walter say?"

"Dumped you as a friend, huh?" Holly asks knowingly. "Well, that makes sense."

I swear, at this moment, nothing would give me greater pleasure than to smash a coconut cream pie into her smug face. But, as I do not have a pie at hand, I simply grit my teeth.

"Let's just say I wouldn't be counting the minutes until his return," Holly states breezily.

CeeCee steps in front of Holly. "It's probably best to just get on with your life anyway, don't you think, Ruby?" She reaches out and gives my arm a quick squeeze. "You've got your two wonderful kids . . ." Behind her, Holly snorts derisively and CeeCee jerks her head around to glare at her. She turns back to me and smoothes her features into a look of serenity. "And you have your bakery. The Muffin Top. You've got so much going for you. You don't need a husband." She chuckles. "Sometimes I wish *I* didn't have a husband."

I appreciate her kind words, but at the same time I realize that she is patronizing me. Because she *does* have a husband to go home to, George Jones, former valedictorian of Harvard and current financial wizard who adores her. I am going home to two forlorn teenagers whom no amount of pecan maple cookies can console.

"Well, I have to go," I say, but before I can push off, CeeCee grabs two bottles of the spotlight Merlot and places them in my cart, thinks for a moment, then grabs a third bottle and sets it beside the others.

"Don't drink them all at once," she says with a wink, but her eyes are full of pity.

* * *

My cell phone is shaking so much, I am afraid that the Big One has finally hit Southern California. As much as I would welcome a natural disaster of devastating proportions at this moment, I quickly realize that it's my hand setting off the Richter scale. I manage to punch in the right numbers only after three tries and am finally rewarded by Isabelle's voice on the other end of the line.

"Ruby? Hi, honey!" Her tone is excessively cheery, like the tone you'd use with a recent amputee who has just come out of anesthesia and has no idea he's missing a limb. "I just went over the May books. It's not as bad as we thought! Okay, it's a little bad, but not as bad as April. That's something, right?"

"Are you in the office?" I ask.

"Sure am. Marcy and Smiley are breaking down out front."

"Is the computer on?"

"Hey, Ruby. You okay? What's up?"

"Izzy, I need to ask you a question." I take a deep breath. "Are you still friends with Walter?"

"That *chingado*? That *puta*-loving, good-for-nothing, *gringo* jerk-off? No way, Ruby. I am never going to speak to his ass again!"

"I mean, on Facebook, Izzy. Are you still friends with Walter on Facebook?" Silence. "Isabelle?" I stare out through the windshield of the car, watching as the croquembouche ladies alight from Bridges with three box boys trailing them like Sherpas. "Izzy?"

"See, I was going to dump him, Ruby, I swear. I just haven't had a chance yet."

"Great!" I cry, a bit too fervently. "I need you to log in

and find his latest post and read it to me." I don't have time to consider the implications of my best friend remaining Facebook friends with my estranged husband. There will be plenty of time for reflection later. Right now I need to know what's going on in his life, and since he refuses to get in touch, I can think of no other way.

"Um, sweetie, no. That's not a good idea. You don't want to hear anything that *cholo* has to say right now."

Stacey Leach and Holly Morgan exchange air kisses with the other four women and head in my general direction, one box boy in tow. I crouch down as far as I can in the driver's seat of my minivan, hoping against hope that I won't be spotted.

"Isabelle," I whisper, as though speaking at full volume will give my whereabouts away. "Get your ample Latina ass on Facebook right this minute and read me Walter's last post."

"What did you say about my ass?" she cries indignantly.

Ordinarily, I do not insult people, especially those I love. Usually, I go out of my way to be kind and complimentary, even when compliments are not warranted. But low blood sugar combined with intense public humiliation has left me unable to stifle my id impulses.

"I called it ample," I repeat calmly. Hey, I could have said "fat" or "humongous" or "monstrous." The truth of the matter is that Isabelle's ass is beautiful, by J.Lo's standards. However, by Kate Moss's standards, it's *gargantuan*.

"You are my best friend, Ruby, and you are going through a rough time right now, so I am going to forgive you for casting aspersions toward my ass. Get it? *Ass-persions?* Toward my *ass?*" You gotta love Isabelle. "But don't think I'm not going to have a long talk with you about this at some later date."

"Fine," I say, peering out the side window as Stacey and Holly pass on the right. Luckily, they are too involved in their own conversation—probably about me—to notice the crazy, soon-to-be divorcée hiding in the Town & Country next to them. A moment later, I scoot up a bit and catch sight of them in the rearview mirror. "Are you on Facebook yet?"

"Be patient!" she retorts crankily. "I can't make this computer go any faster. Okay, okay. Here it comes."

I am clutching my cell to my ear so tightly that my fingers are starting to ache. I tuck the phone in the crook of my shoulder and massage my hand, willing myself not to scream at Izzy to go faster.

"Walter, Walter," she mumbles. "Scrolling, scrolling. Okay, here it is . . . Oh my God."

I feel a tight fist of dread in the pit of my stomach. "What? *What?*"

"Oh, um, Ruby, okay. Are you sure about this?"

"Read me the post," I say, my voice tight.

"All right. Fine. 'Ample ass'! Jesus." I hear her take a breath. My pulse throbs in my temple. "There's a picture of him and, you know, *her.*"

Cheryl.

"They're on a boat."

"Yacht," I hear myself say.

"Whatever," Izzy returns. "And they're all smiling and lovey-dovey. She's not so hot, Ruby. You're much prettier than this *puta.*"

"The *post,* Iz."

"Yeah, right. Got it. Um . . . shit . . . 'Kay. Oooh, it, like, rhymes or something. *True love found / Happiness abounds / Sailing into the sunset / with nary a regret / Good-bye, old life / Good-bye, faux wife / Headed for parts unknown /*

With a love truly my own / Who knew a slice of heaven / Would come at forty-seven . . . What the fuck does 'nary' mean, anyway?"

The inside of the minivan has disappeared and I am sliding down a steep embankment, heading for a black yawning abyss. Isabelle's voice is far away; she calls my name as if from the end of a long tunnel. *Since when does Walter write poetry?* I wonder. *He never wrote* me *a poem.* This is my final thought before the darkness envelops me.

The house is eerily quiet when I walk through the front door thirty minutes later. The living room is bathed in shadows, and my kids are nowhere in sight. I wander through to the kitchen, setting my three illustrious bags of Bridges groceries—which cost me forty-seven bucks—on the counter, and peer into the den. I can just make out the silhouette of my son, sitting on the couch, staring at the muted television which is playing an old Tom and Jerry cartoon.

"Hey," I call to him. He turns to me and does his best to smile, but I can see the strain etched in his youthful features.

"Yo, Mom. How's Granny?"

"Your *grandmother* is having a good day," I tell him. *Unlike me. And* you *apparently.* "Where's your sister?"

He jerks his head toward the ceiling. "In her room. She's been there for about three hours. Crying. Well, she *was* crying. I think she's all dried up." He narrows his eyes at me. "Hey, Mom? You look pale."

"I'll be fine," I assure him. *In about a thousand years.*

"Why is your hair wet?" he asks with mild curiosity.

I shrug, at a loss for a suitable lie. Best not to tell him about my fainting episode or how Isabelle raced from the Muffin Top to Bridges—a trip that normally takes ten minutes but which my friend made in five—and how she'd run into the market and spent six dollars on a liter bottle of Evian, which she proceeded to dump on my head in order to wake me up.

"Colleen's upset, huh?"

He nods, then says simply, "Dad called."

I swallow hard, then silently curse my traitorous heart for leaping in my chest at the thought of Walter calling.

"He called, huh? Here?"

"No, her cell. Then mine. Wanted to . . . I don't know . . . check in, explain things, make sure we were okay."

"And are you, honey? Are you okay?"

He chuffs and shakes his head with bitter amusement. "I told him, 'Bon voyage, dickhead!'"

A bleat of laughter escapes me before I can slap my hand over my mouth.

"Kevin, watch your mouth," I say, instantly turning serious. Because I realize that either Walter told the kids about sailing away with *Cheryl,* or the kids read his Facebook post. Oh, Jesus. That would be bad. I pray with all my might—ironically—that Walter dumped Kevin and Colleen as Facebook friends. But I cannot bear to ask, really don't want to know whether or not they read the horrendous poem that caused me to faint in my car.

"You know what, Mom?" Kevin asks with unusual solemnity.

"What, hon?"

"This is a total nose dredging."

And although I am not familiar with surf speak, I'm pretty sure what my son just said is the equivalent of "this sucks ass."

"It is," I agree, nodding. "Totally."

7

Not the Next Food Network Star

There's good news and bad news. The bad news only begins with Walter's departure and subsequent sailing off into the sunset. Apparently, the day after his soul mate/first mate gave notice, Walter quit his job, relinquishing his family health insurance plan, his 401(k), his life insurance policy, and—oh, yeah—his income. On the Monday after he cast off, I received a phone call from his lawyer informing me that Walter had, *in fact,* filed for bankruptcy, and would not, *in fact,* be able to bring our mortgage current, and does not, *in fact,* intend to pay alimony since he has no occupation, and that there is, *in fact,* not a damn thing I can do about it since he is currently sailing around the South Pacific with *Cheryl.* Also, the no-good bastard has emptied our joint checking account.

On a more superficial note, I should mention that most, actually all, of my social engagements for the foreseeable future have mysteriously been canceled or indefinitely postponed, invitations withdrawn, and lame excuses concocted to spare my feelings, i.e., "We have to cancel because the peach tree has been infested with African beetles." I take solace in the fact that none of my peers are entertaining Walter and *Cheryl* in my stead since he is currently frolicking around Pago Pago, or wherever the hell he is.

Okay, now the good news . . . Um . . . I'm thinking. Let's

see . . . I haven't thrown up since the day after Walter left. That counts, right? And Izzy has managed to add Colleen and Kevin to the health insurance policy we have through the Muffin Top, which is great, except that it's another monthly chunk of change I have to come up with. And if the Muffin Top folds, which may or may not happen, we'll all be out of luck. Wait. I was talking about good news. Fine. Okay. The best news of all is that the kids and I are not homeless . . . at least, not yet.

When my father passed away a month after my mom went into Casitas—and I honestly believe he died because he didn't have Mom around to disappoint anymore, and therefore had no reason left to live—he'd put most of his money into a trust meant for Mom's care. But he'd left a modest sum to me, which I locked up in an account in my own name. I hadn't told Walter at the time, had convinced myself that I would someday surprise him with a month-long trip around the world or an engraved Rolex, which he claimed was the pinnacle of material gain. Perhaps, subconsciously, I had been preparing myself for the exact circumstances in which I now found myself, although I never would have admitted it then. But whatever the motivation, my secret stash has been gaining interest for the past two years, right up until the moment when I ripped 90 percent of it from the clutches of the bank.

Thanks to Dad's bequest, I was able to bring my mortgage current. I dropped off a cashier's check to Franchise Funding, where a haughty receptionist with a bad bouffant and a pencil tucked behind her ear looked at me with such disdain that I wanted to yank the pencil out of her hair and ram it up her right nostril. I immediately labeled her bad fruitcake, which I realize sounds redundant because there has never been a *good* fruitcake, but my label demonstrates just how much I despised this woman on sight. (The fact that she was plucking from my hands a check for tens of thousands of dollars may have had something to do with my negative assessment, but not much.)

Luckily, I was able to get out of the building before Jacob Crazy-Water-Gazing-Dead-Lesbian-Wife Salt made an appearance. The last thing I wanted was to see his (handsome) face and hear another rousing rendition of "I Love Gays." Nor did I want to be reminded of ruining his prime rib dinner and the trousers of his expensive suit. But, apparently, Mr. Salt was busy with "another *foreclosure*," as the receptionist informed me, and if I'd like to wait to give the check directly to him, it would be at least another twenty minutes. I chose not to wait. Instead, I sprinted out of there.

All in all, there is enough money left in my secret account to cover the mortgage until September, at which point I will have to make a decision about what to do. Possibly, Walter will be back on dry land by then, and I can sue him right down to his socks for alimony and child support. But, as his lawyer said, I cannot, *in fact*, count on his return or his ability to generate enough income to support an ex-wife and two kids. (I have come to the conclusion that lawyers use the phrase "in fact" over and over again just to increase their billable time. *In fact, ka-ching, in fact, ka-ching, in fact, ka-ching!*)

In the meantime, Izzy has come up with a couple of ideas for me to make some extra money. And since I told her I would do anything short of streetwalking—not because I am morally opposed to the idea, but because who would pay to have sex with this bag of bones?—I feel duty bound to listen to her suggestions. Hopefully, her ideas are better than her recipes.

Sunday night, eight days after Walter-gate, Izzy and I sit

at the kitchen table drinking hibiscus margaritas and brain-storming. The Muffin Top's meager profits, deduced by Izzy with her illegible figures scratched onto a yellow legal pad, will be enough to pay for my living expenses, *if* the kids and I live extremely frugally. Meaning we will most likely have to give up cable TV, eating out, driving anywhere (with gas at four bucks a gallon), heat in the winter (thank God it's June), air-conditioning in the summer (damn it!), any and all online impulse purchases, brand-name products, and last-minute trips to Bridges Market (okay by me!). Having al-ways been practical by nature, as demonstrated by my nonbelief in true love and my unshakable faith in the suc-cessful outcome of a perfect recipe well executed, I am not concerned with giving up luxuries and unnecessary extras. I am, however, concerned with the mortgage come Septem-ber. Which is where Izzy's ideas come into play.

"Okay," she says, dropping her pen onto her pad. "So the first thing is that I got in touch with the Food Channel about getting you on *Cake-Off*."

"'Scuse me?" My brain is already a little fuzzy, thanks to Izzy's heavy hand with the tequila. But I am not so far gone that I don't shudder with dread at the bomb she just dropped. *Cake-Off* is a show in which three cake designers have eight hours to create a masterpiece which then gets ripped apart by three unforgiving judges who seem to take pride in mak-ing the contestants cry. Even tipsy, I want no part of that.

"They're asking for a résumé and some pics of your work. I'm on it."

"Iz, no," I tell her. "No way."

"It's a very slim chance," she says, by way of reassuring me. "But you'd be perfect for that show. And the prize is fifteen grand. Plus, think of the publicity for the Muffin Top."

I take a huge sip of my margarita, clinging to the phrase "slim chance." *Good.* The drink is disappearing, not surprisingly, because it tastes like punch.

"Also, I called Dolores Fernandez over at PPC," she tells me, after strategically, yet surreptitiously, topping off my glass. "She is very excited about my proposal."

"Which is?" Because of the booze, my words come out sounding like "Weeshees?" But since Izzy speaks fluent margarita, she understands me perfectly.

"Remember when she asked you to teach an extension class in pastry?"

Dolores Fernandez is the course coordinator for Pelican Point College, a very respectable junior college in town that educates kids who are not yet ready for, can't afford, or don't really want to go to university. The perks of PPC include reduced tuition for residents, parking passes for any lot or meter in the whole of the community, and a breathtaking view of the Pacific Ocean for students who want to stare into space rather than gain knowledge. About a year ago, Dolores approached me about replacing the current pastry instructor, who was forced to retire due to the sudden onset of high cholesterol, diabetes, and a penchant for squeezing coed buns. I was flattered by her offer but had graciously declined, for although I know far more about desserts than most, the idea of standing in front of a group of people staring at me and anxiously awaiting my tutelage filled me with unspeakable terror.

I have never been good at public speaking or performing of any kind. This is the one area of my life where I cannot hide behind a placid veneer. I have a number of early childhood memories which, to this day, make me blush with shame. *The Wizard of Oz* in second grade, for example, in which I was given the role of Evil Tree Number Two. During the scene when Dorothy takes an apple—not from *my* tree, but from Evil Tree Number One—the thought of all those people in the audience looking at me (even though they were probably looking at Dorothy) made me faint dead away, right there on stage. An emergency intermission was inserted into the show by Mrs. Greenblatt, the EMTs were called, and I was rushed in an ambulance to the hospital for observation, just in case I'd had a seizure.

In the fourth grade, my Thanksgiving poem had been chosen as the school's best and I was requested to read it aloud at the Wednesday assembly. The subject was "What Thanksgiving Means to Me" and I had written two pages in rhyming couplets about the holiday food, using language so descriptive, even for a nine-year-old, that our principal, Mr. Forbes, claimed he could practically *taste* the pumpkin pie. As I stood at the dais, my knees knocking together, perspiration erupting from my forehead, I peered out at the hundreds of kids gathered in the activity room, all of them staring at me expectantly. I forced myself to breathe deeply, as my mother instructed me to do so as not to lose consciousness. And I have to say, it worked. I didn't faint. Instead, I peed in my pants. Literally. Hot urine squeezed out of my oxygenated bladder, soaked my underpants, and slid down the inside of my thighs, which were thankfully hidden by the dais. After I choked my way through the poem, I managed to escape out the back of the auditorium with no one the wiser. Well, no one except Mr. Dean, the school custodian, who'd spent the next half hour sopping up, cleaning, and disinfecting the stage floor. From that point on, years before my first period, whenever I had to get up in front of anyone, I wore a Kotex maxi pad.

I am fine in one-on-one situations, with my friends and family, and even in large gatherings like parties, where everyone is laughing and drinking and not paying particular attention to anyone else. But put me in a situation that is remotely like public speaking or performing and I practically go to pieces. Therefore, it was a nobrainer to turn Dolores Fernandez down.

But now here it is, Izzy's ridiculous plan.

"So that guy they brought in to replace the perv?" she says between swigs. "Apparently, he doesn't know anything about cakes. I mean, decorating them. He can bake 'em and ice 'em and swirl on 'em and all that, but it's just bare-bones Wilton kind of stuff. And the kids all want to learn how to be the Ace of Cakes. So I told Dolores, I said, 'Ruby could teach an extension class, right in the Muffin Top.' And you know what she said?"

"Wa?" I ask, unable to form hard consonants as my tongue is mysteriously numb.

"She said she'd had exactly the same idea!"

And suddenly, as my tequila-soaked synapses finally begin firing again and it dawns on me just exactly what Izzy is proposing, I bolt to my feet and shriek, "No way!" (Although it sounds more like "Nyoaaaeee!")

Izzy scribbles more figures onto her pad, all the while talking. "Look, Rube, you need money. Bad. And Dolores is gonna give you half the tuition, plus you'll have to charge the kids materials fees and you might as well make a profit there, too. I mean, seriously, I know we have a full-court summer marketing plan in place for the shop, the Fourth, and your kids' events, but you have to be realistic about how much impact those are going to have. The Top's in dire straits right now. Not that I don't think business is going to get better," she adds quickly, "but while we're slow, this'll supplement your income." Scribble, scribble. She underlines a number, puts the pen on the table, and picks up the pad to display it to me. "This is what you'd make with eight kids in your class. That's the minimum you need to keep it on the schedule."

I admit, the figure is impressive, but I'm still not sold. "Tha's for eight kiz. Wha if eight kiz don take da class?"

"They already got eight signed up."

"Wha????"

"First class is a week from Tuesday. And don't look at me like that! Summer session starts next week. I had to make a decision. This first course is just a test, but if it goes well, Dolores said she'd add it to the curriculum. This is a chance for you to keep your house come September, Ruby!"

My heart starts pounding furiously at the thought of teaching a class, of having eight pairs of eyes trained on me for three hours at a clip.

"I can't do it, Izzy! Why can't we get a website instead?"

"Because a good Web designer would cost us twenty grand and we decided not to do anything half-assed." She stands and places her hands on her generous hips. "Look, I know you have this deep-seated, paralyzing, irrational fear of getting in front of people, but so what? Pretend you're someone else, like Kim Kardashian or something."

"Like Kim Kardashian would ever teach a cake-decorating class," I retort, realizing that adrenaline has rendered me sober enough to speak clearly.

"Kim Kardashian couldn't teach a class on how to boil water. But that's not my point. Look at you, Ruby. Your husband is sailing around the world with a *puta* named *Cheryl*. And you haven't fallen apart. You haven't had a nervous breakdown or bought a ticket on the Xanax express. You are strong! You can handle anything!"

Izzy's unbridled (and unfounded) enthusiasm is what got her on the cheerleading squad in high school, despite the fact that they'd had to special-order a uniform in her size. I can't help but be inspired by her words of support. And she is right about me not falling apart. I realize that although I've been having trouble eating, and I've let a few things go around the house, and I've passed several nights covertly crying into my pillow, and I've discovered an untapped affinity for red wine . . . and vodka . . . and tequila, obviously, and I've avoided going anywhere in public lest I see the looks of pity/disdain/fear of contagion on the faces of my former acquaintances, I have been functioning. I haven't been sitting on my couch in my nubby bathrobe watching *One Life to Live* eating Ben & Jerry's by the carton, bemoaning my cursed fate and ignoring my children.

In fact, although I almost hate to admit it, I've noticed that Walter's absence hasn't wreaked nearly the amount of havoc I'd anticipated. In the last week, I've missed him on countless occasions, but if I had to be specific about those occasions, they would include the following: when the lightbulb in the foyer blew; when the downstairs toilet clogged; when Kevin wanted to get his old boogie board from the crawl space in the garage; when the air in my tires ran low; when I needed a spare set of hands while I tried a complicated new recipe. Not once have I reached for my husband in the middle of the night, but then, we stopped reaching for each other long ago. Even the kids seem to be doing all right. Their initial shock has been replaced by a kind of quiet ambivalence. I've always heard that kids are resilient, but I think it goes deeper than that.

I'm not sure when it happened, but Walter slowly edged out to the periphery of all of our lives. This may have been by his own design to make his departure easier for him. But I also acknowledge that this kind of family dynamic just happens. From the time my kids were born, every morning

Walter went off to work, and I was left on the parenting battlefield. Just like all the other moms I knew. Generally speaking, fathers become outsiders, happily, in most cases—the "backup parent." They return from their long days at the office having missed all of the poopy diapers and spit up and unending crying jags that rip through your eardrums until you are nearly insane, and boo-boos that merely need a kiss and injuries that need the ER, and fights between siblings and write-ups from school and talking back and the occasional spilling of glue or Kool-Aid on new carpets, and vomiting from cheese dogs and screams of "I hate you!" Dads get to come home to clean, fed children who have already done their homework and are ready for bed.

Recently, Walter's interactions with Colleen and Kevin have been completely superficial. *How's school? Brush your teeth. No, you cannot use my Volvo. What are you wearing? Ask your mother. Love you, too.* I must be honest and give him his due. He was always there for them, up until a week ago. And he never raised a hand to them, never verbally attacked them, or made them feel small. He liked to make them laugh with silly jokes he got in his e-mail. He was a good father. He was a good husband, too. He never hit me or abused me, he was always there for me, and he didn't mind me barking orders at him when he helped me in the kitchen. But at some point, he stopped being emotionally invested and inextricably involved. So, although the three of us are aware of the shift, aware that a certain energy is missing from our daily lives, it feels less cathartic than it might if that missing presence had been more of a *presence*. Like a cocker spaniel.

That's not to say that I haven't been struggling. I'm not comfortable with my new position, my new place in society, my new responsibilities. I'm frightened of the unknowable future and angry that the past eighteen years feel remarkably like wasted time. I'm filled with rage that I gave my life to a man who could so easily throw me away like garbage. I'm constantly second-guessing myself for the decisions I've made, and racked with guilt over my role in the destruction of my family. And also, I am lonely.

But in the end, I have not crumbled. That's got to count for something, right? And having this realization on the heels of my third margarita, I am led to the conclusion— alcohol-inspired though it may be—that I might possibly be able to execute Izzy's plan. With Helen Reddy's voice warbling through my brain (*I am woman, hear me roar!*) I start nodding at Izzy and saying "I guess maybe I could."

"I *know* you can, Ruby. All you have to do is try." She refills our glasses, hands me mine, and raises her own in a toast. And we drink on it, downing the remaining hibiscus margaritas and thereby sealing the deal.

Which is why I am now standing in the center workstation of the Muffin Top on the following Monday night. The bakery is closed and I'm surrounded by my entire staff, my kids, two of Kevin's surfer friends, Luke and Billy Peters, Colleen's cohorts Rachael and Zoe, elderly Mrs. Sheerborne, who owns the travel agency next door, and some random guy wearing an Air Supply T-shirt who Izzy found loitering outside.

In my hand I hold a pastry bag filled with buttercream as I attempt to demonstrate how to put a scalloped border on the bottom of a cake. My hand is shaking and I am stuttering nervously and the Kotex maxi pad in my underwear is chafing my upper thighs. I can tell that my practice class is not going well from the glazed expressions on the faces of my faux students.

"You have to b-b-be sure that you k-k-keep consistent p-p-pressure on the bag in order to m-m-make an even border." My voice is almost a whisper and I am having trouble breathing. My forehead is beaded with perspiration that I worry might drip onto the frosting. On the plus side, the perimeter of the cake looks gorgeous, but then, I can do a scallop border in my sleep, so that's not saying much.

"Yo, dog," Luke calls out as he grabs one of the other pastry bags from the counter. "Watch this!"

The boy lifts the bag toward Billy's face and begins to squirt frosting over his upper lip, creating a scalloped pink mustache. The lines are uneven, but I have to give Luke props for his first attempt.

Air Supply Guy, with his two-day growth of beard and hands that look like they haven't been washed for a week, grabs another of the bags and starts squeezing frosting into his mouth. "Mmmm."

I glance up at my staff, who form a semicircle on the outside of the group. Marcy instantly paints on a supportive smile and gives me a thumbs-up. Smiley Wilson, a short, muscular man of thirty-five who came to work at the bakery when he lost his job as a mechanic at the local Pep Boys, stands ramrod straight, arms crossed over his chest, unsuccessfully trying to suppress a grin. Pam Whitfield, an attractive sixtysomething former day trader who was forced into retirement long before, as she puts it, her financial prowess became obsolete, is overtly filing her acrylic nails. Izzy, generous hip resting against the sink, has her head cocked to one side and is squinting at me in puzzlement. Knowing my friend as I do, I can guess what she must be thinking: *Should have gone for the streetwalking angle.*

I drop my own pastry bag and push a strand of hair behind my ear. I notice that Mrs. Sheerborne has claimed her own bag and is now competently finishing the border on the cake.

"That's very good, Ida," I croak, and the older woman beams.

A ring tone sounds in the kitchen and the six teenagers instantly check their purses and pockets. Rachael gives a shout of "Aha!" and raises her cell phone into the air victoriously, as if she just won the lottery. She checks the caller ID and grins, then taps the screen and raises the phone to her ear. "Hello?" she coos. "Oh, Brett!"

Zoe and Colleen crowd around her, staring at her expectantly. Zoe nudges Colleen in the ribs and giggles. "No. I'm not doing anything," Rachael says breezily, then allows herself to be ushered over to the display case by the two other girls.

The boys, my son included, are busy having frosting wars while Marcy makes a futile attempt to rein them in.

"Okay, everyone," I say, trying to clear the fear-phlegm from my throat. "Why don't we call it a night?"

"Oh, man," says Air Supply Guy. "I was *told* we were going to learn fondant."

"Yeah, yeah," says Izzy, sidling up to the counter. "That's not till week four. Sign up at PPC and you'll get the whole kit and caboodle."

"If I may say so, dear," says Mrs. Sheerborne as she sets the pastry bag next to the cake and removes her glasses in order to clean them, "your teaching style leaves something to be desired."

Ida Sheerborne thinks of herself as an éclair, which I discovered one afternoon in March when the unrelenting rain left both of our shops empty and inspired us to share a pot of coffee and a couple of cranberry muffins. She'd told me that her husband—long gone now—always called her "my little éclair," and then proceeded to tell me why, which shocked me because I'd never known a septuagenarian to use such candid language. I think of her more as a Bundt cake: simple, straightforward, and ageless.

"I assume you want me to be honest?" she asks, replacing her glasses on the bridge of her nose. When I nod (even though I really don't want to her to be honest), she continues. "It's clear you know your subject, as evidenced by all of the wonderful sweets on display. But you lack organization. I highly recommend you come up with a more detailed lesson plan." I open my mouth to respond, but Mrs. Sheerborne is not yet finished. "Also. You need to wear darker lipstick."

Her last suggestion causes me to gape, and since my mouth is already open, this requires almost no further action.

"Your students are listening to your every word, watching the words come out of your mouth. Your mouth is the wellspring from which all your pearls of wisdom flow." She smiles and pats my hand. "I'm sure you'll do just fine once you work out the kinks."

Marcy has wrestled the pastry bags away from the boys by tempting them with a couple of fudge macadamia cupcakes. She begins to clean up the workstation. Rachael is still talking into her cell phone while Colleen and Zoe give her hand signals and whisper to each other. Mrs. Sheerborne exits, followed by Air Supply Guy, who is questioning her about the cost and logistics of a trip to Bora Bora. At this moment, I'd welcome a trip anywhere.

"Are we excused?" asks Pam, tucking her emery board into her purse.

"Oh yeah," Smiley answers for me, then he gives me a salute and removes his specially made chocolate-brown apron. (For some reason, the former marine refused to wear the *plum* aprons.)

I begin to shake my head as Izzy takes a step closer. "It wasn't *that* bad," she tries as I chuff derisively.

"Yes, it was. It was that bad. It was worse than *that bad.* I suck at this, Izzy!"

"I don't know if 'suck' is the word I'd use," she says.

"How about 'suck big-time'?" offers Billy around a chunk of cupcake.

"Dude! Back off!" Kevin hisses, trying for a whisper.

"Yo, man, watch the ribs!" Billy cries, recoiling from Kevin's well-placed elbow jab.

"That's my *mom,* dude!" Kevin glances over at me. "He didn't mean you, Mom. Right, Billy?"

"Uh, no. No, no. Not you, Miz McMillan. I meant, uh, the, uh, Lakers! Yeah, dude, the Lakers. They suck big-time!" The boy quickly stuffs the rest of the cupcake into his mouth.

I look at Izzy. "I suck big-time."

"No, you don't," she says, but her doubtful expression contradicts her words.

Kevin, sensing my distress, ambles over to me and slings his bony arm around my shoulder. "Mom. You are the best, uh, baker I've ever seen in my entire life."

Despite the fact that he is only fourteen, his compliment warms my heart.

"Thanks, Kev."

"You're better than all those guys on the Food Channel, even. You totally rock cakes. You just gotta chill. You know, be cool." He removes his arm and grabs the counter with both hands. "It's like when I taught Craig Greely to surf, you know? I mean, I showed him all the right moves, like positions and stuff. But in the end, I kind of had to let the waves do the talking. Get it? It seems like that's kind of what you have to do. Let the, you know . . ." He makes a wide-sweeping gesture around the workstation with the remaining cake and pastry bags. "Let the cakes do the talking."

He smiles at me and I can't help but smile back. God, I love my son.

"Dude!" calls Luke. "You gotta try this . . . this . . . this thing! What is it?"

"Raspberry lavender muffin," provides Marcy.

"Yeah, that! It's the bomb!"

Kevin wanders off to join his friends in their diabetic-coma-inducing adventure, leaving Izzy and me to stare at each other.

"Let the cakes do the talking," I repeat thoughtfully.

She hides her skepticism with a nod. "Plus," she says, "you might want to think about a crash course in public speaking."

"Izzy!" I cry, then quickly add, "Do they offer those at the rec center?"

8

Hiding the Crumbs

It turns out that the community center does have just such a class—a kind of Parks and Rec version of Toastmasters. But the course is six weeks, and since I don't have nearly that long to find some instructional mojo, there's no point in my signing up. Instead, with Kevin's sage fourteen-year-old advice in mind, as well as Ida Sheerborne's less than flattering assessment of my teaching skills, I've decided to tackle this challenge the same way I always do, by breaking it down like a recipe.

The ingredients for a successful class are as follows: solid information and knowledge. (I've got this in spades.) A clear and detailed course outline with each session divided into three parts: lecture, demonstrations, and hands-on. (I'm working on it.) The proper equipment and enough supplies for eight students to get jiggy with cakes. (In the last two days I have stocked the Muffin Top with a hundred pounds of fondant, twenty pounds of gum paste, an industrial-size carton of meringue powder, and enough confectioners' sugar to bury a corpse.) And finally, the instructor's ability to get through an entire class without soaking her underwear. (I'm working on that, too, by doing a thousand Kegel exercises a day. But just in case, I have moved past Kotex maxi pads and have invested in a package of Depends.) Roll all of the above ingredients together, and voilà! Successful class.

The thing is, I love cakes. I love everything about them. The way a simple batter plus a little heat equals a moist, mouthwatering confection. The way you can sculpt and form just about anything from a couple of pound cakes. The way a dollop of frosting, a sheet of fondant, and a few well-placed accents can transform a buttermilk cake into a sports car or a cell phone or a plate of sushi. But mostly, I love the way the receivers of cakes look when they first see the creations that were made especially for them, whether it's a rendition of the Taj Mahal or a simply decorated layer cake with buttercream flowers. *Everybody* loves cake. Cakes make people happy.

And this is what I want to convey to my class. A sense of fun and whimsy and enthusiasm. Of course, it can be difficult to impart fun and whimsy and enthusiasm when you are worried about wetting your pants.

But I am trying not to think about that, and every time my terror-induced incontinence comes to mind, a stressipe takes its place. So far I have come up with twelve new recipes to try at the bakery. But I don't have time to test any of them out because I am busy immersing myself in my old cookbooks, professional pastry tomes, online cake-decorating course outlines, and Food Channel programming.

My kids are very understanding about my current obsession and are giving me a wide berth. They're both busy with their own summer activities anyway. I haven't mentioned the whole mortgage-deadbeat-dad thing to them, and they've mistakenly assumed that this extension class is a kind of therapy for me, a way for me to change my focus and get over Walter. And it *is* having that effect on me, as I have little opportunity to wallow or contemplate my existence or wonder where on the planet my husband and *Cheryl* happen to be. But the class means much more than that. It has become a lifeline, a way to save my family and our home, and if I fail, if the class gets canceled because the instructor is total crap, I have no idea what I'm going to do.

Sell the car, sell the house, rent a two-bedroom apartment in the "undesirable" part of town, get a part-time job at the gas station, get robbed at gunpoint . . .

Uh-oh. I feel another stressipe coming on.

Apple-streusel pastry tarts drizzled with sweetened condensed milk and coarsely chopped walnuts.

Okay. I feel much better now.

On Thursday afternoon, I sit on my bed watching my seven-hundredth hour of the Food Channel, an assortment of cake-decorating magazines lying open around me. This morning at the Muffin Top I baked and decorated three theme cakes for Friday pickup: a simple two-layer red velvet cake with cream-cheese frosting and a spray of buttercream roses; a devil's food cake in the shape of a pool table—edible balls and pool cues included; and a two-tier vanilla sponge cake with raspberry filling, covered with a hundred miniature gum-paste shoes of all different types and colors for a sweet sixteen party this weekend. My hands are cramped into claws and I am bone weary.

On the TV screen, an episode of *Cake-Off* airs and three cake designers are furiously trying to build archvillain cakes in the allotted time. I recognize Cody Armstrong, a designer from Texas, in her famous peach polka-dot chef coat, working in Kitchen One. She is calmly attaching rice cereal to armature while one of her assistants rolls out fondant and the other spray-paints what looks like a gum-paste remote control. Cody is considered the grande dame of *Cake-Off*, having won it more times than any other competitor. On top of that, she always looks fantastic, gorgeous, really. Never a blond hair out of place, never a smudge in her makeup, not even at the end of eight grueling hours. She exudes confidence and grace and was featured in a two-page spread in *Marie Claire* a few months back in which her chef coat was conspicuously absent in order to show off her hot bod. (I really hate this woman!)

In Kitchen Two, Thomas Bell, another frequent contestant, is cutting into a three-foot-high stack of cakes, chewing his lip nervously and sweating profusely. Apparently, he is way behind. His assistants scurry around the kitchen behind him. A chef I'm not familiar with stands in Kitchen Three, hands on her hips, staring at her villain cake with wide eyes, her two assistants flanking her. The cake is seriously listing to the side and looks as though it will topple at any moment.

The camera cuts back to Kitchen One, and there's Cody with her can-do attitude. I study her cake, which is in the shape of a diabolical scientist standing atop a warhead, his finger poised on the "fire" button. If I break it down into steps, it's really quite simple. *I* could make that cake. But the cake is not the problem. It's the can-do attitude I'm struggling with.

I glance at my clipboard, on which I've written outlines for the first four classes. I'm just about to make a note in the margin when I hear a soft tapping on my bedroom door. Colleen stands in the doorway. She wears a light pink camisole and denim capris, and with her hair in a braid, she looks about twelve.

"Can I come in?" Her voice is small. "I don't want to bother you if you're working."

I put the clipboard down, mute the TV, clear a space for

her on the bed, then pat the covers. "Come, come. I could use a little break."

She crosses the room and sits next to me. For a moment she says nothing, merely gazes at the TV.

"Is everything okay, honey?" I ask.

"I guess," she says with a sigh. I recognize the sigh. It's the everything-is-*not*-okay sigh. At least it's not the everything-is-total-crap growl, which my daughter is particularly good at, especially around her period.

"What is it, Col? Is it your dad?"

She shrugs. "They're in Hawaii," she offers, and I feel my shoulders tense. Not because I've always wanted to go to Hawaii and Walter promised me a trip, but because I was under the impression that Walter had removed the kids from his friends list.

"Did he post it on Facebook?" I will myself to speak casually.

"I guess." Another sigh. "Martha Applegate's mom is one of his friends. Martha told me there's all kinds of pictures of him and *her*."

Oh God. My poor daughter.

"Snorkeling and waterskiing and standing next to some big volcano."

Too bad he didn't fall in, I think.

"It's just so wrong," she states flatly.

"I know." It's my turn to sigh.

"I miss him. I mean, kind of," she admits. "He could be funny sometimes and he always told me how pretty I looked even when I had a gnarly zit on my face." Which has happened roughly four times since she hit puberty, the lucky girl. "But then, you know, I hear this stuff from my friends and it's like I don't even know him at all. My own dad."

My own husband . . .

"You know?"

I nod. "Yes, I do."

We sit side by side for a long moment, neither of us speaking. I wish there were more I could do to ease her pain, but there isn't. I can only be here for her. I pat her knee and try to change the course of both of our thoughts.

"What do you want to do for the Fourth?" I ask, and receive another shrug. "Do you want to do the park with me or the beach with Kevin?"

"I don't care."

"I can always use your help at the Muffin Top booth."

"Oh, Mom. Please."

"Well, what's Jeff's family doing?" Jeff is a boy my daughter claims is not her boyfriend.

"I think they're going away. Not that it matters."

"Did you two break up?"

"Mom! He was *not* my boyfriend." She hangs her head. "And yes, we broke up because Charlene Vincent showed him her boobs at the End of the Year Dance and I won't show him *my* boobs, so he feels like he has to be *her* boyfriend."

Ah. Just like Walter. Maybe if I'd shown my husband *my* boobs more often, he wouldn't be with *Cheryl*. But then, she hasn't had kids, so her boobs are much better than mine.

"Well, I think you're right not to show *anyone* your boobs for a while."

"I would if I loved the guy," she says, causing me to shudder internally at the idea of Colleen bare-breasted with a member of the opposite sex. "But I didn't love Jeff, even if he was kind of cute."

"Then you made the right choice."

She diverts her focus to the magazines on the bed. "So, how's it coming with the class prep?"

"Um . . ." I stretch my neck then lean back against the headboard. "Not bad."

"You're worried you're going to suck, aren't you?"

Colleen can be very perceptive and never minces words. Usually I admire these qualities. At this moment, not so much. "Maybe a little," I admit.

"But, Mom, you are so great with cakes."

"The cakes aren't really the problem," I tell her, watching as she picks up one of the magazines and starts flipping through it. "The problem is me. I'm not cut out for teaching."

She frowns down at a picture of a marzipan lion sitting atop a chocolate mountain. "But you are, Mom," she says, tossing the magazine away. "Remember when you helped me with my algebra? And that composition on the economics of third-world countries? And what about when you tried to teach me to make Grandma's famous chili? You are, like, so patient. You didn't get frustrated and make it yourself. You kind of walked me through it, showing me what to do."

"But this is different, honey. This is a bunch of people I don't know. Strangers. Eight of them. All at the same time."

"You know what I think? I think Aunt Izzy's right." I give her a sharp look and she dons an expression of sheer innocence. "What? She and I discussed it at great length. Why wouldn't we?"

"At great length, huh?"

"Yes, and I think her idea is brilliant."

"And exactly which idea would this be?"

"You know. The one where you pretend to be somebody else. Like Julia Roberts."

"Izzy said Kim Kardashian."

"Yeah, like *she* knows how to bake a cake. But I bet Julia Roberts does. She has, like, three kids!"

"So I should pretend to be Julia Roberts?"

"Okay, maybe not pretend to be a movie star or anything, because why would a movie star teach a cake class? But you could make up a personality."

"Like Sybil?"

Colleen gives me a puzzled look. "Who's that?"

"Never mind," I say. "But, Col, it'll still be me."

"See, no. You should totally give yourself a complete makeover. Change the way you look."

"What's wrong with the way I look?"

She narrows her eyes at me and I flinch. She won't say it, but ratty sweats, men's baggy T-shirt, hair pulled into a messy knot, and not a stitch of makeup is what's wrong.

"Look, Mom, I love you no matter what. But you haven't had a new hairstyle for, like, forever. And your makeup is so old it smells kind of funky. I know this because I was looking for an eyeliner sharpener 'cause I lost mine, and the smell from your drawer almost made me gag. And I know you wear jeans and plain shirts because of all the batter and stuff at the bakery, but you wear an apron, too, so why not go for it a little? You need a little *za za zing*!"

I'm thinking I don't need a little *za za zing*. I'm thinking I need a lobotomy. Or a hypnotherapist. Or a daughter who doesn't refer to *Vogue* magazine as the Bible.

"Seriously," she says. "I tell my girls all the time. 'When you look good, you can't help but feel good.' And, 'Beauty comes from the inside, but confidence comes from the outside.' And it works, too, Mom."

"It may not work for me, Colleen. I'm not six. I'm . . . well . . . I'm old."

"It's worth a try," she says, and I try to ignore the fact

that she didn't argue with my "old" comment. She jumps up off the bed, her eyes wide and sparkling, and puts her hands on her hips, then stares at me expectantly.

"What, *now*?"

She nods. "Yes. Right now."

I groan. "Colleen, *honey*, I appreciate your enthusiasm. But I really don't think this is going to do any good."

She cocks her head to the side. "You got any better ideas?"

I glance past her at the TV, where Cody Armstrong is receiving her seventh first-place medal, her cherry-red lips smiling wide, her blue eyes sparkling, her blond hair perfectly in place. "No, I don't have any better ideas, Colleen. I'm all yours."

My daughter is good. At sixteen, she could be the host of *Extreme Makeover: Middle-Agers*. I stare at myself in the mirror, transfixed. In two hours, Colleen has transformed me from fortysomething hausfrau into hot mama. My cheeks flame as I take in the details: new bangs and a layered haircut, a fresh application of auburn highlights strategically woven into my brown locks, a simple yet comprehensive application of makeup, a hip-hugging denim skirt that flairs out at the bottom (which Colleen found in the back of my closet), a stretch black Lycra top with ruffled cap sleeves (which Colleen found in the back of *her* closet), a chest-length silver chain on which hangs a medallion that rests just above my cleavage, and chunky silver earrings that look like a party in my ears.

The best part is that I actually look *alive*.

"Whoa, dude!"

Colleen and I turn to see Kevin standing just inside the bedroom door. His mouth is open and his eyes are wide.

"What'd you do to Mom, Col? She's, like, a total babe!"

Colleen smiles gleefully and hugs herself. "I know! Isn't she?"

Kevin comes closer, walks around me slowly, inspecting me as though I am an exhibit in a museum, or a space-age, rocket-propelled surfboard. "Holy shi—crap. It's like a total miracle!"

I am flattered by my son's praise but also a little disturbed. I know I didn't look that great before, but I didn't realize just how *awful* I looked. Or that my *kids* thought I looked awful.

"Now all she needs is a really great name," Colleen says, standing back and admiring me.

"I have a name, thank you."

"Yeah, no, what I mean is, like a catchy kind of nickname. Like the Cake Diva or the Cake Boss."

"What about the Cake Queen?" Kevin suggests, but Colleen shakes her head.

"Too pedestrian."

Where the hell did she learn the meaning of that word? I wonder as my children launch into a heated discussion without so much as an acknowledgment of my presence.

"It has to be a little glam, you know, to match her new look. Like the Cake Empress."

"Empress?"

"Yeah, like Cleopatra."

"That sucks," Kevin says, shaking his head.

"What about the Cake Duchess?"

"I know, I know. Cake Commander!"

"She's not on *Star Trek: The Next Generation*!" Colleen cries.

In the middle of their debate, my cell phone rings. I move toward the bed to answer it and almost trip on the black leather boots Colleen has forced me to wear.

"Where are you?" Izzy asks before I can say hello.

"Home. Where else?"

"You have to get back to the bakery," she tells me urgently. "We got a last-minute cake order. Yellow with chocolate for fifty. In the shape of a roulette wheel."

"What?"

"Oh, and they want the wheel to spin. Pickup, eight A.M. 'cause they're taking it to Vegas."

"Izzy, you're insane. I can't make a spinning roulette wheel for an eight A.M. pickup. Who's the client?"

Izzy pauses. "My mother."

Oh, crap. "Why the hell didn't she order it last week? Or yesterday, for God's sake."

"She kind of did," Izzy says. "At Sunday dinner? She told me but I kind of forgot."

"Damn it, Izzy!"

"Look, I'm sorry, okay? I'll make it up to you, I swear. But she wants the cake bad. She and *Craig*"— she says her mother's husband's name with the same inflection I use when I say *Cheryl*—"are celebrating the fifth anniversary of their first kiss, which apparently happened in the casino of the MGM Grand. And even though I want to douse myself with kerosene and light a match every time I think of her kissing that pasty-faced *borracho,* you know Mama. If we don't come through, she's gonna put a curse on all of us."

I sigh heavily. I'm not concerned about the curse so much as I'm concerned about *Izzy* and the curse. If Izzy thinks she has a curse on her, she will be unable to function until the curse is removed. And knowing Mama, that could be a very long while. I need my business partner and friend, now more than ever.

"Marcy's about to put the cakes in the oven and Smiley's coloring the fondant for the wheel. You'll be all prepped."

"Fine," I grunt. "I'll be there as soon as I can."

"I love you!"

"Yeah, yeah. Hey, Izzy? Why for fifty? Is the whole family going?"

"Nah. They just want enough to share with all the dealers at the MGM."

"I've got it!" Colleen exclaims from the bathroom. "The Cake Goddess! That's it! Ruby McMillan, Cake Goddess!"

I glance at the mirror over the dresser and give myself the once-over. I wouldn't call myself goddess material, but I'm a lot closer than I was three hours ago. And what I can do with a cake could certainly be labeled divine. Maybe Cake Goddess isn't such a bad name after all.

"Kevin," I call to my son. "Get on Google Images for me. I need a picture of a roulette wheel."

"Right now?"

"No," I tell him. "Yesterday."

9

Baked Alaska

A lone customer is leaving the Muffin Top, bakery box in hand, when I arrive thirty minutes later. I enter the shop to the jangle of the bells and see Smiley at the center island, wrapping fondant in cellophane.

"Sorry, we're closing up," he calls out. He flashes me an annoyed look as I continue toward the display case, and when I enter the kitchen his annoyance turns to exasperation.

"Hey! You can't come back here—" His brows jump almost to his hairline as my identity registers. "*Ruby?* Holy effing shit! What the hell happened to you?"

"It depends," I tell him, suddenly self-conscious. "Is that a compliment or an insult?"

"What?" He still looks like he's in shock. "No, you look effing great! Not that you were a bowser before or anything, but you look . . . Jesus . . . effing great!"

I can't help but smile at him, although the "bowser" comment puts to rest any question as to why his marriage failed. "Thanks."

I glance at the center island and see that he has prepped me completely. There are several mounds of fondant in red, green, black, and white, and a hunk of modeling chocolate, all wrapped tightly in plastic wrap. Pastry bags filled with white and black royal icing lie next to the large wooden cutting board along with an assortment of clean knives, utensils, and tools. Four twelve-inch round yellow cakes are cooling on racks and a large bowl of chocolate frosting sits beside them. Smiley has even put together the spinning mechanism for the roulette wheel and mounted it to the base. I am so pleased that he has cut my work in half, I could kiss him, but then I would smear my perfectly applied Passion Peach lipstick and Colleen would have my head on a platter.

"Is Izzy here?" I ask, donning an apron.

"She left right after she talked to you," Smiley says as he pulls the last of the sheet pans from the dishwasher and stows them on a shelf.

"Coward," I say under my breath. "Marcy's gone, too?"

"She had a date."

"Marcy?" I stop and stare at him. "*My* Marcy? Has a date?"

"Yeah, and on a Thursday night, no less." He pulls off his own apron and tosses it into the laundry bin.

"You mean, a date with an actual person?"

Smiley crosses his arms over his chest and chuckles. "Well, I didn't actually see the guy because she was meeting him at the restaurant, but I'm pretty sure he exists in reality."

"I hope she doesn't go and fall in love or anything," I say aloud before I can stop myself.

"Oh, yeah." Smiley grins. "That would really suck."

"You know what I mean." I finish tying my apron and shake my head ruefully. "What would I do without her?"

"And here I am, just chopped liver." Smiley puts on a theatrical frown.

"You are not chopped liver," I tell him sincerely. "You are warm, chocolate pecan pie with a scoop of vanilla-bean ice cream on top."

He stands on the other side of the island, staring at me

thoughtfully. "You know, I think that might be the nicest thing anyone's ever said to me."

"Well, it's true. And thanks for setting everything up for me, Smiley. I really appreciate it."

"I know you do." He executes his usual salute and heads for the exit. When he reaches the door, he turns back to me. "Good luck with the roulette wheel. Don't forget to lock up and make sure you set the alarm before you leave."

"Yes, Dad," I joke.

"Oh, and Ruby? You really do look effing great."

An hour later, I am working on the top of the roulette wheel. Triangular strips of colored fondant for the green, red, and black slots are cut, and I carefully place each strip onto the wheel, constantly referring to the photo Kevin got from Google Images. When I finish this task, I will line and number each strip with royal icing, and when the icing hardens, I'll paint it with edible gold powder dissolved in vodka. There is still so much to do—frost the cakes, place them on the base, cover them with chocolate plastic, test the mechanism for the spinning wheel, add all of the details. Details alone take hours. I glance up at the clock and see that it is just past seven. I could be here all night.

Just keep going, Ruby.

To help me along, I brew a fresh pot of coffee, and soon, with the aroma of French roast permeating the air, the chocolate and fondant roulette wheel begins to come to life. I place the last fondant strip into its slot and reach for the bag of royal icing, gazing at my new masterpiece. I love this moment in the process of cake creation, the point at which the object I am trying to simulate comes into focus out of sugar and chocolate. The rest of the world falls away. There are no errant husbands or threats of foreclosure, no children in their precarious teens, no gossiping housewives, no bad economy or terrorist plots. Only me, my hands, my tools, and the cake.

I am just piping the final border and number on the wheel, the zero slot, when I hear the jangle of the bells. It occurs to me that I never stopped to lock the front door. I frown down at my work, continuing to pipe, resenting the interruption in my concentration, but more annoyed that I brought it on myself by not heeding Smiley's command.

"We're closed," I say, rounding out the zero with royal icing.

I look up to see Jacob Salt standing next to the display case, watching me intently. I am so surprised I almost drop the pastry bag onto the wheel, which would be a devastating mishap and set me back two hours. Luckily, I manage to keep hold of it and set it gently down on the counter.

"Sorry to interrupt," he says amiably.

Perhaps it's due to my recently acquired single status, but for the first time in years, I feel a stirring in my belly at the sight of a handsome man. Admittedly, it's not just my midsection that's stirring; the sensation spreads a little farther south as well. If I thought Jacob Salt looked good in a suit, he looks downright sexy in charcoal slacks and a hunter-green dress shirt with the sleeves rolled midway up his muscular arms. The collar on his shirt is unbuttoned far enough to reveal a smooth tanned chest. His sandy-blond hair is thick and has a slightly untamed look to it and complements the chiseled features of his face. His green eyes are round with lashes so long I can see them from where I stand, and framed by deep and utterly fetching laugh lines. He holds himself stiffly, his posture perfectly erect, adding to his height of roughly six two.

I quickly look away, lest he think I'm ogling him, which I may very well be, but since I've never been much of an ogler, I can't be sure.

"We close at seven on Thursdays," I say, grabbing a rag and wiping the powdered sugar from the counter. I don't know why I'm not greeting him with a "Hi, Mr. Salt" or a "How are you, Jacob?" or something equally polite. But I suspect that I am deeply mortified by his presence and conversely astounded by the sudden reappearance of sexual attraction in my loins. I can't even remember the last time I *thought* about my loins. *Why am I suddenly thinking about my loins?* Especially since this rebirth has been inspired by a man who was going to foreclose on me two weeks ago. Not to mention the fact that he's nuts! Egads!

"I was hoping to catch Ruby McMillan," he says, his words clipped, his expression studious. "Is she here?"

Is he kidding?

Okay, so I do look a little different, thanks to Colleen, and he did spend 90 percent of our first encounter staring at his water glass, but *really?*

"I'm Ruby."

As recognition dawns, the features of his face relax into a smile. "Hi," he says. He slaps a palm to his forehead, then gestures to the cake. "Of course you are. Sorry."

"No worries."

"I'm Jacob Salt," he informs me unnecessarily. "Remember? The Josefsberg party?"

"Of course," I tell him. *How could I forget?* I cross to the sink with various tools that need to be washed. "How are you, Mr. Salt?"

"Jacob, please."

I set the tools down and turn to face him. "You look, um, different," he says. "You had your hair done."

Among other things, I think.

"It looks . . ." He suddenly narrows his eyes at me and cocks his head to the side. ". . . um, very nice." His emphasis on the word "nice" is unmistakable. He thinks I'm hot. Score one for Colleen. And hell, Ruby, too.

"Thank you." Am I blushing? Oh God. I suspect I might be. I'm suddenly a mass of jumbled contradictions. I know I look good—from my new do, to the formfitting Lycra top that dips below my apron and makes me look more busty than I am, to the hip-hugging skirt which accentuates my derriere. And yet I am still me—unused to and uncomfortable with attention from someone, anyone, of the opposite sex, especially someone as good-looking as Jacob Salt. I want to throw my shoulders back and laugh like a hussy, and at the same time I want to cower and slouch and hide my head. Because I am me, I quickly choose the latter, dropping my gaze to the floor as I turn toward the ovens. I grab two of the yellow cakes on the counter and carry them to the center workstation.

"As I said, we close at seven." I attempt a throaty timbre to match my boobs, but my words come out sounding strangled instead. I try again. "But I do have some muffins and cupcakes left over from today." Better.

"Oh, that's not why I'm here," he tells me. He starts to put his hands in his pockets, changes his mind, and lets them drop to his sides. "I just wanted to talk to you. I was in the neighborhood and thought I'd stop by."

I retrieve the other two cakes and the bowl of chocolate frosting, then set the bottom layer on a cardboard round and place the round on top of my cake stand. I feel Jacob Salt's eyes on me and my heart starts to thump crazily in my chest. I am so flustered that I fumble the metal spatula and it clatters to the floor. A cake goddess would never do that,

I remind myself as I retrieve the utensil and toss it into the sink. I grab another spatula from the drawer and am careful to wrap my fingers firmly around it.

"What did you want to talk to me about, Mr.—uh, Jacob?" I ask, studiously avoiding his eyes. I focus on the frosting because chocolate buttercream is safe and something tells me that looking at Jacob Salt for too long might be dangerous. I can hardly believe I'm having these thoughts. I feel like an adolescent, although I was precociously practical even then. My pulse never raced in the presence of the football star or the lead in the senior play who was voted "Most Handsome" and was rumored to have slept with every female in the production, including the drama teacher. This is completely new for me and definitely not pleasant. "Don't tell me my cashier's check bounced. I thought that was impossible."

"No, no. You're current. I just, you just . . . when you dropped the check by, I didn't get an opportunity to speak with you."

"Yes, I know. You were busy ruining another family with a foreclosure."

Where the hell did that come from? I can only assume that an unexpected emotion, i.e., being instantly attracted to someone who shows up in my bakery, makes me cranky. Or maybe the Cake Goddess is really a snarky bitch.

"I don't enjoy that particular aspect of my job," he replies with a grimace.

"I'm sorry," I say quickly, releasing my hold on the spatula. "I didn't mean—"

"Obviously you're busy. I should go." He turns his back to me and I find myself moving toward him.

"No. Please don't. I'm really sorry." I am halfway to the display case when Jacob Salt reaches the door. "Look. I made some coffee. Why don't you have a cup?" He stops, hand on the doorknob, as I try to sweeten the deal. "And I think I can rustle up a chocolate caramel cupcake to go with it."

His shoulders relax and he turns around to face me. "I haven't had dessert yet," he confesses.

"Well," I tell him, "you came to the right place."

I have resumed my work on the roulette wheel while Jacob Salt sits at the counter, enjoying a cup of French roast and a chocolate caramel cupcake. He sighs contentedly, rhythmically, as he eats, and for some reason, each of his exhalations sends a tremor through my entire body.

What the fuck? Excuse the expression.

Normally, it gives me great pleasure to hear my customers' groans of satisfaction. But when I say pleasure, I mean contentment, validation, a serene sense of accomplishment. I do not mean that my vagina is performing the *William Tell Overture*.

"Oh, that's *good,*" he moans.

I feel a spasm in my nether region and my hand jerks reflexively, causing me to ruin the perfectly applied frosting on the side of the cake. I take a calming breath, force myself *not* to look at Jacob Salt, and repair the damage.

"That's *really good,*" he murmurs around a mouthful.

I have heard it all before, mind you. It's a natural occurrence for a baker with an excellent product. The sounds of ecstasy over a wonderfully rich dessert, the frenzied outburst on the heels of that first delectable bite, the warm, fuzzy ministrations of love for a gooey-centered cookie fresh from the oven. The exclamations of "This is better than sex!" or "This is like a party in my mouth!" or "This is *orgasmic!*"—

which is my personal favorite, probably because the only orgasms I've had in the last two years have been caused by eating something I've baked. And, furthermore, plenty of men have eaten my sweets, handsome men, even. But no reaction I've ever heard has affected me like this.

"Oh God. It's incredible!"

Another spasm downstairs. *What the hell is wrong with me?* Where is Rational Ruby when I need her? If I didn't recognize the woman in the mirror earlier, I certainly don't recognize the body I currently inhabit, which twitches at every moan and murmur made by a complete stranger. I thought my vagina was retired! And here it is, back in the workforce. *Twitch twitch.* It's like I've been possessed by a nymphomaniac!

Concentrate, Ruby! You have a cake to finish!

I do a quick cleanup of my station, using all of my determination to drown out Jacob Salt and his vocal appreciation of the damn cupcake. Then I grab the remaining chocolate plastic, remove it from the protective cellophane, sprinkle the clean counter with cocoa powder, and begin to roll it out. Thickness is key—too thin and any imperfections in the frosting will show through, too thick and the weight of the chocolate plastic will flatten the cake beneath. I work briskly, moving the widening sheet of chocolate at regular intervals to keep it from sticking to the counter, and within moments, I have a sixteen-inch circle an eighth of an inch thick. I gently pull up the edge of the circle, then ease my hands under it, sliding them to the other side until both of my forearms are covered. I take a breath, then all at once raise my arms, bringing the sheet of chocolate plastic with me. I pivot to my right and lower my arms over the sides of the cake, laying the chocolate over it.

With my smoothing tool, I affix the chocolate plastic to

the cake while ensuring a straight, flat surface. I drop the smoother and grab my paring knife. Using my left hand to pull the edges of the plastic down to the bottom of the cake, and being careful not to form any wrinkles, I cut away the excess with the knife. A moment later, I stand back to inspect my work. The cake is covered, no seams, no wrinkles, and perfectly smooth. I nod to myself and give myself a mental high five. Covering a cake can take several tries and several batches of fondant or plastic, so it's always a relief to get it right the first time.

"Wow!" Jacob's voice startles me and I realize that I almost forgot he was here. "You're amazing."

He stands beside the cash register gazing at me with something akin to awe. Warmth spreads through me instantaneously.

"Thanks," I say, unable to suppress a smile, then quickly add, "It's not brain surgery."

"Oh, anyone can do brain surgery." He grins. "All you need is a power drill."

I laugh out loud, and it occurs to me that I haven't heard myself laugh in a while. I kind of like it. Jacob looks immensely pleased by my reaction.

"Do you mind if I take a closer look?" he asks, gesturing toward my workstation.

"Uh, yeah, sure," I stammer, and without hesitation, he strides over to me.

He bends slightly to peer at the roulette wheel and produces a soft whistle that whispers through my every nerve ending. "This is remarkable. It looks just like a roulette wheel." He straightens and lets out a self-conscious chuckle. "I mean, I know that's the point. It's supposed to look like a roulette wheel, but it really does."

His green eyes meet mine, and for a split second, under Jacob's intense gaze, I lose the ability to breathe. A mere twelve inches separate us, and the energy that sizzles between us is undeniable. This is a romantic comedy scene, a chapter out of a Harlequin book, a completely un-Ruby-esque moment, and I have no idea how to deal with it.

"Mrs. McMillan," he says, clearing his throat.

"Ruby. Call me Ruby."

"Ruby," he repeats. Slowly, tentatively, he lifts his hand toward my face and I suddenly wish I'd worn a maxi pad or one of my newly purchased Depends because, by God, I am going to wet my pants. His fingers graze my temple, but instead of a tingling caress, I feel a slight tugging on my skin. When he pulls his hand away, I look down and see an inch-long strip of green fondant between his fingertips.

Oh my God! I am an idiot. There was no movie magic happening! He doesn't think I'm hot. He thinks I'm a dork!

"Uh, thanks." I manage to suck in a gulp of air and look down at my forearms, which are covered with cocoa powder. The floor around me is sprinkled with cocoa, along with a fine dusting of powdered sugar, and I make a mental note to get the broom. I don't want to slip in these boots, and the powder will surely cause an accident if I don't take care of it. Hurriedly, I make for the sink and start washing the cocoa off my arms and hands.

"Ruby," he says again. "I came by tonight to apologize."

I glance over my shoulder at him.

"For my behavior at Ted and Miriam's party. I was a complete nincompoop."

I am still mortified by the whole green-fondant-on-the-face thing, but I can't help commenting on his vocabulary.

"Did you actually use the word 'nincompoop' in a sentence?"

The corners of his mouth curl up in a smirk. "I happen to like that word. It's very descriptive and certainly appropriate."

"I don't think you were a nincompoop at all," I assure him. *I* was the nincompoop.

I head for my workstation, then hesitate because Jacob Salt is standing right where I need to be and the thought of brushing against him fills me with a delirious kind of dread. He seems to read my mind and moves out of my way.

"You were a little preoccupied is all." I sidle up to the counter and organize my station, surveying the cake as I line up my tools. I haven't placed the roulette wheel on the spinning riser yet, and I still have to mount the base cake onto the stand. *Mount . . .* my brain seizes. *Mount mount mountmountmount.*

I try to ignore Jacob's proximity, but it's very difficult since I can feel his breath on my neck. Suddenly an image of Jacob Salt and me having sex on the floor of the kitchen flashes through my mind, surprising the heck out of me. This is not a vision I would ordinarily have, for many reasons, not the least of which is that the floor of the bakery is worn linoleum, which would be extremely uncomfortable. But also because the idea of having sex with a (practically) total stranger is unheard of for Ruby McMillan, or even Ruby Simmons, the woman I was before I married Walter. I never had casual sex with total strangers, neither one-night stands nor brazen interludes with dashing men who disappeared before the clock struck midnight. I was never that kind of gal. But for a split second, as I reach for the PVC pipe (how appropriate) I can't help but wonder what it would be like to fornicate with reckless abandon.

Jesus, Ruby! "Fornicate"? Could you be any more parochial?

Okay, "do the nasty." What it would be like to "do the nasty" with the man standing next to me, although perhaps we could do it against the display case rather than on the floor . . .

Ruby, get ahold of yourself. I think. *This man might send your hoohah into a frenzy, but that's only because he's the first attractive man you've had any real interaction with since your husband left. Jacob Salt is not interested in you. He is not going to have sex with you on the floor or against the display case or anywhere else. He's a nice man who feels sorry for you because your husband left you, because you're this close to losing your house, and because you like to wear edible clay on your face. Now get to work!!!*

PVC pipe in hand, I take a breath to clear my head, then set about twisting the pipe into the base of the cake stand.

"I was preoccupied," he confesses, his voice more serious. "I was having a bad day. Of course, not as bad as yours, I realize, but bad nonetheless."

He watches as I pick up the cake and carefully center it over the PVC pipe, then push it down. The top of the PVC erupts through the cake and I can't help but think about sex again. I have executed this maneuver hundreds of times and have never, not once, thought about sex, but there it is. I ease the cake down the penis—uh, PVC—to the base, feeling perspiration pop out on my upper lip. Jacob Salt is still talking, completely oblivious to my lascivious thoughts.

"I upset you that night. I was inconsiderate and insensitive, and I hope you'll accept my apologies."

I dab at my upper lip with the back of my hand, then grab the metal rod on which the spinning platform will rest and insert it into the PVC. *Oh. My. God. Insertion.* I mentally shake my head, reach for the platform, and screw it onto the rod. *Screw. Jesus!* Is it possible I have reverted all the way back to elementary school? *Concentrate!*

With an oversize metal spatula, I gingerly lift the roulette wheel onto the platform.

"You see," Jacob continues, "earlier that day I learned that my ex-wife is having a baby with her, um, partner. I'd always wanted kids. And we tried for a while. But it never happened."

I absently process his words as I cut a small hole in the middle of the wheel where I will attach a handle. I think about Jacob Salt's wife and wonder what she's like. I have never had any gay tendencies, not even in college when half of my friends were experimenting with other women's labia. So it's impossible for me to imagine turning away from a man as attractive as this for another woman. Despite his formal air and his ramrod-straight posture, he is a hunk. Plus his sense of humor and intelligence simmer just below the surface. He is a baked Alaska if ever I met one.

I stop what I'm doing and place my hands on my hips. There is no way I am going to finish this cake with a baked Alaska around.

"I don't know why I'm telling you all this," he says with a small grin. "I haven't found a therapist in town yet."

"Mr. Salt—"

"Jacob. And that was a joke. I'm not in therapy. Not that there's anything wrong with that."

"Jacob, you really don't need to apologize. I'm the one who should be apologizing to you." He starts to shake his head. "I ruined your meal. And your suit. I should pay for your dry cleaning. If you drop off the bill, I'll be happy to reimburse you."

He holds up his palms to stop me. "No, no. That's not necessary. The slacks were fine, just a little wet. They dried."

He regards me for a moment, and this time, since I assume there are no more cake decorations adorning my person, I know he is scrutinizing how I look. His eyes travel down to my cleavage, linger for a few seconds, then snap back to my face, and I can feel my cheeks flame even as I see rosy splotches appear on his. He jerks backward, one step, then two, and it's the second step that does it. If he'd only taken *one,* everything would be fine, but it seems my boobs are just too much for him because he scrabbles backward, and as he does, his shoe slips in the cocoa and powdered sugar which I forgot to sweep up, and then both feet go out from under him and all seventy-four inches of him collapse toward the floor. His arms flail madly as he tries to gain purchase on something, on anything that will keep him from going down. And as he does, his forearm smacks against the cake with enough force to knock it from the counter. I watch helplessly, with the world in instantaneous slow motion, as my precious roulette wheel cake goes flying. I lunge for it like an action hero, sailing though the air, my arms outstretched, but I am a precious second too late. The cake, roulette wheel, base, and platform all hit the kitchen floor at the same moment I land on an unprepared and comically prone Jacob Salt.

The first thing I notice is that Jacob Salt doesn't have an ounce of fat on him, for he cushions my landing not at all. His stomach, chest, arms, and upper thighs are solid as a rock. The second thing I notice is that his mouth is working, but no sounds are coming out. Such is the degree of his agitation, and I'm pretty sure it has more to do with the ruined cake than it does with the fact that he has a woman sprawled out on top of him. The third thing I notice, despite the fact that my roulette wheel has been completely and utterly destroyed, and I will likely be here until dawn, is that my woman parts are orchestrating again, only this time, I think it's Mozart.

"Oh my God." His voice finally breaks through.

"I'm sorry," I tell him, trying to disentangle myself.

"*You're* sorry? Are you kidding? Look what I've done!"

I don't want to look, can't bring myself to gaze upon the devastation. I start to get up only to have my boots slip out from under me, causing me to fall back upon Jacob.

"Ooomph!" he groans.

"Sorry!"

I might actually find the situation humorous, might also enjoy the feel of having a man beneath me, if only Jacob Salt were not gazing at the cake with the kind of horrified expression you might wear when gazing upon a dead body. A dead body you've just murdered.

"I killed your cake!" he exclaims as I manage to push myself to my feet.

He stands awkwardly, his eyes riveted on the destruction. His entire backside is covered with a film of cocoa and powdered sugar. His hands clench and unclench as he shakes his head.

"I . . . I . . . I just don't know what to say," he says. "This is a catastrophe!"

"It's my fault," I say softly, still not allowing myself to look at the cake. "I should have swept up that mess."

"No, I'm a numbskull. What can I do to help?"

I say nothing, merely shrug. Finally, after a few more seconds of blessed ignorance, I follow his gaze and turn to face what's left of my cake. A lump forms in my throat as I survey the wreckage: the bumpy mound of yellow layer cake, the broken base and platform, the savaged wheel with strips of green, red, and black fondant strewn around it like confetti. I blow out a breath as the full implications of this disaster hit me.

Mango and papaya compote with cherry cinnamon glaze—

No. No time for stressipes. I have another roulette wheel cake to make.

I guess no one's getting lucky tonight.

10

All-American Apple Pie

"Madre de Dios!" Izzy cries as she approaches the Muffin Top booth at the Pelican Point Fourth of July Festival. I know her excitement has nothing to do with the tray of s'more bars I hold, even though they are impressive. My friend has been making herself scarce around the bakery since her last-minute roulette wheel order, so she hasn't yet seen Colleen's makeover. She gushes in Spanish for a moment, then punctuates her final sentence with the words "Raquel Welch." I flush at her compliment, because I know that Raquel Welch is the stick by which Izzy measures all beauty.

"It's a miracle!" she says as she sidesteps into the booth and stares at me appreciatively.

I set the tray down on the red, white, and blue tablecloth that covers our table. The stall is about eight feet wide, and every inch of the table in front is covered with sweets: chocolate and vanilla cupcakes topped with edible American flags, three varieties of cookies, fudge brownies, and now the s'more bars, which I dreamed up the day of Walter's departure. We're selling everything for a buck, which won't yield us any profit, but we're hoping to entice people to come to the bakery by getting them to taste our treats. Napkin-lined baskets with free samples—broken cookies and small chunks of brownies—sit at both ends of the table for those not willing to pay bottom dollar.

"Colleen's good," I agree as I begin to rearrange the sweets in a more eye-catching manner, placing small wooden crates under some of the trays to give them different heights and hiding the crates with linens. I am wearing a pair of formfitting blue capri pants with a red-and-white halter top that dips almost to my bra line in the back. My hair is wavy and windblown, courtesy of Colleen's leave-in lotion and her hair dryer, my lips are crimson, and huge silver hoops spring from my ears. "She won't let me leave the house unless she's had at me."

"Well, you should pay her," Izzy says, giving me a toothy smile.

"I would if I could afford to," I return.

The park is done up in grand Independence Day style with red, white, and blue banners, balloons, streamers, and flags decorating every booth, lamppost, and picnic table in sight. Most of the booths, which have to be reserved by January because of the popularity of the event, are occupied by local businesses wanting to drum up summer sales. (Adelle's Bakery is conspicuously absent because her business is doing great, but I wouldn't be surprised to see her streaking through the park later today, possibly wearing a strap-on penis.) There are stalls with games for the kids: the ring toss, the shooting gallery, the basketball throw. There is a dunk tank, and it's rumored that the mayor has a time slot later in the day. The Muffin Top will host a pie-eating contest in the afternoon, and I have three dozen banana cream pies stowed in a large cooler in the back of the minivan for the event. The aroma of grilling burgers and hot dogs permeates the air, mingled with roasted nuts and the sticky-sweet scent of cotton candy.

Izzy tugs at the hem of my halter top. "Hey, Ruby. Thanks for the cake. Mama loved it."

"I'm glad," I return with a grin. "God knows we don't need any curses."

"Seriously. I owe you one."

"You owe me *two*," I say, thinking of the second roulette wheel with its numbers that were somewhat fuzzy due to the fact that I piped them with my eyes closed. Izzy doesn't know about the catastrophe, only that the cake was ready for Mama's 8 A.M. pickup.

"Yeah, two. Hell, I owe you three!" She laughs. "It was a damn great cake. I hope you took pictures for our book."

Which I did *not* do because by the time I finished it, I hadn't a single functioning brain cell left. But, hell. Knowing Mama, she probably captured images of the roulette wheel with every single dealer at the MGM Grand (and she's probably already posted them on Facebook).

It's early, just past noon. Things won't pick up for another hour at least, at which point the park will be filled to capacity with Fourth of July revelers. Now is my chance to peruse the other booths before we get slammed. I ease myself out from behind the table and step back to inspect our display. Nice. A veritable buffet of delectable, mouthwatering delights. How could anyone resist?

"I'm going to do a round," I tell Izzy. "You'll be okay?"

"Who are you asking?" she replies, hands on hips. "Just get back in time for me to get a dog. I've been starving myself all week so I could gorge today."

I laugh, knowing that when Izzy says she starved herself, it means that she refused second and third helpings and stuck to only one scoop of ice cream for dessert.

"I'll be back," I promise, sliding on my sunglasses and heading out.

The booths line three sides of the great field, facing in, so that the people working them can watch the contests and relay races and the ever-popular water-balloon toss. As I wander down the perimeter, I catch sight of Kip Fielding setting cones along the grass. This brings to mind a Fourth from years past, before the Muffin Top, when the kids and I won a couple of races: Colleen and I, the three-legged race, and Kevin and I, the mother-son flag relay. I try to remember where Walter was while the kids and I were chasing down our blue ribbons. Perhaps my subconscious is trying to expunge all memories of him from my mind, but I cannot for the life of me place Walter in the events of that day. I know he was here, we came as a family. But he was not *really* here. Even then.

I shake my head to clear it, passing Goldman's Hardware booth, where Dave Goldman is busily lining up mini bottle openers engraved with his logo. I give him a smile and a wave. He merely nods in my general direction, but doesn't offer me one of his freebies, and I have to assume he doesn't recognize me. Either that, or he is one of Walter's Facebook friends and can't bear to look directly at me because he is still reeling over a post in which Walter and *Cheryl* are bungee jumping naked from a coconut tree atop a Hawaiian cliff.

Pumpkin pecan soufflé with brandy maple reduction.

Oooh. I'll have to file that one for Thanksgiving.

I walk along the stalls from various local businesses, stopping here and there to peruse. Kendra Shiner, from the Book Bag, gushes about my new hairstyle, even asks me for the card of my stylist, and dons an expression of downright betrayal when I tell her that my daughter performed the task with a couple of boxes of dye and some kitchen scissors. Paddy's Pub owner, Patrick Shanahan, doesn't recognize me

at all, but then he isn't wearing his glasses today. The croquembouche ladies are gathered in the Pelican Point High
School booth, passing out flyers for upcoming events and
taking direct donations for extracurricular activities. They
have a fair crowd, even this early, and I manage to pass them
unnoticed.

I sigh, relieved, when I come to Ida Sheerborne's booth.
Her table is covered with pamphlets advertising a host of
travel destinations and a couple of plastic trays containing
little globe key chains. She smiles automatically when she sees
me, then her smile crescendos when she realizes who I am.

"Ruby, my God!" She flaps her hand at me in a come-
here gesture, then takes a moment to admire me. "Wow! I
said to put on some lipstick, not turn into Angelina Jolie!"

I chuckle, pleased by her exaggerated praise. "Thanks,
Ida."

She nods knowingly. "I recognize this, you know. It's the
my-husband's-gone makeover! Very good. I got one after
Ralph passed. Whether they die or leave you, makes very
little difference. We women must soldier on, but better to do
it with style!"

She points to a box on the table with a slot on top and
pictures of different parts of the world glued to the sides.
"It's a raffle. You must enter. The winner gets a trip to their
choice of any of the places represented. You really should
consider a vacation, Ruby, even if you don't win. God knows
you deserve it. The raffle ticket is only five dollars, and we
have, let's see, the Caribbean, London, an Alaskan cruise,
Hawaii—no, you don't want to go anywhere in the South
Pacific—oh yes! The south of France! That would be perfect
for your new look."

"Ida, I have never won a raffle in my entire life," I tell her
honestly.

"Well, there's always a first time, right?"

I know the chances of my winning are slim to none. Still, I reach into my pocket for some bills and hand them over, then write my info on a ticket and toss it into the box.

"Well done," she says, her eyes twinkling. "And, anyway, it's for a good cause. We're helping to feed the starving children."

"Which ones?" I ask.

"All of them," she replies, and hands me a globe key chain.

I see him when I am twenty yards away from the Muffin Top booth. There is no mistaking the excellent posture and lovely backside, even from a distance, although the last time I saw the backside in question, it was covered with powdered sugar and cocoa powder. He is dressed casually in a pair of jeans and a navy-blue collared T-shirt, and I can't help but be impressed by the fact that he wears so many different styles so well, can't decide whether he looks better in jeans than he did in his suit. As I slowly walk toward our booth, I wonder what he would look like wearing no clothes at all.

"Ruby!" calls Izzy, flashing me a toothy grin. "Here she is!"

Jacob Salt turns around to face me, and a guarded smile spreads across his face.

"Hi, Ruby." My name carried on his lovely baritone sends a shiver through me.

"Hi, Jacob. Happy Fourth of July."

"Right," he says. "The same to you."

A small bit of melted chocolate decorates his chin and I surmise that Izzy has been plying him with free samples. I grab a napkin from the table and reach up to wipe away the smudge, then remember myself when he jerks his head back.

"Uh, here." I push the napkin into his hand, my fingers grazing against his palm. For a split second he grips my hand, and I can feel his warmth pulsing into my fingers. Immediately he releases his hold.

"You, uh . . ." I cough to cover the fact that I'm stammering as a result of his fleeting touch. "Chocolate, uh, on your chin."

He grins and quickly swipes at his face with the napkin. "It seems I've recently gained an appreciation of sweets."

"Jacob and I were just having a little chat," Izzy says. "Between mouthfuls, that is."

She gives me a knowing stare, then raises her eyebrows a couple of times in swift succession for emphasis.

"Yes, I came by specifically to apologize to you. Again," he chuckles, and gestures toward the table. "But since you weren't here, I managed to sample just about everything you have to offer."

"Oh, you haven't sampled *everything*," Izzy says, trying to suppress her grin. I would really like to punch her just about now.

"Really?" Jacob asks, oblivious. "There's more?"

"Lots more." She takes the napkin from Jacob and pitches it into the waste can. "So, Jacob mentioned the fact that he murdered your cake."

"It was more like involuntary manslaughter," I reply, and Jacob chuckles again, a low rumbling from deep in his chest that rolls through me and turns my innards to mush.

"Ruby was very gracious about it," he says. "She even took the blame."

"Is that so?"

"I should have swept up the mess. I know better than that."

Izzy purses her lips in mock consternation. "I guess you must have been distracted, hmm?"

"Mmm, yes," I say, deciding that I will kill her later.

"Well." Jacob shifts his weight from side to side, looks around. "This is my first Fourth. I mean, not my *first* Fourth, obviously. Here. My first Fourth in Pelican Point. This is quite the event."

"Does Franchise have a booth?" I ask because I can't think of anything else to say. Okay, not true. I can think of lots of things to say, like *Your ass looks great in denim* or *Your voice is like warm butterscotch syrup*. But neither feels appropriate.

"Oh yes," he says, then points to a stall on the far side of the field. "Our booth is over there. You can't really make out the banner from here. 'Franchise Funding. Ruining Families Is Our Specialty.'"

Surprised, I look up to find him giving me a Cheshire smile.

"Sorry. I couldn't resist."

I laugh despite myself. "Apology *not* accepted."

Izzy is still staring at us quizzically when a couple of older ladies with identical caps of short silver hair approach our booth, oohing and aahing as they inspect our offerings. She frowns at the interruption, then tears herself away from our conversation and moves toward the would-be patrons.

"I do have to get back to my coworkers," Jacob says regretfully. "But I wanted to discuss something else with you before I go."

He's going to ask me out, I guess, and am surprised by the way my pulse races at the thought.

I try to keep the expectation from my voice. "Yes?"

"I need a cake," he says simply. "Franchise is having a fifty-year celebration at the end of the month."

I feel myself deflate, then chide myself for my stupidity. One, he is not interested in me beyond my cake skills. Two, I am a recently abandoned wife who doesn't even have divorce papers.

"Sure. I can do that."

"Wonderful!" he exclaims. "Terrific. Great." Shift shift. "Oh, and one other thing . . ."

Again with the pulse-racing thing. "Yes?"

"Could I have six cupcakes to go?"

I duck my blushing head and scoot behind the table, then hurriedly package up his request. The sooner Jacob Salt leaves this booth, the sooner I can reclaim my calm facade. I hand him the bakery box and he offers me a ten. I make change and thank him.

"So, hopefully I'll see you later," he says, and I nod noncommittally. "I hear the fireworks are really something."

"They are," I agree, and wave him off. I force myself to look down at the table and pretend to busy myself with restocking the cupcakes. Still, I can't help but sneak a quick peek at his retreating backside. Yummy.

"Mmm-hmm."

Oops. Did I say that out loud? Izzy is suddenly beside me, her eyes riveted to Jacob Salt. "I heard that," she says.

"I was talking about the s'more bites. They are yummy. With a capital Y."

"You lying piece of shit. That man is hot! Well, you know, for someone with a stick up his butt."

"Is he? I hadn't noticed."

"You are so full of *caca del toro*!"

One of the older ladies giggles and Izzy and I look over

at both of them. They exchange a conspiratorial glance with each other, then turn toward us. "I heard his ex-wife is a lesbian," the taller of the two says in a mock whisper.

"Huh!" Izzy exclaims, nodding vigorously. "Well, she would have to be one totally irreversibly gay bitch to let that man out of her sight, wouldn't she? 'Cuz he is a fucking babe!"

The rest of the afternoon rushes by in a haze of red, white, and blue. The Muffin Top booth is one of the more crowded, with customers four and five deep for most of the day, and I am relieved that I asked Marcy and Smiley to help out. My kids stop by around three, on their way to the beach celebration with their friends (and their friends' parents, who I trust will supervise). I am so busy, I barely have time for quick hugs and kisses, and I can't help but feel guilty about not spending the holiday with them. I tell them so even as I am bagging a dozen cookies for a young mother with four kids hanging on to her, tugging at her shirt and screeching "Chocolate chip! Chocolate chip!" But Colleen and Kevin put my fears to rest by telling me they understand. In a way, I think they are relieved that I will not be around. My presence would remind them of Walter's absence, of the fact that our family has splintered. They will enjoy their Fourth far more without me.

"We can be together when you get home, Mom," Kevin suggests. "Bring the leftovers and we'll all pig out!"

I tell him I will, but at the rate we're going through our stock, it'll be a miracle if we have anything left at the end of the day.

At five thirty, Smiley and I head for the nearby picnic tables, carrying the banana cream pies and a bag of plastic bibs for the pie-eating contest. Over the PA system, the MC, otherwise known as high school principal Gerald Lowe, announces the contest, and within moments all three picnic tables are filled with rollicking, laughing contestants. A crowd of onlookers has gathered to cheer them on. Out of the corner of my eye, I see Jacob Salt approach the area and tentatively ease onto the end of one of the benches, forcing a girl of about twelve to scoot over.

Smiley begins setting pies in front of everyone. I take my place between the tables, avoid looking at Jacob Salt, and curse the fact that I am not wearing Depends. I clear my throat loudly.

"Okay, everyone," I call, and all eyes turn toward me. "Here are the rules."

"Can't hear you!" someone says.

I take a breath and remind myself that I am the Cake Goddess and that I currently look like a million bucks. This thought makes me stand up straighter and I clear my throat again.

"Okay! Rules!" I shout with a voice I don't recognize. "You have to eat the whole pie! Not *most* of it. *All* of it! No hands allowed. If we see any evidence of pie on your fingers, you will be disqualified. When you're done, stand up where you are."

That was good, Ruby! I tell myself.

I am slightly giddy over my first successful public speaking gig, even if it's only a pie-eating contest. Empowered, I hold up my hands for quiet, and surprisingly, all of the contestants go silent.

"Now, this can get messy," I say, starting to enjoy myself. "We've brought some bibs. Anyone who wants one, just raise your hand."

Most of the pie eaters are kids not concerned with getting

banana cream filling on their shirts (although I'm sure their *moms* are concerned). I scan the tables and my eyes come to rest on Jacob Salt. Slowly, surreptitiously, he raises his arm, an embarrassed look on his face. I grab a bib and walk over to him.

"This is a surprise," I say.

"I'm representing Franchise," he clarifies. "My coworkers said I have the biggest mouth, but I think it's because I'm the newbie. Anyway, they really want the prize." Which is a box filled with an assortment of our best items. "Can you blame them?"

I laugh and shake out the bib. Bending over slightly, I drape it around Jacob's shoulders and am treated to a delirious waft of his scent: soap, a subtle woodsy cologne, and maleness. My fingers are shaking ever so slightly as I knot the tie.

"Good luck," I tell him, then return to my place.

"Ready?" Smiley officiates. "Set? Go!"

A hilarious display of good-natured gluttony ensues as the contestants voraciously attack their pies. Although I went heavy on the whipped topping to keep them light, eating an entire eight-inch pie without hands is no easy feat. Much to my surprise, a teenage boy bolts to standing within sixty seconds, his smiling face covered with goo.

I glance at Jacob and see that he has barely made it through the top layer.

"Stop!" Smiley yells as I hurry over to the boy. He is roughly Kevin's age, thin as a wisp, with longish brown hair falling over his eyes.

"That was so good!" he exclaims. I glance down at the pie tin, see only the barest hint of crumbs along the bottom, then grab the boy's hand and raise it into the air.

"We have a winner!"

The crowd erupts into applause as Smiley trots over with a damp towel for the victor, then heads back to our booth to get a bus tub. The other contestants make sounds of happy annoyance as they disentangle themselves from the picnic tables and use the napkins I provided to clean themselves up. I tell the teenager, whose name is Christian, to come by the Muffin Top booth to collect his prize, then I begin to clear away the mess. As I'm stacking the partially empty pie tins, Jacob wanders over. He pulls the bib over his head and tosses it into the trash can, then starts to help me collect the tins.

"Thanks." I keep my voice neutral, even though his proximity is making me a little goofy.

"My pleasure." He laughs. "Seriously, I don't dare go back to the Franchise booth right now. My coworkers are going to have me transferred back up north for my poor performance. They were really counting on your sweets. I can't believe that string bean won! What do you think he weighs? Eighty pounds soaking wet?"

"Kids," I agree. "Makes you wonder where they put it. My son can eat an entire large pizza by himself and still have room for dessert."

"You have a son?"

I nod. "And a daughter, too."

"One and one. That's nice."

I look up to see him gazing at the pie tin in his hand, much the same way he was gazing at his water glass the first night we met. I wonder whether he is thinking about his ex-wife, her child, the children he doesn't have and possibly never will. I want to reach out and touch him, and the impulse is so intense, it feels like an ache. But before I can act upon it, Smiley arrives with the bus tub, jolting Jacob from his thoughts and me from mine. The three of us pile the tins in the tub and Smiley hauls them away with a grunt.

"Well," Jacob says, straightening to his full height. "That was fun. My first pie-eating contest, and I must admit I was a complete failure at it."

"I'm sure you have many other talents." The words tumble out of my mouth automatically, as though I am talking to one of my kids, but the double entendre hits me immediately. Jacob's eyes flash for a split second and I swallow hard. "Thanks for your help," I quickly add, then grab the bag of unused bibs and scurry away from Jacob Salt and his penetrating green eyes.

Penetrating. There. I said it.

The fireworks are scheduled to start at nine o'clock and they last for half an hour. At eight forty-five, a short bespectacled young man wearing plaid Bermuda shorts and a white golf shirt stops by the booth to say hi to Marcy. Assuming that this was her date from Thursday night, and noting the smile that lights up her face when she sees him, I release her from her duties so she can watch the show. I offer Smiley the opportunity to leave the remaining cleanup to me, but he refuses, telling me that once you've seen real combat, fireworks pale by comparison. And since Izzy left with her husband, Bobby, an hour before, I am glad for Smiley's assistance.

We work without speaking, following our usual routine, boxing the minimal leftovers and stowing trays in bus tubs. The rhythmic, thundering explosions from the show are our soundtrack. I'd assumed that the mindless work would keep me from falling into a funk, but I can feel my spirits lower with each cacophonous bang. By the time we finish, I feel like crying. Smiley takes the last load of trays to the mini-van, and I move to the front of the booth.

The constant bursts of light in the night sky illuminate the audience on the great field, and I see all of the people gathered there; the children and parents and grandparents, the men and women, the old and young. And within these groups I see lovers, husbands and wives, married for years or merely months, boyfriends and girlfriends of all ages, teenagers experiencing their first heart-pounding crushes. They all gaze up to the heavens in wonder, the fireworks reminding them of that first kiss or the first time they made love or the first time their beloved's touch lit upon them. They hold hands and steal glances at each other, smiling and sighing at their mutual recognition of that which the light show reminds them. Fireworks are intrinsically romantic, a metaphor for those passionate, all-consuming emotions that burn within us.

But I, Rational Ruby, have never gazed at fireworks and felt my heart pound within my chest. I have never rested in my lover's arms as the sky erupted in colorful flames. Even with Walter, on Fourth of Julys past, I would watch with appreciation for the technical and artistic skills of the people who put on the show, but at the same time I would always be thinking about work, or a recipe, or how I might enter-tain my kids for the remainder of the summer. And even when Walter entwined his fingers with mine, probably in an attempt to capture the same feelings the other people were experiencing, I would give his hand a quick squeeze, then release it, usually in order to grab a tissue to wipe a runny nose or open a snack for one of my kids or pick an errant thread from my sweatpants.

Just as hearts do not have wings, fireworks do not ex-plode within our souls over love. Or so I always thought.

Yet the way my body has responded to Jacob Salt during our last two encounters causes me to question my own beliefs. Not that I am in love with this man; I hardly know him. But my reaction to him is something I have never experienced before. And I wonder if this is because he is the first man to inspire such feelings in me, or because I've never *allowed* myself to feel them. And if the latter, then why? Because I am rational and practical and pragmatic? Because I like order? Or because I am afraid? These kinds of feelings are scary, yes, and they can lead to disaster, as I have witnessed firsthand. But I've recently discovered that they are also warm and gooey and produce a wonderful adrenaline rush.

I am middle-aged. I have spent the better part of my life building walls around my life to keep myself safe. But that safety was an illusion, as demonstrated by the Walter and *Cheryl* fiasco. I wonder, as I reflexively search for Jacob Salt among the sea of upturned faces, what else I've been missing out on in my quest for security, and whether it might be time to break down those cinder-block walls of control.

At the end of the evening, I don't win Ida Sheerborne's raffle. But I try not to take it as a sign. I never believed in signs anyway.

11

Mise-en-Place

"Hi. My name is Ruby McMillan, and I am the Cake Lady."

Okay, so I have downgraded from Goddess, but I'm fine with it. I didn't feel much like a goddess, despite my new look. And my mother always said that if I were a lady, all else would follow, so I guess eventually I might be able to tack on the goddess moniker. But for now, as I look at the faces of the seven students gathered around my center station, Cake Lady works for me.

The assembled group is made up of a variety of types, all but one female. The lone male is a kid of about twenty, short and thin, his hair slicked into place by a copious amount of gel. He wears a white, collared dress shirt tucked into slacks, and black-rimmed glasses that he keeps pushing back up to the bridge of his nose. *Calvin,* says his name tag. Jessica and Francie are irreverent eighteen-year-old freshmen who can't stop giggling through the layers of curly blond hair that fall into their pert round faces. If I didn't know better, I would think they were twins. Stephanie is a sophomore, planning to transfer to a UC school to pursue veterinary medicine once she earns enough credits. She seems studious and intense, quietly scanning her surroundings and taking notes even though I have yet to begin my lecture. Carol is a twenty-eight-year-old redheaded beauty who is studying acting at

PPC after being forced to quit a very lucrative career as a catalog model. I can tell just by looking at her that she has never spent any appreciable amount of time in a kitchen. Blanche is the oldest in the group by far, including me. I peg her to be in her late fifties, with a helmet of closely cropped silver hair, a tanned weather map of a face, smiling blue eyes, and a trim athletic body. Amy is a full-time culinary student at PPC who is aiming for the Cordon Bleu. She wears her mousy-brown hair in a severe ponytail and gazes around my kitchen, nodding with approval.

I glance at the clock, which reads 7:10. The eighth student hasn't shown yet, one Shane O'Neil, and I have a brief moment of panic when I realize that without the full eight, the course will be dropped from the curriculum. But I quickly square my shoulders and push the thought from my mind, reminding myself that I don't have time for anxiety. Anxiety and panic are useless emotions that will undermine my efficiency as an instructor. And also, I am not wearing Depends.

I made a conscious decision to forgo the compromised-bladder accessories, acknowledging this as my first step toward emancipation. I may end up soaking my underwear, but at least I will have made a valiant effort just by leaving the incontinence pads at home. I know it sounds pathetic. Small steps, right? Still, my heart is pounding in my chest, and I'm sure that if my students looked closely at me, they would be able to see my pulse throbbing in my neck.

"Cake Lady," says Francie on a giggle. "I like that."

"For the next eight weeks, I plan to introduce you to the wonderful world of cake confection," I announce, satisfied with the volume and timbre of my voice. I sound confident, assured. *I know cake*, I tell myself. *I know cake*. "Because there is no prerequisite for this class, I'll assume that you are

all at different levels of culinary expertise." A few compla-
cent nods. "I will take into account your prior experience
and you will be graded not in comparison with your class-
mates, but by your own personal learning curve. We will
cover all areas of cake creation, and as you improve in the
hands-on classwork, I will give you more challenging assign-
ments." I hear a sigh from someone, then a yawn from another. I'm losing them already. Yes, I sound competent, just
like a professor. Competent and *boring. Oh God. I knew it.
I'm BORING!*

I take a deep breath and look around at the faces of my
new students. I was barely Jessica and Francie's age when I
made my first cake from scratch without assistance from my
mother. It was dry and crumbly, and although it was supposed to be a Buster Brown saddle shoe, it more closely resembled a large dog poop. But even though it was a failure, I
found the process exhilarating, and I refused to give up,
going on to make a spaceship that looked like a Frisbee, a
monkey that looked like a bear, and a tree that ended up
being a bush because there was no structure inside to keep
the trunk from collapsing in on itself. I glance through the
sliding-glass door of the refrigerated case and see the champagne bottle and the laptop computer, and give myself kudos
for how far I've come.

"Okay, look. Let's take a minute and talk about why
you're all here. And don't tell me it's for the units, because
there are a whole lot of other fluff classes with the same
amount of units that cost less money and take less time. So
give me a better reason. Who wants to start?"

Just then, the bells on the front door jingle loudly and all
eyes turn to see a kid of about twenty enter the bakery. He
wears jeans and a faded Quiksilver T-shirt and has a huge
backpack slung over his shoulder.

"Heeeere's Johnny!" he calls out to no one in particular. "Sorry I'm late. I was studying for a psych quiz and lost track of the time. Whoa! Major cake shit happening, huh?" Dropping his backpack onto the counter, he saunters past the display case and into the kitchen.

"Hey! What's shaking?" He inserts himself between Jessica and Francie and receives a burst of giggles in return. He runs a hand through his hair and smiles unself-consciously. His gaze wanders over the rest of us and lands upon Blanche. "I'm Shane O'Neil. You must be the chosen one." He grins. "I hear you really know your way around a cake. It's awesome that you're willing to share your pearls, you know? I'm really sorry I'm late. It won't happen again."

I have completely lost my train of thought at the arrival of Shane O'Neil. Not solely because he is the complete antithesis of a cake-decorating student, with his James Dean demeanor and his easy smile. But also because he is perhaps one of the most gorgeous men—uh, boys—I have ever laid eyes on. His hair is dark and shiny and tousled in a manner that Walter could only dream of. His pale complexion offsets the deep blue of his eyes, which are outlined by lashes so thick and long, my daughter would kill for them. And he has a cleft in his chin that is part of a three-for-one special with the two dimples on either side of his mouth.

At the risk of sounding like a dirty old lady, I have to say that this kid is sexy with a capital *S-E-X*.

White and dark chocolate frozen mousse pâté with milk-chocolate pastry cream . . . Oooh. Gotta write that one down.

Shane is still staring at Blanche expectantly and I manage to rein in my renegade thoughts.

"Uh, actually, *I'm* the instructor," I say. Shane shifts his focus to me and grins unabashedly.

"Wow. Really? This class just keeps getting better."

I force myself to keep my expression neutral. Blanche shakes her head and sighs gruffly.

"Oh, hey, no offense . . ." He squints at her name tag. ". . . Blanche."

"None taken, young man," she says grudgingly. "You suffer from the same condition that plagues all of your gender."

"Thank God for that!" he returns genially. "So. Where were you all before I so rudely interrupted?"

"We were just discussing all of your reasons for being here," I say. "Perhaps you'd like to begin, Shane."

He lowers his head with mock embarrassment, the corners of his mouth betraying yet another grin. As he leans against the counter, I am struck by a sense of familiarity, of having met this kid before. I search the recesses of my brain for a clue but come up empty. Which is strange, because Shane O'Neil is not someone you would easily forget, especially if you were a female of breeding age.

"Well, ma'am. I, uh . . ." He blows air through pursed lips. "I'm here on a dare."

I groan inwardly. A frat boy, has to be. A night of reckless revelry and Jack Daniel's–inspired drinking games, and here he is. I wonder how many sessions the dare demands and whether he will drop out before or after the three-week cutoff when the course will be safe from deletion.

"Really, a dare," I say, my tone tinged with disapproval.

"I'm afraid so. See, my niece? She's nine. She got diagnosed with leukemia last year, and even though she's in treatment now, and her doctors are really optimistic, you know, she's kind of using the whole thing to get her family to do crazy shit for her." He rolls his eyes, but he's still smiling, and I feel a warmth from him that is unexpected. "Her birthday's coming up and my sister and I were talking to her about what kind of cake she wants, and she kind of got on me like, 'What do you know about cakes, Uncle Shane-Man? You've never made a cake in your entire life.' And telling me that I'd be more likely to fly to the moon on a hot-air balloon than make a cake, and so I told her that *I* was going to make her the best damn cake she's ever had. 'Course, my sister will order one as a backup, but you know, I couldn't back down from her challenge."

Everyone stares at Shane with a revised opinion, including me. Even Blanche is smiling.

"I'm not going after that story," Amy says. "How could any of us top that?"

"My mom told me a class like this would be a great place to meet girls," Calvin offers, glancing around shyly.

"Okay, Calvin," says Amy. "You topped it."

And suddenly the kitchen is filled with the laughter of nine very different people, and the sound inflates me like a gorgeous, delectable chocolate soufflé.

"The first thing we're going to talk about is *mise-en-place*. Loosely translated, it means 'everything in its place.' This is a concept I live by. And it's important to design your kitchen with this in mind. What do you need today? What will you need tomorrow? Is everything where it should be? Is it close at hand? Are there things taking up space that you no longer use?"

I talk for a while about various kinds of professional kitchens, from four-star restaurants to fast-food joints, and what the *mise-en-place* might look like in each. I ask questions and get the students to respond, and although I have numerous moments of stress throughout (*Am I boring them? Will they be back next week? Do I have something green sticking out of my nose?*), I find myself starting to relax. When I finish the lecture, I give them a tour of the kitchen, showing them the racks of dry ingredients, spices, oils, and flavorings in the pantry, the butter and dairy products in the fridge, all of the tools lined up neatly in drawers and on magnetized racks, rags and aprons stacked on metal shelves. We spend a few minutes at each station; they ask questions and I explain what certain ingredients and items are used for, and why they might be placed where they are. The appliances, for example, which range from a stand mixer to a juicer to a food processor, all lined up on the counter in order of which gets used the most.

"Everything is where it should be so that the kitchen can run smoothly."

"Have you ever seen so much freaking flour in your entire life?" Shane asks.

"I have." Amy, of course.

"Seriously, you could build a cathedral with all that flour!"

"I haven't done a cathedral, but I have done a few churches," I tell him, returning to the center station. I grab a stack of stapled handouts and pass them out. "This is a course outline which will tell you what to expect from each session. The last page is a sort of *mise-en-place* checklist, of all the items you need to make and decorate a cake, from a simply frosted two-layer to a . . . well . . . a cathedral. I want you to study it, because there will be a quiz first thing next Tuesday. We won't be doing a hands-on tonight, but next week, each of you will bake a cake." A chorus of oohs and aahs greets me. "That's it for tonight, but you're welcome to stay for a little while, get familiar with your new kitchen, look at the cakes or my cake book."

I gaze at the faces of the students who will share my kitchen with me for the next five weeks. I want to leave them with more than "that's it."

"Cakes are fun, guys. I'll admit I've shed more than a few tears over breakage and things that didn't work as I'd planned, or challenges I thought I couldn't overcome. But I love making cakes. And my hope is, by the end of this class, you'll love making them, too."

The kids and Blanche disperse. Francie, Jessica, and Amy head for the fridge, and Blanche, Calvin, and Carol go to the counter, where I have laid out my enormous cake album. Stephanie spreads her handout across her notebook and starts to slowly circle the kitchen, making notes in the margins. Shane stands on the other side of the counter, watching me as I collect the remaining checklists.

I can't help but feel unnerved by his gaze. "Did you have a question, Shane?"

He cocks his head to the side. "I was just thinking that you look familiar."

I don't mention that I had the same thought.

"But you're definitely someone I would remember."

Oh my Lord. Is this kid flirting with me?

Ruby! He's twelve! He is not flirting with you!

He scrunches up his face, thinking. "Wait a minute! 26735 Cherry Lane?"

I stop and stare at him. "Yes?"

"That's it! McMillan! Right. You were on my very first route!"

Recognition slams into me much like Maxwell's Silver Hammer as I realize that ten years ago the man-child before me was my paperboy.

Oh God. I feel so old.

* * *

Wait a minute. I'm not old, I think as I climb the stairs of my home. *It's all relative, right? I mean, to an eighty-eight-year-old, I am a virtual spring chicken.*

But to a kid of twenty?

Oh God. I'm old.

The kids are in their rooms. Colleen is going over her Little Princess schedule and Kevin is playing a computer game which thankfully has very little blood spatter. They both seem a little subdued right now, so after giving them kisses and hugs, I leave them to their respective occupations and return downstairs for a little quiet time of my own.

In the den, I turn on the overhead light, collapse onto the couch, and stare at the wall next to the TV. The built-in shelves are lined with books, trophies, knickknacks, and assorted paraphernalia that I have taken great pains to organize. I kick off my shoes—canvas wedges with straps around my ankles that were a compromise Colleen and I came to when she dressed me this afternoon. She wanted funky spiky-heeled things that would have been murder in the kitchen, and I wanted my beloved cross-trainers that keep my toes from swelling to the size of bananas. Although the wedges are not as comfortable as sneakers, I have to admit they did not bother me as much as I feared, and the added height gave me an extra boost of confidence. Still, removing them feels great, and I stretch my bare feet out in front of me, rotating my ankles and splaying out my toes.

As the sound of popping joints assaults my ears, I think back over this evening's class, satisfied with how it went. I can't say that I enjoyed every minute of it, but the students seemed to like me, I kept them interested, and I didn't wet my pants.

As I lower my feet to the coffee table, my eyes wander back to the shelves across the room, and my gaze lands on one of the trophies—Walter's bowling league trophy from last winter. And suddenly a memory flashes through my mind from our fifteenth wedding anniversary. We'd had a party, inviting several couples whom we called friends, and some of Walter's work colleagues, not including *Cheryl*. After dinner, we gathered everyone in the living room and served champagne for a toast. Walter had deferred to me, and I'd stood there and stammered for about thirty seconds, my face hot with embarrassment.

"Forgive her," Walter had said on a laugh. "My wife has trouble with public speaking." He'd then gestured to the cake on the table in the adjoining dining room, which was in the shape of the number fifteen and had edible sugar crystals all over it, signifying our anniversary year. "But when you can make a cake like that," he'd said, "you don't need the ability to form coherent sentences!"

Everyone had laughed, even me, because it seemed funny at the time. But looking back now, from my current perspective, which is one of resentment and indignation, I see just how patronizing and condescending he was. Even though his words were disguised as a compliment, they were actually meant to emphasize my weakness.

My husband often made jokes in reference to our relationship, like "What do you see in me, Ruby?" or "I don't know why you ever married me, Ruby!" Not the way he said it the morning he left—four weeks ago now—but with a wink and a chuckle. "I'm not good enough for you, Ruby." Ha ha ha. "I don't deserve you, Ruby." Nudge nudge. Always laughing, always irreverent. But I realize now that these jokes were rooted in his secret fears, his belief that he wasn't good enough for me, or that *I* thought he wasn't good enough for me. And his dig at my expense during our anniversary party was one of the ways he proved to himself that he *was* good enough, or more specifically, that *I* wasn't too good for *him*.

And he did this regularly, in other arenas, using humor to undercut me, even though I was oblivious to it at the time. "Are those *new* sweats you're wearing honey? Gee, I hope you didn't break the bank on them!" Hardeehardeehar. "Here's the gingko biloba you asked me to get. You don't remember? I'm not surprised." Chuckle chuckle. "Don't quit your day job . . . Oh, that's right. You don't have one!" Snort snort. (That was before the bakery, and it had stung.) He honestly thought he was being funny, but he was really just trying to make himself feel better by bringing me down.

And now all his hooey about "deserving to be happy" and "being worthy of true love" becomes clear. As much as he believes he has found his soul mate and the life he was destined to live, he is also proving something to himself. He is punishing me for his own projection of how I felt about him. And the truth is I never felt one way or the other. I never thought I was too good for him or that he didn't deserve me. I honestly never thought about it. I knew why I married him, and I loved him, and I made a life with him. I made a choice and stuck with it. And if there were telltale signs that we weren't "perfect" for each other, "good enough" or "deserving" or "worthy" never came into play for me as they did for him. So here I am, left with the stunning epiphany that Walter ended our marriage because of something he assumed I felt that wasn't even true.

Now I *really* want to kill him. The *jerk*.

Gazing at the trophy, I think of *mise-en-place*. Everything in its place. I live by this concept. I keep all areas of my life tidy and ordered, compartmentalized. Perhaps I am too structured. Perhaps the fact that I approach situations like recipes, breaking everything down into ingredients and steps, keeps me from seeing and dealing with the gray areas. Or even seeing the myriad colors of the rainbow. Possibly it would do me good to allow a little havoc to be wreaked here and there. All things to consider. But at this moment there is one thing I do *not* have to consider, one thing I am absolutely sure of: Walter's bowling trophy no longer has a place in my den.

I jump to my weary feet and cross to the shelf, then peer down at the inscription on the trophy. *Walter McMillan—Best Score—40 and Over.* Resisting the urge to dump the damn thing into the trash, I stomp to the garage and rescue three large cardboard boxes from the recycling pile. I haul them into the house, drop two of them at my feet, then peer at my surroundings as if for the first time.

For someone who has been existing on the periphery of my life, Walter certainly has left his mark everywhere in my home. *My* home, I think. Not his anymore. I head for the shelf, grab the trophy, and stow it in the box. Next goes the hand-carved Bolivian humidor, empty of cigars because Walter is allergic to smoke. A glass paperweight with his company's (or should I say *former* company's) logo on it; a silver plate stamped with a Scottish crest which he got off the Internet but told everyone was his actual family crest; books he brought home, like *How to Get More Bang for Your Buck,* and *Religious Practices of the Algonquin Tribe,* and *How to Laugh Your Troubles Away: The Lunatic's Guide to Happiness* (actually I might keep that one), and a book I've never noticed before called *Cannibalism Today* (that's just weird). By the time I am finished with the shelf, the box is half full.

Suddenly energized, I carry the box to the kitchen, then set about eradicating Walter from the rest of my domain.

Metamucil? Gone. Two-pound bag of prunes? Outta here. Dairy-free butter replacement? See ya. Powdered creamer, muesli, Cheez Doodles, decaf (what's the point?), Sweet'N Low (why bother?), men's multivitamins, bulk package of Oriental noodle soup? Bye bye.

Within minutes, the box is filled to the brim. I lug it to the garage and set it down, then quickly return to the house. My heart is pumping and I am experiencing a sense of euphoria that is foreign to me. But I like it. And I want more. I grab the other two empty boxes and head for the stairs.

It's time to make the master bedroom all mine.

12

Stirring the Pot

"Wow, Mom, you look great! And I haven't even done your makeup yet!"

I beam at my daughter as she saunters into the kitchen and makes her way to the fridge. It's eight thirty and I've already been up for a couple of hours, trying two new stressipes, a sweet calzone turnover with ricotta cheese and blackberries and a puff-pastry bread pudding with a Frangelico cream sauce. Both items have turned out great and the aroma of baked sweets permeates the air.

"Mmm, smells good," Colleen says, peering at the casserole dish of bread pudding and the sheet pan on which rests the golden turnover, creamy ricotta oozing out the sides. I know my daughter will try neither, at least not when anyone is looking, for fear she will ruin her reputation as a health nut. But there have been times when I've returned to the kitchen to find a corner of brownie cut away or one less cranberry oatmeal cookie on the cooling racks. I have never called her on it, merely filed the information away as parents do with their children. Her circumspect pilfering of sweets is not in the same category as finding the Victoria's Secret catalog under the mattress in Kevin's room or coming across one of my favorite crystal candleholders in Colleen's hamper. But, for a parent, knowledge is power, and we gather the goods on our kids for later use.

"Try some," I urge, and Colleen vehemently shakes her head.

"You know I don't eat that stuff, Mom," she says, and grabs her whole-grain bread from the fridge. She yawns audibly and sighs. "I'm so tired this morning!" she exclaims with her sixteen-year-old theatricality. "Probably because I only slept for eight hours."

Eight hours. Sheesh. I, myself, didn't get to sleep until after 1 A.M., following my ruthless Walter purge, but I am feeling surprisingly refreshed nonetheless. Packing up his clothing and toiletries and various and sundry personal effects was like losing twenty pounds or getting a face-lift or winning a date—canoodling included—with Johnny Depp. I feel liberated and hopeful and, as Kevin would say, ready to Carpe the Diem.

"You're using that facial scrub I gave you, right?" she asks, taking a step toward me and inspecting my face with the intensity of a dermatologist. "Your skin is, like, totally glowing. Isn't that scrub the bomb?"

"It is," I agree, trying to remember the exact spot where I stowed the avocado-and-rosemary paste that smelled like Italian guacamole. Oh, that's right. The trash.

I stir the hazelnut cream sauce as Colleen returns to the fridge. "Hey, where's my dairy-free butter spread?"

Oops. "I thought that was your father's."

"Mo-om!" Kevin calls from the garage, where he has been painstakingly waxing his surfboard for the last half hour. He appears at the kitchen door, holding up a book. "What's my *Cannibalism Today* doing in a box in the garage?"

"That's yours?"

"There's a whole load of sh—stuff out there. Like Dad's trophies and his shaving kit and sh—stuff."

"That's right," I say, glancing from Kevin to Colleen,

who has set her loaf of bread on the counter and is now looking at me curiously. "I went through the house last night . . . well, most of it, and got rid of your father's things."

They both look at me as though I've just told them I ate a chinchilla for breakfast.

"Why?" Colleen asks.

"Why do you think?" I reply sharply. "Could it maybe have something to do with the fact that your father doesn't live here anymore?"

"He's only been gone a month!" Colleen cries.

"How long would you like me to wait?" I ask, my hackles rising. I shut off the flame under the cream sauce and set down the wooden spoon, then put my hands on my hips and regard my kids. "A year? Ten years? What is the appropriate amount of time for me to keep his *shit* after his stunning departure?" I rarely raise my voice in anger, and I can tell my children are shocked. A tense moment of silence passes.

"But . . ." Kevin's voice is soft. "But . . . what if he comes back?" His question surprises me, since my son has had only terse words for Walter whenever he's come up in conversation.

I look at their horror-stricken faces and I suddenly realize that their ambivalence toward their father's abandonment was not due to their resilience or acceptance or Walter's peripheral existence. They were ambivalent because they assumed, in their naive teenage way, that his absence was only temporary.

"First of all, I don't think your father is coming back," I say calmly. "But even if he did, do you really think I would take him back? Wait, what I mean is, do you really think I *should* take him back?"

Colleen and Kevin exchange a quick glance, which reveals that they have already discussed this.

"What if he's, like, really sorry and gets down on his

knees and begs you to forgive him?" Kevin asks. "Couldn't you, Mom? You know. If he's really, *really* sorry."

"Then we could be a family again," Colleen interjects before I can answer. "You wouldn't have to, you know, live together like a real couple." I see a blush rise to her cheeks. "You could have separate beds . . ."

"Like on *I Love Lucy*," Kevin chimes in.

"Yeah. Or separate bedrooms," Colleen continues. "I mean, it's not like you have sex anymore anyway!"

"Why do you say that?" I ask, shocked.

"Because, you're, like, *old*!"

Oh dear God.

"And just what do you think your father and *Cheryl* are doing on that boat in the middle of nowhere? Playing Parcheesi?"

"It's a yacht, Mom," Kevin corrects.

"Whatever!"

"But that's different. Dad's a guy." Colleen says this as though she were citing an actual statistic.

"So it's okay for him and not for me?"

"I'm not saying it's not *okay* for you to have sex." She shudders slightly at the thought. "I'm just saying that you *don't* have sex. And I know this, because if you *were* having sex, Daddy wouldn't have been *compelled* to go have sex with someone else!"

I am stunned speechless. I have no possible reply. I love my daughter intensely, but at this moment I can't stand the sight of her. And Kevin, her accomplice, championing his father the way he is, makes me want to cry.

Four-layer chocolate lasagna with phyllo sheets, mascarpone, and fresh raspberry puree.

Not helping. Not this time.

I feel like lashing out at them and coming clean about all

of the putrid garbage Walter has dumped, not just on me, but on them as well. The mortgage in arrears, the lack of health insurance and alimony and child support. I know this revelation would hurt them, as much as I am hurting right now. But it is my obligation as a mom to keep their emotional pain to a minimum and not to cause them more distress than I already do by default. So even though my base urges crave their misery—as in, misery loves company—my maternal instincts take over and I keep my mouth shut.

Telling them about Walter would not only hurt them but would also kill whatever love they have left for him. And even though that would give me a perverse satisfaction, Walter is still their dad. At some point, whenever that might be, Walter will be back in their lives, and they'll need to draw upon their depleted reserves of love in order to forgive him.

My voice is soft when I speak, my shoulders glued to my ears as I struggle to remain calm and keep my tears at bay. "You are oversimplifying things, Colleen," I tell her. "I wish to God it were as simple as you think it is." What I want to say is, *If I'd thought your father was going to leave me for some blubber-butt accountant named* Cheryl, *I would have dosed up on some pheromones and screwed him from here to Timbuktu.* But I am Rational Ruby, the queen of restraint. So I turn on my heel and leave the kitchen before I can betray myself. Just before I reach the stairs, I hear my son's voice from the kitchen.

"Dude, that was way harsh."

No argument here.

My hand shakes as I lift the eyeliner toward my lids. I have already applied a thin veneer of foundation, which took three tries to get right. The tip of the pencil is mere millimeters from my right eye, and my fingers are shaking so badly I'm afraid I'm going to blind myself. *To hell with makeup,* I think, setting down the liner. Lipstick will have to do. No chance of blinding myself with lipstick.

As I withdraw a muted red lip stain from my drawer, I catch sight of Colleen in the vanity mirror. She enters the bedroom, carrying with her a lovely burgundy cap-sleeved top with faux gemstones embroidered into the swooping neckline. She sets the top on the bed then hesitantly approaches the bathroom. I can tell she is working hard to keep her expression neutral.

Neither of us says a word. She picks up the eyeliner and I automatically turn to face her. I close my eyes and immediately feel the tip of the pencil against my lids. Her touch is light, skilled, and a moment later she is done. She carefully places the liner back in its slot and picks up the mascara, biting her lower lip in concentration as she lengthens and thickens my lashes. When she finishes with that, our eyes lock briefly. I know she wants to say something, but she remains mute, grabbing the blusher and brush and setting to work upon my cheeks. She lines my lips, dabs on some lipstick, then steps back to appraise me.

She nods, and our eyes meet again. Her guard has slipped, and her blue eyes shimmer with unspoken regret. She slowly lifts her hand up, reaching for my hand, and I am reminded of when she was a little girl and we would be walking through a bustling park or a busy mall, and she would reach for me, afraid of getting lost in the crowd, her tension palpable until her fingers found mine. It's been ages since she's clung to me, since she's sought the safety and security of my grip. I feel a lump rise to my throat as I lift my hand toward hers, our fingers finding each other's.

What Colleen never knew, what I never told her lest I

shatter the illusion of Mom as Great Protector, was that I needed to hold her hand as much as she needed to hold mine. I pull her into my arms and embrace her while she weeps. And for the first time in my daughter's life, I allow my own tears to spill into her lovely golden hair.

"Whoa. Definitely a chick moment."

We both turn to see Kevin. Colleen immediately wipes her eyes and sneers at her brother. "You're such a weenie, Kevin."

"I got one. Don't know if I *am* one." He smiles crookedly, then gives me a somber look. "Yo, Mom. Sorry. You know. Sorry."

I nod, not trusting my voice.

"Oh no!" Colleen cries. "Your makeup! It's smeared! We're going to have to start all over again!"

"This is my cue to exit stage left," Kevin says, slipping out the bedroom door and disappearing down the hall.

Colleen nudges me back toward the vanity, grabs some cold cream and a face cloth from the side rack, and turns on the faucet, waiting for the water to heat. She glances up at me, holds my gaze, her expression meaningful.

"Mom?" she says softly.

I reach up and tuck a strand of her hair behind her ear. "I know, honey," I tell her. "I know."

Noon finds me at my workstation in the Muffin Top, assembling a strawberry shortcake for a three o'clock pickup. A couple of twentysomething moms are at a table in the seating area, chatting and nibbling on red velvet cupcakes while simultaneously rocking their strollers with their feet. An older man with a thick head of white hair, a cartoonish white mustache, and spectacles sits at the counter reading the newspaper. His name is Jonathon Carr, a transplanted Brit who has been in the country for fifty years but still sports an almost unintelligible Cockney accent. Fortunately, "muffin" is easy to translate.

Pam Whitfield stands at the sink, washing and topping the strawberries while I brush the shortcake layers with strawberry liqueur. Pam comes in at eleven on Wednesdays to relieve Marcy, who, after opening three days in a row, takes the rest of Wednesday off. Pam is a good worker, if a little slow and somewhat overly concerned with her nails. She is popular with our older customers and has been known to offer stock tips while serving coffee. According to my patrons, she is always right.

She carries the colander of strawberries to the counter, withdraws a cutting board from the rack, and starts to slice the fruit.

"So," Pam says casually as she concentrates on keeping her slices consistent, knowing that if she doesn't, I will take over the task. (I am not an evil dictator, but uneven slices can throw off the balance of a shortcake, and we can't have that.) "I heard about this big pharmaceutical company that's coming out with some new wonder drug around Labor Day. It's going through clinical trials right now, and apparently they're going to push it through the FDA."

"Is that right?" I ask, although I have no idea why she's telling me this. Unless the new drug is some sort of antidepressant and Pam thinks I need one. I take the pan of perfectly sliced strawberries from her and begin covering the base cake with them.

"This particular company has been flagging for the past few years, so their price per share is pretty low." A lightbulb flashes on in my brain as Pam continues. "If you were to, say, buy a thousand shares right now, you could make a fortune come September."

I don't have enough money to buy even a single share, and I suspect she knows this, but I also know that she is trying to help me.

"I made a killing last year in a similar situation," she says, wiping the blade of her paring knife before starting in on the next strawberry.

I glance at my employee. Pam Whitfield is a napoleon if ever I knew one, with layers of crisp pastry sheets sandwiched between rich cream and a perfectly appointed top. Her two-carat pendant sparkles at me from where it hangs on her chest, and I don't doubt that the three strands of diamonds which adorn her wrist are genuine. I have often wondered why she bothers to work when she clearly doesn't need to, but I have never questioned her about it. For some reason, I choose today to ask.

"Pam, just out of curiosity, why . . . um, what makes you . . . well, why do you work at the Muffin Top? I mean, clearly there are other things you could be doing with your time . . ."

She crosses to the sink and begins to wash her hands. "I love the smell of a bakery," she answers simply, grabbing the scrub brush and going to work on her nails as though there are massive amounts of dough beneath them, when in reality there may or may not be a few strawberry seeds.

I shrug and return my attention to the shortcake, using a spatula to scoop some stabilized whipped cream from the stainless-steel bowl. Of my three employees, Pam is the most tight-lipped, except for her moneymaking tips. I know she was a stockbroker, and she was forced to retire, but I don't know exactly why. I know that she has been married twice but have no clue as to what ended her marriages. She shows up on time and leaves the moment her shift ends, but I have no idea what she does outside of the bakery; I never see her at town functions or social events. I know she lives in one of the pricier neighborhoods, but I have never been to her home. I realize now, as I spread a heaping dollop of whipped cream over the strawberries, that I have never really shown much of an interest in my coworker, and perhaps respecting her privacy is only part of the reason.

I hear Pam sigh, turn to see her dry her hands on a towel. She wanders over to my station and gazes at the shortcake under construction.

"My grandfather owned a bakery," she says wistfully.

I set the spatula down so that I can give her my attention, even though she is not looking at me.

"Every Sunday my mother would take my brothers and me to the shop and we were allowed to spend the whole day there. My brothers were older, they got to help with the baking. But I was Grandpa's official taste tester. By the end of the day I was so sick from all of the sugar." She laughs at the memory. "But I loved every minute of it. He died when I was ten and the bakery got torn down to make room for some chain drugstore." She runs her finger along the countertop, then taps the edge of the stainless-steel bowl with her nail. "I'm comfortable, Ruby, I admit. But I'm also alone. Fifty-five next year. No husband, no children. My brothers are both gone, heart attacks in the same damn month, do you believe? My house is full of expensive things and *AARP* magazines. I've already been around the world several times. But I like it here. It reminds me of Grandpa." Finally, she looks up at me. "It reminds me of family."

I feel tears threatening for the second time today over the wealth of personal information Pam has just given me. *Since when have I become so sentimental?* I ask myself. But her memory has reminded me of a time with my own mother. We were in the kitchen of the house I grew up in, side by side, stirring batter for an angel food cake, Mom teaching me how to gently fold in the egg whites, her hand guiding mine.

I reach over and squeeze Pam's fingers, silently thanking her for opening up to me. She quickly straightens her back and pulls her hand away. She is not being rude or rejecting my gesture of intimacy, merely signifying that our sharing session has concluded.

"Of course, I do wish I could actually bake!" she jokes, lightening the mood. She grabs the empty tray and crosses to the sink. "I've always wanted to be able to make a cake."

I smile. "You're welcome to come to my class. Free of charge."

She squints at me dubiously. "Uh, that's a nice offer."

"I've improved considerably since the practice class," I tell her. "Really, I have."

"I believe you, Ruby," she says, though her tone suggests she doesn't believe me at all. "But Tuesday nights are bad for me. *NCIS*. I just love that Mark Harmon. He can eat crackers in my bed anytime. What a hunk!"

At that moment, in walks Jacob Salt. Or should I say, "Baked Alaska." He wears charcoal slacks, a pin-striped shirt, and a navy tie with gray accents and carries a briefcase in one hand. He stops at the display case, his eyes drawn to the sweet treats within, then looks up at me. He gives me a wave and a smile that could melt all one hundred pounds of Callebaut chocolate in my pantry.

Pam turns around and leans back against the counter. "Oh my," she whispers.

"Hi, Ruby," Jacob says.

"Hi, Jacob," I reply, my pulse doing that thing it does whenever this man is around.

"I thought I'd come by and talk about the cake. For the celebration?"

"Oh. Great." I gesture for him to come into the kitchen, but he shakes his head and dons a schoolboy grin.

"I think I'll stay on this side of the counter," he says, glancing at the strawberry shortcake. "Safer that way."

I laugh and move to the sink to wash my hands, and I have to elbow Pam out of the way since Jacob Salt's presence has turned her to stone. She stares at him admiringly even as I nudge her over a few feet.

"Maybe Jacob would like some coffee or a refreshment?" I remind her.

"Yes, of course!" She seems to realize that she is gawking, instantly comes to life, and moves toward Jacob. "What can I get you? Our special today is white and dark chocolate pâté, one of Ruby's latest creations. It is to die for!" Her bracelet shimmers as she gesticulates dramatically.

Oh no! Not the pâté! I can only imagine the moans and groans of pleasure my new dessert will inspire in him, and I really don't think I can handle any vaginal gymnastics right now.

"That sounds a bit too rich for the lunch hour," I hear Jacob reply, and I let out a sigh of relief. "Perhaps a cup of coffee?"

"Coming right up!"

I dry my hands on a clean towel, remove my stained apron and toss it into the hamper, then head to the display case.

"I meant to come by earlier in the week," he tells me. "But I've been swamped at the office."

I usher him over to the counter. Jonathon Carr, a few

seats away, gives us a cursory glance, then returns his attention to his paper.

"It's a rather complicated design that we have in mind. You might have to scale it down a bit."

He sets his briefcase on the Formica countertop, clicks it open, and withdraws a manila envelope. He hands it to me, and as he does, his fingers brush against mine. A shiver runs through me at this fleeting touch, and I snatch the envelope away from him to sever the connection. *This is a job,* I remind myself sharply. *Jacob Salt is a customer. Nothing else.*

"Let's see what you've got," I say, perching on a stool. Jacob closes the briefcase and tucks it under the counter, then takes a seat next to me. He holds himself straight despite the fact that the stool has no back.

I open the envelope and pull out a single eight-by-ten black-and-white photograph. The subject is a white clapboard, three-story house with a wraparound porch. Although I have very little knowledge of architecture, it looks to me to have been built in the early part of the twentieth century.

"This is the first house Franchise wrote a mortgage on, back in '63. It's still standing, too, only now it's a bed-and-breakfast. Just outside of Santa Barbara. We thought you might be able to make a replica out of cake."

My mind is already two steps ahead of him, working out the structural necessities that such a cake would impose and the materials I would use for the facade. Gingerbread covered with long strips of fondant, textured and brushed to look like wood? No, white chocolate plastic would be sturdier, and I can texture and paint it more easily. Dark chocolate for the roof tiles—I'll need at least a couple of hundred; oh, man, my hand is cramping at the thought—dotted with black luster dust to give them a realistic shimmer. The porch overhang creates a bit of an issue, but I can stick long metal pins through white chocolate plastic beams, which will give them added strength.

"How many are we serving?" I ask, noting the dark trim around the windows. Jacob doesn't answer immediately, and I glance up to find him watching me curiously. I suddenly wonder if I have whipped cream in my hair or a strawberry slice stuck to my forehead.

"Oh, sorry," he says with a chuckle. "I could see the wheels turning. I thought smoke might come out of your ears."

I grin. "I get a little intense when it comes to cakes."

"That's why you're so good." Our eyes meet, but Jacob quickly drops his gaze. "At cakes," he clarifies, obviously embarrassed. "Good at cakes." He clears his throat and looks down at the picture. "There will probably be between a hundred and fifty and two hundred people. The San Francisco office is coming down, as well as the team from San Luis Obispo. San Diego's coming up. Plus, we're inviting all of our clients. I doubt the ones from the other cities will make the trip, but a lot of the locals probably will."

Pam arrives with Jacob's coffee, setting it down on the counter in front of him, along with a pitcher of cream and a ramekin filled with sugar and Splenda packets.

"Thank you."

"Oh, my pleasure," Pam says gratuitously. "And let me know if you need anything else. Dow Jones stats, market advice, *anything*." She winks at me, then breezes past the display case to check on the young mothers.

"That's a large group," I comment, watching with approval as Jacob Salt stirs real sugar into his coffee. Walter used Sweet'N Low. I seriously should have known better than to marry a man who sweetened his drinks with sac-charine. "Will you have room at Franchise for that many people?"

He shakes his head. "We're renting the banquet room at the Regency. It should be quite a to-do. The staff's been working on it for months."

Something occurs to me and I squint at Jacob as he takes a sip. "I'm surprised you didn't have a cake already lined up for the event."

A splotch of color explodes on his cheeks, and I suspect it has nothing to do with the hot coffee. "Actually, we did," he says slowly. "But we, uh, decided to switch bakeries."

"Really?" *Just keep your mouth shut, Ruby. Be happy for the job and leave it alone.* "And why is that?"

Jacob has no choice but to look at me. He opens his mouth to answer, closes it, opens it again. Just as he is about to speak, Izzy appears, accompanied by the tolling of the bells on the front door.

"Well, if it isn't Mr. Salt."

He whips around to face her, relieved by the distraction. "Please call me Jacob."

"Absolutely, Jacob," Izzy returns, giddy at the sight of him. I wonder if he is aware of the effect he has on women. From his formal manner, I would guess not. "I'm here to cook the books!" she exclaims on a wink. "Or should I say, *bake* the books? Get it? *Bake* the books? Instead of *cook* the books?"

Jacob laughs heartily, sincerely. Izzy's sense of humor may be wanting, but her enthusiasm is infectious and she could charm the skin off a snake. Alternately, when she's really pissed off, she could skin the same snake while it wrig-gled in her hands.

"So, what are we doing?" she asks, moving between our stools and draping an arm around each of our shoulders. "Oooh. Pretty house."

"Ruby is doing a cake of this house," Jacob says. "For our celebration."

"Do you have any pictures of the back? The sides, maybe?" I ask, peering at the lone photograph.

Jacob grimaces, then shakes his head. "This is it. But like I said. The house is still there. I suppose I could ask one of our brokers in the Santa Barbara office to go out and take some photographs."

"That would be great."

"But it would be even better if you saw the house for yourself, huh, Ruby?" Izzy suggests. "Take your own pictures from every angle. I know how you are. It's only, what, a two-hour drive up there? You could go up and come back in one day." She warms to her idea, drawing me in to her breast and shaking me. "Or spend the night! Santa Barbara's beautiful! I'm sure there's a hotel nearby."

"Actually, this very house is a bed-and-breakfast," Jacob says.

"Oh my God! You could stay there! That's perfect! You deserve a little getaway, you know, with all that's happened. You could stay there and really study the place." She leans away from me and into Jacob. "Ruby is very detail-oriented," she says conspiratorially.

"I couldn't possibly go," I interject before she can get herself into a lather. "The kids."

I say "the kids," but what I really mean is that I cannot possibly afford an overnight at a bed-and-breakfast. Nor the gas it would cost to get my minivan there and back. As it is, I have scaled back our cable service to the minimum channels, sacrificing HBO and the like, which only bothers me when one of my customers, or Izzy herself, starts discussing what happened the other night on *Boardwalk Empire*. I also had to let Enrique go, his green thumb replaced by my own black thumb. I find it ironic that I can make gorgeous colorful, lifelike flowers out of gum paste, but I'll be damned if I can coax a real flower to grow from the ground.

I've cut spending in other areas as well. Without Walter, the kids and I eat out far less often than we used to, saving me a bundle. And frozen dinners, which I previously eschewed, now fill my freezer, since they are far cheaper than a trip to McDonald's. (And yes, although they have a mother who can make them braised lamb shoulder with burgundy reduction sauce and caramelized shallots, my children go absolutely gaga over the Hungry Man dinners and far prefer them to my cooking. Go figure.)

I was never given to reckless spending, except when it came to gourmet food items. Sacrificing these has caused me a fair amount of heartache. Passing the gourmet cheese section in Trader Joe's and not being able to buy that sevendollar hunk of Danish bleu—well, let's just say that my eyes well up and I curse Walter anew. But I'm counting every penny that comes in and goes out, and an overnight in Santa Barbara would cost a boatload of pennies.

"I can stay with the kids," Izzy offers. "They'll love it! Having Aunt Izzy for a night? I'll bring over some of Mama's chimichangas and frijoles and her Ouija board and we'll party!"

"Izzy," I say, my tone soft but curt. "I can't."

She catches my expression and immediately understands my reticence.

"Oh, shit, yeah, no, you're right, it's a bad idea." She talks rapidly, her voice shrill. "Santa Barbara's crazy with tourists this time of year anyway. You'd probably never get a room. And all those college kids from UCSB on the loose? *Dios mío*. I hate college kids. They remind me how old I am, and I *really* hate that! Know what I mean?" She nudges Jacob, who has been silent for the last few minutes, and draws a smile out of him. "Still, you could go for the day, see the place for yourself, and come right back, right?"

"I don't think the minivan could make the trip," I say quickly. "It's making funny noises again." This isn't a lie. My van has been known to sound just like Chitty Chitty Bang Bang, although the noises mysteriously come and go.

Jacob Salt clears his throat, then speaks in almost a whisper. "I could take you."

Izzy and I go still, then she immediately steps behind him and gives me a big thumbs-up behind his back, grinning like a madwoman, her head bobbing up and down.

Without looking at me, he says, "I have no plans on Saturday. We could get an early start, drive up, you take your pictures, and then we head back."

"I, uh, have to work," I stammer, because the thought of being trapped in a car with Jacob Salt for four hours has unexpectedly awakened my vagina.

"Saturday's your day off," Izzy reminds me. I am so going to hurt her later.

"I . . . um . . . that would be . . ." I shrug, my eyes wandering over his strong profile. *Make up something fast, Ruby. You cannot be trusted to be alone in a car with him.*

"That would be great," I say, unable to come up with a good excuse. I make one last attempt to derail this plan. "Are you sure you don't have anything better to do?"

Jacob shakes his head and looks at me, his expression unreadable. "Well, I was planning to foil a terrorist plot, but apparently the terrorists are taking this weekend off."

Izzy bursts into laughter. "Those damn lazy terrorists," she says.

"Actually, you'd be doing me a favor. The only thing I had planned was laundry, and I'll take any excuse to put it off."

Wow. What a compliment. I'm more fun than laundry. Eat your heart out, Walter.

"And in the interest of the cake, of course . . ." he adds.

"Then it's a done deal," Izzy announces, looking as though she's going to burst with glee. "You are quite a devoted employee," she tells him, grinning broadly. "Franchise Funding is lucky to have you! Pam?" she calls. "Bring Mr. Salt some of Ruby's pâté. On the house."

13

Mini-Meringues and
Plucky Penuche

The next few days are filled with a number of activities which I'd hoped would keep me from thinking about my impending day trip with Jacob Salt. But the idea of Saturday's drive lingers in the back of my mind. I haven't been alone, in close quarters, with an attractive man in a long time. Not that Walter is *un*attractive—but he doesn't hold a candle to a certain mortgage broker who runs our branch office. I know Jacob's offer was based upon his concern for the cake and his general niceness, not to mention his aversion to laundry. His interest in me goes no further than my culinary capabilities. He is not going to ask me to mount him while he drives. But the way I feel whenever I am in his presence makes me worry that I might do so without an invitation.

This thought alone has inspired several stressipes, because, really, Rational Ruby engaging in car sex? The image is not only comical, it's horrifying! At forty-three, the logistics of such an act are hard to fathom.

Then why are you fathoming them?

I am asking myself this question for the tenth time on Thursday morning as I arrange trays of cucumber sandwiches and mini-scones on the banquet table in the main hall of the Pelican Point Rec Center. Colleen and her co-counselors have set up a midcourse tea for the Little Princesses and their families, and the Muffin Top is providing the finger food and tea at a reduced rate (read: free of charge).

Ten round tables have been covered with lacy linens, napkins, and porcelain cups and saucers. Colleen is in the side kitchen, filling the teapots from the forty-cup urn I prepared this morning. (I chose chamomile, sweetened with a touch of honey, because, let's face it, nobody wants to see twenty little girls dressed in tea attire running around like banshees, high on caffeine.) Izzy and Zoe are setting handwritten name cards at each place, constantly referring to Colleen's chart. Rachael helps me with the buffet, placing lace doilies beneath the trays and stacking the plastic-that-looks-like-porcelain plates in easily accessible rows.

Colleen stresses punctuality in her course; therefore, it is no surprise that at exactly ten thirty, the hall door opens and several Little Princesses enter, their parents and siblings in tow. I stand by the banquet table with my hands clasped behind my back in the subservient pose I always adopt when serving, and watch the crowd. Colleen's students all wear dresses that cost more than anything in my wardrobe, with yards and yards of tulle and satin twirling out around them. Their hair is perfectly appointed; either scraped into buns with nary a strand out of place (likely thanks to Aqua Net) or burned into ringlets that would make Shirley Temple proud. Shiny patent-leather shoes encase delicate feet, and gloves cover dainty hands. The parents' attire is more casual, but still reflects the occasion; not a pair of jeans or a T-shirt in sight.

Colleen heads into the fray with Rachael and Zoe on her heels. With my daughter and her friends overseeing, the girls formally introduce their families to one another, shaking hands and giving the occasional curtsy. Izzy sidles over to me, a grin pulling at the corners of her mouth.

"You ever dress like that when you were six?" she asks in a whisper.

"I wore dresses, occasionally," I answer quietly. "Not like those. And only to church socials."

"You couldn't catch me dead wearing something like that when I was a kid. Mama tried. How she tried. Please, Izzy, *dame los pantalones, por favor. Dios mío, pareces como un hijo!* Give me those pants, for God's sake. You look like a boy!"

I give her a sideways glance, taking in the swell of her ample chest and her curvaceous hips, both accentuated by the snug Lycra top and brown suede skirt she wears.

"Times have changed, huh?"

"Speaking of clothes," she says coyly. "What are you wearing on Saturday?"

I'm still annoyed with her for instigating the whole bloody affair. "A tent," I retort. "I'm wearing a tent."

"The hell you say," she snorts.

"It's not a date, Iz," I say firmly. She makes her eyebrows do a quick up-down-up-down thing in response, gleefully mocking me. I roll my eyes and shift my focus back to the party.

Colleen calls for everyone's attention, rebuking those who don't quiet immediately with an admonishing look. "Thank you all for coming to our Little Princess Teatime. For the last few weeks, our Little Princesses have been learning so much about what it means to be a girl in today's world. They are discovering themselves, while also learning manners and etiquette and the proper way to behave in the many different social situations that arise." A groan erupts from one of the big brothers. "For example . . ." Colleen seizes upon the unsuspecting kid's faux pas. "Keeping our negative feelings to ourselves and being supportive of loved ones who wish to better themselves."

I watch my daughter, amazed by the ease with which she addresses the assembled group. So natural, I think. Her words flow freely and her manner is completely self-assured. Calm, confident. Obviously, she doesn't get this particular gift from me, but I am responsible for creating her and carrying her in my womb and giving birth to her and raising her, so I do get some of the credit. (I begrudgingly acknowledge that Walter deserves some credit, too, but I am not generous enough to give him more than a sperm-size chunk of it.) And Colleen deserves most of the credit anyway. She has worked hard to nurture her own talents and has made a commitment to these girls that is uncommon for someone her age. As I watch her expertly maneuver through the crowd and guide each family to their seats, I am filled with pride.

After a brief presentation about the Little Princess class, the girls and their chaperones are invited to the buffet. While the group gathers at the banquet table, Zoe, Rachael, and I move to the rounds to pour the tea and Izzy remains stationed with the food.

As I finish with one of the tables, I see Holly Morgan move toward me, carrying a plate on which there is nothing but a few pieces of fruit. She wears an ivory pencil skirt, size two, and a sleeveless pale blue turtleneck which emphasizes her high, round breasts (courtesy of Dr. Phil Feinstein). Her blond hair is teased, her makeup perfect.

Oh crap! I'd forgotten that Holly's youngest daughter, Iris, is a Little Princess. I glance past Holly and see the four-foot-tall replica of her mother standing next to the mini-scones. The six-year-old scrunches up her nose in a most unladylike fashion as her father tries to explain what the pastries are.

"Oh, Ruby. Look at you," Holly exclaims in mock surprise. For a brief moment I actually think she is going to compliment me on my new do. What an idiot I am. "I didn't know you were waitressing now!" She leans in to me conspiratorially. "I guess you have to do whatever it takes to make ends meet, right? There's no shame in waitressing, you know. It's a very noble profession."

That's it! I draw my arm back like a bow then release it, and my fist hurls toward Holly Morgan's smug face, landing a solid blow to her nose, which snaps with an echoing crack as blood spurts from her nostrils.

Okay. Not really. This is my daughter's day, after all. I can't ruin it by throwing down with one of the guests, much as I'd like to. And besides, Holly would be forced to buy yet another new nose and the only business I plan to send Firming Phil is my own.

"The Muffin Top provided the food," I say calmly, although I suspect she already knows this.

"Oh, right," she says with a patronizing smile. She sets her plate down and pulls out her chair. "So, Ruby, did you hear the latest about Walter? On Facebook? About his run-in with a tribe of natives on this little island near Hawaii? It was a hoot!"

I shake my head and force myself to don a placid expression. "Uh, no, I didn't catch that one. But I did hear about Rea's new Facebook fan page," I say sweetly. "'Spit or Swallow,' is it? Very popular with the football team apparently."

Holly almost falls into her seat, her eyes blinking rapidly. Before she can regain her equilibrium, I turn and head to the next table to pour the tea, wondering where the heck that comment came from. That was not the Cake Lady. That wasn't even the Cake Goddess. That was definitely the Cake Bitch. Oooh. I like *her*.

I should feel remorse for the comment, and in my previous life, I would have. As I head back to the buffet table, I realize that being left, being suddenly single, being ostracized from my former world has released me. Before now, I would have worried about the repercussions of making such a nasty remark, which would have included rejection or rebuke from my peers. But my peers have already rejected and rebuked me, and there is nothing they can do to me now that would injure me further. A great weight lifts from my shoulders at this knowledge, and a small satisfied smirk spreads across my face.

"What did you say to Holly Morgan?" Izzy asks me when I take my place next to her. "She looked like she was going to have a seizure."

I say nothing, but my smirk slowly morphs into a full-fledged grin.

Twenty-four hours later, I am on the long stretch of Pelican Point Beach. Once again, I am catering for my children, having brought a metric ton of goodies to the First Official Beach Cleanup Fund-raiser of the summer, hosted by the Eco-Surfers, my son's band of merry waveriders. They have a great day for it, too, not a cloud in the bright cerulean sky, the sun shining down upon the beach, causing the sand to shimmer as though it's full of tiny gemstones, the temperature rapidly climbing into the mid eighties.

The kids have pamphlets with information on the harmful effects of litter, including photographs and a frightening blurb on Trash Island in the Pacific Ocean. (Although the island itself is horrendous, I secretly hope that Walter and

Cheryl will get marooned upon it.) The Eco-Surfers have also brought biodegradable trash bags for beachgoers and are handing them out with enthusiasm.

Even though it's not yet noon, a crowd has gathered around the Muffin Top's table of treats. Since all of the profits are going to the cleanup fund, I have upped the asking price to two dollars per item, but no one is complaining. Cash is thrust into my hand as cookies, brownies, muffins, and bars are consumed with abandon.

Due to the success of the Little Princess Teatime, Colleen is feeling charitable today and has come to help out her brother and me. She stands beside me, making change with the speed of a magician and restocking napkins and take-away sleeves as needed. She wears a red halter top and bikini bottoms and has tied a half apron around her waist, which does nothing to conceal the lithe, firm body beneath it. I myself am wearing a pair of cutoff denim shorts which Colleen talked me into and which ride up a bit in the crotch, but if I do say so myself, they also show off a pair of legs I'd forgotten were not damn bad. (I was forced to shave my legs last night, much to my chagrin, and had to settle for one of Walter's abandoned Schicks, since my pink Daisy disposable razor was completely rusted from disuse.) A pale plum tank top and my own half apron complete my ensemble. I usually shy away from sleeveless shirts in order to hide the upper-arm jiggle that plagues most middle-aged women—save for Madonna—but Colleen assured me that my biceps look great (praise be to stirring by hand) and the heat of the day called for as little clothing as possible.

A group of ten-year-olds has the table surrounded, poking at the array of goodies with fervor. Colleen puts her hands on her hips and frowns at them. "You touch it, you buy it!" she declares loudly. "Keep your sandy little fingers off the goods until you make up your mind."

One boy in particular, a towheaded kid so painfully thin a light breeze might blow him away, looks up at Colleen with huge brown eyes. He elbows the boy next to him.

"Dude, she's a Betty," he whispers loudly.

Colleen tries to hide her grin.

"I guess," the other kid says with a shrug. "If you like 'em that old."

Colleen's eyes go wide as I snort with laughter. But my laughter fades as I realize that if this boy thinks Colleen is old, he must think I'm an *antique*.

"I only got a dollar," the first kid says glumly as his friends hand over their money in exchange for their delicious loot.

Colleen leans down and smiles at him. "I'll give you a discount," she coos, and I watch the boy's face light up. He places his single dollar into Colleen's outstretched hand and grabs an enormous chocolate-chunk cookie, smiles wide, and takes a bite.

"Phanks!" he says around his mouthful, and starts to walk away.

"Come back in about ten years, mister, and we'll talk," Colleen calls to him. She turns to me. "Old! Me! Do you believe that?"

"It's all a matter of perspective," I say. "Compared to them"—I gesture to the remaining two kids trying to decide between a couple of items—"you are old." *And compared to YOU*, I think, *I'm a freaking dinosaur!*

"Whatever," she says, shrugging.

While Colleen finishes with the last two boys, I use the slight lull to restock the trays, noting that my reserve of brownies is already dwindling. The white chocolate cranberry muffins are not selling well, but the chocolate-chip and chocolate-chunk cookies are going fast.

"Hey, Cake Lady!"

My former paperboy, Shane O'Neil, walks toward the table wearing black board shorts with Peanuts characters on them and nothing else. I can't help but notice that his tanned, toned torso really shouldn't be allowed out of the house unclothed—and don't ask whether this is the mother in me talking or the wanton harlot, because I honestly don't know.

"How're you doing?" Shane asks, smiling warmly at me.

"I'm well, Shane, thanks. How are you?"

"Terrific. I don't have any classes today, so I'm great. Looking forward to Tuesday, though. I've got the *mise-en-place* memorized already. I used anagrams. 'Best to step forward when entering Vatican.' Butter, tapioca, sugar, flour, whisk, eggs, vanilla. 'Course, they're out of order, and I kind of peppered the tools in between."

I smile, impressed. "That's really good, Shane."

"I have a bunch of them," he admits. "A few of them I can't repeat out loud, at least not in mixed company." He sports a naughty grin.

"I think I'd like to hear those ones especially."

What did I just say?

"I couldn't possibly share them with you," he says, shaking his head, and I feel like an idiot for my remark. He must think I'm a desperate, horny, pathetic older woman—

"Unless my grade depends on it," he adds, and when I look at him, his lids are at half-mast and he is giving me a lazy smile.

That's flirting! It is. He's flirting with you!

No, he isn't.

Yes, he is.

Rice Krispies peanut-butter balls coated with caramel and rolled in chopped peanuts.

"Well, I think it's terrific that you're putting so much effort into the class already," I quickly comment, trying to sound professorial. "You're going to do great, I'm sure."

He lowers his head shyly, pleased with my praise, and his shiny dark hair falls across his forehead. His gaze lands on the plethora of sweets. "Wow! Calorie fest!"

The last of the ten-year-olds have completed their purchases and are now scampering off toward their parents. I glance over at Colleen. She stands frozen, gazing in my direction. Her jaw has practically dropped to her chest, and if I didn't know better, I would swear she was drooling. I clear my throat and she quickly pulls herself together—thankfully closing her mouth—and inches closer to where Shane stands.

"Hi," she says with forced indifference. But I can tell that her heart is pounding from the bright pink spots that have appeared on her cheeks. And I understand why. Any woman with a pulse would be drawn to Shane O'Neil. And Colleen has a pulse. I have one, too, although I refuse to admit that mine is racing because that would be a little creepy.

Shane looks up and sees Colleen. "Hi."

"This is Shane," I say to my daughter. "He's in the cake class."

"So, you're one of my mom's students, huh?"

"Wait, you're her daughter?" Colleen nods and bats her eyelashes flirtatiously. He glances back and forth between us. "No way! She's too young to have a daughter as old as you!"

I know Shane is trying to compliment me, but Colleen,

having been referred to as old twice in the past ten minutes, visibly deflates. She struggles to keep her confident smile in place while simultaneously swallowing a gulp of air.

"Your mom's really something," he confides as though I'm not there. "Her cakes are amazing! I only hope she can teach a dope like me how to make something that looks halfway decent." He winks at her, and she puffs up a bit in response. "Otherwise there'll be hell to pay."

"Yo, Uncle Shane-man!" a young girl calls to him, trotting over from down by the shore.

"Ah, here's the devil that will make my life miserable should I fail in my mission!"

He takes a few steps toward her and holds his hand out, but she playfully bats it away.

"I'm fine, I'm fine," she tells him gruffly. She is slight—no taller than four and a half feet tall—and extremely fair, with a thick smear of fluorescent-pink zinc oxide on her nose. She wears baggy shorts revealing skinny legs and knobby knees, and an oversize T-shirt that bears the legend GO GAGA! An Angels baseball cap covers a head, which, on closer inspection, appears to have not a single hair upon it.

Shane slings an arm around her and pulls her toward our table. "This is my niece Annabelle," he announces proudly. "Annabelle, this is the Cake Lady, remember I told you about her? And her daughter, um . . . I'm sorry, I don't know your name."

"Colleen," my daughter breathes. "My name is Colleen."

"Colleen, right. Say hi to Mrs. McMillan and Colleen," he instructs his niece.

"So you're the one who's going to help Shamrock here make my birthday cake, huh?" Annabelle says without preamble. I peg this girl as nine going on thirty-five. But then, considering what she's going through, I'm sure she is mature beyond her years. I silently thank God for my two healthy children, one of whom is currently ogling my student, and not very covertly. Colleen is so mesmerized by Shane that she barely gives Annabelle a second glance.

"She's the one, Annie," Shane says. "And you should see what she can do!" He gives me an admiring look that actually makes me blush. "Her cakes are outrageous!"

"You have to make mine yourself, Uncle Shane," Annabelle replies, unimpressed. "If she does the work, that's cheating and it doesn't count."

"Am I allowed to help?" I ask, and receive a guileless look from the girl.

She considers my question for a moment, then shrugs. "I guess that would be okay," she decides. "But only help. No taking over."

I feel the urge to salute her, stifle it, and smile instead. "It's a deal. I think your uncle will do just fine."

"With you as my teacher, how could I not?"

Annabelle rolls her eyes. "Maybe because you're a total loser in the kitchen? He can't even make microwave brownies!"

"You shouldn't eat that shit anyway, Annie. It's full of preservatives."

"You said 'shit.' I am so telling my mom."

"Would you like something sweet, Annabelle?" I interject, amused by their repartee.

She looks down at the table and frowns, crinkling her nose at my confections.

"Not now, thanks," she replies, then turns to Shane. "I'm gonna try that skim board again. Hopefully I won't end up on my ass this time."

"Watch your mouth!" Shane cries, swallowing his laughter.

"I will if you will!" she fires back. She sticks her tongue out at him and skips off in the direction of the water.

Shane grins at me and shrugs. "She's something, huh?"

"She's very sweet," Colleen says, and Shane laughs.

"'Sweet' doesn't exactly come to mind, but she's a good girl." He looks at me apologetically. "Don't take it personally, you know, about her not wanting your goodies." He gestures to the trays. "The treatment's making her a little nauseous, you know."

"I understand," I assure him.

"But I sure would love something. Only I have a big problem. I can't possibly decide on just one!"

A couple of people wander over, eco-bags in hand, and Colleen immediately moves to help them. I pull several sleeves from the pile and fill them with an assortment of cookies and bars and hand them to Shane, which he happily accepts. At the last minute, I go to one of the coolers and grab a muffin from within. These particular muffins are from a recipe I created, with oats, flaxseed, shredded carrots, nuts, and honey instead of sugar, and I make them for myself and the staff because they help with energy during a long shift. (I did try to sell them at the Muffin Top once, but they lay untouched in the display case until I finally had to throw them out. Apparently, people don't want healthy crap when they come to a bakery. Who knew?) I sleeve it and add it to Shane's bounty.

"That's for Annabelle," I tell him. "It's very easy on the stomach and it's chock-full of good things."

His easy manner evaporates and his expression turns serious, as though he is contemplating an outcome for his niece that would be better left uncontemplated. "That's really nice of you. Thanks."

Without thinking, I reach across the table and place my

hand on Shane's wrist and give it a gentle squeeze. "She'll be all right," I tell him.

He glances down at my hand, then looks up at me and smiles gratefully. "I know she will. She has to be." Suddenly he grins. "I don't think even God could handle her right now."

I chuckle and pull my hand away. "I have a feeling He has a lot more things planned for her here on earth."

"You mean like taking over the planet?" he asks. We both laugh for a moment, then he glances over his shoulder toward the water. "I better go make sure she doesn't break her butt. My sister would kill me. How much do I owe you?"

"Well, you get the student rate," I say. "Free."

"Wow. Thanks!" He starts to turn away, then looks back at me and gazes at me intently. "You really are something, Cake Lady."

I wave him off to hide my embarrassment, then busy myself with rearranging the trays, even though they don't need to be rearranged. Just as I raise my eyes to steal a look at Shane, he turns around, cocks his head to the side, and treats me to an entrancing smile. Then he gives a two-finger salute and continues on his way.

Penuche, I think. Shane O'Neil is penuche. An amazing candy that melts in your mouth and demands your full attention to consider the many different sensations and layers it reveals as you consume it. Penuche could inspire anthems. It's the Brad Pitt of candy.

"Oh my God!" Colleen exclaims as soon as her patrons walk away. "Oh my God, oh my God, ohmyGod! He is hot!"

Yup. Penuche.

Colleen has her eyes glued to Shane as he trots toward the water, where Annabelle is trying her luck on the skim board. The expression on my daughter's face is similar to one you might wear if you were gazing at a truly fabulous dessert, or if you were a lion about to pounce on your wounded prey. I wouldn't be surprised if she suddenly licked her lips and revealed sharpened fangs the size of candy corns. As we watch (yes, I am watching, too, because there are only so many ways I can rearrange the cookies), a young woman about Shane's age approaches him. Her sun-bleached mane is long and layered, and she tosses it back for effect as she gives Shane a coy wave. Her body is perfectly tanned and lithe, but voluptuous in the right places, and her stomach is decorated with a sparkling diamond navel ring. The hot-pink micro-bikini she's sporting is so small she might as well be naked. She touches Shane on the arm with apparent familiarity and he smiles at her.

"Do you think that's his girlfriend?"

I glance at Colleen. Her brows are knitted together in a frown. "I don't know, hon. Maybe. Hey, can you grab a tray of brownies from the cooler?" We don't need more brownies, but she needs a distraction. Without a word, she complies and I do my best to make room on one of the trays. At the shore, I see Annabelle toss the board down and jump upon it, grinning with glee as she slides across the sand. Shane and the young woman clap enthusiastically for her. Colleen returns with the tray.

"I wonder if Annabelle's mom has looked into getting a wig for her," I say thoughtfully. "Do you know where she can get one?"

"What? Who?"

"Annabelle. She needs a wig."

"Why would a little girl need a wig?" When she looks at me, her clear blue eyes reveal that she is utterly clueless.

"She's going through chemo, honey. She's lost all her hair."

"Who?"

"Annabelle!" I cry.

"Oh," Colleen says absently, returning her attention to Shane O'Neil. "I didn't notice."

No kidding, I think. *I can't imagine why.*

Late that night, I stand at my closet, peering in, waiting for an ensemble to jump out at me. I hold my cordless phone in one hand, listening to Izzy's advice with only half an ear.

"Comfortable," she is saying. "You're going to be four hours in the car at least, so nothing that wrinkles easily. But it's gotta be cute," she continues without pausing. "You know, chic. Probably the bed-and-breakfast people are gonna wonder why there's some strange woman taking pictures outside, and you don't want to look like a hippie or a transient or anything."

"When have I ever looked like a hippie or a transient?" I ask, trying not to sound offended.

"Do you want me to be specific?"

"That's not nice."

"Okay, transient is pushing it. You never looked like a transient. But that tie-dye T-shirt you wore to the bakery for like a month? Not even a hippie would be caught dead in that."

"It's colorful."

"If your customers were 'shrooming, it would be perfect. If you were going to a Grateful Dead show? Rock on, sister-friend. But don't wear it tomorrow. Or ever again, as far as I'm concerned. Burn it."

"I don't even know why we're having this conversation," I say seriously. "This isn't a date, you know. This is a job. Jacob Salt is doing me a favor. He's not interested in me. So it doesn't matter what I wear."

"Um, let me just interject, if I may," Izzy says. "Jacob Salt is one of the few eligible middle-aged men in town."

"So what, Iz? I'm still married, in case you've forgotten."

"In whose eyes? God's?" she fires back. "You think Walter still thinks he's married to *you* while he's boinking that *chingada puta* in the freaking South Pacific?"

This pulls me up short and I say nothing. I hear Izzy sigh. "Look, I'm sorry about that, but come on, Rube. So what if Jacob Salt isn't interested in you?"

"He's not," I reply tersely, still wincing from her words. "And I am not interested in him."

"Okay, fine. He's not. You're not. But you're still spending the day in the company of a fucking babe. You owe it to yourself to look your best."

I breathe in and exhale loudly, feeling a stressipe jab at my subconscious. I ignore it. "Fine. You're right."

"Damn straight I am," she says. "So what are you going to do?"

"I'm going to wake up Colleen."

14

Here's Mud Pie in Your Eye

At the stroke of nine o'clock the following morning, I hear a car pull to the curb. It's hard to believe I can hear the sound from my kitchen, but I am a mother. Mothers have almost preternatural hearing. My mom could hear me tiptoeing across the carpet of my bedroom on the second floor in the back of the house when she was in the garage. It's a gift we mothers are blessed with the minute our kids are born, and it probably fades once they move out, but during that interim period of eighteen years or so, we are like bats. Except for the blind part. (Although the first time I saw Colleen wearing a tube top that exposed her midriff, I kind of wished I was.)

The kids are seated at the kitchen table eating their respective breakfasts. When the car door slams shut, they both look up from their plates.

"Your ride's here, Mom," Kevin announces pleasantly.

Colleen says nothing, just watches me curiously as she takes a small bite of multi-grain toast.

Last night, I had thrown caution to the wind and taken the kids to our local Italian restaurant for a celebratory dinner. I felt they deserved it after all of their hard work and the success of their endeavors. Over garlic bread oozing with butter and melted mozzarella, I told them about my jaunt to Santa Barbara, that a customer was taking me, and that

I would be back before dark. Neither thought anything about it at the time. Even when I woke Colleen out of a heavy sleep to help me decide on an outfit, she didn't question the situation, was simply thrilled I was taking the whole makeover thing so seriously. But this morning, I can see the wheels spinning in her brain, as if she is trying to work something out.

"Mom?" she calls to me. I prepare myself for her inquiries. *Why did you wake me up last night? Why was it so important for me to do your makeup this morning? Why do you look like a hornet's nest was just let loose in your stomach? Who is this guy giving you a ride, anyway?*

"Do you think Shane O'Neil likes Coldplay?"

Oh, boy. I am relieved not to be at the center of my daughter's thoughts, but also a little concerned by her instantaneous fixation on my student. She's had crushes before, all of which she vehemently denied, but none matches the intensity of the one she currently has on Shane.

The doorbell rings and we all look toward the front of the house.

"I don't know, honey," I say as I place my coffee mug next to the sink and head for the hall. "You like Coldplay, right?"

"She likes Chris Martin," Kevin jokes.

"Who's she?"

"*He,* Mom. Lead singer," Kevin faux-whispers.

"Right." Sometimes moms are complete morons, aren't we?

"I do *not* like Chris Martin," I hear her say behind me as I walk to the foyer.

My palm feels a bit clammy as I reach for the doorknob, and I realize that every muscle in my body is tense with anticipation. If I didn't know better, I would think I was a teenager going to her first prom. But I do know better, and I also know that I never did go to prom, which I'm sure was a complete waste of time, even if the other girls in my class talked about it for weeks afterward as though it were the be-all-and-end-all of high school existence.

I take a deep breath before I turn the knob and force myself to relax. *This is not a date, Ruby. This is not a date.* Although that may be true, I'm glad I look good, thanks to my daughter. She has outfitted me in a pair of white cotton pants and a formfitting yellow top with elbow-length sleeves and a neckline that plunges ever so slightly at my cleavage. I wear a pair of Colleen's canvas espadrilles, yellow to match my top, and a simple gold chain adorns my neck. My makeup is light, for daytime, but subtly highlights my eyes and my cheekbones.

This is not a date, I remind myself one last time. Still, you can't blame a girl for wanting to be attractive to her, um, ride.

I pull open the door to reveal Jacob Salt on my front porch. He is dressed in khaki slacks with a light cotton pull-over sweater in a shade of aquamarine, the sleeves pushed up to reveal those wonderful forearms. His wavy hair is tousled and a light growth of stubble on his face reveals that he shucks his razor on the weekend, a fact that doesn't bother me in the least because I have been known to shuck my own razor for months at a time. He seems a bit more relaxed than usual, his posture less stiff, his thumbs tucked into his front pockets.

Wow. He looks good.

"Hi, Ruby," he says, smiling down at me.

His voice is so deep and melodic that just those two words make me want to cross my legs, which is damn difficult when you're standing up.

"Hi, Jacob."

He doesn't comment on how I look, nor does he offer me a corsage. Oh, well. We stand there for an awkward moment, with me wondering how I am going to survive alone in a car with him and him staring at me expectantly.

"Ready to go?" he asks after a few seconds, and I nod.

"Just let me get my bag," I say. "Come in," I add as an afterthought, and he wordlessly follows me down the hall, leaving the front door open as if in preparation for a quick escape.

Kevin is at the sink, dumping his cereal bowl into soapy water, and Colleen is still at the table, staring dreamily into space while chewing her bite of toast the requisite thirty-seven times.

Okay, so I know *this is not a date,* but still, there is a strange man in the house—who is not Walter—and I have to introduce the kids to him. I realize, as I walk into the kitchen with Jacob on my heels, that I am slightly unnerved by the situation. I wonder how I will behave if and when I actually have a date. My anxiety instantly evaporates because as soon as Kevin sees us, he marches across the room and puts his hand out to Jacob.

"Hey! I'm Kevin. How's it going?"

Jacob smiles and shakes Kevin's hand. "I'm Jacob Salt."

"Yo, cool name. Like the spice of the earth! You know, the world's economy practically revolves around salt."

"I didn't know that," Jacob says evenly.

"Oh, yeah. We learned about it in SS."

"Social studies," I translate, crossing to the table to retrieve my carryall, which is loaded with my digital camera, my wallet, Kleenex, the makeup kit Colleen put together for me, a PowerBar, my cell phone, a notepad and pen, and a few items that were already floating around in the bag prior to this morning, although why I put a rectal thermometer, a smiley-face eraser, and a Statue of Liberty bottle opener in my purse in the first place, I have no idea.

"And this is Colleen," I say, placing a hand on my daughter's arm.

"Hi," she murmurs faintly.

"How are you?" Jacob asks, and thankfully it is more of a rhetorical greeting, because Colleen has taken another bite and is furtively chewing once again.

I sling my bag over my shoulder, then move to the counter and grab the paper sack I prepared earlier. "Okay, guys, so I'll see you later, all right? If you need me, call my cell. If there's an emergency, call Izzy."

"Yo, Mom, chill. We'll be totally kosher."

I kiss Kevin's forehead and glance at Jacob, who is watching us with interest.

"It was nice to meet both of you," he says, then turns and heads for the front door. I exhale quietly, offer the kids a wave, and follow him out into the sunshine.

"I have a GPS, but I also MapQuested to see alternative routes," Jacob is saying as he maneuvers his BMW onto the main thoroughfare outside of my tract of houses. "I think the 405 to the 101 will be the most time-efficient, although PCH is a much nicer drive . . . visually speaking."

While the Pacific Coast Highway would ordinarily be my choice, that particular route, with its traffic and stoplights and jaywalking surfers, would automatically add at least half an hour to our journey. We've only been in the car for two minutes and already Jacob's subtle cologne is doing funny things to my psyche and his proximity is making it difficult for me to maintain a normal pulse rate. I try to keep my gaze firmly fixed on the road ahead, but I can't help sneaking sideways glances at him, and when I do, I can't stop myself from appreciating his chiseled profile. The paper sack sits in my lap, crinkling loudly every time I shift position, which seems to be quite a lot as I cannot seem to get comfortable.

For the first time in my life, I have a crush on someone. Because this has never happened before, I can't be completely sure, but the signs are all there. I am acting just like my teenage daughter. My mouth is dry. I feel like giggling over absolutely nothing and I am just dying to know whether Jacob Salt likes Coldplay. (Kidding! But really, I do wonder what kind of music he enjoys.)

"405 okay?" he asks.

"You're the captain," I say lamely, and cringe with embarrassment. But when I look up at Jacob, he is smiling amusedly.

Wow. He really has nice teeth.

I am almost forty-four years old. And I have a crush on Jacob Salt. I didn't even have a crush on Walter, and I married *him*. Think what I'd do for the man sitting beside me.

How do I handle this? I ask myself. Having no prior experience, I am at a loss. I try to think about it like a recipe. *What are the ingredients necessary to battle middle-aged infatuation?* Denial? Feigned ignorance? Mood-altering drugs which come with that warning about deadening sexual arousal? Mix 'em all together and you'll be fine? The problem is, I am almost enjoying the way this man makes me feel. *Is that wrong?* As Izzy so eloquently pointed out, for all intents and purposes, I am single. Why do I have to do anything? Why do I have to pretend I'm not infatuated?

All right, so maybe I don't have to pretend with *myself*. But I definitely should pretend with him. After all, he hasn't done anything to inspire these feelings. He has behaved in a completely platonic manner, maintaining a professional distance even as he held the car door for me and waited until I was safely belted before easing it shut. Aside from the choice of our route, he hasn't said anything. I sure hope he'll engage in a bit of chitchat; otherwise, I'll have nothing to take my mind off of my newly recognized crush, my decision not to fight it, and my complete bewilderment over both of the above.

Jacob expertly guides the Beemer into the fast lane, and then, as if in answer to my prayers, he speaks. "Your kids are terrific."

I nod enthusiastically. "Oh, yeah. They're great. I think I'll keep them. Of course, it's too late to give them back now."

I realize how stupid that sounds. Uh-oh. Another irrefutable sign of a crush. Analyzing every word that comes out of my mouth. This is going to be a *long* trip.

But Jacob chuckles softly, relieving me. When his laughter fades, he glances over, his face suddenly somber. "How are they doing? Your kids."

"Great. Fine," I answer automatically, and his brow furrows.

"I mean, you know, how are they dealing with . . . everything?"

Oh no. We have bypassed small talk and gone straight to "serious discussion." I want small talk back. I let out a sigh.

"I'm sorry," he says quickly. "I didn't mean to pry."

"No, no. It's okay." Another sigh escapes me. "I think they're fine. Most of the time. But I think it hits them, occasionally, like ripping off a Band-Aid. You forget about the wound until you uncover it, you know? They've got great friends, really supportive, so that helps. And I try to talk to them, but I'm the mom, so what do I know? They're old

enough to understand what's happened, at least intellectu-
ally. They're smart, they get it. But then, you know, *intel-
lectually,* how do you wrap your head around the idea that
your father has completely abandoned you for some random
woman?" I shake my head at the idea of leaving my children
behind. It would be like unscrewing my arms and legs and
heading out into the world limbless. I just couldn't do it. Not
for any reason.

"And how are *you* doing?" he asks quietly, without taking his eyes off the road.

I laugh mirthlessly and say nothing. Not because he is
prying, which he is, but because I'm not sure how to answer
the question. Six weeks ago, Walter left. And during that
time, I have been publicly humiliated, left financially bereft,
dumped by my social network, have pulled myself up by my
bootstraps, had a makeover, started teaching a cake class,
developed a crush on a handsome man who happens to be
driving me to Santa Barbara. How am I?

"I'm fine," I say at last.

"Really? I mean, it's got to be hard."

"We didn't love each other anymore," I say simply, although I know this is not the entire truth. Can I bear to say
the absolute truth out loud? Can I, Rational Ruby, reveal
all? To a virtual stranger?

"The truth is," I hear myself say, "I never loved him the
way he wanted me to." There. I said it. And no disaster has
befallen me. Not even a stressipe has come to mind.

Jacob glances at me before returning his attention to the
Saab exactly five car lengths in front of us. "And what way
was that?" he asks.

In for a penny, in for a pound, as my mother used to say.
(Now she says, "When God closes a door, somewhere else

He opens a window," but I don't think that applies here.) "You know. I didn't love him *that* way."

He nods thoughtfully. A long moment passes. "Ruby? May I ask you one more question?"

I don't think I can possibly handle any more pointed questions from this man. "Sure."

A grin appears at the corners of his mouth. "What on earth do you have in that bag? The aroma is driving me crazy."

By the time we reach the 101, Jacob has laid waste to four of the white-chocolate-macadamia-nut cookies, miraculously consuming them without getting a single crumb on his person. I made the cookies this morning as a thank-you because they are a no-brainer when it comes to sweets, reliable and delicious. The white chocolate is still warm, the outside of the cookies are golden brown and crisp, and the insides are perfectly gooey, and Jacob has been vociferously appreciative of their merit. Let's just say that my legs are clamped together like a steel trap.

"I usually wait until after noon to eat sweets," he tells me. "But I just can't help myself."

"I had a T-shirt once that said 'Life's Short. Eat Dessert First.' I loved that shirt."

He laughs. "A wise proverb," he agrees.

He has relaxed visibly since our earlier discussion; his manner is more at ease, his posture less stiff, and the tension lines on his face have faded dramatically. In short, he is even more attractive to me now.

"You know, this is my favorite kind of cookie," Jacob reveals.

"Mine, too."

"My ex-wife used to make them for me . . . back in the day." (Read: back when she liked penises.) "Of course, she used those frozen premade dough balls. Her niece sold them through the school, for a fund-raiser."

I nod. Jacob has returned to "serious mode," as if it is his turn to get something off his chest. I remain silent.

"She's a great girl, Phoebe. Wow, she must be fourteen by now. I haven't seen her for three years. Well, that's divorce for you. You don't just separate from your spouse. You lose their entire family, too."

"You liked your in-laws?"

"I didn't dislike them," he replies. "Kristen's parents were—are—a little straitlaced." This comment strikes me as humorous coming from Mr. Straitlaced himself, but then I realize that I don't know Jacob Salt at all. Maybe he secretly cross-dresses or slathers himself with mayonnaise or watches clown porn.

"I used to play golf with my brother-in-law. Joe. Every Sunday at the country club. That stopped faster than you can say 'Rosie O'Donnell.' It's not even that you take sides. You just have nothing in common anymore."

I think of my own in-laws, Lorraine and Todd McMillan, who were killed in an auto accident five years ago. Of course, their loss hit our family hard at the time, especially Walter, but I'm relieved that they aren't here to see what he has done. They would have been mortified. But then, maybe if they were still alive, Walter wouldn't have left. From the moment we buried them, Walter started waxing on about his own mortality, about the speed with which time flies, about how it all can come to a screeching halt at any instant. Perhaps the idea of his leaving was formulated even then, years ago, when he was confronted with his own fragile place in history and the finite number of hours and minutes and seconds he had left on the planet.

Or maybe he's just an ass. Yeah, that's probably it.

"What about you? Are you close with your, uh, husband's family?"

"Walter is an only child. Like me. His parents died a few years ago. So . . ."

"I don't mean to sound callous, but in some ways, that's better."

I shrug. "Do you have brothers or sisters?"

"One of each. Lucas is a stockbroker in Manhattan. He actually handles Ted and Miriam's money. He and his second wife have twins. And Deborah lives in Wyoming with her husband and their three kids."

"Pretty spread out," I remark.

"Yes," he agrees. "But we all converge upon our parents at the holidays. It's sheer chaos for days."

He absently reaches into the cookie bag, which sits between us on the center console, then suddenly withdraws his hand and tsks. "These are addictive. What do you put in them?"

"Love," I answer automatically, and instantly want to open the car door and hurl myself onto the 101 going eighty miles an hour. In all the times I've been asked that question, I have never before given that answer. I've heard other people say it and thought it was completely idiotic.

Maybe I need a therapist.

But Jacob takes my answer in stride, probably because he is watching the road and hasn't noticed that I've started to sweat like a pig.

"The most important ingredient," he says.

And best to be kept relegated to sweets, I think, crossing my legs for the twelfth time. *Amen to that.*

Gingerbread

The sun is high in the dazzling blue sky by the time we reach Santa Barbara. After taking the designated off-ramp, we spend fifteen minutes weaving through lovely suburban neighborhoods adorned with lush foliage and beautifully maintained homes. Jacob makes left and right turns as dictated to us by the Australian-female voice of the navigation guide on his car's GPS, which he turned on just outside of Ventura proper. The voice emanating from the device has begun to irritate me, not because it is especially annoying, but because it's actually quite sexy. Every instruction she—it—gives sounds like a lascivious suggestion; each turn she—it—tells us to make comes across as an invitation to foreplay. I know it's irrational to harbor feelings of jealousy toward a piece of modern technology. I never felt remotely resentful of Walter's intimate relationship with his Black-Berry, for example. But the fact that Jacob has chosen this sultry, accented voice—no matter that it is disembodied—irks me.

Why'd you pick that *one?* I want to ask. And, *How do you feel about Nicole Kidman?* But, of course, I keep these questions to myself.

Thanks to *her* perfect directions, we roll up on the Sunny Hills Bed and Breakfast at eleven thirty sharp. Jacob slows next to an old-fashioned wooden sign which bears the name of the inn and, beneath that, the words CHEZ ROB.

"Chez Rob?"

"It's one of the best restaurants in town, apparently," he explains as we pass the sign and pull into a gravel parking lot. "The chef is from New York."

"You have arrived at your destination," the Aussie harlot announces. I immediately reach over and shut off the GPS, and in my peripheral vision, I see Jacob glance at me. I ignore him. I'm just glad to be rid of that voice.

Several cars are parked in unmarked slots, and Jacob pulls the Beemer between two of them and turns off the ignition. We sit side by side in silence, both of us taking in the B&B.

The house is much larger than it appeared to be in the photograph, and in much better condition, having been recently restored. The clapboard siding is white, the trim a deep hunter green. The wraparound porch is wide and accommodating, with a number of plush chaise longues, tables, and a cozy-looking porch swing, currently empty. Window boxes line each of the ground-floor windows, filled with a variety of impatiens bursting with color. The grounds are manicured, but inviting rather than sterile, with vibrant green grass, a couple of maple trees, and a border of rosebushes on the perimeter of the porch, crowded with large, blooming flowers so perfect they almost look fake.

"Wow," I breathe. "It's amazing."

Jacob seems equally riveted as he stares through the windshield. "Let's take a closer look, shall we?"

As we simultaneously alight from the car, I realize that my right foot has fallen asleep. I stand for a moment, leaning on the Beemer, trying to hide my discomfiture. Jacob reaches his arms high over his head, then bends at the waist and touches his toes, stands straight, and stretches his neck. I would be enjoying the show were it not for the zillion microscopic daggers stabbing at my foot. I whimper softly as I try to take a step, stumble, and fall back against the car.

"You okay?" Jacob asks, coming around the hood.

I stifle a yelp. "Fine. Great. Terrific."

He narrows his eyes at me. "Foot asleep?"

I crack a smile through my pain. "Yup."

"Yes, you have that look." He grins, then scrunches up his nose in mock sympathy. "I hate it when that happens."

"Just . . . give me a minute."

The older I get, the longer it takes for my limbs to wake up once they've gone to sleep. Therefore, if I don't urge my right foot along, we could be here all day. I grit my teeth in anticipation of the torture my appendage is about to inflict upon me, then lift my right leg and stomp my foot into the gravel. Once, twice, three times. The result is so excruciating I almost see stars.

"A masochist, eh?" Jacob says with a throaty chuckle.

"No. Just impatient," I retort.

A mischievous smile spreads across his face as he tucks his hands into his pockets and rocks back on his loafers. "Don't you just wish you could do this?" he asks, and to my utter amazement, he begins to do a soft-shoe number, right there on the gravel of the B&B parking lot, whistling "Tea for Two" as he goes.

I feel my jaw slacken with surprise and almost forget about the pins and needles assaulting my foot. He shuffles first one way, then the other, his shoes tap-slide-tap-sliding beneath him. Watching him, I am overcome with childlike delight. This memory will be burned into my brain for the rest of my life. I have never seen a display of such unselfconsciousness, especially from someone I thought was so controlled. What's more astonishing than the fact that Jacob is tap-dancing in the first place is that he isn't half bad. When he brings his little solo to a close, I am compelled to applaud.

"A man of many talents," I say, and he gives a little bow. "Very impressive."

He grins modestly. "I like to get my Gene Kelly on every once in a while, although, I admit, this is my first public performance."

"I'm flattered," I tell him honestly. He did that for me. For *Ruby*. I am pleased at the thought, but try not to reveal just how much. "And in answer to your question, no," I say. "I don't wish I could do that. I'm more of a salsa kind of gal."

Where did that come from?

"I can see that," he replies, meeting my eyes. We stand for a moment, staring at each other over six feet of gravel. I feel my stomach clench at his green-eyed gaze. He looks away first, crossing his arms over his chest and inspecting the pebbles at his feet. "I've been known to tango on occasion."

I have a vision of Jacob with a red rose clamped firmly between his teeth, and a giggle escapes me.

"You don't believe me?"

"No, I do," I assure him.

"Well, it's been a while. Thirty years, to be exact. Miss Pimm's ballroom-dancing class. I was fifteen and had a huge crush on Mary Gillespie. She was taking the class and I thought I could impress her if I took it, too. Cost me forty-five dollars of my own money. Paper route."

Lord, another paperboy! "So what happened?" I ask, testing my foot with a few subtle taps. "With Mary Gillespie?"

"She ran off with the varsity quarterback," he says, shaking his head with mock solemnity. "I learned a very important lesson, and it had nothing to do with dancing."

"I'll bet."

As soon as I can move my foot without too much agony, I head to the rear door of the Beemer and withdraw my bag from the backseat. I pull out my digital camera and loop it around my neck, then sling the strap of my bag over my shoulder. Jacob falls into step beside me, and we make our way toward the inn. His arm brushes against mine and I shiver.

He's a customer, Ruby, I warn myself. *Your crush notwithstanding, he's here because of cake.*

On the cobblestone path, I stop and raise the camera to snap a couple of shots. Jacob stands aside, hands in his pockets, and waits for me to finish.

"Those balconies are new," I say, pointing to the second floor. He nods, following my gaze. "So, the question is," I say thoughtfully, "do you want the original house or the current house?"

"Which do you prefer?"

I am loath to add another complicated feature to the cake, but Jacob is the boss. So to speak. "It's really up to you."

"I think the balconies are lovely," he says. *Damn.* But he's right, they are lovely. And now that I think about it, I can incorporate them fairly easily, since they are merely an extension of the overhang that covers the wraparound porch.

"I can see your brain working." I look over to find him smiling at me and I have to clutch the camera tightly to keep from dropping it on the walkway.

"I just need to take some pictures of the sides and the back of the house," I say quickly. "Then we can go." I raise the camera to hide my face, make a show of lining up a shot.

On the LCD, I see the front door of the inn open. An older, bespectacled man wearing a seersucker suit emerges, and I am so taken aback by his ensemble that I lower the camera to make sure I'm not imagining things. Nope, he's real, although he looks like he just stepped out of a black-and-white movie, bow tie, pocket kerchief, and all. He bounds toward us, rubbing his hands together.

"Ah, you must be Mr. Salt," he announces, reaching us in seconds flat. "Welcome, welcome. I am Henry Forsythe, proprietor of this wondrous establishment." He shakes Jacob's hand enthusiastically, then turns to me. "And Ms. McMillan, I presume?" I nod, puzzled, as he grips my free hand and pumps it up and down like a seesaw.

He smiles pleasantly at me and I instantly think of peanut brittle: a little nutty, very sweet, and though old-fashioned, a confection that pleases almost everyone. "Mr. Salt tells me you are going to re-create our little B-and-B in cake. How remarkable! I take it you will only be creating the facade and not the interior?" I nod. "Hmm. Yes, I understand, but should you like to view one of the guest suites, you know, for ambience and inspiration's sake, we have several unoccupied rooms at this time and you are welcome to see them."

He finally releases my now-tingling hand and turns back to Jacob. "Your reservation is for noon, but you may be seated anytime. Unusually, we are underbooked today. Apparently, there is a crafts festival going on downtown, and inexplicably, some people prefer to buy papier-mâché pigs than dine at Chez Rob." He shakes his head with regret. "Well, it's only once a year. Anyhow, I am at your service!" He bows slightly and retreats to the porch, disappearing through the front door.

I give Jacob a questioning look. "Reservation?"

"I called last night and spoke to Mr. Forsythe," he admits. "Some of my colleagues in the local branch have raved about this place and I've always wanted to try it. I thought since we were here . . . It *is* lunchtime. And we do have to eat before heading back."

No, you don't have to eat, Ruby! You have a PowerBar in your bag. That'll do! Do not have lunch at Chez Rob with this man! Your crush will grow to Romeo and Juliet proportions. And we all know how that one ended!

"Oh . . ." Jacob seems to realize. "I'm sorry. You have to get back, don't you? Well, that's all right, I'll just let Mr. Forsythe know."

He ducks his head and starts toward the porch.

"I *am* a little hungry," I say, and he stops. "I'm sure Chez Rob beats the McDonald's drive-through."

He smiles. "That's a safe bet. But you never know. I have a soft spot for Big Macs." He pats his stomach, which looks about as far from soft as a brick wall. "I suppose we could risk it, and if it's terrible, we could still hit Mickey D's on the way out of town."

I just love a good plan. "I'm in."

My digital camera is safely stowed in my shoulder bag, its memory card filled with shots of the house taken from every possible angle. The bag lies at my feet, tucked under the table of the cozy booth where we sit, in the back corner of Chez Rob. I feel slightly underdressed in my cotton pants and yellow shirt, despite Henry Forsythe's assurances that lunches are *très* casual, but I soon relax when I realize that the few other patrons in the restaurant are dressed much the same.

The interior of the Sunny Hills Bed and Breakfast is replete with antiques and plush, comfy furniture, its decor tasteful country. The lobby boasts three velvet sofas in immaculate condition, along with solid, hand-carved mahogany tables, crafted in an earlier era when furniture was made to last. Several shelves filled with all kinds of books, both old and new, line the walls, and a corner nook accommodates a complimentary coffee-and-tea station. An informal dining room adjoins the lobby, where the traditional inn breakfast is served, along with, as I was informed by Henry, tea in the afternoon and a wine-and-cheese hour in the evening. The lounge is reminiscent of a gentlemen's club, with overstuffed easy chairs and low-standing tables. In the corner of the bar, at the threshold of the restaurant, stands a shiny black grand piano.

Chez Rob is situated in the back of the ground floor, with its own entrance for diners who are not staying at the inn. The decor is decidedly old school with floor-to-ceiling oak panels inlaid with beveled glass and brass chandeliers with bulbs that glow like candles. The lighting is dim—yes, I will need my reading glasses, darn it—and the tables are covered with cream linens and the requisite amount of utensils for fine dining. The glassware—red wine, white wine, water glass, aperitif pony glass—are set in formation at each place and are all genuine crystal. The salt and pepper shakers are the only whimsical accent on the table. They are in the shape of a man and woman, and they fit together in an embrace. Coincidentally, the man is the salt. If I believed in signs, I would take this as one.

Although I am trying to stifle my attraction to Jacob, it's difficult not to be affected by the romantic surroundings, even for someone not inclined toward the romantic. As Jacob checks his e-mail on his iPhone, I consider the unlikelihood of my being here at all. This was not part of my recipe for the day. Eight weeks ago, it was not part of the recipe for my life. The whole situation seems suddenly bizarre and surreal, and not for the first time I wonder just what the heck I am doing.

You're having lunch, Ruby. No big deal. Don't make it a big deal, just enjoy.

I scan the room and notice a waiter lingering at the service bar, surreptitiously glancing in our direction. There are three other parties in the dining room, seated in separate areas to offer each more privacy. A man and woman in their mid to late twenties sit a few tables away, their hands linked, their eyes locked. The woman giggles and the man pulls her hand to his lips and kisses it. I quickly shift my gaze to the salt and pepper shakers and stare at them for a long moment.

Jacob pockets his phone. "I'm sorry," he says. "That's very rude, I know."

"Don't worry about it," I tell him, sounding generous even though I covertly checked in with Colleen and Kevin from the ladies' room, to tell them I would be later than expected.

"We're in escrow on a house in the Cove, and the buyers are having some last-minute reservations," he says. "Something about the feng shui of the kitchen. And the pool is kidney-shaped instead of spleen-shaped or something. Between you and me, I think the wife's a little cuckoo."

The waiter appears at our table and hands us each a single sheet of parchment paper with the menu items handwritten in swirling calligraphy. He removes our napkins from the place settings and lays them in our laps. Jacob grins at me and thanks him.

"Chef has several specials today," the young man says with a solicitous bow. His short brown hair is slicked back, his face clean-shaven, and his uniform is perfectly pressed. "Beginning with a sautéed Dover sole on a bed of braised radicchio with a *limoncello* reduction. Also, we have a crispy sweetbread sandwich on brioche with a gremolata-mayonnaise and a watercress salad with vine-ripened cherry tomatoes. Additionally, we have the prix fixe menu, which as you can see, is a five-course tasting menu, all of which are Chef's choice. Each course is prepared with locally grown produce and paired with a wine from one of our nearby vineyards."

I gaze at the menu. Even without my glasses, I can see that no prices are listed, and I am filled with dread. Prices are only omitted when they are high enough to give patrons a coronary. I left my credit cards at home, as I have done since the whole foreclosure thing came about. (I purposely placed them in the bottom of my lingerie drawer, being that this particular drawer gets the least amount of action.) I brought a small amount of cash and my debit card with me. Since I've kept most of my remaining funds in my secret account, only transferring into my checking as needed for the mortgage and other living expenses, I'm not sure if the debit card will cover lunch. How mortifying would it be to have my card rejected when I pay my half of the bill?

"I think we need a minute." The waiter nods to Jacob and backs away. Jacob leans forward, resting his forearms on the table, and gives me an earnest look. He seems to sense my distress. "This is on me," he says quietly.

I shake my head. "No, I can't let you do that."

"I insist. This was my idea, and it's my pleasure. And anyway, I can write it off as a business expense." He winks and I feel myself relax. "Please."

"Thank you," I say. "That's very nice of you."

It's still not a date, I tell myself.

A busboy materializes out of nowhere and places a breadbasket on the table. Then he silently pours water from a crystal decanter that is fogged with condensation. As he fills Jacob's glass, I am reminded of Ted and Miriam's party and my first impression that Jacob was off his rocker, what with the story of his dead/lesbian wife.

"What?" Jacob asks.

I start to say something, then close my mouth. He cocks his head to the side, intrigued. "Seriously," he says. "What is it?"

"The night we met, I noticed that you were fascinated by your water glass." He colors slightly and I regret my words. Maybe he has a water fetish. Maybe he has an irrational fear of drowning. Maybe he spent time in prison for hijacking a Sparkletts truck.

"Yes," he says slowly, "I guess I was." He is pensive for a moment and I feel myself tense. But then he grins and I am able to breathe again. "That day . . . I think I mentioned that my ex-wife called me to give me her news . . . about the baby. It was a shock, I admit, and I was having difficulty coming to terms with it, you know. Not that Kristen noticed. She went on and on in her inimitable way about how excited she and her wife were. Told me all about her birth plan, as if I'd be interested in every detail. How they were going to have a 'water birth' so the baby would be welcomed into a familiar environment, and once the baby came, they were going to do some kind of dance around the placenta, which, if you ask me, is absolutely revolting, and—" He stops suddenly. "Am I babbling? I do that sometimes."

"No, not at all." Actually, he is, and it's absolutely adorable.

"Anyway," he continues, "that phrase, 'water birth,' just kept rolling around in my head for the rest of the day. And suddenly there was water everywhere I looked. I couldn't escape it. At the Josefsbergs'? The ocean? The infinity pool? The fountains?"

"The water glass?" I offer, and he chuckles.

"It was more than I could take. I mean, I'm happy for Kristen, of course. But also a little envious. I wanted children, very badly. And we tried for a couple of years. We even saw a fertility specialist, went through the whole process. Kristen had her eggs harvested and I . . . well, I did my part. The day before the, uh, implantation, she broke the news to me. About being gay. That was it."

He is pensive for a moment. I try to think of something to say but come up empty.

Jacob sighs, then manages to smile. "I never even knew there was such a thing as a birth plan."

I shrug. "Well, we make all kinds of plans about how that particular event is going to go down. But, you know. You have to be flexible. I was going to have a natural birth with Colleen. No drugs. Just me, breathing through labor, blissful in the knowledge of the impending miracle."

"That's not how it happened?" Jacob asks, a grin tugging at the corners of his mouth.

"I screamed for an epidural with my first contraction." He laughs. "Seriously. I mean, birth is a violent, messy episode. I vowed the next time I was going to find a doctor who would put me into a coma as soon as labor started and wake me up when the baby was all clean and nice and wrapped in a blanket. Of course, I couldn't find a doctor who would do that. But it was easier with Kevin. He practically fell out. One sneeze and there he was!"

I suddenly realize what I'm doing—talking about giving birth to a man who never had kids but desperately wanted them—and I stop short. Again, Jacob reads my mind.

"It's okay," he says. "I like hearing about it. I wouldn't say I've come to peace with my situation, but I'm learning to accept it."

"You know," I say, without thinking, "you could still have a child. You're not old. You could find a woman, I mean, someone younger, someone who's, well . . ."

"Of breeding age?" he offers, then shakes his head. "I'm not going in search of a woman in order to procreate. That seems so pathetic. Love is difficult enough to find without putting parameters on it. Besides, younger women don't interest me. I've dated a bit since the divorce, and I'm better suited to women in my own age group." He gives me a pointed look, his green eyes flashing, and a single thought races through my brain.

Oh my God, this is *a date*. I'm in his age group, after all. Beneath the table, my knees start knocking together.

"Look, Ruby," he begins. "I know you've been through a great deal these past few weeks, tremendous changes and such, and you're probably not ready for—"

A deafening shriek interrupts Jacob, and we both turn toward the source of the sound. The woman at the nearby table jumps out of her seat and rushes into the man's arms. He laughs, patting her like a child, as she gazes adoringly, first at the ring on her finger, and then at him.

"Yes!" she cries. "Yes, yes, yes! I will!"

The man kisses her passionately as the waiter swiftly moves to their table, champagne bottle in hand. He expertly pops the cork as the busboy procures two flutes and begins to pour, murmuring congratulations. The few other diners in the room applaud them, even me. Though, in truth, my applause is forced because I'm annoyed that Jacob was so rudely interrupted by their joy. Couldn't the man have waited until after Jacob finished his sentence before popping the question? I mean, really, is that too much to ask?

The man and woman untangle themselves and look around the room, as if seeing the other parties for the first time. They smile and call out their thanks as the applause dies down.

Jacob has a wan smile on his face. "That's nice, isn't it?"

"Oh yes, young love," I agree, although this is another area in which I have no expertise. I was young, yes, but the whole wildly-in-love, unabashedly-climbing-into-each-other's-lap-in-public thing didn't resonate with me. When Walter asked me to marry him, at the Chart House in Westwood Village, he was so nervous, he almost couldn't get the words out. And I, having been prepped by his mother, had been expecting the ring. I'd had to finish the proposal for him, which he'd taken as a sign, saying something like 'We must be perfect for each other, Ruby, if you already knew what I was going to ask!' After he slipped the diamond on my finger, I remember ordering another glass of red wine to go with the scrumptious prime rib in front of me. Walter, too excited to eat another bite, had giddily started planning our nuptials.

I look over at Jacob and quickly squash the memory. Walter isn't here. He's with *Cheryl*. I'm here. And Jacob is here. And he is about to say something that just might turn me inside out, that might possibly give me a clue as to why some people—like the young woman across the room—look so freaking happy in the presence of a man.

"You were saying?" I prompt. His brow furrows in puzzlement, then his expression clears and he directs his gaze at me. My palms start to sweat with anticipation.

"Oh, yes. Well, I was going to say that you—"

"Are you ready to order?"

Damn it all to hell.

"Ah, right," Jacob says to the waiter. "Yes. I think we should try the prix fixe." He looks to me for approval. "Don't you?"

I nod. *Absolutely. The prix fixe. Order anything. Order a plate of beetles, just get the waiter out of here and finish your sentence!*

"Very good choice, sir. And madam." He bows and removes the menus from the table and saunters toward the kitchen.

"So . . ." I laugh nervously, feeling myself blush. I am literally on the edge of my seat with anticipation. If I scoot one inch forward, I will end up on the floor. "Go on."

Jacob chuckles. "Okay. You've gone through a lot lately, and you might not be in any position . . . that is, you might not be inclined to . . . well, what I mean is, I would very much like to—"

The cell phone in his pocket blares an old Rolling Stones tune ("Satisfaction"—I can relate!) and he withdraws it. As he checks the caller ID, I feel like cursing out loud. This has gone from comical to downright frustrating. But then, maybe it's fate or God or the Powers That Be intervening. Perhaps I am not meant to hear what Jacob has to tell me, or he is not meant to say it.

"I'm so sorry, truly I am," Jacob mutters, shaking his head regretfully. "I have to take this."

"Of course. Please," I say magnanimously as he rises from the booth and crosses to the lounge. I sigh heavily and lean back in my seat. I know what's going to happen now. I've seen enough movies. When Jacob returns, he will have forgotten about the conversation or will have decided not to go forward with his thoughts. Though it may sound cowardly, I am praying for either. Jacob's right. I have been through an ordeal. I am not ready to date anyone. A crush is okay; its repercussions are minimal because it's one-sided. Acting on a two-way attraction is far more complicated. Best to keep it simple.

You are such a liar, Ruby. As practical as it may be, simple sucks. You've been trying to keep things simple your whole life, and look where that got you.

I reach into the basket for a warm, cheesy breadstick and glance over at the newly engaged couple. They drink their champagne and gaze at each other intently, ignoring their food. My eyes slide to Jacob, who stands at the far edge of the bar speaking quietly but forcefully into his cell phone. For a brief moment, as I surreptitiously admire his backside, I allow myself to finish his sentence.

You've gone through a lot lately, and you might not be in any position . . . that is, you might not be inclined to . . . well, what I mean is, I would very much like to . . . start seeing you on a nonprofessional level . . . Or, *what I mean is, I would very much like to . . . take you to bed and make wild passionate love to you . . .* Okay, maybe not *that*. But there's no question he was about to suggest some kind of romantic adventure. Is there? Could I be totally wrong? Could I have misread his words?

You've gone through a lot lately, and you might not be in any position . . . that is, you might not be inclined to . . . well, what I mean is, I would very much like to . . . refinance your mortgage . . .

I mentally slap my forehead as I bite into the flaky, delicious breadstick. Even as I ponder our conversation, I can appreciate the scrumptious morsel. It has just the right amount of cheese and a hint of garlic (thank goodness for breath mints) and that melt-in-your-mouth quality that only puff pastry can achieve. I wonder if *Chef* will give me the recipe.

Jacob returns to the booth, his cell phone pocketed, and I hurriedly try to swallow the remains of the breadstick.

"Once again, I apologize," he says, folding himself into his scat. "The buyers backed out."

I grab my water and take a long swig, hoping to wash down the pastry, which feels like a clump of clay in my throat. "That's too bad," I croak.

"Their Realtor called my boss at Franchise. At his house. Completely up in arms because he is going to lose a fat commission. He claims that the mortgage I wrote is the reason the couple changed their minds, which is utter nonsense. I mean, honestly, the wife is a nut!"

"I hope your job isn't in jeopardy," I say, meaning it.

"No, no. Frank has met the couple. He knows the deal. Still. It's damn frustrating."

As he drums his fingertips on the table, I wonder how I can bring us back to our earlier topic. I am just about to say something completely idiotic, like *So, what were we talking about before your boss called?* when Jacob's eyes light up. I sit at attention, thinking he is about to make his declaration, then realize he is looking past me at something across the room.

"Good! The first course. I have to admit, I rarely drink alcohol this early in the day, but I am definitely looking forward to a glass of wine!" He smiles sheepishly as the waiter sets down two plates in front of us. "But don't worry. I know I'm our designated driver. I promise not to get drunk. They're only tasting servings anyway, right?"

The waiter nods solemnly, but his eyes are twinkling. "Of course, sir. Tasting portions only."

16

A Little Sugar and a Little Spice

The meal at Chez Rob is a culinary masterpiece, each course more tantalizing than the last. We linger over the seared fois gras appetizer and the salad of mâche and teardrop tomatoes with a pomegranate-infused olive oil dressing, which are paired with a fabulous Sauternes and a crisp Riesling, respectively. To my relief, neither wine makes me burp. In fact, the sauternes is so sublime that Jacob and I feel compelled to order a second glass.

At some point, after the salad and before the entrée of braised lamb shank with veal reduction and cassis glaze, I realize that I'm enjoying myself immensely. I have forgotten my troubles for the time being, and not merely because of the wine. Jacob is a terrific dining companion. He manages to combine childlike wonder with adult appreciation of every dish placed before him. He is also a terrific conversationalist, regaling me with funny anecdotes about his outdoor adventures: jogging on the streets of San Francisco and seeing the six-foot-five, African-American-male Marilyn Monroe impersonator who sashayed down Lombard Street singing "Happy Birthday, Mr. President"; or the first—and last—time he tried to snowboard when he crashed into the ski lift and broke the nose of a fifty-eight-year-old woman who was waiting to get on; or the unusual trails he's hiked, like the one that led him straight into a nudist colony.

As our waiter sets our entrées before us, Jacob tells me the story about when his father taught him to fish. When he cast out for the first time, he accidentally hooked his father's nose. I laugh so hard I almost spew wine through my own nostrils.

"I would never have taken you for a nature enthusiast," I comment.

"Because I'm such a stiff?" he asks, his green eyes sparkling.

"You're not a stiff."

"I am when I'm indoors," he assures me. "But when I get outside, I don't know, I guess I feel released. Like from prison. Wow. This is really good." He stabs his fork at his lamb shank and the meat literally falls off the bone.

I breathe in the savory aroma of rosemary and cassis, then try a bite, and I have to strain to keep my eyes from rolling to the back of my head. "Mmmm."

"What about you?" he asks. "Do you like the great outdoors?"

I shrug. "I don't have much experience with it. My parents never took me camping, my dad didn't see the point. 'We've got indoor plumbing and a television,' he used to say. 'Why would you want to sleep in a tent and go to the bathroom in a hole you have to dig?'" I shake my head at the memory. "I was in Girl Scouts one summer, but I had a run-in with a colony of fire ants that scarred me for life."

Jacob laughs, his eyes crinkling at the corners. "Best to steer clear of fire ants."

"So I discovered," I say, laughing with him. "Walter didn't like camping either. He thought taking a picnic to the park was roughing it. Ironic, huh? Now he's sailing around the world."

"Sailboats have bathrooms, so it's not that rough," Jacob says, trying to make me feel better.

"Anyway," I say, steering the conversation away from Walter. "Between my kids and the Muffin Top, I don't have a lot of time for other pursuits. I haven't taken a vacation in years. And now we're just trying to keep the bakery afloat, so unless we close down . . . well, I won't be hiking the Adirondacks anytime soon."

"Is that a possibility? The Muffin Top closing?"

I let his question hang in the air as I take another bite of lamb shank. "I don't know," I say after a beat. "I hope not."

Jacob chews thoughtfully. "I'm surprised you don't have a website."

"We should. But that would require money, which we don't have."

"Right." He thinks for a moment, then says, "You know, you could start a Facebook fan page. They're free if you have an account."

"I'm avoiding Facebook."

He frowns. "Right. What about those do-it-yourself websites? They're reasonable."

"Again, that would require something I don't have, which is technological acumen. I know how to turn my computer on, get my e-mail, surf the Web. But beyond that . . ." I shrug. "I should have been born in another century, you know, one where a byte was something you got from a bug or a dog or a snake."

He laughs. "I love computers. I could spend hours and hours just sitting in front of my Mac. The possibilities are endless."

"You're a contradiction," I point out, and notice that my consonants have gone a little soft.

"How so?"

"A man who loves the great outdoors but also loves to spend hours on his computer?"

He grins. "I prefer to think I'm well balanced." He drains his glass of petite Syrah and looks pointedly at my almost empty glass. "Another?"

"Um, well, it is rather good, and it goes so well with the lamb shank, and I still have a lot of shank to get through."

He winks at me then signals for our waiter.

An hour later, we both lean back in our seats, allowing ourselves room to digest. The melon sorbet, wonderfully piquant, is fighting for space with the exquisite *île flottante* I've just finished. Jacob lazily signs the check while I try to focus on the face of the grandfather clock across the room. Unfortunately, even as I squint, I cannot read the numerals, and my fortysomething vision has little to do with it.

I am tipsy.

Jacob closes the sleek black folder which houses the— likely exorbitant—bill and looks over at me. His eyes are slightly glazed, but otherwise he looks fine.

"Ready?" he asks, and I nod. I scoot to the edge of the booth and push myself to my feet. My legs wobble beneath me like Jell-O and I have to hold the back of the chair to keep from falling over.

Uh-oh. Okay, not just tipsy. I am drunk.

Jacob is fine, I tell myself. He's taller than me and outweighs me by at least forty pounds, so the wine won't have affected him as much. I watch as he manages to get to his feet.

"That second glass of petite Syrah may have been unwise," he declares a bit loudly, although there are no other patrons to disturb, as the place is empty save for us.

I stifle my own grin. "Unwise, yes." Three syllables were never so difficult to say.

"But it sure seemed like a good idea at the time!" he exclaims jubilantly.

"That it did," I reply.

Jacob's expression turns serious as he carefully moves around the booth toward me. He lays his hand over mine, and I notice how large his hands are, masculine and tanned and strong. The warmth of his palm spreads through my entire arm. "Ruby. I have to tell you something very important, and I hope it doesn't upset you."

My heart starts to pound in my chest. "What is it?" I ask.

He gazes at our hands for a few seconds, then looks up, his mouth twitching at the corners. "Ruby . . . There is no way in hell I can drive."

I laugh, amused, and Jacob joins me.

"I'm so sorry," he says, straightening to his full height and removing his hand in the process. I notice that he is slurring his words, ever so slightly. "I shouldn't have let myself drink this much. I was just . . . having such a good time. The food and . . ." He sighs. "And the company. I haven't enjoyed a meal this much in ages."

"Me, too, Jacob," I tell him, wishing his hand were still on mine.

Despite the wine and the woozy way I'm feeling, I urge myself to think clearly. Glancing at my watch, I see that it's just after four. The kids will be fine. I left them some money for pizza, just in case I was late, but I still have to get back to Pelican Point. A cab is out of the question, as it would cost about a million dollars for the two-hour drive, and an airlift helicopter would only take us home if we were involved in a near-fatal accident and I want to *avoid* a near-fatal accident at all costs.

"Why don't we take a walk on the grounds," I suggest, hearing "grounds" come out as "grounz," but Jacob doesn't notice. He nods enthusiastically.

"A walk sounds great. I can walk. Just don't let me operate any heavy machinery."

"I don't think they have any," I tell him. I release my hold on the back of my chair, testing my legs for their integrity. As Jodie Foster said in *Contact*, "I'm okay to go. I'm okay to go." I take a tentative step, relieved that my legs are not buckling, then take another. Good. Okay to go.

Jacob straightens and follows, and within seconds, his long stride takes him past me. When he reaches the bar, he stops and turns, and I am surprised at how self-possessed he looks for a drunk.

Out of nowhere, Henry Forsythe appears, his eyes bright behind his glasses.

"Mr. Salt, Ms. McMillan!" he gushes. "How did you enjoy your lunch?"

"It was amazing, Mr. Forsythe, thank you." Jacob's words are completely coherent, and when I glance up at his face, I see that his features are tense from the strain of making them so. "We thought we might take a stroll around the garden."

"Ah, yes, a wonderful idea. Wonderful!" Henry Forsythe is all graciousness and hospitality, but I can tell he is no fool. He knows we are completely blotto. But he doesn't appear to mind; in fact, he seems tickled by it. "You know, it is a long drive back to Pelican Point. Should you decide you'd like to stay the night, in order to get a fresh start in the morning, I do happen to have a suite available."

"I don't think that will be necessary," Jacob replies, not a slur to be heard. "But thank you."

"Please enjoy the grounds for as long as you'd like," he

says graciously. "And you are welcome to the coffee-and-tea service in the lobby."

I nod my appreciation as the two men shake hands. Jacob turns to me and juts his elbow out, inviting me to tuck my arm through his. I do, and I'm instantly treated to the warmth of his body and the wonderful scent of soap and cologne. If I weren't already drunk, that scent would cause me to fail a sobriety test.

With the sun lowering in the sky and a light breeze cooling our wine-flushed faces, we meander down the cobblestone walkway, arms linked, enjoying the lush foliage and the many varieties of flowers blooming in the beds that border the path. Ahead, maple trees and olive trees create a canopy over the cobblestones, their leaves fluttering ever so slightly. When we reach the copse of trees, fallen leaves crunching beneath our feet, we can just make out a pond about a hundred feet farther down the lane. In silent agreement, we move toward it, stepping beneath the natural tunnel of branches.

"This is beautiful," Jacob remarks, inhaling deeply.

"It is."

The weakened sunlight streams though the leaves, creating a kaleidoscope of patterns on the ground, on us. Jacob stops, forcing me to stop beside him. Slowly, he turns, unlinking our arms while simultaneously moving me to face him.

"Ruby," he says.

No amount of alcohol in the world could keep my heart from slamming against my ribs at that one word. He takes a step closer and brushes his fingers against my chin, softly at first, then purposefully urges my face upward so that I'm looking into his green eyes.

"I would very much like to kiss you," he says quietly. "Would that be all right?"

No, that would not be all right. That would be fucking amazing.

He takes my silence as assent, leans over, and gently touches his lips to mine. I can't help but think that this is the first time I have kissed a man other than Walter in twenty years. Oh, Lord, I hope I still know how to kiss someone new.

But it's already over. Jacob's lips are soft, that much registered, but the brevity and chasteness of the kiss makes me feel cheated.

"Was that okay?"

"No," I say without thinking. He flinches, startled, but before he can pull away, I throw my arms around his neck, yank him toward me, and crush my mouth against his. I can feel his surprise in the stiffness of his posture, the tension in his lips, but a fraction of a second later, he relaxes. And a fraction of a second after that, our kiss explodes into a wondrous melding of mouths.

Jacob quickly takes charge, wrapping his arms around my waist and hugging me closer. His tongue flickers past my lips and electricity charges through me. I press against him and he abandons what's left of his restraint; his tongue probes, explores, intertwines with mine, and I suddenly feel like lava cake, my insides molten chocolate. And somewhere in the back of my mind it occurs to me that I have never been kissed like this in all my forty-three years, but I turn the thought off so as not to miss even a millisecond of this amazing experience. And we're still going, our lips locked, our tongues tasting each other, our breathing labored as we cling ever more tightly to each other, and someone is moaning and I realize it's me . . . no, it's him . . . no, we're both moaning, and *Oh my God,* no wonder we're both moaning because this feels so incredible and I could suck face with this man all day, all night, and into next year.

Okay. I get it. I understand what all the hoopla is about. Finally.

He breaks away first, inhaling huge gulps of air as though he's just come up from a deep-sea dive, and rests his stubbly cheek against mine. I can feel his pulse pounding in his neck in unison with my thundering heart.

"You know," he murmurs in my ear, "it might not be a good idea for either of us to get behind the wheel today." He presses his body against me and the underlying meaning of this statement becomes perfectly clear. I don't trust my voice to sound remotely normal, so I simply nod. He pulls away slightly and looks down at me, his green eyes blazing. "I should tell you . . . I mean, you should know that I haven't . . . I mean . . . it's been a really long time . . ."

"For me, too," I manage to say. "For me, too."

He clasps my right hand in his left, whirls me around, and hauls me in the direction of the inn. When we find our new best friend, Henry Forsythe, plucking at a flower arrangement on the front desk, I see that a pianist has begun to play the grand piano in the lounge, and the song he plays is "I've Got a Crush on You." And I realize that along with all of the other things He is, God is a DJ, and a darn good one at that.

"Izzy." My voice comes out in a hoarse whisper.

"Ruby, where are you?"

Crouched on the ledge of the tub in the bathroom of the Chrysanthemum Suite in the Sunny Hills Bed and Breakfast.

"I'm still in Santa Barbara," I wheeze, not wanting my

words to carry into the next room, where Jacob is awaiting my return, and probably disrobing.

"You were supposed to be home hours ago, *chica*. You okay?"

No, I'm terrible. I have stubble under my arms and on my legs, and my pubes look like an Amazonian rain forest. And for all the amenities this inn provides, there is not a single disposable razor in sight. Four toothbrushes, toothpaste, a set of plastic tweezers, mouthwash, hair products, lotion, and a floral shower cap, but no razor. Seriously? I thank my lucky stars that I gave myself a cursory shave on Thursday night before my Friday on the beach, but the hair sprouting out is coarse and impossible to ignore. Oh, why couldn't my grandparents have been of Nordic descent?

"I need you to do me a favor, Iz. Can you go over to the house and spend the night with the kids? I . . . um . . . I . . . uh . . . well, it looks like I'm going to have to crash up here tonight."

Long pause. "O-kay."

"Can you do it?"

Another interminable pause.

"Oh, yeah, 'Jacob Salt is not interested in me and I am not interested in him and we are not interested in each other and this is not a date—'"

"Izzy!"

"No problem, Rube. Bobby's working late anyway. I'll go over right now."

"Thank you."

"You realize you have a lot of 'splaining to do."

"I'll figure out something to tell the kids."

"I didn't mean the *kids,* Ruby. What's going on?" I can hear the smile in her voice. "I want details. Where are you? In a room? At the B-and-B?"

"In the bathroom," I admit.

"Where's the hunk?"

"In the suite. Waiting."

"What the hell are you doing talking to me?"

"I haven't decided whether I'm going to leave the bathroom. Ever."

"Why the hell not?"

"I've never done anything like this, Iz. I've never been so . . ." I try to think of the right word. *Spontaneous? Reckless?* "Irresponsible," I decide.

"Well, it's about freaking time you were! Now get your ass out of the bathroom and go have some amazing sex! You deserve it!"

"I don't know if I can," I confess. "I'm . . . I'm . . ."

"Scared shitless," she finishes for me, and I sigh.

"Yes."

"It's okay, Ruby. You'll do fine."

"Please don't tell me it's like riding a bike."

"No. More like a horse. And by the looks of him, I bet Jacob Salt is a real stallion."

Oh God. I can't do this. "Walter's the only man I've been with for twenty years. I didn't plan for this to happen, Iz. I didn't even shave this morning. What if the friction of our leg hair starts a fire?"

"Ruby, you are not going to embarrass yourself. You are a beautiful, desirable, amazing woman. You have the soul of a lover, even if you don't know it. Just be you. And, by the way, despite rumors to the contrary, body hair on women doesn't matter. Men like having sex. They'd have sex with monkeys if it weren't against the law."

I laugh and hang up the phone, then push myself from the rim of the tub and regard myself in the mirror. My makeup hasn't smudged very much, except for my lipstick, which is completely gone, but my lips are now swollen and rosy—like Angelina Jolie!—from my make-out session. My hair looks fine, my body fairly toned and somewhat shapely, my breasts accentuated by the tight yellow top. I look good. But more than that, I have a glow to me that has been absent for, oh, twenty years. I look energized and alive and enthusiastic.

I, Ruby Simmons McMillan, am about to have sex. *Me!*

Before I can change my mind, I turn and grab the door-knob, then ease the bathroom door open. The suite beyond is cast in shadows. "Jacob?" My heart pounds as I step into the room. I move toward the bed, expecting Jacob to call out to me. Instead, I hear something which simultaneously fills me with relief and crushing disappointment. I needn't have worried about my hairy legs, or my guilt over being reckless, or the possibility of embarrassing myself in bed. Because the sound I hear is snoring. Jacob is fast asleep. And fully clothed.

My house is like a beacon in the darkness of the early morning, the porch light burning brightly. Walter would never have left the light on had he been home. But then, if Walter were home, I wouldn't be pulling up to the curb at three o'clock in the morning with a man I almost had sex with the night before.

The "almost" part is upsetting, but I know it's for the best. I am not ready for a relationship. I'm not equipped for spontaneous, alcohol-fueled sex. Things happen—or don't happen—for a reason, and I have to accept that fact.

Back at the inn, in the Chrysanthemum Suite, I'd stood over Jacob's inert, but noisy, form, considering my two options. Wake him up and ride him like a—yes, Izzy—stallion, or leave him be. I chose the less favorable but more practical of the two options and had let him sleep. It seemed inappropriate to climb into the bed next to him, so I grabbed a pillow and reclined on the daybed in the adjoining room. Sleep was, as usual, elusive. The anticipation of sex had rendered me sober, and my brain kept replaying the events of the day in static motion, like a scratched DVD. Finally, somewhere around ten o'clock, I drifted off, only to be awakened two hours later by a firm nudge. I was so disoriented, I almost screamed, but Jacob's voice instantly brought me back to where I was.

"Ruby," he had said quietly, and I stumbled to my feet. "I'm so sorry."

"Don't apologize." I tried for a light, casual tone, but I may have sounded curt instead.

"I guess I shouldn't drink at lunch. At least not two bottles of wine." He reached out to me then, clasping my hand in his, and I gave his fingers a cursory squeeze before letting them go. I didn't realize it at the time, but on the long, silent drive home, I came to the conclusion that my reflex—releasing his hand so quickly—was an undeniable act of rejection.

"Well," he'd said, his voice suddenly stiff. "I'm fine to drive now. We can head out if you'd like." He wasn't looking at me, but at the floor. "Unless you'd rather stay."

"I should get back," I'd said, without a moment's hesitation.

I know I could have played it differently. I could have held on to his hand. I could have thrown myself at him and let him drag me back into the bedroom. I could have said I wanted to stay. So many "could haves." But I didn't. And now here we are, seated next to each other in the idling Beemer. The console between us feels as wide as a chasm.

He shifts into park and shuts off the ignition, puts his hand on the door handle.

"You don't have to walk me up," I say quickly.

His hand drops to his thigh. I think of his soft-shoe in the parking lot of the inn and I want to smile at the memory. But I can't. A great weight of sorrow for all of the things I've missed out on is pushing down the corners of my lips—lips that are still tingling from Jacob's kiss. Oh, why didn't I jump him? The Cake Goddess would have jumped him. Even the Cake Lady would have jumped him. But Rational Freaking Ruby took over. I hate her.

"Thanks for today," I say. "Or, uh, yesterday."

"You've got everything you need?" His tone is detached, impersonal, and he is looking at me like I'm a supermarket checker and he doesn't have enough cash. "For the cake?"

I nod. "It'll be great. I promise."

"I'm sure it will." His expression softens and he offers me a smile. "Well . . ."

"Well . . ."

Say something, damn it! Give him some clue that despite the awkwardness of the situation, you like him!

"Okay, bye." Despising every inch of myself, especially the practicality and cowardice that coexist within me, I grab my bag, push open the car door, and step out into the pre-dawn light.

Jacob waits behind the wheel as I climb to the porch and slide my key into the lock on the front door. But before I can turn and wave one last good-bye, the Beemer silently pulls from the curb and disappears down the block.

"I was expecting some kind of postcoital glow," Izzy says.

It's 7 A.M., far too early for Izzy, but I'd accidently awakened her when I tiptoed into my bedroom to get my toothbrush after a few fitful hours of sleep on the couch. Thinking

I was a homicidal maniac, she leaped to her feet and came at me brandishing the cordless phone. Such a move may not sound frightening, but when a crazy six-foot-tall Latina comes at you, she could be holding a banana and you'd be scared shitless. Once both of our breathing had returned to normal, and my teeth were absent the fuzzy sweaters they'd been wearing, Izzy dragged me back to the master bed with her. And although she could have gone back to sleep—lucky narcoleptic that she is—she opted to stay awake and grill me for details.

"But I don't see any glow." She sits cross-legged on my bed, a pillow in her lap. "How come I'm not seeing any glow? Was it that bad?"

"It wasn't," I reply, leaning back against the headboard.

"It wasn't bad? Then it was good?"

"It wasn't. Period. He fell asleep."

"Oh my God, seriously? Like right in the middle of it? That's bad."

"Not in the middle of it," I say. "Before. When I was on the phone with you." I peer at Izzy as though it's her fault.

"Don't give me that look, *chingada*. You called me, re-member?"

"Yeah, yeah, I remember. But if you hadn't answered the phone and I'd just left a message, I might be glowing right now."

She starts to giggle, and after a moment I join her. "Your lips are chapped," she declares, then raises her eyebrows questioningly. "Good kisser?"

I nod on a sigh. "Oh, yes." Just thinking about it makes my stomach flutter.

She smiles dreamily. "Kissing is the best part, you ask me. Plus, you can tell how he's gonna be in the sack by how he kisses."

I nod again. "Of course, I'll never know."

"Oh, come on. That's not the end of it. He'll call you and you'll go out on a proper date and start things up where you left off and be doing the bump and grind in no time."

"It's not going to happen, Izzy. I blew it. I acted like I didn't want to have anything more to do with him."

"Then you call *him*. Explain yourself. Very eloquently express to him the nature of your feelings—that you want to jump his bones."

I am quiet for a moment, then I shrug. "No. It's for the best, you know? I'm not ready to be jumping anybody's bones. I have too many unresolved issues in my life to add any more."

"Bullshit," she says with a level gaze. "And that's all I'm going to say on the subject 'cause you know already." She fingers the comforter, picking at a stray thread. "But, uh, speaking of those unresolved issues in your life, Ruby . . . You might just have one more to deal with."

I narrow my eyes at her. "Meaning?"

"Well, see, now, I'm going to tell you something because it's my duty as your best friend, and you are not going to like it at all, but I have to remind you that it's not right to kill the messenger, or maim her, or hurt her in any way."

I lean forward expectantly. "What, Izzy?" She studiously avoids my gaze as she continues to pull at the thread. If she keeps this up, she's going to unravel my entire bedspread. "Izzy! What. Is. It?"

"Okay, so I guess you're not the only one around here who has the hots for someone."

I immediately think of Colleen because Kevin's only romantic inclinations revolve around his poster of Elle Macpherson (who, by the way, is older than me, but a refreshing choice for a fourteen-year-old, in my humble opinion).

"Who is this Shane guy, anyway?" Izzy asks. "*Dios mío*, all afternoon, Shane this and Shane that. He's in your cake class? Colleen's got it bad for him."

I know where this is heading, can feel it with my maternal ESP. "How bad?"

"Well, she went and did something that she figured he would like—"

"What?" I demand.

"I just want you to know that I had nothing to do with it. It was before I got here—"

"Izzy. What. Did. Colleen. Do?"

She stops pulling at the thread and looks at me. Then she gives me the information I seek. Were I not the master of control, the top of my head would have blown off like Mount Vesuvius.

"Let me see it."

I know already that something is very wrong. At 7 A.M., Colleen is usually clinging to the last vestiges of her beauty sleep, dead to the world and curled into a fetal position. But this morning she is wide-awake, lying on her back, her covers tucked tightly under her chin.

"See what?" She tries for innocence, but the panic in her eyes betrays her.

"You know what," I say. Izzy stands at the door of her bedroom, my reluctant wingman. "Isabelle told me about it."

"Oh, Aunt Izzy!" Colleen cries, directing a pointed glare at my friend.

"Don't you go and blame Izzy."

"You grown-ups are all in this together. Persecution of the young based on jealousy and covetousness. It's an age-old conflict."

Her attempt to avoid my ire by diverting the conversation will not work this time. My daughter is smart enough to know this. Still, I can't blame her for trying.

"Yes, yes, Colleen. It's grown-ups versus teenagers, the final showdown. They should make a movie. Now let me see it."

Her eyes dart back and forth like a deer in headlights, her fingers grasping her covers with such force that her knuckles are white with tension.

"Colleen. Now."

"I think there might be a problem," she whimpers, and her tone is so odd, so much like a frightened child, that I feel my blood pressure rise.

I sit down on the edge of the bed and place my hand on hers. "Colleen, honey, let me see it." My tone is firm but gentle because I sense her nervousness is only partially the result of being caught. I tug the bedding out of her viselike grip, and slide it down below her waist. With trembling fingers, she grasps the hem of her nightie, which is bunched up around her hips, and slowly draws it upward. I see her wince and realize I am holding my breath. A second later, I stare in horror at my daughter's previously lovely stomach.

Her entire abdomen is swollen to pregnancy proportions, but her navel is the worst. I can barely make out the glittering diamond protruding from the skin just above her belly button for all the puckering, angry red flesh surrounding it. I keep my expression neutral so as not to frighten Colleen, but then Izzy shrieks. "*¡Dios mío!*"

"It's bad, isn't it?" Colleen refuses to look down, and I don't blame her. "Oh God, it's really bad, right?"

I lay a palm on her belly and her skin is fiery hot to the touch.

"Yo." Kevin appears behind Izzy, his face puffy with sleep. "Whazzup? Estrogen meeting on a Sunday morning?"

I lean closer to Colleen's savaged midsection and can see the unmistakable sign of infection: greenish-yellow ooze leaking out around the stud. I stifle a revolted grimace.

"Holy shit—shoot!" Kevin cries, stepping past Izzy to get a better view. "Seriously, dude, that is sick!"

"Shut up, Kevin!" Colleen snaps. "Mom?"

"It's okay, Col. It's infected, that's all. We're going to have to take a trip to the walk-in clinic. Now."

"Yeah, dude," Kevin says. "And you better get your UZI 'cause the freaking Alien is about to pop out!"

17

Just Desserts

I have always thought of God as a kind and benevolent being, not one who sits on His throne in heaven peering down at us mortals, waiting for us to screw up so He can visit upon us plagues of swift punishment. But karma is a different story. I absolutely believe in karma. What rational person doesn't? Karma is about weights and balances. Karma is about equations: Person + Bad Choice = Consequence. Karma is also a vengeful bitch.

So I'm not surprised that when—for the first time in my life—I behave in a reckless and irresponsible manner, I am treated to a comeuppance of karmic proportions. Sometime between Kevin's beach fund-raiser and our celebratory dinner Friday night, Colleen went to the mall, brazenly ignoring the family rule about body piercings, and paid a Russian immigrant named Svetlana to violate her precious belly button. Along with the diamond stud, Svetlana bestowed a microscopic bacterium upon—and *into*—my daughter's midsection. And while I was chugging down wine at a four-star restaurant and making out with my mortgage broker, that tiny bacterium was multiplying at light speed and transforming itself into a raging staph infection.

Colleen is taking it as well as expected, alternately crying over her swollen midsection and promising vengeance against the whole of the Soviet Union, even though she knows the Soviet Union no longer exists. For her, having to wear draw-string sweatpants is a far more cruel punishment than any I could mete out, and she merely rolls her eyes when I ground her for two weeks.

"Like I'd go anywhere looking like *this*!" she shrieks, yanking at the faded blue fabric gracing her lower body. She is parked on the couch following our Sunday-morning trip to the clinic, with a blister pack of Zithromax on the coffee table in front of her, along with wadded-up tissues and a stack of fashion magazines. Her face is unusually pale, her hair stringy and lifeless. "Two weeks is no big deal. This will take longer than that to clear up, I bet."

She is so unfazed by my punishment that I feel the need to make an addendum, not only because I want to regain my parental control but also because I need her to understand the gravity of her actions. "When the infection clears up, you're going to give me ten hours at the bakery."

"What? Are you crazy?"

When Colleen turned sixteen, I offered her a full-fledged job at the Muffin Top, which she vehemently declined. She absolutely loathes cooking, especially baking, because she might end up with food/dough/unidentifiable goo under her French-tipped nails, or, God forbid, chip one of them in the cooking/baking process. Thus, my addendum to her punishment has just the right impact.

"That is so not fair! Why don't you just send me to clean the sewers or pick up trash on the freeway!"

"Watch your tone with me, young lady," I warn her. "You violated my trust, Colleen. You did something you knew was off-limits. Your father and I made it perfectly clear—"

"Oh yeah, well, Dad's not here, is he?" she spits back, and the venom in her voice is like a slap in the face.

"No, he's not. But I am."

"What do you care what I do with my body, anyway? Navel piercings are chic." She gestures to the magazines. "Not that *you'd* know what chic is! You can't even put clothes together without my help!"

I'll admit, that one stings.

"You're just old—" She catches herself. "Old-fashioned! You don't believe in belly-button rings because you could never get one!"

I resist the urge to retort, *I could if I wanted to!* because, really, who am I kidding? I may be in good shape, but after carrying two children, the folds that form on my otherwise toned stomach would obscure a stud the size of a kumquat.

"It's my life, Mom!"

"No, Colleen," I say through gritted teeth, my voice icy calm. "Until you're eighteen and living under your own roof, one that you pay for, your life is mine. And you will follow my rules or suffer the consequences."

"No wonder Dad left," she snaps. My mouth opens reflexively, but no words come out. I take a breath and wait a few beats, to give her an opportunity to apologize or back-pedal or make some kind of contrite gesture, but she ignores me, grabs one of her magazines, and begins to heatedly flip through it.

I am aware that my children hold me at least partially responsible for Walter's departure, but to hear the accusation straight from her lips, spoken without compunction, without remorse, makes me feel horrible and guilty all over again. Tears threaten at the corners of my eyes.

This is what you get, Ruby. This is what you get when

you shuck simplicity and order to the wind and invite chaos into your life.

I push myself off the armrest of the couch and head for the kitchen, stopping at the breakfast nook. "For your thoughtlessness and hurtful behavior, you can make that *twenty* hours at the bakery."

Although I might be stooping to her level, I can't deny my satisfaction at Colleen's groan of misery.

The upside of the whole navel-piercing fiasco is that it has overshadowed all other issues, derailing any possible discussion of *Where Mom Was* and *What Mom Was Doing* for the entirety of Saturday. Or so I hoped.

But no, apparently karma is not finished with me.

"Mr. Salt seems nice," Kevin says, passing behind me while I separate laundry in the garage.

"Yes," I reply, resenting the knot that seizes my chest at the mere mention of Jacob's name. "He is nice."

My son gives me a pointed look, then grabs a screwdriver from the tool shelf and heads for his bicycle. The surfboard rack on the side of the bike has come loose, and as I watch, he kneels down to fix it.

At fourteen, Kevin is unable to master nonchalance, but he attempts it anyway, pretending to concentrate on his task. "How do you know him again?"

"He's our mortgage broker, honey," I say, tossing some whites into the washing machine.

"And you're doing him a cake?"

"Yes. I'm making a cake for his company party."

"So that's why he took you up to Santa Barbara . . . to show you the house . . . you know, the house you're going to make the cake look like?"

My temples start to throb, a sure sign of an oncoming headache. "Yes, Kev. That's why."

"So, it wasn't like a date or anything."

Uh-oh.

"No, hon. Nothing like that." *Well? It didn't start out as a date!*

"Good," he says with a firm twist of the screwdriver. I pause mid-sort and look at him. He glances up at me, then returns his attention to his bike. "It's just kind of soon, don't you think? For you to be, uh, dating someone. I mean, when Luke broke up with Evie Moffett, he waited like six months before he asked Carley Bishop out."

"Six months, huh?"

"Yeah. And they were only together for like a year. You and Dad were together for a lot longer than that."

By Kevin's calculations, I should wait about nine years to start dating again. An image comes to mind of my fifty-two-year-old self hitting the local singles' bars. The thought makes me suddenly depressed.

"Well, my situation is a little different from Luke's," I say.

"Oh, I totally know that, Mom. You're old—uh, older. You don't have a lot of time left to find someone else."

Did I say "depressed"? Try "suicidal."

"And it's not like I don't want you to find someone. I do. Honest. I've been thinking about it, you know? You deserve to be happy and stuff. But just not right now. You know what I mean?"

"I know what you mean, Kev."

I dump a scoop of detergent into the washing machine, then close the lid with a thunk. Kevin jerks his head toward me as I shove the dial to on.

"You're not upset, are you, Mom?"

I take a deep breath and don a placid expression. Kevin is so sweet, such a good person, that I can't bear to cause him further distress by revealing mine.

"No, honey. I'm not upset at all."

I give him a smile, then turn and go into the house. I pass Colleen, who doesn't even glance in my direction, move through the kitchen, and head for the stairs. In my bedroom, I grab a pillow from the bed and take it with me into the bathroom, then shut the door, sit on the lid of the toilet, shove my face into the pillow, and burst into tears.

To: *Ruby McMillan*
From: *Karma*
Subject: *Another Banner Stunt from Your Good-for-Nothing Cheating Husband*

Hi, Ruby—

I thought it best to let you know that I received a call from Walter's attorney this morning requesting all tax documentation, P&L statements, and Accounts Payable and Receivable records for the past five years for the Muffin Top. As your faithful servant, I declined the request in no uncertain terms, citing that, lacking a subpoena, I was under no legal obligation to procure such documents. But Ms. Stein, as she calls herself, gave me the impression that such a legal demand will be forthcoming. I can only assume that this is related to spousal support and the equitable separation of your and your husband's assets. I'm sure you have already retained legal counsel and therefore should consult with

him on this matter. But if you are in need of a reference,
one Jonathon Ruget handled my own divorce and I was
very satisfied with his services.

Very humbly yours,
Elliot Humboldt
CPA, Logan, Humboldt & Meyers

Cell-Phone Message-Center Voice: *You have no new*
messages. That's right, loser. He did not call. And he's not
going to, Ruby, so stop calling your voice mail to check. If
your phone says there are no new messages, then there are
NO NEW MESSAGES!

Two short weeks ago, I was paralyzed with fear over the
thought of cake class. But this evening, I didn't even glance
at the package of Depends under my sink when I went in
search of a fresh container of deodorant. My teaching anxiety has been replaced by the other, more disturbing issues in
my life. And as I got dressed, carefully choosing my ensemble and applying my makeup in an attempt to prove Colleen
wrong—I *can* do chic—I realized I was actually looking
forward to class. It would be a safe haven, an oasis where I
would be able to leave my troubles on the doorstep and lose
myself in the wonderful world of cake making. Rebellious,
resentful, staph-infected daughters; worried, well-meaning-
yet-hurtful sons; sleazy lawyers of creepy, ne'er-do-well, future ex-husbands; and stringently silent cell phones would
have no power over me.

And for the first hour of class, all of the above is true,
especially since the subject tonight is the cake itself, the base
upon which all accents and decorations are built. I am able

to relax into the meditative art of making cake batter, lecturing on the chemical composition of cake as I mindlessly sift dry ingredients, cream, butter, and sugar, prepare pans, and stir the velvety concoction together. I explain why the perfect balance of acid and alkaline is needed; the leavening properties of baking powder and baking soda and eggs; the result of using butter as opposed to oil; which kinds of frostings highlight certain kinds of cakes, and which should be used for different decorating purposes.

"Your cake may look like the Taj Mahal," I say, scraping the batter into the pans, "but if it doesn't taste good, what good is it? The most important aspect of any cake is the flavor. All other characteristics aside, the bottom line is that a cake's true purpose is to be eaten; therefore, it should be delicious."

I am happily in a zone, my words pouring out smoothly, my hands working on autopilot. I feel great. But Karma has not yet delivered her crowning disciplinary action, which comes in the form of a twenty-year-old man-child.

"You look great tonight, Ruby," Shane O'Neil said as soon as he'd walked into the bakery. Then he'd given me a look which I couldn't decipher at the time. But now that ninety minutes have elapsed, I can no longer ignore or deny what's going on. For the entirety of tonight's class, Shane has been *accidentally* brushing against me, effusively complimenting me, and gazing at me like, well . . . like . . .

Like you're Jamoca almond fudge and he's the spoon?

My rational mind tries to deny this as I set dirty bowls in the sink. I'm old enough to be his mother, after all.

Haven't you ever heard of a MILF?

So, it goes both ways, as one part of my psyche argues with the other. While I possess no practical experience with having a crush on someone, I've also never dealt with someone having a crush on *me*. If I were, say, Demi Moore, I might know how to handle this, might be flattered that my former paperboy thinks I am worthy of his attention. But, alas, I am me, so I'm kind of shit out of luck on this one.

It's your own fault, Ruby. You were practically drooling over him at the beach.

I was not drooling! I was simply appreciating one of God's wonders—

Yeah, his six-pack abs!

But that was Friday, before Shane O'Neil became the unknowing harbinger of a tortured teenage abdomen. He is no longer penuche to me. In fact, it is impossible for me to look at him as anything more than what he is, my student. I can acknowledge his good looks, but now I do so with the perspective of a fortysomething mother of two.

"That's a great color on you," Shane says as I check the status of his layer cake.

I know I look good, having chosen a rose-pink, cap-sleeved top and gem-encrusted blue jeans which accent my waist and rear end. But I don't want *Shane* to think I look good. I want him to share my children's opinion of me: the unchic hag who will be so decrepit and undesirable by the time my appropriate grieving period is over that no one will want me anyway.

I ignore his compliment and look at his cake. He has the right amount of frosting between the two layers and has begun to frost the outside, but there are ridges and lines across the surface from using uneven pressure with the spatula.

"You want to rotate the stand while you apply the frosting," I say, demonstrating.

He moves closer and I detect a hint of cinnamon in the air between us. Big Red gum perhaps.

"You make it look easy," he murmurs, and I feel his

breath on my ear. I shiver reflexively, and he seems to infer that I am reacting to him on his level. He presses his side against mine.

I quickly move away, my eyes darting around the room to make sure that none of the other students are looking in our direction. Amy is almost finished with her cake, and it looks perfect. Blanche touches up the top of hers, smoothing out the buttercream. Francie and Jess, at side-by-side stations, giggle and covertly lick their fingers, their cakes only partially complete. Carol furtively mixes her frosting while, next to her, Stephanie rotates her cake stand, scrutinizing her cake for all its imperfections. Calvin busily applies a third layer of buttercream to his terribly lopsided cake.

"Shane," I say with an authoritative edge to my voice.

"That muffin you gave Annabelle was awesome," he tells me. "I haven't seen her scarf food like that in a long time." He steps toward me. "You're amazing, you know."

"Shane." I try again, but this time, my voice wavers.

Don't look at me like that, please! Like you're a T. rex and I'm a bloody piece of Ornithomimus *flesh. I'm going to be forty-four next month. I was a college graduate before you were born. Your mother and I used to play tennis at the club. Stop it right now before I put you over my knee and give you a spanking!*

Blueberry lemongrass pot de crème *with coconut milk and coconut shavings . . .*

"Do you think maybe we could talk after class tonight?" he asks, and I feel myself start to sweat. I recognize the perspiration right away. This is not the result of my last few sleepless nights when I tossed and turned and finally got up and stormed my kitchen, baking myself into a coma by trying seven new stressipes (only two of which were any good). This is not the product of my recent familial anxiety, and this certainly is not a reaction to a gorgeous twentysomething with smoldering, ocean-blue eyes who is hitting on me.

This is a hot flash.

I turn away from Shane and clap my hands together. "Okay, everyone. Once you're finished frosting your cakes, I want you to start piping borders. Remember to keep consistent pressure on your pastry bags to keep your scallops even, just like I showed you earlier."

"Ruby?"

I hear Shane's voice behind me, but I don't turn, don't even glance in his direction, just make a break for the back hallway. I bypass my office and head for the bathroom, where I take a moment to splash cold water on my face. As I gaze at my reflection, I recognize the flaming cheeks which only hint at the inferno raging within me. And suddenly the waistband of my jeans has magically shrunk four sizes, it feels like it's cutting through my abdomen, compressing my diaphragm and making it impossible to breathe. I claw at the top button like a rabid animal, freeing it from the hole, and the pressure eases slightly, but not enough, so I yank the zipper halfway down until I can actually take a full breath. I untuck my blouse and start flapping it up and down, using it to cool myself.

At that instant the phone in the bakery rings, echoing through the hall from both the kitchen and my office. I know the answering machine is on, but I automatically move toward the sound, reaching my office door just as my recorded voice announces a greeting.

"Hi, you've reached the Muffin Top! We can't get to the phone right now, but if you would like to place an order, please leave your name and number after the beep!"

"Hi, Ruby, this is, uh, Jacob Salt."

I rush into the office and grab for the phone, but stop

myself before I lift the receiver. My brain is fuzzy with hormones, but one rational thought manages to break through
the fog: *He has your cell-phone number, but he called the
bakery while it's closed. He doesn't want to talk to you.*

The lack of warmth in his voice proves my assumption.
He sounds curt, reserved.

"We would like to take care of our bill for the cake, so if
you could please fax an invoice to our office, we would appreciate it. I assume it will be in the range we discussed.
Also, the celebration will begin promptly at six on Saturday, so if you would be so good as to have it delivered by
five thirty . . . we . . . uh . . . well, again, we would appreciate it."

He doesn't hang up, but instead clears his throat as if he
is about to say something else. I want to pick up the phone
so badly my hand shakes. But I have no idea what I would
say or how I would handle his studied detachment.

"Well, I guess that's all. We'll look forward to getting
your invoice." About as much as he would look forward to
getting a venereal disease, if his tone is any indication.
"Thank you."

The machine beeps as the call disconnects. Slowly, I relax
my fingers and release my grasp on the receiver. Sudden
tears, which have nothing to do with the hot flash, spring
into my eyes. As I reach up to wipe them away, Shane O'Neil
steps into the office and closes the door behind him.

This is not happening.

"How's your cake coming?" I ask reflexively, although I
can tell from his expression that he is not remotely concerned about his cake, or anything else that has to do with
baking. I suddenly feel like I am starring in a spin-off of
Cougar Town.

"Ruby," he says, his voice low and husky. He looks at

me the way I might gaze upon a chocolate fudge cake with raspberry sauce, or possibly a naked Jacob Salt. As he approaches, I feel the desk pressing against the backs of my legs, preventing me from moving an inch.

"I know what's going on," he says, closing the gap between us. "I could see it. And I feel the same way."

Okay, recipe for dealing with unwanted attention from a young stud muffin . . . Um . . . I'm pretty well screwed here. I glance down and am horrified to see that not only is my waistband yawning open, but my shirt has bunched up under my bra and my granny panties are exposed for all the world to see. Although it's not the world I'm concerned about, but Shane O'Neil, who is staring at my midsection with wide eyes and an insatiable grin on his face.

"Shane, I think you have the wrong idea . . ." I hurriedly zip up and button my jeans.

"Don't do anything on my account," he says teasingly, shifting his gaze first to my cleavage, then to my face.

His bangs fall across his forehead and I have the instinctual urge—*maternal* instinct, I assure you—to brush them aside. Knowing this gesture would be taken the wrong way, I clamp my arms to my sides.

"I've been thinking about you constantly since Friday, Ruby. I can't get you out of my mind."

He reaches out and touches my face with his fingertips and I can't help but squirm. I bat his hand down then move away from him, circling behind the desk.

"Shane, you're my student."

"I know. I know." He follows me around, stalking me like prey. I wedge myself between the wall and the desk chair, then shove the chair in his path. "But out there? Just a few minutes ago?" he continues. "It was written all over your face! You were blushing and . . . and . . . and glowing and sweat—perspiring! I know you feel it, too."

"No, Shane, no! That was a hot flash! Something middle-aged women get!"

He takes a step closer, shoving the chair out of his way, a Cheshire smile on his face.

"Middle-aged women!" I repeat for emphasis. "Me, Shane. Middle-aged. You, Shane, just out of diapers."

"Age has nothing to do with this, Ruby, and you know it. We have a connection. I saw how you looked at me on the beach. And tonight? I just knew when I walked in. You're wearing my favorite color on a woman."

Oh God, why did I pick this *shirt?*

"It's a sign."

I am backed against the far wall, cornered between the fax/copy machine and the filing cabinet. I don't feel threatened, or worried that at any moment he will turn violent and attack me. I probably outweigh him by ten pounds anyway, and years of kneading and rolling and stirring has made me strong. But the intensity of his fervor is unsettling.

"I want to be with you, Cake Lady," he says with such incongruous lasciviousness that I have to laugh. But my laughter is short-lived because Shane lurches forward and grabs me, then kisses me with all the frantic energy of a twenty-year-old. I am shocked into paralysis.

For one peculiar and fleeting instant, as Shane slides his lips down my chin and kisses me on the nape of the neck, I wish I were the kind of woman who could be flattered by the pursuit of a man twenty-three years her junior. A woman who could bask in the sunlike rays of his attention and enjoy the sheer physical pleasure he has to offer. A woman who could take on a Svengali-like role and mold her fledgling lover to her own desires, teach him a few things about what feels good and what women really want. But then I remember the karmic retribution I earned from my earlier transgressions—this particular situation included—and I return to my senses, wholeheartedly inviting Rational Ruby to take the helm of this sinking ship. I push my arms up between the two of us and shove at Shane forcefully with my open palms.

"What—what—" I try to avoid his mouth, much the way Sigourney Weaver tried to evade the Alien's snapping jaws, but with far less success. "What about your girlfriend?" I shriek, pressing hard against his chest.

"What girlfriend?"

"The one on the beach!" I cry as he swoops in and manages to steal another kiss.

"Julie?" He laughs merrily. "No way! I am so not down with that! She's not my type. She had her belly button pierced, for crying out loud! That is so not my style."

You've got to be kidding.

"*You're* my style, Ruby. You're beautiful and talented and mature and, man, I just want you so bad!"

"Shane! Stop it! Right now! This is crazy! The rest of the class is down the hall. Anyone could just come right in and catch us and then I'd be fired for inappropriate behavior. Do you want that?"

He suddenly goes still, contemplating my words. He shakes his head almost imperceptibly, then lowers his hands.

"You're right. You're right."

Thank God, I think, breathing hard.

"I'll lock the door."

"No!"

I shoulder around him, heading for the door, but he is spry—of course he's spry, he's *young*—and before I am halfway across the room, he grabs my hand, pulls me to him, and envelops me in a kiss that would be remarkable if I were nineteen again. There is no finesse, only enthusiasm. And as I stand there, wondering how I am going to extricate myself from this absurd situation, I hear the door to the office open with a creak. Although my vision is obscured by Shane, I know instantly that the person standing in the doorway is not a student. I recognize the subtly sweet scent of afterbath spray that has been a constant in my life for the past four years. Ever since she hit puberty.

Karma's laughter echoes through my head just as Colleen's anguished scream shatters my eardrums.

"She's here," Izzy assures me, unnecessarily because I can hear my daughter fuming in the background.

Class has long since ended. All of my students, including Shane, left over an hour ago, proudly carrying their cake boxes with them. I'm seated at the desk in my office, holding the phone with one hand and massaging my forehead with the other. My eyes are constantly drawn to the blinking light on the answering machine.

"She's pretty upset, Ruby. You want to tell me what happened? I can't really make it out, something about you stealing Shane away from her or something? Can you fill me in?"

"I did not steal Shane away from her," I say calmly. "He came after me. He's got some kind of crush on me."

I hear Izzy say something to Colleen, but the words are garbled, as though she is pressing the phone to her chest. A second later, Colleen's voice, clear as daylight, screeches through the phone line.

"Is she kidding? He attacked *her*? He has a crush on *her*? God, she's like forty-five years old—"

"Forty-three!" I shout into the receiver before I can stop myself. "I'm forty-three."

"She's forty-three," Izzy repeats.

"She may as well be a hundred!" Colleen cries. "What would Shane O'Neil want with *her*? He's hot. She's not. She tried to seduce him, that's it! To get back at me! To punish me for piercing my belly button and being a brat!"

"That is ridiculous."

"I know. It's ridiculous," Izzy says while my daughter has an absolute fit. "Maybe you ought to let me talk to her for a while, okay? Let her chill out with her aunt Izzy. She can even stay over, okay?"

"Damn right!" Colleen yells.

"Language!" I cry.

"Language!" Izzy repeats.

"I am never speaking to her again!" Colleen says defiantly. "I never want to look at her again! How could she do this to me? She knew how I felt about"—*hiccup*—". . . about Shane! How am I supposed to . . . to . . . to coexist with a person who does something like that? Maybe when Dad comes back, I can go live with him and *Cheryl*!"

Ouch.

"Colleen," Izzy barks at my daughter. "That was uncalled for."

"I'm hanging up now," I say faintly. I think back to the Fourth of July, when I told myself it would be good to let go, to try living spontaneously and without parameters and walls. What was I thinking?

"I'll call you later," Izzy promises, and I hear the line go dead.

18

The Cake's the Thing

Early Thursday morning I am at the Muffin Top, painstakingly making miniature flowers to fill the twelve gum-paste window boxes hardening on parchment paper. The Franchise celebration is two days away and I am in crunch mode. I have spent twenty-four of the last thirty-six hours here, returning home only to shower and grab what little sleep I can.

My home is a battle zone now, and although I am clinging to my composure, every moment I spend in my children's presence chips away at my armor. True to her word, Colleen is not speaking to me, communicating her disdain for my existence with her every breath, glower, sigh, and shrug. Kevin is only partially aware of the details of our contretemps, but the few he has gleaned—that Mom and some studly guy his sister has a crush on were going at it in the office of the Muffin Top—have driven a wedge between him and me as well. Since I must have been a willing participant in whatever high jinks were occurring Tuesday night, I have violated the terms of the marital grieving period Kevin dictated to me. So, basically, he hates me, too.

Cake. Ah, sweet and wondrous cake. My salvation. While the thought of Jacob Salt still confuses me, I am thankful for the celebration cake he has commissioned. It's the only thing keeping me sane. I don't have the time or energy to dwell on my personal problems. My focus must remain firmly and unequivocally on the task at hand. Of all the cakes I've ever made, this one has to be perfect.

Following the e-mail from our CPA, Izzy took a good hard look at the Muffin Top's finances. Unless we bring in some serious new business, not only will I not be able to pay myself enough to keep my house, but we'll have to consider closing shop altogether. My castle cake for the Josefsbergs' party would have been a marketing coup, if not for the Facebook fiasco. Walter may have gained a few Facebook friends, but the Muffin Top didn't gain a single customer. My hope is that the Franchise cake will impress some of the mortgage company's clients. Our inexpensive ad in the *Pennysaver* certainly isn't having any effect.

So, even though my hands ache from all the detail work and I am almost dizzy with fatigue and my calves are starting to seize from standing so long without a break, I carry on, making certain every minute adornment is perfect.

At six thirty, I hear the lock turn on the front door and Marcy enters, easing the door open as she always does to keep the jingling of the bells to a minimum. ("It's like a friggin' air-raid siren before coffee," she often jokes.) When she sees me, she offers me a wave.

"I hope you went home at some point, Ruby," she says, crossing to the display case and peering in to see that I have already stocked it. "You do need to sleep."

"I got a few hours," I tell her, sliding a tray of tiny flowers onto a rack.

She moves toward the center island and glances at the window boxes. "These came out great."

"Thanks," I reply absently.

"And the flowers. Nice. How do you make them without going blind?"

I flick at my reading glasses by way of an answer.

"You want me to start on the walls? Gingerbread, right?"

I nod, starting in on orange flowers. A hundred down, four hundred more to go, each hundred a different color.

"Should I make the dough?" she asks, pulling an apron from the rack. I look up and am shocked to see that Marcy's hair is brown. Not brown and pink or brown and purple. Not blue, not jet black, just brown. The stud in her nose is also gone, and she wears a pair of khaki slacks and a simple blue cotton shirt with a button-down collar.

"Marcy?" I say her name as though she is a body snatcher sent to earth in Marcy's place.

"I know. I look like a geek. But Owen thinks I look better with my natural color."

"You look terrific."

"Honest Injun, kimosabe?" she asks. I don't think I've ever seen her look so unabashedly hopeful.

"Honest Injun," I reply in Marcy-speak.

"Well, you look great, too, Ruby-dooby-doo." She smiles and puts her arm around my shoulder. "We're quite a pair, huh? Me going from punk to precious and you going from middle-aged mom to hot mama. We should be in *People* magazine! You know, like the fat-to-thin issue?"

I laugh because it feels good to do so. And I am secretly pleased that even though Colleen has quit her position as Mom-makeover-maven, I am still carrying on her legacy. At first I wondered why I was even bothering to take time with my appearance, but then I remembered the adage that if you look good, you feel good. And since I actually feel like shit on the inside, I was hoping that looking good on the outside would sink through my skin and affect my emotional state. It's not really working, but I've decided to give it more time. Like until I run out of mascara.

"So, you like this Owen, huh?" I ask, rhythmically piping petals with royal icing.

"Well, you know, I guess, yeah. He kind of makes my heart go pitter-pat." I glance at her and notice she is blushing. "I don't want to put a hex on it or anything, but it might be possible that he's, you know, the guy."

I'm happy for her, I really am. Happy for this strange and terrific girl who may have found someone who appreciates her for who she is. Still, I can't deny the prickle of jealousy that creeps through me.

She moves toward the island and leans against the counter, watching me. "Did, you know, you feel that way with Walter? Did he make your heart go pitter-pat?"

I keep my eyes on my orange petals. "No. He didn't," I admit.

She sighs, apparently relieved. "Good. I mean, what with your situation and all."

"I made the dough already," I say, desperate to change the subject. I don't want to talk about Walter. I don't want to be reminded of the conflicting emotions that have been coursing through me these last few days. How I felt at the dinner table last night with my two sullen teenagers; that I would have given anything for Walter to be there, to tell one of his dumb jokes that would always make the kids smile, no matter how many times they'd heard it. Or how I'd woken at three in the morning, wishing Walter were there to make his famous hot milk concoction that tasted horrible but invariably got me back to sleep. Right now I don't have room for introspection while I'm trying to create something beautiful. The Sunny Hills Bed and Breakfast might end up looking like a crack house.

"It's in the walk-in. And I cut the patterns for the walls."

Marcy nods. "Right. I'll start rolling."

We work in companionable silence for the next hour, up until the bakery opens, when Marcy has to abandon her gingerbread duties to wait on a few early morning customers. I nod greetings to familiar faces but keep to my checklist of preparations, only stopping long enough to use the bathroom or sip at a cold cup of coffee.

By nine o'clock, five hundred flowers are drying on the racks and six huge sheet pans of gingerbread are cooling on the counters. While Marcy inventories the display case, I begin the arduous task of cutting the gingerbread. I carefully lay the wall patterns down, then grab a pizza cutter and cut through the warm dough. A patron calls to me from the counter, but Marcy hurriedly steps in to help him, joking that one doesn't interrupt Michelangelo while he's suspended under a ceiling. After finishing the long lines, I set the pizza cutter down and reach for an X-ACTO knife, then use the sharp, delicate blade for the smaller cutouts: windows and notches. When all of the cuts are complete, I remove the patterns, shuffle them together, and place them in an oversize envelope in case I need them again—meaning, in case one of my walls breaks. (Please, no!)

I take a breath and wipe the perspiration from my forehead, then glance up to see a stocky woman standing by the display case, staring at me suspiciously. I can't place her at first, but then I realize she is the fruitcake from Franchise Funding. She sports the same oversprayed bouffant, but her number two pencil is conspicuously absent. I take a step toward her and smile amiably.

"Good morning. Can I help you?" I pretend I don't know who she is, although I'm not sure why. Oh, yes. Shame. That's why.

"Are you Ruby McMillan?" she asks, her nasally voice as grating as I remember from our one and only previous encounter.

I nod and she thrusts an envelope in my direction. "This is for you. From Franchise Funding. For the cake for Saturday evening. We received the invoice yesterday, and I was asked to drop this off."

"Oh, thank you," I say. I grasp the envelope and try to wrest it from her fingers, but she refuses to relinquish it.

"It's an *awful* lot of money for a cake, if you ask me. Who are you, anyway, the Ace of Cakes?"

I feel my smile splinter. "No, I'm the Cake Lady." My voice has a slight edge, as though I am saying "I'm the Terminator" or "I'm Dirty Harry . . . Go ahead, make my day."

"Well," she says snootily, "I'd never even heard of the . . . what's this place called? The Muffin Top? . . . until Mr. Salt told me about you. We were going to use Adelle's, over on Park? But Mr. Salt insisted. He seems to think you're worth it."

My smile returns—I can't help it—accompanied by a warm woozy feeling in my gut.

"Anyhoo, for what we're paying you, I expect the cake will be tremendous."

"I hope you'll be happy with it," I say. "Would you like to sample a muffin or a cupcake?"

"I don't eat sweets," she says too quickly, and her girth belies the statement. She covertly glances into the display case, then looks back at me. "But, uh, perhaps I could take a few muffins back to the office. You know, for the others."

"Of course. For the others."

I fill a bakery box with an assortment of muffins and cupcakes, leaving out Izzy's inedible of the week, a cherimoya-and-rock-salt scone that could double as a paperweight, and hand it to the woman whose name I don't know and really don't care to ask. She makes a superficial motion to pay me, but I wave her off.

"It's on the house."

Without thanking me—which really makes me want to smack her—she gives me a two-finger wave and saunters out of the bakery. Once she is gone, I grab the envelope from where I left it next to the register, turn it over in my hands, and withdraw the check. I look at the amount, exactly what I asked for, and it does seem hefty, written in ink. But if I were to deduct the cost of ingredients, electricity, overhead, and labor, I'm getting roughly minimum wage.

I sigh, then stuff the envelope into the pocket of my denim skirt and head back to the center island, where a thousand other tasks await me.

By Friday afternoon, I have finished with all aspects of the house itself: the walls, which I reinforced with white chocolate plastic then overlaid with strips of fondant to simulate wood siding; the porch, treated similarly; the roof, which I covered with a thousand dark chocolate tiles brushed with black shimmer dust; the windows, made with isomalt, a kind of sugar substitute used to create edible glass; and all of the minutiae that I was able do ahead: the window boxes, shutters, porch swing, and chairs.

Six sixteen-inch cake layers—two red velvet, two yellow, two chocolate—are in the convection oven. While they bake I work on the cake board, a three-foot square of quarter-inch plywood that will bear the burden of a cake weighing hundreds of pounds, which I am fashioning to look like the grounds of the Sunny Hills Bed and Breakfast. As I cut tiny rectangles of rust-colored fondant—bricks for the walkway—I can't help but think of my Saturday afternoon with Jacob.

I've been trying *not* to, but the cake makes it difficult. When thoughts of Jacob surface, I force myself to remember the price karma exacted from me. Today, that's not difficult because Colleen—her navel almost back to normal now—is making good on her punishment of working in the bakery. Her scowling presence is a constant reminder of my sins.

Although I had no intention of holding her to the twenty hours I assigned—I know, I know, *bad* mother!—she has taken it upon herself to prove that she is a better person than I am. (*Yes, my mother is a boyfriend-stealing ho, but I am a paragon of virtue, a saint who serves her penance no matter how unjust.*) When she arrived around noon, after Little Princess class, she greeted me with a frown and told me she would do whatever I asked, as long as I had Smiley make the request. I, in turn, made it clear that I would tell her what I needed her to do as the need arose, and if she didn't like it, she could take her self-righteous self home immediately. Not wanting to be booted off of her moral high ground, she had buttoned her lip and donned an apron.

Now she stands at the sink, lavender latex gloves up to her elbows, rinsing out a bowl that was filled with batter, wrinkling her nose in disgust. As soon as she places it in the industrial dishwasher, Smiley appears with a crusted muffin pan and hands it to her apologetically. She grunts, catches me looking at her, and proffers up a smile for my employee, one she won't deign to give me.

I begin to place the bricks into the outline of the walkway on the cake board, constantly referring to my photograph in order to capture the herringbone pattern, and leaving gaps which I will fill with royal icing to mimic cement grout. In my peripheral vision, I see Colleen removing her latex gloves.

"Colleen. I need you to bag some royal icing for me. Plain white."

"You could say please," she snipes, drying her hands on a clean rag. "Then again, I guess people like you don't say please, do they?"

I roll my eyes and shake my head simultaneously. I've tried to set the record straight with her, but she refuses to listen. And I'm tired of defending myself to a stubborn, hormonal sixteen-year-old. I'll just have to weather the storm, for as long as it lasts, which may well be until she's thirty. But at least she hasn't brought up moving in with her father again. She knows she went too far with that threat and is probably afraid I'll take her up on it if she makes it again.

"The bags are in the third drawer and the royal icing is in the bowl under the damp cloth. Number two tip. Please."

As I set the last brick into place, a pastry bag lands next to me on the counter with a thunk.

"Thank you," I say sweetly.

"You're not welcome," my lovely daughter retorts with an unlovely grimace, and I wonder what moron decided that corporal punishment is bad for children. I'd really like to have a long chat with him about Colleen.

Since the bakery has been empty for a couple of hours, and Colleen is here with me, serving her time, I decide to let Smiley go early. Ten minutes after he walks out the door, I realize I made a mistake.

I'm assembling the house, and for some reason, the royal icing is taking too long to dry. As I press the left wall against the front, the right wall starts to slide away from the facade. Panicked, I reach my hand out and catch it before it tumbles onto the cake board, where it will certainly shatter.

"Colleen!" I shriek. "I need you!" She stands on the far side of the kitchen, wrapping leftover muffins with twenty-four-inch plastic wrap. She looks over at me and cocks her head to the side, her expression bored.

"I'm not kidding," I tell her, my voice shaking, one hand holding the renegade wall, the other frantically trying to keep the second wall and the front of the house in place. "Please, come here *now*."

She seems to intuit the seriousness of the situation and moves quickly to where I stand.

"Okay," I whisper, afraid that even the merest exhalation of breath will topple the whole house. "Carefully, put your right hand where my right hand is, and slide your left onto the front wall. *Easy*. Don't press hard, just hold them up."

As Colleen takes the burden of the left wall, I remove my hand and use it to ease the right wall back in place.

"How long do I have to hold this?" Colleen asks as though I'm forcing her to touch an eviscerated squid.

"Awhile." I feel a trickle of sweat roll down my temple but can't do anything about it. We stand there, side by side, Colleen studiously ignoring me as I stare at the royal icing, wishing I had laser vision that would make it harden more quickly. It occurs to me that although my daughter and I are physically closer than we've been in days, we have never been further apart. I want to say something to her, something meaningful. Remind her that she is my baby girl and I love her more than anything and that I would never do anything to hurt her. That her happiness is more important to me than my own. That whatever she imagines I've done, she should remember the things she *knows* I've done that were only intended to make her life rich and safe and full of joy.

I am just about to open my mouth when the bells on the front door jangle. Colleen and I turn toward the door and simultaneously groan when we see Shane O'Neil saunter into the bakery.

"Oh, perfect!" Colleen says.

"You're kidding," I agree.

"Hey, ladies," he calls to us. "What's happening?"

Colleen starts to pull her hands from the cake, but I stop her with my stern voice. "Don't. Move."

"Wouldn't you like to be alone?" she asks snidely.

"We're a little busy here, Shane," I say.

"Oh, yeah, I can totally see that," he says. "But, well, I just got out of class and I had to come by. I mean, I've been feeling really bad since the other night, Ruby, and I just wanted to apologize to you."

"You're apologizing to her?" Colleen looks dumbstruck by the idea.

"Oh, yeah. I was a complete jerkweed. Sorry, my mom hates that word."

"It's a compound word, actually," Colleen offers.

"Right," Shane says skeptically. "Anyhow, I guess I kind of misinterpreted some signals, Ruby, which I've been known to do on occasion . . . like the time I thought this old lady was getting purse-snatched, but really she was just giving her grandson his book bag. I chased that kid for three blocks, scared the crap out of him! Plus, some of my buddies and I watched *The Deep* last week, and I've kind of had this whole Jacqueline Bisset thing going, and you kind of remind me of her a little bit."

"It's okay, Shane—"

"No, it's not. I'm so embarrassed. And I really like your cake class and I don't want it to be weird now. But if you want me to drop out, I will."

"That's not necessary," I tell him.

"Wait!" Colleen cries. "*You're* apologizing to *her*?"

"Yeah!" He grins self-consciously. "I totally tried to jump your mom's bones!"

Colleen scrunches up her nose, the same way she does when dealing with goop. "But . . . why?"

Thanks a lot, Colleen.

Since I don't want to rehash those particular five minutes of my life, and because I recognize the fact that I now have a spare set of hands, I quickly change the subject.

"Shane. Go wash your hands. We need you."

He gives me a puzzled look, then seems to understand and springs into action, dropping his backpack and rushing to the sink. He hurriedly washes, then crosses to my workstation, holding up his hands like a surgeon. I instruct him to take my position, and he quickly complies.

"Gently," I say. "Nice and easy."

Holding the walls, he looks over at me beseechingly. "I really am sorry, Cake Lady."

"You're forgiven," I tell him, then I head for the opposite counter, where the bowl of royal icing awaits. As I thicken it with some powdered sugar, I hear Colleen whisper to Shane behind me.

"You really jumped her? She didn't attack you?"

"No way. Your mom's a professional. She'd never do that."

"But why would *you* jump *her*?" As if she still can't wrap her mind around it. In all fairness, *I* still can't wrap my mind around it.

"Are you kidding? She's awesome! Just look at what she can do! Not to mention the fact that she's hot." I start to feel warm and fuzzy until I hear his next sentence. "You know, for someone her age."

And there it is.

But I'm not going to complain. He came to his senses and

vindicated me in front of my daughter. I know when to count my blessings.

I grab a pastry bag and toss a number ten tip inside, scoop some icing into it, and return to my station.

"You think my mom's hot?"

"Oh, sure," he answers, as if I'm not there. "She dresses cool, and, you know, always looks kind of glowing—but not too much makeup, like some of the girls in college—just the right amount."

"You know what's so ironic?" Colleen says, sounding both coquettish and brainy at the same time. "I outfit her. I totally put her together, pick all of her clothes and do her makeup. She doesn't leave the house until I've had my way with her." She glances up at me furtively to see whether I will betray her, as she has not been "having her way with me" for almost a week. I raise my eyebrows teasingly.

"That's right," I say. "If it weren't for her, I'd look like a bag lady."

Colleen smiles at me warmly, appreciatively, and I realize just how much I've missed her.

"Not a *bag lady*," she says with a laugh. "But, you know. She was a little, um, plain before I took over."

As the two of them continue to hold the cake, I pipe another layer of icing into the jambs, one that will hopefully dry more quickly and give added strength to my walls. Otherwise, Colleen's and Shane's arms are going to fall off.

"So, do you want to be a cosmo—cosmic—cosmetic— what's the word? You know, makeup-and-hair person?"

"Cosmetologist? No. I'm planning to major in biochemistry with an emphasis on molecular biology."

Shane looks over at me. "Is she kidding?"

I shake my head. "Nope." I refrain from adding that she intends to use her education to invent a line of organic and environmentally friendly cosmetics as opposed to curing cancer.

He turns back to Colleen. "How old are you again?"

"Sixteen," she replies guilelessly. "But I've already taken two college courses, and I'm taking three more my senior year. So I'll be going into Stanford with, like, ten credits already."

"Wow. I had no idea what I wanted to be when I was sixteen," he says, as if it were an eon ago. "I'm still trying to figure it out."

"That's okay," Colleen says generously. "You shouldn't commit to something unless you're really passionate about it."

"I'm taking a psych class right now. I'm kind of into it. I was thinking I might like to be a psychologist or a counselor who works with sick kids . . ."

"Because of your niece?"

He nods and gives Colleen a meaningful look, which she returns in kind. The pastry bag almost slips from my fingers as I realize that Shane and my daughter are having a *moment*. Three nights ago, he was ready to pounce on me, and now, in the space of three minutes, he has transferred his affection to Colleen. *Men.*

Not that I am jealous. In fact, I'm relieved that he has dismissed me. But the age difference between the two of them is a point of concern. Clearly, from an emotional and intellectual standpoint, they are on the same level—Colleen actually might be more mature. But physically speaking, their four-year gap is akin to the Grand Canyon. I am suddenly seized by a vision of Colleen being on the receiving end of Shane's lascivious pursuit. My hand reflexively squeezes and a huge dollop of icing plops onto the cake board.

Frangelico sabayon with citrus infusion and finely grated lemon essence . . .

My stressipe is interrupted by the bells on the front door, and I am reminded—not for the first time—of a British farce in which every time the bells sound, a new character enters to wreak havoc on the status quo. I might as well be a prophet, because it's Izzy, and she is about to completely rock my world—and not in a good way.

"Oh, yes, certainly. Great! Absolutely! No problem!" She's on her cell phone, talking animatedly and gesticulating like a madwoman. When she sees me, her eyes go wide and she jabs a maniacal finger at her phone. "Is that one assistant or two? Two? Terrific. Yes. I'll tell her. Great. Thank you so much!"

She punches the disconnect button, then gives me a jubilant expression, throwing her hands up in the air for emphasis. "That was the producer of *Cake-Off!* From the Food Channel!"

I feel my throat constrict.

"Ruby," she cries, "you're on! The show tapes September second and third, then airs on the twenty-first. It's the season premiere!"

This time I do drop the bag, and luckily, it lands in the center of the board without smacking into any of the walls. I feel faint, can barely draw breath.

"September third is my birthday," I squeak.

"Right!" Izzy agrees. "It would be a helluva birthday present to win fifteen grand!"

I look at Colleen, who is beaming excitedly, then at Shane, who is grinning like a kid on Christmas morning, then back to Izzy.

"Yo!" Shane cries. "The Cake Lady's going national!"

19

S'mores, Please

I live in what is essentially a beach town, and although I enjoy the occasional foray onto the sand and will venture to the shoreline to dip my toes into the foamy surf, I do not swim in the ocean. Ever. Never have, in fact. There are large creatures lurking beneath the waves intent on doing me harm. So, too, while I enjoy—would even say that I am enamored of—cake making, I am not even remotely interested in participating in a cake competition. Cake designers are a vicious, cutthroat group, and the slightest show of weakness will provoke them to eat you alive faster than you can say *"Jaws."* My fear of public speaking aside, I wouldn't willingly dive into a pool with those sharks if my life depended on it.

Of course, in a way, it does.

But right now I have more pressing things to consider; for example, how to get my two-hundred-pound Sunny Hills Bed and Breakfast cake to the Pelican Point Regency Banquet Hall without disaster befalling it. Tomorrow, I'll figure out how to excuse myself from the cake-off. Today, I have a delivery to make.

The clock in the bakery reads 3:05. I have ample time to go home and change out of my gum-paste/fondant/icing/chocolate-splattered clothing, shower, dress, remove the rear seats from the minivan, and return to pick up the cake. Smiley and Marcy will help me load it into the van, and I have already called the Regency to make sure there will be a couple of strapping gentlemen awaiting my arrival.

As I remove my apron, I watch Izzy circle the cake, her digital camera in hand, snapping pictures from every angle. For *Cake-Off,* she informs me. And although I have no intention of appearing on the show, I am letting her get her photographic groove on. The confrontation we are certain to have can wait.

"This is freaking amazing!" she exclaims for the hundredth time. And it is, by far, my best creation to date. I have captured the Sunny Hills Bed and Breakfast perfectly in flour, sugar, and chocolate and have dubbed it *Franchise BegINNings.* Every detail, right down to the porch swing, which actually *swings,* has been re-created. I think of how tickled Henry Forsythe would be, and make a mental note to e-mail him one of Izzy's pictures.

"I'm off," I say, passing Smiley. He stands at the register making change for a couple of teens who are gaping at my masterpiece. "Don't let anyone near the cake."

"I thought about running crime-scene tape around it," Smiley says with a grin, "but I didn't want it to be a self-fulfilling prophecy. Are you sure it's safe with Izzy so close?"

"When she's done with the photographs, make her leave the kitchen," I instruct him, and he nods. "Use force if you have to."

He gives me a salute, and I head out.

I arrive home ten minutes later to find a note from Kevin, telling me he's at Luke's, working on the surf club's Labor Day festivities. Colleen doesn't answer my hello, and as I climb the stairs, I hear the shower running in the hall bathroom.

When I reach the master bedroom, I stop in the doorway. A shimmering, smoke-blue sleeveless cocktail dress has been carefully placed atop the comforter, the price tag still attached. On the floor beside the dress sits a pair of high-heel navy suede pumps. I cross to the bed and reach down, stroke the fabric of the dress, then lift it up by the hanger and hold it against my body. I gaze at myself in the mirror over the dresser, and I'll be darned if my eyes don't light up like sparklers.

"I knew it would look great on you," Colleen says from the hall. She is wearing a terry-cloth robe and has a towel wrapped around her head.

"It's beautiful," I agree, still admiring my reflection. "Did you find it in the back of my closet? I don't even remember buying it."

"You didn't," she says, walking over to me, a smile playing on her lips. "I did." She gestures to the shoes. "*Those* I found in the back of your closet."

I turn to her, puzzled. "You bought this? For me?"

She nods. "You deserve it, Mom. I've been a total witch to you. And not just about the whole, you know, bakery-Shane thing. I've been blaming you for Dad leaving, and the truth is, it didn't have anything to do with you. Shane's right. You are awesome. I've just been too selfish to see that."

My eyes suddenly brim with tears.

"I'm really sorry, Mom."

I reach out my hand and she takes it. "It's okay, honey," I say, my voice surprisingly strong. "I mean it. The past two months have been hard on all of us. And you know, as much as I'd like to be the victim and place the blame completely on your dad, I know that there are things he needed from me that I didn't give him. Not because I couldn't, but because I didn't want to. There are things I used to believe about how life works and how love works, but lately, I've been thinking maybe I was wrong. I'm not sure anymore. But I do know that whatever your dad did, it was because he really believed it was the only thing he could do."

"So you don't hate him?" she asks.

I ponder the question. "Maybe a little."

She giggles and I join her, and we laugh together for a long moment. Then she releases my hand and bends over to retrieve the suede shoes.

"You are going to look so amazing tonight," she tells me.

I shake my head and lay the dress on the bed. "It's going back to the store." She opens her mouth to protest, but I cut her off. "You can't afford to buy me a dress. Heck, Colleen, *I* can't afford to buy me a dress. As sweet as it was of you, you're taking it back."

She crosses her arms over her chest. "I am not."

"Colleen, you are."

"I bought that dress with my own money from the Little Princess class. I've put half away for college, like you asked me to, and you said I could use the other half however I saw fit. *Your* words."

"Colleen—"

"Besides, I got it at Clara's Boutique. It was on clearance, and Clara gave me an extra discount because her daughter, Giselle, is in my class. Really, Mom. It was a total steal. And I want you to look amazing tonight."

"Honey, I'm just dropping off the cake. I'm not staying for the celebration. This is a little too flamboyant for a delivery gal."

"But you got an invitation," she says. And I had, along with all of the other homeowners whose mortgages are with Franchise. I'd automatically tacked it to the corkboard in the kitchen, then completely forgotten about it. "You should totally go."

The urgency in her tone gives me pause. "Why?"

"That man who took you to Santa Barbara?" she says as she strokes the suede shoes. "He's going to be there, right? Mr. Salt?"

"That's right."

"Well? Don't you want to see him?"

Now I am deeply suspicious. "What makes you say that?"

She meets my stare, a knowing look on her face. "Izzy told me about him—"

"Damn it!"

"And before you get all indignant, she told me about him to talk me off the ledge about you and Shane. She said you really like Mr. Salt."

I'm about to deny the accusation, but instead I sigh and sit down on the bed. "I like him a little," I admit. "But he's not . . . he doesn't . . . he's not interested anymore."

"Do you know that for a fact, or are you assuming? Because you know what they say about when you assume something."

"Colleen," I say, exasperated, "it doesn't matter. It's too soon for me. I'm not ready. I'm not even divorced."

Colleen takes a seat beside me and pats my knee with her hand, much the way I do whenever she needs maternal support. I think of the irony of the two of us switching places. Eventually, we all switch places with our children; they become our caretakers. I just didn't expect it to happen while I still had my teeth.

"Do you remember what you told me," she says, "you know, when I turned fourteen and started to really think about my future? You said to always make sure I thought long and hard before making decisions. You told me to always have a solid plan in place. To never be impulsive and always use my head." She pats my knee again for emphasis. "I'm sorry, Mom, but that was all a bunch of crap. Sometimes, you just have to fucking go for it. Excuse the expression."

Words of wisdom from my sixteen-year-old daughter. I clasp her hand and smile.

"Are you sure the dress will fit me?"

She looks at me like I asked her if the sun is hot.

"Now go take a shower," she commands. "I'm breaking out the L'Oréal!"

If it's good enough for Andie MacDowell, it's good enough for me.

"Oh, and Mom . . . ?" she says before I reach the bathroom. "You better find that Wonderbra you bought when you were high. You're going to need it."

Three burly, dark-skinned busboys stand at the receiving entrance of the Pelican Point Regency. Between them, they look like they could hoist a life-size replica of the Statue of Liberty. I lean into the back of the minivan, inspecting the B&B to make sure that nothing has come loose or cracked or shifted or otherwise fallen apart. The cake looks perfect, probably due to the fact that I drove at a whopping fifteen miles an hour all the way here, drawing several raucous horn-honking fits and one rather violent flipping of the bird from other drivers.

"*Chingada,* man, that is *muy asombroso,*" one of the men says, peering over my shoulder.

"Okay, guys, let me be honest with you," I say, summoning the Cake Bitch for effect. "It's heavy and it's fragile. Just the slightest tip or bump will have the same effect as a ten-point-one on the Richter scale." They each give me a blank stare. "Earthquake? *Muy grande* earthquake? Everything comes tumbling down?" Nods all around. "So, basically, you drop it, you die. *Te mato*." (I learned that one from Izzy's mom.)

The banquet hall might as well be a mile away. With all of the twists and turns we have to navigate, the enormous kitchen and endless hallways, I feel as though I'm doing a triathlon. After ten long minutes, with the muscles in my arms burning, and my breathing labored, and my compadres grunting, the four of us set the cake board down on the display table at the far end of the vast room.

"Gracias! Gracias!" I cry with relief. I hand each of them a five, which they accept with big smiles, then set about arranging the linens on the table to hide the edges of the cake board. I am secretly praying that Jacob will not catch me before I've had a chance to freshen up—meaning dry my armpits and reapply my lipstick—but when I look around at the spacious hall, I see only hotel staff hustling about with last-minute preparations and adding steaming hotel pans to the hot chafing dishes on the boundless buffet table.

A banner spreads across the front wall, displaying the legend HAPPY 50TH, FRANCHISE! Overhead, above the dance floor, thousands of balloons are suspended in a net, ready to be released at the assigned moment. I make my way past dozens of round tables set with napkins and glassware and utensils, each place setting accompanied by a noisemaker and a small gift bag silk-screened with the Franchise logo. In the far corner is a mini control booth, and a short man with dreadlocks stands behind it, earphones atop his head and a clipboard in his hand.

My watch reads 5:45. I make my way back to the service entrance. Not wanting to deal with the scorn my car provokes from valets everywhere, I choose the self-parking lot, and it takes me another ten minutes to hike to the hotel en-

trance. As I walk through the majestically appointed lobby,
I see Jacob Salt by the door to the banquet hall, engaged in
a conversation with an older couple. He looks dashing in a
charcoal suit, and my insides do a little dance. I hurriedly
duck into the ladies' lounge, where I am greeted by a young
woman in uniform who holds out a hand towel as though
she's been expecting me.

I accept the towel, dampen it at the sink, and carry it
with me to a stall, as there is no surreptitious way to wipe
your armpits and I certainly don't want to be caught out
by anyone I might see at the celebration. I use the towel on
my forehead, the back of my neck, the bottom of my back,
then finally on my underarms, relieved to discover that my
Lady Speed Stick is working because although I've been
sweating, I still smell like a baby's bottom—pre-poopy dia-
per. I pee, then head out to wash my hands and fix my
makeup, touching up the foundation I wiped away, powder-
ing my nose, and painting my lips with the fiery-red color
Colleen insisted upon. As I leave, the young woman nods at
me approvingly, and I quickly fish a couple of dollars out of
my purse and toss them in her tip basket.

The cocktail hour is from six to seven in the Bay Lounge,
another enormous space with fully stocked bars on three of
the four walls and bistro tables arranged at intervals in the
middle of the room. Jacob is nowhere to be seen, but many
guests have arrived, most of whom are in line for drinks or
standing at tables, drinks already in hand. I know several of
them, but I make no move to mingle. Instead, I head straight
for the bar, keeping my eyes fixed on the floor.

I am nervous, and rightly so. This is one of the first social
occasion I've attended since Ted and Miriam's party, and we
all know how that turned out. Also, I have no idea how
Jacob is going to behave in my presence or whether he will

actually speak to me at all. I still have adrenaline coursing through my veins, which always follows the tense and hazardous delivery of a delicate cake. Suddenly I am desperate to relax.

"Vodka soda, please, with lime," I tell the bartender, who nods and complies. I grab my drink, scoot around the bar to the far corner, then take a big sip.

"Ruby?" I look up to see Miriam Josefsberg approach, holding a martini glass in one hand and waving at me with the other. As usual, she looks dynamite in a diaphanous peach calf-length gown. "Ruby! My God, it's you!"

Miriam hasn't seen me since the party, although she has made numerous attempts to reach out to me. I realize that I have been shunning her, as my former acquaintances have shunned me, partly out of shame, partly out of being discombobulated by suddenly being single. But she seems not at all bothered and kisses me warmly on the cheek.

"You look fantastic!"

"Thanks to Colleen's artistry."

"It's more than that," she says. "You look . . . happy." She leans closer and whispers conspiratorially. "Is it the pool boy?"

I laugh out loud. "You know I don't have a pool, Miriam!"

"The landscaper?"

"I had to let him go," I reply, wistfully thinking of Enrique.

"Pity," she says. "If Teddy ever left me, I'd jump every single one of our maintenance crew." Which would keep her busy for about a decade. "Seriously, Ruby, how are you?"

"I'm doing fine, thanks."

"Well, you look better than fine. Anything from Walter?"

I shake my head. "You?"

"Are you kidding? I dumped him ages ago, dear. The buffoon. Made Teddy dump him, too, and you know how much Teddy loves his Facebook friends. Did you get in touch with David Greenberg?"

"I called, but I'm not sure I can afford him." I think of all the bills piling up and my secret account that will be empty by Labor Day. "He's pricey."

"As I understand it, with Norma Devane, he took his fee out of the settlement, didn't ask for anything up front."

"That would be good," I say. "Anyway, I still have time. I figure I can wait till the bastard . . . uh, Walter comes back."

"Well, the best defense is a good offense, Ruby. That's what Teddy always says. Oh, here he is now."

I follow her gaze to find Teddy walking toward us with none other than Jacob Salt. They are in the middle of a conversation, but when Jacob sees me, he freezes midsentence.

"Ready for another, darling?" Ted asks, then does a double take when he realizes who I am. "Ruby!" He envelops me in a bear hug that threatens to squeeze all of the air from my lungs. Ted is a big guy with a big personality and a big heart to match. He is a red velvet cupcake with cream-cheese frosting and sprinkles on top—you just can't help but be happy when you're around him. "You look wonderful! How the hell are you?" He looks over at Jacob. "Oh, Jacob, you know Ruby McMillan, right?"

Jacob nods and smiles fleetingly. "Of course I do. The Muffin Top did the cake for tonight."

The Muffin Top? *Uh-oh. Not a good sign.*

It doesn't mean anything. Take it easy. Take another sip. I do.

"Really?" Miriam asks.

"I'm not surprised. She's the best, isn't she, Mir?"

"The very best," Miriam agrees. "I'm sure it's extraordinary, although I don't see how it could be better than our anniversary cake."

"That was a humdinger!" Ted adds.

"I trust you received the check?" Jacob says, glancing around the room.

"Yes, the fruitca—uh—your receptionist dropped it by. Thank you."

"Well?" Miriam says, directing her gaze at Jacob. "How is it? The cake?"

I hold my breath in anticipation of his review. I know the cake is amazing, but to hear it from him, to hear how he chooses his words, might reveal some subtext: i.e., how he feels about me. If he says, for example, *It's terrific,* and leaves it at that, he might as well just tell me to take a flying leap. But if he says, *I have never before beheld such a spectacular display of confectionery genius,* I may still have a chance to get naked with him.

"I haven't had the opportunity to see it yet, actually."

My heart drops along with my spirits, and I take another sip of my drink.

"Perhaps you'd like to show it to me?" I look up to find Jacob staring at me with his penetrating green eyes. Although I can't read his expression, my pulse quickens beneath his gaze.

"Uh, sure. I'd be happy to." To Miriam and Ted, I say, "See you in there?"

"Let's sit together," Miriam suggests, and I nod, then hurry to keep up with Jacob's long strides.

The lights are dim in the banquet hall and candles glow from the tables, creating a festive, intimate feel. The mingled aromas of prime rib and roasted chicken hit me as soon as we enter, and my stomach rumbles with anticipation. Instrumental jazz wafts through the speakers, softly now, though I suspect it will be cranked to a deafening volume soon. A single spotlight has been trained on the cake, and as we draw closer, I grow tense. Not because I think Jacob won't like the cake. But because he and I are alone together for the first time since Sunday morning.

Jacob stops a few feet from the display table. Hesitantly, he circles the cake, taking in every line and angle, and when he is directly behind it, he raises his eyes to me. The corners of his lips curve upward.

"Remarkable. Stunning. Absolutely breathtaking," he says, his voice low.

I exhale. "Thank you."

"And the cake isn't bad either."

It takes me a moment to process his words, but then their meaning finally connects with my gray matter.

"What did you just say?"

Jacob moves around the table and comes up beside me, looking suddenly unsure. "Well, what I meant was, the cake is fantastic. It's incredible, better than I could have imagined." He glances over at the edible inn, then back at me. "And . . . also, you look stunning tonight."

I feel myself blush all the way down to my Wonderbra. "Are you flirting with me?"

He furrows his brow. "Is that all right?"

"No. I mean, yes. Yes! I just didn't think . . . I mean, we haven't spoken since . . ."

"Look, Ruby, I've been wanting to call you since Sunday. And then I called the bakery on the pretense of getting an invoice, when what I really wanted to do was apologize for my behavior. And then I realized that I wasn't sorry for getting drunk, because if I hadn't gotten drunk, I would never have . . . well, you know, instigated things between us, and I really wanted to instigate things between us, so what I was actually sorry for was passing out on you like a common drunk and possibly making you think that the only reason I started anything in the first place was because I *was* drunk. I'm babbling right now, aren't I? Boy, I could really use a drink."

He slaps a palm to his forehead and the two of us burst into laughter. I carefully swipe at my eyes, and as our chuckles fade, Jacob takes my hand.

"I thought maybe I was too curt, or rude," I admit. "I have a habit of holding things in, of not saying what's going on in my head . . . or my heart, and I was worried you might have taken it the wrong way."

"Are you kidding? I was surprised you even managed to be civil to me after what I did."

"You were tired!" I say in his defense.

"It was a long drive," he says, nodding.

"And a long lunch," I add.

"Next time, maybe we should order à la carte."

My heart skips a couple of beats. "Next time?"

He reaches for my other hand and turns me to face him. "Look, Ruby. Tell me now if it's too soon for you. Because I'd really like to see you . . . as in, date you. Spend time with you." He pulls back a little and regards me intently. "You might be doing that thing you just told me you do, because I have no idea what you're thinking right now."

In the words of my illustrious employee Marcy, I'm thinking that this man makes my heart go pitter-pat. Along with another organ which shall remain nameless at this time. But since I've never really felt this way before, I'm not certain what the correlating facial expression should be. Finally, I decide on a smile.

"I'd really like to see you, too."

He slides his arms around my waist and pulls me in for a warm embrace. It feels so good, so right. I close my eyes and rest my head against his chest.

"That's a beautiful dress," he whispers, his breath on my skin.

"Thanks. I wore it for you."

Did I just say that?

"I like it very much," he says, still holding me close. "By the way, congrats on the *Cake-Off* thing. I've set my TiVo already."

I pull away and look up at his smiling face. "How do you know about that?"

"Izzy's a new Facebook friend. She posted it this morning."

I roll my eyes, thinking of how I might kill my best friend and whether or not it would be possible to take the whole institution of Facebook down.

I pull the minivan into my driveway, still giddy from the Franchise celebration. This has been the most romantic, magical night of my life. Enemy of romance that I've always been, I realize I've set the bar very low up until now. But every nerve ending in my body is tingling with delight, my senses feel heightened, the stars are practically blinding in their radiance, and the man on the moon is smiling at me, I know he is.

Jacob Salt has turned me into a complete sap.

As much as I would like to report that we took a room at

the Regency and resumed where we left off in Santa Barbara, we didn't. Instead, we spent the evening eating and drinking and dancing to rock and roll and disco and jazz, whooping it up with Ted and Miriam as though the four of us had been socializing together for years. When it came time to cut the cake, Jacob took the microphone and spent five minutes gushing with praise over my work and invited all the guests to patronize the Muffin Top for their celebratory needs. As the evening wound down, the music turned soft and slow, and Jacob and I danced together, our arms around each other, keeping rhythm to the languid beat of the music.

He kissed me chastely, as his coworkers and boss were present, but I'd seen the promise of passion in his eyes when he said good night. He told me he'd call me tomorrow, and just like a schoolgirl, I will count the minutes.

With wobbly steps that have nothing to do with alcohol, but, instead, with the suede pumps that are starting to make my feet cramp, I reach the front door. When I put my key in the lock, the knob twists in my hand. I feel a tiny prick of fear. It's after eleven. The kids should be in bed. The front door should be locked.

Before I allow any number of horrifying images to gallop through my brain, I step inside the foyer. All of the lights inside are blazing and there is no sign that anything is amiss. My maternal sixth sense picks up nothing alarming.

I walk down the hall to the kitchen, calling my kids' names as I go. "Colleen! Kev!" When I reach the archway to the kitchen, I stop. Colleen and Kevin sit at the kitchen table, staring at each other but not speaking.

"You guys left the front door unlocked," I tell them as I walk into the room. On first glance, they seem fine, but on closer inspection, I see that they both look completely shell-shocked.

"Hey. What's going on?"

They turn to me slowly, simultaneously, two cogs in the same machine.

"Dad called," Colleen says hollowly. "He's coming home."

I stir grated bittersweet chocolate into hot milk, watching as the white liquid turns brown. When it thickens, I pour the luxurious concoction into three awaiting mugs. I carry the mugs to the table, set two in front of my children, and take the seat between them. We sit there for a long while, talking sporadically in low voices, allowing the hot chocolate to soothe our nerves. Just after midnight, I finally kiss Colleen and Kevin good night and send them to bed. They are both feeling better, and for that I am thankful.

Their news doesn't surprise me. Eventually, Walter would have to return. At some point, I have to face the tangible consequences of a separation, a divorce. I have been given a pass these last few months, I've been able to ease into my new life without facing the legal and practical issues that need to be dealt with. It was just a matter of time. And now that time has arrived.

Walter is coming back. Not tomorrow, perhaps not even next week. But he is headed into my orbit, for better or for worse.

After rinsing the mugs, I grab a piece of paper and a pen and make myself a note to call David Greenberg first thing Monday morning. Then I tack it to the corkboard and head to bed.

20

Recipe for Disaster

In the dayroom of Casitas en la Mesa, the residents are having an impromptu sing-along. Ralph McNeary, eighty-six with a head of wild white hair reminiscent of Einstein, sits at the piano tickling the ivories. Ralph doesn't know his name, or the names of his children and grandchildren and great-grandchildren, can't remember the nurses or other staff members. But he can play any musical-theater tune he ever learned. Since my mom thinks she's one of the greatest musical-theater heroines of all time, she and Ralph get along great.

My mother sits beside him on the piano bench, facing the room and clapping her hands while she leads the residents through "Do-Re-Mi." Most of the assemblage is singing with her. A few merely stare into space, like Irene Zapruder, who clutches a stuffed bunny to her chest, and Joseph Cleary, who only recently came to Casitas and is still trying to understand what's happening to him.

I stand at the back of the room, watching. In some ways, it's downright comical; a roomful of old people performing an energetic, if painfully off-key, rendition of a song from *The Sound of Music,* clapping and stomping their feet, losing their places during the round, and giggling like little kids as they struggle to catch up. But the tragedy of so many lives ruined, of all these souls losing everything they have—far more than material wealth—keeps me from appreciating the humor.

But at least they have this. And they have Mom.

When I was very young, my mother sang to me all the time. Show tunes and old vaudeville ditties and little snippets of familiar songs with lyrics she'd make up as she went along. One in particular sticks with me, to the tune of "Frère Jacques," and it went something like this: *Little Ruby, making poopy, how are you? How are you? You are such a big girl, sweetest in the whole world, I love you. I love you.* As I grew up and Mom grew older and life's complications weighed more heavily upon her, her singing became less frequent, and when she did sing, the songs were often filled with sorrow and regret. I remember a lot of country and western during my teenage years.

But here she is, smiling wide, singing joyfully, her eyes bright and shining. Not a care in the world. I am both comforted and heartbroken.

Cherry McKenzie, a therapist at Casitas, comes up next to me and gives me a wink. At fifty-one, Cherry doesn't have a line on her face, perhaps because her cornrows are so tight, or possibly from clean living, or maybe, just maybe, she is an angel. She exudes warmth and generosity of spirit with every breath she takes and refers to all of the residents as her special friends. I think of her as dark chocolate, not because she is African American, but because she is as comforting as . . . well, chocolate.

"My special friends love this," she whispers to me. "It seems like it's something that makes them feel normal again."

"You in the back!" my mother calls to us. "I see you there! Come along now, sing out! *'Tea, a drink with jam and bread!'*"

Cherry and I exchange a glance, then join in. "*'That will bring us back to do!'*"

"How are you?" my mother asks, sitting next to me on the couch in her living room. The one-bedroom apartment is cheerful and simply furnished. The walls are off-white, the curtains sunny yellow, and the floors blond wood. There are no personal accents, no photographs of family which might cause distress, no crayon drawings under magnets on the fridge, no lumpy clay paperweights made in second grade for Grandma. Serene, prosaic landscapes are hung in every room, interspersed with mirrors to magnify the sunlight which streams in from the many windows.

"I'm fine, thanks," I tell her. I have to remind myself that we no longer have our traditional roles to play. Neither mother and daughter, nor friends. She is comfortable with me, which is a blessing. But today she studies me closely, as though there is something familiar about me. I try not to make too much out of her scrutiny.

"You look wonderful," she announces, taking my hand into hers. "You really do."

I swallow hard in an attempt to suppress the cauldron of emotions simmering within me.

"You look . . . happy," she adds. "You're actually glowing. You must be in love!"

"I don't know about that . . ."

"You look just the way I did when Baroness von Schrader told me I was in love with the Captain. I was horrified, too, of course, but I couldn't deny it." Her expression turns dreamy. "Is he wonderful?"

"Yes," I answer, thinking of Jacob. "He is." Then I shake

my head. "But my life is just so full of complications. Walter's coming back, God knows when, but he's coming. Like a hurricane. And this cake competition, *Cake-Off,* that Izzy got me into. I mean, I can't do it. Business is bad, and we need the money. *I* need the money, but there's no way I can put a cake together in eight hours on national television."

"You make cakes?"

Her question stops me short. I have been complaining about my life to a woman whose only memories of *her* life are imagined.

"I do. I make all kinds of desserts," I tell her. "But mostly cakes."

"How wonderful. Are you good at it?"

I shrug, attempting humility, then nod. "I am."

"Then why on earth wouldn't you do this, this . . . What did you call it?"

"*Cake-Off.*"

"Yes. Sorry. My memory." A flicker of regret crosses her features, then she smiles. "If you have a gift, it is your duty to share it with as many people as possible."

"But I'm terrified." Just the thought of it makes me nauseous.

"Oh, my dear, I was terrified of the Nazis. We all were. But we didn't give in to them. We fought them, didn't we? You can't run away from your fears, you have to face them."

Somewhere in the back of my mind, I knew this was coming.

"It's like the Mother Abbess says." She starts to sing. "'*Climb every mountain . . .*'"

I try to interrupt her. "I'm not running away from my fears, Mom. I just have certain goals. And this isn't one of them."

"'*Ford every stream . . .*'" she continues. She's not listening to me.

"I just wanted to have a good life. A good marriage. Healthy kids."

My mother is still singing.

"A gardener."

She stops singing long enough to pat my hand. "That's very practical of you, dear. But perhaps your dreams should be bigger than that."

Or perhaps I should allow myself to dream at all.

I consider this as my mother serenades me with Rodgers and Hammerstein's finest.

"I know what you're going to say," Izzy fires at me as soon as I walk into the office. "That you're not going to do it. No way, no how."

"Izzy—"

"But if you just think about it for a few minutes without bringing your bladder into the equation, you'll see that it makes sense."

"Izzy—"

"We don't have a lot of options here, Ruby. I know how much the bakery means to you. This is an opportunity for publicity out of our wildest dreams, even if you don't win, which I know you will, because you're so fucking awesome! And that's fifteen thousand dollars right there!"

"Izzy—"

"But even if, for some reason, you don't win first prize, everybody watches that show, even the ones who don't admit it! The Muffin Top will be famous."

"Izzy!"

Her mouth hangs open as if she is about to continue with

her filibuster, but she thinks better of it. She waits me out as I take a deep breath and turn my eyes skyward.

"I'll do it," I say. And in less than one second, she is out of her chair, around the desk, and at my side, dispelling the theory that larger women cannot move with superhero speed. She wraps her arms around me and jumps up and down, forcing me to jump up and down along with her.

"Should I leave you two alone?" Smiley asks from the door, a clipboard tucked under his arm.

"She's gonna do it, she's gonna do it!" Izzy sings.

"You keep bouncing her like that and she's going to have a stroke," Smiley observes.

"Oh no," Izzy says, coming to a halt. "We don't want that! Ruby's representing! She's gotta be in tip-top shape for *Cake-Off*."

"You're doing it?" Smiley sounds skeptical. "I thought you said never in a million years. Or was it a billion? Wait, I remember. It was 'not in a billion years, not even if they held my children at gunpoint.'"

Izzy raises her brows. "Wow. That's harsh."

"I was exaggerating," I say defensively.

"Well, it doesn't matter now, because she's doing it. And we have a lot of preparing to do, so if you'll excuse us . . ."

"Did you need something, Smiley?" I ask.

"Uh, yeah. We're almost out of a lot of things," he says, referring to the checklist on his clipboard. "Cake flour, all-purpose, cocoa powder, powdered sugar, granulated sugar. All the staples. We got plenty of butter, but the eggs are running low."

I glance at Izzy. While it's my duty to check the inventory and make sure we have everything we need, it's her duty to actually order the ingredients.

"Iz? Why are we out of flour, for God's sake?"

Her cheeks turn red. "Well, we're kind of having an issue with one of our vendors," she says as she takes a seat behind the desk and shuffles through a pile of papers. "You know, America's Best? They're a bunch of *cholos*. I don't think we should order from them anymore."

"What's the problem?" I ask, even though I have a sneaking suspicion that I don't want to know.

"Okay, the problem is, they want money and we can't pay them."

"I thought we were on net thirty with them."

"We were, but they changed the terms on us to fourteen. And we kind of fell behind, and now they want COD plus." Meaning we have to pay them for every order at the time of delivery, plus a percentage of the outstanding balance.

"And, um, how much are we into them for?"

She shrugs, pretends to study a sheet of paper. "I don't know, something like three thousand and something."

Smiley whistles. "That's a lot of freaking flour."

"Did you try Frisco?"

"Yeah, but no good. We owe them like a grand."

"What about Nyberg and Oliver?" She shakes her head.

I sigh heavily and turn to Smiley. "Make a list of absolute essentials. Nothing special, just the things we need to get through the next two weeks. Pull out some petty cash and hit Costco."

He nods.

"Just the essentials, Smiley."

"What, no truckload-size box of glass cleaner?" he asks, then disappears out the door.

I turn to Izzy and narrow my eyes. She looks up at me and frowns.

"You look worried," she says.

"I *am* worried."

"Yeah, but you actually *look* worried. You hardly ever look worried. You mostly look sort of calm."

"Well, I'm turning over a new leaf," I tell her. "To look how I feel, and right now I *feel* worried."

"So what inspired this new leaf?"

I feel myself blush.

"Or should I say, who?"

"You're trying to change the subject, Izzy. Why didn't you tell me how bad things are?"

"It's not *that* bad. It's the same all over. Adelle can't get anything from those *putas* at Nyberg and Oliver either. It's the economy. Look, you got enough on your plate, Ruby. The Muffin Top finances are my headache, not yours."

"They're mine if I'm out of work."

"That's not gonna happen. We're gonna get through this. Things are going to turn around, I just know it. We got the *Cake-Off* in less than two weeks, for God's sake! That's gonna shake things up around here. Frisco, America's Best, N and O! All those bastard suppliers are going to be knocking down our door to get our business. You just leave all this to me and concentrate on getting ready for the competition. You've got a lot to do between now and then."

"Like what?" I ask.

"You don't have anything in the oven, do you? 'Cause this is going to take a while."

Reflexively, I pull my cell phone out of my pocket and glance at the LCD. I've been checking it regularly, anticipating Jacob's call. My heart sinks for the tenth time today when I see that I have no messages.

He'll call, I tell myself. *He said he would, and he will.* But my inner cynic is snickering at me.

"Have a seat, Rube. You'll need to be sitting down."

I toss my cell into my purse and grab the chair opposite Izzy. Three minutes into her dissertation on the *Cake-Off* experience, I forget all about my phone and Jacob Salt. It's a good thing I brought my Tums.

Last year, Miriam Josefsberg introduced me to a blog called *Something New*, written by a housewife-turned-blogger named Ellen Ivers. I read it to this day. In it, she catalogs all of the weird, wacky, and wonderful new things she tries on a weekly basis, hoping to inspire other fortysomethings to do the same. I don't spend a great deal of time surfing the Web, but this blog spoke to me. And although I was heartened by the fact that I try new things all the time, I had to admit that those things were only recipes. I've never run a half marathon, for example, or gotten a Brazilian (really, why?), or sampled blowfish (I'm not the kind of woman to risk death for other people's entertainment). But I was inspired to sit down and make a list of new things I'd like, or was willing, or ought, to try.

Go to China was on the list, and *Grow an organic vegetable garden,* and *Make a digital scrapbook*. Not once did I ever consider adding *Enter nationally televised cake competition* to the list, and this is why. Because it's a bad idea.

The *Cake-Off* contract has a list of rules longer than the Constitution, and according to the fine print, the show will own everything I touch and all that I am for the entirety of the two-day shoot. I will have eight hours to make a cake that must reflect the chosen theme *comprehensively*. Creativity is stressed and weighed heavily by the judges, so while I must adhere to the theme, I must also be wildly imaginative. My cake must be at least three feet high, and the amount of cake used to create my thematically correct and uninhibitedly inspired masterpiece has to feed two hundred people. And it has to taste good. No pound cake strengthened with Elmer's Glue. One of the production assistants will scurry around the competitors' kitchens and grab little pieces of discarded cake to present to the judges. It doesn't have to be the most delicious or moist cake—it doesn't have to rock the judges' world—but if it tastes bad, I'm screwed.

The structural elements may be nonedible, but all decorations must be edible. And unlike the cakes themselves, which are made in advance, the decorations must be made the day of the taping. I am allowed two assistants and I can choose anyone—as long as both are over eighteen and have no warrants sworn against them in any of the fifty states. But if one of my assistants cuts off her finger or drops dead of a heart attack, if a light from the set falls on her head causing a concussion or brain damage, again, I'm up a creek. Assistants may not be replaced during the competition.

Cake-Off isn't live, but there is a studio audience, and this worries me far more than the cameras. All those countless, faceless viewers out in TV Land won't be watching until weeks later. But the audience will; a hundred and fifty people sitting on uncomfortable chairs all day long, just waiting for someone to screw up, for something to break, melt, crack, or—*yeehaw!*—come crashing to the ground.

Just for good measure, the judges like to throw a curveball in the middle of the competition. It doesn't always happen, but it happens enough. Like during the *Star Wars Cake-Off,* they brought in Mark Hamill, Carrie Fisher, and Harrison Ford to give pointers to the contestants creating their likenesses. The designer who was doing Han Solo was so flustered by Harrison Ford's presence, she couldn't even finish. Once, during a Mother's Day show, the judges sent the competitors' mothers in to replace their assistants. Although mothers know best, none of these mothers knew much about cake and this surprise did not bode well for any of the participants.

The day after the competition, there is a postmortem in which the three designers are filmed together and separately and are forced to rehash the entire competition. (Bad enough you should lose, but then you have to give a running commentary, a play-by-play of each and every step that led you to your failure.)

Have I mentioned the theme for my particular episode? This theme proves that God has a sense of humor, that He is the ultimate jokester and has currently turned His attention to Ruby McMillan. Forget about the Middle East and the homeless and the starving. Let's have a little Fun with Ruby. Because the theme is *fairy-tale romance.*

See? Bad idea.

By five o'clock Sunday evening, I'm having serious second thoughts about competing, but I already signed the contract, and Izzy already faxed it back to the producer of *Cake-Off,* one Madeleine Gingrich (no relation to Newt), who will find it waiting for her in her office Monday morning. So unless I drive up to the valley and break into the Food Channel studios and steal the contract from the fax machine without getting arrested, I am officially committed.

In the three hours since I told Izzy I would do the show, I have come up with eight stressipes. Marcy is on board to assist me, having enthusiastically agreed when I called her on her cell while she was out with her pitter-pat man, but I am still short one assistant. I asked Smiley, but he declined, saying that his appearance on national television might compromise national security. I don't know if this has something to do with his time in the service, or if he's just full of crap, but I didn't ask and he refused to be more specific. Pam Whitfield gets back from her vacation on the second, and although she could probably return early, I didn't press her. She is a hard worker, but not a *fast* worker, and speed is imperative.

"Don't look at me!" Izzy says, gathering the contract together and placing it into a file folder marked CAKE-OFF in bold red letters.

I wasn't looking at her, but past her at the wall behind her head. Because, although in every other aspect of my life Izzy would be my first choice of backup, when it comes to cake, I prefer her to stay in the safety of our office, where she can do no harm.

"The camera adds fifteen pounds," she tells me. "I'd look like a freaking Amazon. Plus, I gotta lead your cheering section, you know? Nobody knows who you are yet, so they won't be clapping for you too much. But don't worry. I'm going to be clapping my ample ass off."

I laugh, then grab my purse from the floor and sling it over my shoulder.

"Are you out of here?"

I nod. Having spent an hour reading through the competition guidelines and another two hours baking and prepping for Monday morning, I am thoroughly exhausted. I want to go home and see my kids. I want to take a long, hot bath. I want to climb into bed with some milk and cookies and watch television, anything other than *Cake-Off*. I want to sleep for fourteen hours, which would only be possible if my name were Van Winkle instead of McMillan.

"What are you doing on your day off?" Izzy asks.

"Getting in touch with a lawyer regarding my impending divorce from my creep of a husband," I answer. "Oh, and I have to design a fairy-tale romance cake."

Izzy chuckles. "Good luck with that."

I give her a little wave and leave.

21

Cherries Jubilee

The summer days are long, so it is still full light when I pull into my driveway at five thirty. I get out of the minivan and head for the house, but when I reach the walkway, my pace slows. Kevin is doing his best with the manual lawn mower I scored on Craigslist, but the rest of the yard needs work. The bushes and hedges lining the perimeter are overgrown and need to be cut back, the roses in the flower bed near the house could use pruning, and the impatiens along the cobblestone path are pretty much dead. Maple leaves pepper the entire area.

I am not close with my neighbors—an aloof Hungarian couple on one side and a single thirtysomething dot-com success on the other who may or may not be gay—but we are all pleasant to one another. We exchange greetings when we see each other and I bring them cookies for holidays. Both of their yards are pristine and well kept—of course, they use Enrique. And I'm sure my neighbors are disturbed by the eyesore of a yard in between them. I sigh and continue toward the house. Perhaps when I have time, after the damn *Cake-Off,* I'll brush off my gardening gloves and do some work on my property. I've never been good with plants or growing things, but I can rake leaves. And there must be some information on the Internet about trimming hedges and pruning roses.

I step into the foyer and am greeted by the aroma of freshly popped popcorn and the sound of laughter coming from the kitchen. Deep laughter. *Male* laughter. I swallow hard as I take a tentative step toward the kitchen.

Oh God. Walter! He's back.

Only, it doesn't sound like Walter. It sounds like . . . The laughter comes again; this time Colleen's lilting giggle and Kevin's staccato machine-gun spray are mixed in with the hearty baritone chuckle. I clutch my purse strap and venture to the back of the house.

"Oh, man!" I hear Kevin exclaim. "That was off the hook!"

When I reach the kitchen, I stop dead in my tracks. Jacob Salt sits at the table flanked by my two children. The three of them look up at me, still smiling from whatever amusement I interrupted, then the kids quickly return their attention to the open MacBook between them.

"Hi, Ruby," Jacob says, smiling warmly. I realize that although I wanted to hear his voice today, I didn't expect to hear it in person . . . in my *kitchen* . . . with my kids present. I am suddenly equal parts infatuated schoolgirl—thumping heart included—and protective mother. I knew Kevin and Colleen and Jacob would be forced to deal with each other at some point. I just didn't know it would be tonight.

But here they all are. The world tilts ever so slightly on its axis and I feel the way I always did in high school when we were given pop quizzes—I would have aced them if I'd been prepared. And I am not prepared for *this*. My stomach clenches even as I realize that the three of them seem completely at ease with one another.

"Yikes! Look at him go!"

Jaunty music, mixed with the revving of an engine, comes

from the computer's speakers. Colleen watches the screen with a mixture of horror and fascination. Kevin is smiling broadly.

Jacob stands and takes a step toward me. He is dressed more casually than I've ever seen him, in jeans and a navy-blue T-shirt with large white letters that read FBI: FRANCHISE BUILDING INSPECTOR. He looks great, so wonderfully tall and classically handsome, and as he draws nearer, I can feel my pulse throb in my temples and my neck and my wrists, and I want to kiss him so badly, but . . . what is he doing in my kitchen?

"Yo, Mom," Kevin calls.

"Hi, Mom," Colleen adds.

"We were just a watching a YouTube video," Jacob says with a grin. "World's Dumbest Stunts. It's a guilty pleasure of mine." He reaches out and touches my arm lightly. Just the barest glance of his fingertips sends an involuntary shiver up my spine.

"How long have you been here?" I ask, trying to ignore the sensation.

"Just a little while," he says.

"I didn't see your car out front."

"It's such a great evening. I walked over." He senses my reticence. "I'm sorry. I should have called. It's just . . . I have something I want to show you. Something I've been working on all day." He shifts his weight, suddenly uncomfortable. "Kevin and Colleen said you'd be home soon and . . . well, they invited me in."

I glance at my children. "They did?"

"I hope you don't mind, but I showed it to them first. To get their input."

"Wait till you see it, Mom," Colleen interjects. "It's so cool."

I look at my daughter but she is still watching YouTube. I can just make out the hazy form of a man on a motorcycle flying over a pond full of what looks like refuse. Sure enough, he crashes into the soupy muck, accompanied by a musical crescendo.

"You know, we can do this another time," Jacob says. "You must be exhausted."

I take a deep breath and blow it out on a sigh. "No, now's good. I'm sorry. I'm really glad to see you."

"Are you sure?"

I nod and smile and he relaxes.

"Okay, guys. Let's show your mom the surprise." He pulls out the chair in front of the computer and gestures for me to sit. Still clutching my purse, and somewhat off-kilter from the reality of Jacob and my children hanging out together, I lower myself into my seat. "Kevin," Jacob says, "you mind if I take your spot?"

"Huh? Oh, yeah, definitely!" Kevin immediately jumps up and Jacob takes his place to my right. For a brief and surreptitious instant, I close my eyes and inhale his soapy scent.

"Okay, what is it?" I ask, quickly opening my eyes and scooting closer to the table. I see the frozen image of the motorcycle rider standing in the middle of the swamplike pond, covered in grunge.

Jacob leans in and reaches for the keyboard and his arm brushes against mine. As he enters a Web address, I stare at the spot where our arms touch, then quickly distract myself by rummaging through my purse for my reading glasses. I put them on and set my purse on the floor.

"Here we go," he announces, his excitement palpable. He glances over at me, then turns back to the screen. My eyes follow his.

Three seconds later, the Web page loads and I am staring at the Muffin Top logo.

"I had to use the Muffin Top Bake Shop dot com," he says, "because apparently there's a Muffin Top Bakery in Duluth. But it kind of works, with the rhyme and all."

"Isn't it awesome, Mom?" Kevin asks from behind me.

I nod, speechless, because it is. The Web page is simple but elegant with muted tones of mauve and plum. The copy uses the same Park Avenue font as our signs and menus. Jacob has placed our waterfall logo on the right side of the page and the muffin tops spill all the way to the bottom. In the center is a photograph of the Franchise celebration cake, and below that, one of Miriam and Ted's castle cake, both with bold captions describing the cakes and the events. The left margin has six buttons: *Cakes, Cupcakes, Muffins, About Ruby, About Izzy,* and *Bakery News.* Below the buttons are the bakery's address, phone number, and a Map-Quest link for directions.

I click on the *About Ruby* button and am surprised to see a picture of myself, taken at the Franchise celebration the previous night. I'm laughing at something, my eyes are sparkling, and if I do say so myself, I look hot in the sleek blue dress.

"I took that," Jacob confesses. "And the one of the cake. I got the castle shot from Miriam and Ted this morning."

"I'm not sure this picture is appropriate," I say, blushing. "Shouldn't I be wearing an apron?"

"You look awesome, Mom," Kevin states.

"Of course she does," Colleen says. "And I get all the credit." I arch an eyebrow at her. "Well, most of the credit," she concedes.

I return my attention to the Web page and read the paragraph-long bio:

> Ruby McMillan, the Cake Lady of Pelican Point, is the head pastry chef and cake designer of the Muffin Top Bakery. Her incredible cakes can be called nothing less than art, and have graced the tables at city functions, corporate events, and countless birthday celebrations throughout the county. Ruby can make any idea, theme, or fantasy come to life with flour and sugar, creating edible masterpieces that go beyond your wildest dreams of what cake can be. Her children, Colleen and Kevin, say that as amazing as she is at making cakes, she is an even better mom.

My throat tightens and I hiccup with emotion.

"We added that last part when I showed the kids the site," Jacob says quietly.

"It's true, Mom," Colleen says, and Kevin nods.

"Totally."

"This is wonderful," I say, my voice thick. "How did you, I mean, what did it—"

"I used MySite. It's a Web hosting company that has a do-it-yourself website building program. Very inexpensive, cheap really. They provide templates, but you can personalize your site if you know HTML. I know a little."

"I don't know what to say," I tell him, overcome. This is the best gift I have received in ages, born of Jacob's time and energy and his desire to do something nice for me. For *me*. I couldn't be more touched if he'd brought me a dozen roses. I press my hand against my chest as though by doing so I can hold my emotions in, and I realize that this reflex, this need to keep myself together, is unnecessary. A tear squeezes out of the corner of my eye and I let it slide down my cheek without wiping it away.

"Thank you, Jacob," I say meaningfully.

"It's very basic," Jacob says. "But we can add to it as we go." The "we" part makes me smile. "Eventually you're going to have to link to Facebook, maybe even think about tweeting."

"Not a chance," I say adamantly. "No tweets for me."

"You know how I feel about tweeting," he jokes, "but social media is a really important marketing tool nowadays. You could start a blog; we could add a button right here." He points to the space between *Bakery News* and the address. "A blog would be a perfect lead-in to a cookbook."

"Okay, okay," I say, holding up my hands in protest. "One thing at a time. Let me get used to the website."

"Fair enough." He chuckles and I really like the way the corners of his eyes crinkle. "The important thing," he continues, "is that you now have a Web presence, which is really important, especially with the *Cake-Off* coming up. I put in a little blurb about it under *Bakery News*."

"But Mom's not doing *Cake-Off*," Colleen says, and Jacob turns to her. "She doesn't like getting up in front of people."

"Yeah. She, like, totally freaks. She pees in her pants."

"Kevin!" Colleen and I shriek at the same time. I glance over at Jacob, my face hot, and see that he is biting his lower lip, violently suppressing his laughter.

Kevin shrugs. "Well? It's no big deal. The first time I caught a wave, I totally whizzed in my shorts, dude. At least I was in the ocean."

I smile despite myself. "Actually, I *am* doing *Cake-Off*."

"You are?" Colleen asks.

"For real?" Kevin echoes.

I nod. "The bakery needs the exposure. If we don't bring in some business, we're going to fold."

Jacob and my children are respectfully quiet at the mention of the Muffin Top closing, but after a beat Colleen's face lights up.

"Mom, that's so rad! You're going to be on TV! I get to do your makeup, right? OMG, you are so going to rock that show!"

"Only if I don't pee in my pants," I snipe good-naturedly.

"It's cool, Mom," Kevin interjects. "You could just get yourself some Depends."

I smile enigmatically, thinking of the jumbo pack under my bathroom sink. "Yes, I suppose I could."

I spend a few minutes clicking all the buttons, reading and admiring what Jacob has done. The kids soon lose interest and carry the bowl of popcorn over to the kitchen counter, sharing it between them as they text their friends. With their total immersion in their cell phones, Jacob takes the opportunity to casually drape his arm around my shoulder and begins to draw lazy circles on my arm with his fingertips. My own focus is completely torn, between his lovely caresses and the several Web pages he has built, which are, as he said, basic, but also terrific, well written, and visually pleasing.

After a while my stomach growls and I realize that my eyes are starting to cross. I remove my glasses and push back from the table. "I could look at this all night," I announce, and Jacob grins, clearly pleased with himself. "But dinner isn't going to cook itself." I stand up and he follows suit. "I'll probably be up half the night looking at the website on my own computer."

"Make notes, anything you don't like, or anything you want that isn't there. We can set aside some time to work on it together."

"That would be great." I smile up at him. "I really can't thank you enough."

"You have. Already." I can tell that he wants to kiss me, and I would love nothing more if my children weren't here. "Well," he says. "I should let you get to your dinner."

"Is Mr. Salt going to stay?" Kevin asks. Surprised, I look over to find my son nodding his head at me.

"Why don't you all let me take you out?" Jacob suggests.

I shake my head gently. "That's really nice of you, but I took some steaks out of the freezer two days ago and forgot about them. They're still okay, but if I don't cook them tonight, they'll turn into a science experiment. You're welcome to stay. There's plenty."

He chuckles. "I love steak. Thanks. And maybe I can help."

I give him the fish eye. "I hope you're better with entrées than you are with cakes."

"Roulette wheel!" we say at the same time, then we both burst into laughter with my children looking on.

"Mr. Salt seems like a really good guy."

I turn from the sink to see Kevin approach. He walks past me, opens a drawer, and pulls out a dish towel, then positions himself to my left. Without responding to him, I swivel back toward the faucet, rinse the plate I'm holding, then give it to my son. He thoughtfully dries it and sets it on the counter in time for me to hand him another.

"The website's awesome, huh?"

I nod. "It is."

"He did all that for you, Mom."

"Yes."

"He must like you a lot."

I carefully clean a wineglass, then run it under the hot water. Kevin gingerly takes it from my grasp.

"I got it," he says, then gently dries it. "You like Mr. Salt, too, don't you?"

"I do, Kevin. I like Mr. Salt a lot. Is that a problem for you?"

He shrugs. I pull another dish from the soapy water and rinse it.

"I know what I said last week. About you waiting awhile before you start dating? I probably shouldn't have said that. It's not really my business, you know?"

"You're my son, Kevin. My business is your business, just like yours is mine. That's what being a family is all about." I turn off the faucet and face him. "I do like Jacob. I'm not going to lie to you. He makes me feel a certain way—a way I've never felt before, not even with your dad. I don't know what it means. I just know it's there. But if I thought, for one minute, that my feelings for Jacob would break something between you and me, it wouldn't be worth it."

He stares at the dry plate in his hands as if all of the answers in the world are written upon it. "I think you should go out with him. Mr. Salt."

"You do?"

"It won't break anything between us, Mom. It might be a little weird, and the timing is kind of sucky, but, you know. He likes you and you like him. That's the important thing."

"You're pretty grown up for fourteen," I tell him, then tweak his ear with soapy fingers, leaving a streak of foam in his hair.

He cracks a smile but quickly turns serious again. "Dad's coming home soon," he says quietly.

"Yeah," I agree. "I don't know what that means either, to be honest."

"Life is complicated," he says with a nod.

"It sure is."

"That's why I like surfing." He wipes the final dish and sets it on the counter. "Just you and the wave. Nice and simple."

"Maybe I should learn to surf," I say, and am rewarded with an unbridled laugh.

"That would require swimming in the ocean, Mom."

I shudder at the thought. "Maybe in another life. Till then, I'll leave the surfing to you."

Halfway through Tuesday's cake class, I approach Amy. The subject tonight is fondant, using the Play-Doh–like confection to cover cakes. I love fondant because it hides a panoply of sins, making even the most poorly frosted, crumb-riddled cake look sleek and glamorous. My students spent the first hour watching me demonstrate and are now practicing rolling it out, a task which is time-consuming and difficult. As with piecrust, fondant must be moved regularly to keep it from sticking to the work surface. Powdered sugar is helpful, but too much will make the fondant dry and cause it to crack easily. Shortening can turn the fondant gummy. Many successful bakeries have mechanized rollers, but here at the Muffin Top, we do things old school (read: we can't afford to buy one).

Amy has just successfully rolled her pink fondant to an eighth-of-an-inch thickness and is eyeing the cake she plans to cover. I stand back for a moment, watching. Her brown hair is pulled tightly into a ponytail and her makeup is minimal. She stands with her hands on her hips, biting her lower lip in concentration. After a moment she tucks the fondant over the rolling pin and, with one quick and confident move, lifts it from her work surface and carefully lowers it over her cake, exactly the way I demonstrated earlier. She unwinds the rolling pin, allowing the fondant to spill over the side of the cake, then uses her left hand to smooth it while cutting away the excess.

"Well done!" I exclaim.

"Thank you," she says, all business. "I've actually never worked with fondant before. Cool stuff."

I hand her the smoothing tool, like a nurse handing a doctor a scalpel, and she gently rubs it over the fondant, erasing all imperfections on the surface of the cake.

"Can I try a ribbon around the base?"

"I don't see any reason why not," I tell her. "You're a natural."

A smile seeps into her no-nonsense expression. "You think so?"

"I think any kitchen, any *restaurant,* will be lucky to have your talents."

"Thanks." She gathers up the leftover fondant and kneads it together, then begins to roll it out.

Over the last few classes, I have come to think of Amy as marble pound cake: confident, sturdy, without embellishment or affectation, but with a streak of whimsy running though her. She is extremely competent and at home in the kitchen and already knows a great deal about all kinds of food. But she is willing to learn new things and is a quick study. Which is why I am about to ask her a very important question.

"So, Amy, are you enjoying working with cake?" I think I know the answer, but it doesn't hurt to ask.

"Very much," she says, her eyes on her work. "Savory's more my thing." She sounds almost apologetic. "I like creating appetizers and entrées, salads and soups. But I think it'll be great to be able to whip up a beautiful cake for birthdays and celebrations, that kind of thing. So customers won't have to bring in their own. You know, when I'm a chef."

"Being well rounded is a plus," I tell her, watching her roll the fondant into a wide swath. "Not too thin, okay? You can eye the length or use a tape measure, but it has to be long enough to wrap around the cake. You'll cover where it joins together with a bow, so don't worry too much about how the ends look."

She nods. "Okay."

"So, listen, Amy, I want to ask you something."

"Yes."

"Yes, what?"

"Yes, I'll be on *Cake-Off* with you."

"How did you know—"

She stops rolling and looks up from her work surface and her gaze slides past me. I turn around to find Shane O'Neil staring at the two of us, sporting a sheepish grin.

"But how did *he* know?"

Amy shrugs and resumes rolling. "I think he might be dating your daughter."

On Wednesday morning, I am seated in the plush office of David A. Greenberg, attorney-at-law, in downtown Pelican Point. The small firm resides in a two-story brownstone on the main thoroughfare, situated between Starbucks and Clara's Boutique, and the second-floor windows overlook city hall. A dozen framed, gold-sealed certificates hang on the walls, and although I can't read the writing—they could say *David A. Greenberg Has Successfully Ridden Space Mountain,* signed by Mickey Mouse—I'm impressed. Photographs of a smiling brunette and two brown-haired boys line the enormous mahogany desk, which is empty of any papers, files, or other office detritus.

David Greenberg is an attractive man in his late thirties with a full head of wavy brown hair and a strong, generous nose that somehow works on his face. He wears a tailored suit the color of bittersweet chocolate and a matching tie, but despite his choice of color, he strikes me as a snickerdoodle: a plain, no-nonsense cookie beneath a facade of cinnamon sugar. His manner was warm and welcoming when I arrived but has turned cool and efficient as we have gotten down to brass tacks. He takes notes on a yellow legal pad as I describe my situation. He doesn't bombard me with questions and only occasionally makes noises of understanding. When I finish my tale of woe, he takes a few minutes to read what he has written, then gazes out the window thoughtfully.

"Miriam and Ted are good people," he says, apropos of nothing.

"Yes. They're great friends."

"There's no question that you've been wronged, Mrs. McMillan." He is still looking out the window, and I feel myself tense. Why isn't he looking at me? "Your husband is clearly at fault."

"I should say so," I agree.

"The thing is, I'll be frank with you. I'm expensive."

I swallow hard.

"I'm expensive because I'm worth it," he adds. "But I don't see how you'll be able to cover my fees. With what you've told me about your situation, it doesn't appear that you are in a position to retain me."

"I thought, uh . . ." To my horror, my voice quavers. I take a breath and start again. "I hoped you might consider extending the same courtesy to me that you did with Norma Devane."

"Miriam mentioned our agreement, huh?" He smiles ruefully. "Sadly, that wouldn't apply here. Charles Devane is worth a fortune; therefore, after Norma Devane was given her rightful share of his assets, she was able to compensate me in full. If your husband is truly destitute, as he claims, I do not foresee a financially fruitful outcome for you." He shakes his head regretfully. "I really am very sorry, Mrs. McMillan. You are in an unfortunate position."

Sweet-potato pudding with ginger-snap crumbs and crystallized ginger chunks . . .

I stand quickly and gather my purse. "Well, thank you anyway," I say in a coarse whisper as I make my way to the door of his office.

David Greenberg also stands. "I would be happy to give you some names of other lawyers who might be willing to represent you at a discounted rate or perhaps put you on a payment plan of some kind. Or both."

"That's all right," I assure him. "I'll figure something out." I grab the doorknob and twist, but my hand is suddenly slick with perspiration and it slides ineffectually over the brass. I clutch the knob more tightly and finally manage to get the door open.

"Oh, Mrs. McMillan," the lawyer calls to me as I step into the hall. "Because you are a close personal friend of the Josefsbergs, I'll be giving you a discount on this morning's consultation. Only one hundred dollars. You can settle up with Tess on your way out."

One hundred dollars?

I know that I should thank him, but the Cake Bitch has

no intention of doing so. Calling him a snickerdoodle was a mistake, an insult to cookies the world over. David Greenberg is most definitely fruitcake.

"You're a prince," I snap before I can stop myself, then I quickly slam the door behind me.

22

Hello, Cupcake

Fairy-tale freaking romance. What the heck do I know about fairy-tale romance? The recent developments with Jacob Salt can't be counted as a fairy-tale romance even though the feelings seem magical, because, let's face it, there is no such thing as a forty-three-year-old fairy-tale princess. I am simply not well versed in this particular area. Even as a child, when my mother subjected me to nightly readings of "Sleeping Beauty" and "Snow White" and "Cinderella," I rejected these stories and was quick to point out all of the holes in their plots.

She's dead, Mommy. No one sleeps for a hundred years. And even if she did, she'd still get all old and wrinkled and the prince wouldn't kiss her prune-y lips.

Why poison an apple to make her go into a coma? Why not just kill Snow White? That's a pretty dumb evil queen, if you ask me.

A prince would never marry a servant, not even Cinderella. It just doesn't happen, Mommy, because of the caste system.

Thankfully, my mother gave up the fairy tales and put me on a regimen of biographies, memoirs, and true-crime books. At the age of six.

It's Friday afternoon and I'm sitting at my kitchen table, pencil in hand, oversize drawing tablet splayed out in front of me. The page is blank. As is my mind. Colleen is staying at Zoe's tonight and Kevin is at Luke's, both of them more than happy to give me the space and quiet I need to come up with an idea for the *Cake-Off* masterpiece. They are more excited about the competition than I am, which isn't really saying much because I'm dreading it with every corpuscle of my being. I've even devised a few schemes to get out of competing, from breaking every bone in my right hand to faking my own death. But since the former requires me to maim myself with a hammer and the latter requires me to hire accomplices in the form of Izzy's relatives, both are out of the question.

I know I'll feel better once I have a design, but the pressure and gravity of the competition has rendered me brain-dead.

I stand up and stretch, bend at the waist and touch my toes, roll my neck and shoulders, and begin to pace the kitchen, circling the island cooktop and counter, mentally repeating the mantra *fairy-tale romance, fairy-tale romance*. For a moment I consider a rendition of "Cinderella," using the Grimm version rather than Disney, but the image that comes to mind, that of the stepsisters with their toes hacked off in order to fit into the slipper, seems a bit violent for the Food Channel. And, anyway, "Cinderella" is perhaps the most overdone fairy tale in history and I am supposed to be innovative and original.

It would help if I could relate to my subject matter on some level, and in that way, "Cinderella" would be the obvious choice. Like her, I've undergone a transformation—the old Ruby would never be teaching a cake class or appearing on national television—and also like her, I have had a complete makeover, although my fairy godmother happens to be my daughter. "Sleeping Beauty" and "Snow White" are out of the question, because those two gals had no trouble what-soever falling asleep . . . or staying asleep, for that matter. I can't relate to them at all. And Sleeping and Snow, like Cindi, are clichéd.

I blow out a frustrated sigh and gaze across my kitchen at the jar of honey on the counter. I come to a halt, feeling synapses firing in my brain. Something about the golden liquid has unearthed a long-forgotten memory.

Honey, I think. *Honeycomb.* And then I hear my mother's voice, quietly reading to me, before we moved on to *In Cold Blood.* "'One day, a rose offered the princess some honeycomb. "But do not show the ambassador," the rose warned her.'"

"Mommy, roses can't talk. They don't have mouths. Or vocal *cores.*"

"This is a magical rose, dear."

"There's no such thing as magic."

"Shall I stop reading?"

"I guess you can finish, since we've gone this far."

It was the story of Princess Mayblossom, I recall now, a French literary fairy tale from a collection of leather-bound volumes that my great-grandmother, who was from Calais, gave to my grandmother, who gave it to my mother, and my mother, in turn, gave to me. I never reread the story, but I cherished the book itself, as it was one of the few items we had that had been handed down through the generations.

"Where is that book?" I ask the empty kitchen, thinking hard. Not in the family room, I know, because I went through those books when I rid the house of Walter's pos-sessions. Same for the master bedroom. I didn't give it to Colleen, which is something I should have done by now—in fact, I should have done it years ago. But I have no recollec-tion of the last time I saw the book.

I head to the garage and aim for the corner storage area where boxes, including the ones filled with Walter's stuff, are stacked chin-high. The contents of all the boxes are labeled in my neat block letters, and it takes me only a few moments to find the one marked RUBY'S/PERSONAL, 1985–1995. I extract it from between two other boxes and set it on the floor of the garage, then kneel down and pull at the seal until it comes free.

I lift the lid and stare down at paraphernalia from my past: notebooks from my college days, yearbooks, photographs—framed and in stacks held together with rubber bands—diplomas, one from high school, one from university, and another from my Wilton cake-decorating course, dozens of thickly stuffed manila envelopes with receipts and documents. And as I gaze at these items, I see clearly, for the first time, how sterile my life has been. There are no love letters, no chains made from gum wrappers, no knickknacks with stories attached, no pillows with sentimental mottoes stitched into them, no ticket stubs from concerts, for although I have been to many in my time, I never had any emotional attachment to any of them.

I try to push this disturbing realization away as I rummage through the box for my great-grandmother's book. I find it at the bottom, beneath a manila envelope labeled MEDICAL INFORMATION/1989–1991. I run my fingers along the spine, then over the worn red cover. Age has faded the gold letters scrolled across the front, but I can still read them: *Fairy Tales of Madame d'Aulnoy*. I open the book to the inside cover and see a short passage penned in cursive, written in French, and beginning with the only three words I recognize, *Ma Chère Catherine*. My Dear Catherine. Clearly a note from my great-grandmother to my grandmother, Catherine Barclay. Below this inscription is another, written by my grandmother to my mother, this one in English, and although I have to squint, I can just make out the words.

My Dear Estelle: May the stars in your eyes shine brightly always, lighting even the darkest day, and the love in your heart keep you warm through all the winters of your life. All my love, Mama.

And finally, at the bottom, I recognize my own mother's writing and the single, simple sentence she inscribed before she passed the book on to me. I never bothered to open it when it was given, merely thanked my mom and placed it on a shelf. I have never read the words she wrote to me before this moment.

My Dear, Dear Ruby: Be strong, be smart, but try to believe. Love, Mom.

The back of my throat tingles and my tears are sudden and fierce. I roll onto my butt and sit on the cold, dusty cement floor. And I cry. For the unsentimental girl whose belongings reveal a painfully anemic life, and for the mother whose message urged her to *believe* something, but now has no memory of ever doing so. I cry for the many decades between the writer writing and the reader reading, all the opportunities I had to ask, *Believe* what, *Mom?* Opportunities that are lost forever.

My cell phone rings from the kitchen, a welcome diversion that forces me out of my pity fest and back into the house. Clutching Madame d'Aulnoy's tome in one hand, I reach for my cell with the other. The caller ID shows Jacob's name, and I feel my spirits lift.

"Hi, Jacob," I say, setting the book down on the counter and perching on one of the stools.

"Hi, Ruby." The warmth of his voice spreads through me and I feel my shoulders relax. I haven't seen him since dinner Sunday night, but he has called every day and we have fallen into an easy banter with a subtle underlying sexual tension. It's new to me, but I like it.

"How are you doing?" he asks. "How's the design coming?"

"Um, it's not," I confess. "I might be suffering from the cake designer's version of writer's block. I don't know the exact name of the syndrome."

"Cake block? That doesn't really work, does it?" I can tell he's smiling.

I glance at the book. "I may have found something that will help, inspiration-wise," I say.

"Is it legal?"

I laugh. "Yes. It is."

"I don't want to keep you from it . . . but . . . well . . . you probably won't want to take the time to cook tonight, and you do have to eat, so I'd like to offer my services."

"You're going to cook for me?"

"Absolutely not. I will not do anything that might jeopardize our relationship at this early stage. But I'm terrific with takeout. I could order up some Chinese and bring it by. I wouldn't have to stay, since I know you're working."

"I don't think so," I tell him.

"You're right. It's not a good idea. You have a lot to do."

"What I meant was, there's no way you're going to bring me food and not stay. *That* would be a bad idea."

"What time shall I be there?"

An hour later, we are seated at the kitchen table, surrounded by Chinese take-out cartons. Jacob scoops some lo mein onto our plates while I regale him with the story of Princess Mayblossom, which I read twice after his call.

"The princess is an only child, all her siblings died before she was born, so the king and queen are crazy worried about her safety. And this fairy, disguised as a hideous old woman, she has a grudge against the king, so she puts a spell on the princess that she'll be miserable for the first twenty years of her life."

"Sounds like adolescence," Jacob jokes.

"Okay, so the king and queen decide to put the princess in a tower to keep her safe—you know, to minimize the misery."

"Like Rapunzel."

"Only with shorter hair. When she's about to turn twenty, the king and queen send a portrait of her around to all the princes in the area."

"Match-dot-com for the Middle Ages."

I laugh. "Right. So, one king decides his son would be perfect for her, and he sends an ambassador to make an offer. The princess gets her servants to cut a hole in the tower, and when she sees the ambassador, she instantly falls in love with him. She persuades him to run away with her and they flee to a desert island."

"And they live happily ever after?" Jacob raises his eyebrows as he picks up the carton of beef with broccoli and dumps some onto my plate.

I shake my head. "He's the ambassador."

"And?"

"He's not the prince. You ever heard of an Ambassador Charming?"

"I see your point."

"All right, so on the island, the ambassador starts complaining about hunger and thirst, and when the princess can't provide him with food and drink, he instantly loses his affection for her. One day, a rose offers her honeycomb, but warns her not to tell the ambassador. She does, of course, the idiot, and he snatches it away from her and eats it all. Then an oak offers her a pitcher of milk and tells her not to show the ambassador, but still, she does, and he snatches it away from her and drinks all of it. At this point, the princess realizes what a chump she's been . . ."

"And what a jerk the ambassador is . . ."

"Well said, yes. The next day, a nightingale offers her sugarplums and tarts, and this time she eats them all herself. The ambassador is furious and threatens her, so she uses a magical stone to make herself invisible. So now a group of men are sent to the island, and the princess makes the ambassador invisible, too, and he manages to stab so many of the men that they have to retreat. But being that he's starving, the ambassador tries to kill the princess, and she kills him instead. She is brought back to court, and when she sees the prince, she discovers how much finer he is than the ambassador and falls madly in love with him."

"This time, for real, right?"

"Right. And *they* live happily ever after."

"Wow. Quite a tale. I like it. And probably not a lot of people have heard of it. Very little chance someone else will do a Princess Mayblossom cake. The ending is a little bloody, though, all that stabbing."

" 'Rapunzel' meets *La Femme Nikita*."

He chuckles. "Now all you have to do is reconstruct that in cake. In eight hours."

I push some rice around on my plate, working up the nerve to ask Jacob a question.

"What?" he asks.

"Will you come? To the taping?"

He seems surprised, but pleased, and smiles warmly. "Yes, I'd like to."

"It's on a Thursday, so you'll have to miss work."

"I'll clear my schedule."

"You'll probably be bored. It's a long day. Your butt might go numb."

"I'll bring a pillow. If you want me there, I'll be there."

My eyes meet his. "I want you there."

"Then it's settled."

Jacob expertly handles his chopsticks, maneuvering a huge bite of lo mein into his mouth without dropping a single noodle.

"You're good with those things," I observe.

"Thank you. I have excellent fine motor skills." He lowers his eyes at me and my heart flutters, in conjunction with my southern region. "Maybe sometime I can show you."

"I'd like that," I say, grinning. "Were you thinking of any time in particular?"

He lays his chopsticks on his plate and scoots closer to me. "Yes. I was thinking, anytime would be good." He leans in and touches his lips to mine and my whole body vibrates in response. His lips part and his tongue darts into my mouth, and then, with practiced ease, he reaches his hands around my middle and lifts me onto his lap. Fireworks, literal explosions of light, fill my head as he presses his mouth against mine, fervently exploring with his tongue while his fingers run from my hips to my breasts, caressing me softly, tracing patterns over the fabric of my blouse.

I feel sudden pressure against my thigh, and I reflexively pull away and glance down at his jeans. He laughs without embarrassment and strokes my cheek.

"I discovered something about myself this evening," he says, drawing my face toward him so that he can graze his lips against the base of my throat.

"What's that?" I breathe as tremors of delight rock me down to my toes.

He kisses my ear, then runs his tongue over my earlobe, stopping only long enough to say, "Fairy tales make me horny."

"Me, too," I murmur. I stretch my arms around his shoulders and slide my fingers through his thick hair. I pepper his neck with gentle kisses, intermittently flicking my tongue against his skin. He moans softly, then grabs my face and kisses me again, more urgently this time, his lips closing around my lips, his tongue fervently seeking my own. His hands move down, across my breasts, to my waistband, and I feel him tugging insistently at my shirt, freeing it from my jeans, and a second later, his palms are spreading their warmth along the skin of my bare stomach, his fingers creeping up underneath my bra.

And while my body is responding to him, matching his passion with every breath, every heartbeat, I can't completely lose myself in the moment. I want to—God, how I want to—but a tangle of thoughts weave through my head, making it impossible to give myself over to him. I think of my children, of their confusion and pain over the last few months, and of how they might handle this new intrusion in their lives. They have both given me permission, but the promises of youth quickly falter under the burden of reality, and they might not be so accepting of Jacob if his presence were actual rather than hypothetical. I think of Walter, of our lovemaking—God, why am I thinking about *that* right now?—our sedate and scheduled joining that still managed to give me pleasure despite the lack of imagination from which we both suffered. I wonder if Walter feels the way I am feeling at this moment when he makes love to *Cheryl*: that complete rightness; that mind-bending, frenetic energy of lust.

Jacob's fingertips have found their way to my nipples, and I flinch. Immediately he freezes and withdraws his hands. He looks down at me searchingly as I gaze into his burning green eyes.

I take a deep breath and let it out slowly. "I'm sorry," I tell him.

He seems to understand. He puts his arms around me and pulls me to him, and I rest my head against his chest. His heartbeat thunders against my cheek, almost hypnotic in its rhythm.

I force all thoughts of my kids and Walter from my mind and find myself thinking of my mother, of her words written in my great-grandmother's book. *Be strong, be smart, but try to believe.* Believe in what, Mom? In fairy tales? In magic? In myself?

And suddenly I recall a conversation we had right before I left for college. We were in my room, packing up all of the things I would be taking with me, my mother carefully folding my clothes and laying them in my suitcase. My father was away on business, the catchphrase that meant he was likely doing something he shouldn't have been. Mom was humming softly, but her brow was furrowed, betraying her underlying sorrow.

"Do you regret anything, Mom?" I'd asked her. "I mean, you know, with Dad?" It was a question I had never asked before, since I always thought I knew the answer.

She paused in the middle of folding a long-sleeved T-shirt and looked straight at me. "Why would I regret anything to do with your father?"

I rolled my eyes at her. "Because of what he, you know, what he does. The way he is now."

"I wouldn't change any of my choices, dear, especially not your father."

"Because you have me, right?"

"Ruby, I would have had you no matter which man provided the seed. A different version of you, perhaps, but you nonetheless. I have no regrets because I fell in love with your father with all of my heart and all of my soul."

"Oh, brother," I'd sniped.

She'd laughed softly at me. "We only live once, Ruby. We don't get to come back and do it again. I believe in true love, and I have felt that every day of my life. Has it hurt me? Yes, deeply. But would I change it? No."

I'd watched her as she resumed folding my things, had scrutinized every line and furrow on her face—etched, it seemed to me then, by heartache. And I had rejected her denial that she wouldn't change a thing. Who wants heartache? Heartache hurts. And I had made a decision, purposely and uncontrovertibly at that moment, that I would not follow in her footsteps, that I would guard my heart at all costs.

And now, as I fold myself against Jacob's chest, I understand that I was wrong about my mother, and I was wrong to pattern my life as the polar opposite of hers. Estelle Simmons lived fully and completely. She experienced soaring joy and sinking despair, outrageous victory and blinding defeat, overwhelming passion and all-consuming love: the rainbow of emotions that human beings are capable of feeling. And I have lived in a tower, closing myself off to those feelings, convincing myself that to remain in a static state of contentment was to be happy. But I have been deceiving myself. When Mom instructed me to try to believe, I now suspect she was instructing me to believe in *everything,* in all that life has to offer. Good and bad.

Jacob eases me slowly from his chest and glances at the Chinese take-out cartons on the table. He gestures to our plates.

"I guess we should finish."

"Yes, we definitely should."

I slide off of him only to throw one leg over his chair and straddle him. He looks up at me, surprised, but when I pull him to me and plant my lips on his, he is more than ready.

We grope our way to the second floor, laughing and kissing and shucking our shirts like giddy teenagers. But at the door of the master bedroom, I pause, my eyes landing on the king-size bed. Jacob, who has his arms around me, follows my gaze.

"If you're uncomfortable . . ." he says quietly.

"No," I assure him, stretching up on my tippy toes to kiss him. "It's about time I had some fun in that bed."

He laughs. "If you're sure."

"I am," I say. "It's just . . . I really have to pee."

A smile spreads across his face. "I promise, I will not pass out on you this time. But please hurry." He pulls me to him and I feel the outline of his erection. The thought of what's to come—pun intended—propels me out of his arms and into the bathroom, where I quickly do my business. When I open the bathroom door, Jacob is standing at the sink in the vanity, rinsing his mouth with mouthwash.

"Lo mein breath," he says with a grin.

"I didn't mind," I say truthfully. With a shrug, I grab my toothbrush, dab some toothpaste on it, and set about scrubbing my teeth. As I do so, Jacob moves behind me and unclasps my bra. My cheeks flame with embarrassment as he slides the straps over my arms, one at a time. His eyes are smoldering as he looks at me in the mirror. He runs his hands over my back, around my waist, caressing every inch of exposed flesh, kneading my breasts and pinching at my nipples. I feel myself grow hot as he presses himself against me. I quickly rinse my mouth just as his hands clasp the buttons of my jeans. He tugs them free and shoves them down to the floor, kissing the line of my spine as he goes. I carefully step out of them, then grasp the counter with both of my hands, staring at the two of us in the mirror, overwhelmed by how erotic this moment is. Jacob gently eases down my underpants and slides his fingers down, over my butt, farther and farther until I feel his fingertips gently tickling my labia, then stroking, teasing, caressing until I am moaning with desire. I look up to see that he is watching my reflection, smiling with almost animal glee.

I turn to face him and am confronted with his sinewy golden chest. The top button of his jeans is already undone, exposing the elastic of his briefs. I grasp his fly and pry it apart, shove at his jeans, but they catch at his waist. He helps me, sliding them down to the floor, where they land in a heap next to mine. His black briefs barely contain his erection: it juts out violently, as if demanding to be set free. I oblige, and I catch my breath when I behold the gorgeous penis before me. Smooth and long, thick and hard. I tentatively reach for it as Jacob swoons in and tenderly assaults my neck, my cheeks, my ears, my breasts, with his kisses. His shaft twitches as I close my hand around it. I squeeze, ever so gently, inciting a groan of pleasure from Jacob.

"I want to be inside you." His words are guttural, all passion. I nod, and he grabs my ass with both of his hands and scoops me up. With my legs wrapped around his waist, he staggers to the bed and lowers me upon it. He pushes my legs farther apart and wedges himself between them, and I feel the tip of his penis nudge against me. With his hands clasping my hips, he thrusts his full length inside me, and every nerve ending in my body seems to fire at that exact moment and I cry out with pain, because I am filled to bursting and it hurts, but it hurts so good, and a moment later, it doesn't hurt at all. And I finally understand those phrases— *we fit perfectly together* or *I was made to be with him*— because we do fit perfectly, like a hand in a tailored glove. I clasp my legs behind his back and grab his buttocks, urging him to plunge even deeper into me, and we both moan as we find our rhythm, and a tidal wave of sensation floods through me as we rock back and forth, deeper, harder, until I think I cannot bear the pleasure of it.

He stops suddenly, and I look up and meet his eyes, and in them I see something beyond lust, something that looks like love, and it scares me because I know he sees the same thing reflected in my eyes. I squeeze him tighter, and he resumes, slowly at first, gently, then building up steam and turning frantic until we both explode in a climax, the kind I had only ever dreamed of, read about, but it's real, I can now say without equivocation, and *Oh my God*.

Jacob falls against me, spent, his labored breath hot against my cheek. I wrap myself tightly around him, feeling our juices commingle as they seep out of me.

"That was incredible," he says haltingly, his heart jackhammering against my chest. "It's never been like that . . ." He stops, perhaps afraid to say too much.

"It's never been like that for me either," I whisper.

He rolls over to my side, easing his weight off of me, but

maintaining contact along the length of our bodies. Then he throws a possessive arm around my waist and nuzzles his face into the crook of my neck.

As I lie in the bed I shared with my husband for so many years, I allow myself to think of him. Walter and I made love a thousand times, and it never bore any resemblance to what Jacob and I just did. For a brief moment I hope he is experiencing the same with *Cheryl,* because everyone deserves to feel that kind of passion and ecstasy, even Walter. Then I remember what he did to me, and I take it back. I hope seasickness has rendered him impotent.

"What are you thinking about?" Jacob murmurs, his eyes already at half-mast.

"Walter," I say, and feel Jacob tense. "Not before," I assure him. "Just now. I wasn't thinking about anything . . . before. You kind of took away my ability to form rational thought."

"Good," he says throatily.

We lie that way for a long time. Jacob's breathing grows deeper and steadier, and I watch the ceiling, drinking him in, crazily comfortable with him beside me, until I can keep my eyes open no longer and sleep whisks me away.

At first, the sound of Jacob's cell phone is part of my dream, whispering through my subconscious. Slowly, it pulls me from a deep sleep and I open my eyes. Jacob doesn't stir. He snores softly, his arm still clasped around my waist.

I glance at the clock as the ringing stops and see that it is just after two. I know that a call in the middle of the night is either a wrong number or bad news, and when the phone sounds again, I nudge Jacob gently.

"Jacob, your phone."

"What?" His voice is thick with sleep.

"Your phone's ringing."

Anxiety twists inside of me, but Jacob merely looks confused. He swings his legs over the side of the bed and pushes himself to his feet. As he crosses to the bathroom where our discarded jeans lie, I take a second to admire his nakedness, then get up and head for my dresser. I grab a pair of sweats and a T-shirt while Jacob fumbles for his phone. The ringing stops before he can answer.

"Shit," he mumbles.

I pull on my clothes when the phone sounds again.

"Jacob Salt," he says on the first ring. "Hello? Hello—Kristen?" He glances at me. "Kristen, what is it? Are you all right? Is the baby okay?"

I watch him, concerned, but he shakes his head and gives me the okay sign. "Okay, just calm down. The baby's fine. You're fine." He moves back toward the bed, jeans in hand, and sits. "Wait a sec, just hold on." He sets the phone down and pulls on his jeans. "I'm so sorry," he whispers to me.

"No worries. I'm going downstairs for a few minutes."

He nods absently then picks up the cell. "Okay, I'm back," I hear him say as I shuffle from the room.

Down in the kitchen, I quickly close all of the take-out cartons and stow them in the fridge, then dump our plates in the sink. I wipe the table with a rag, then sit and pull the drawing tablet over to me. I tell myself not to think about the phone call, that it has nothing to do with me, that it's none of my business. I tell myself it's not karma, because how could I possibly be punished for something that felt so good? But despite my efforts to reassure myself, a sliver of unease trickles through me. To keep it at bay, I focus on the blank page of the sketch pad. And after a moment I allow myself to revisit the feel of Jacob in my arms, to bask in the afterglow of our lovemaking.

Fairy-Tale Romance Cakes.

I slowly begin to sketch, my pencil moving over the paper with bold, confident strokes. Minutes later, I peer down at the tablet and smile. The drawing is bare-bones with no embellishment, but even so, my design is on paper, and it isn't half bad.

Jacob appears at the archway to the kitchen, fully clothed down to his shoes. He face is pale and drawn and I feel my smile fade.

"I have to go," he says simply, bouncing on the balls of his feet.

"Is everything okay?"

"The baby's fine." He inspects the floor. "Kristen's . . . hormonal."

"That happens," I say, trying to keep my tone light. "Do you want coffee?"

He shakes his head. "No, thanks. I . . . I'm sorry, Ruby. Last night was wonderful, but I . . ."

"Do you want to talk—"

"No. No. I'm fine. Really. Something's just come up. I can't really explain it right now." He avoids my eyes and I have to bite my lip to keep it from trembling. "I may have to go up north in the next few days. I probably won't be back in time for *Cake-Off*."

"It's no big deal," I lie, offering up my best smile. "Are you sure you're okay?"

"I'm sure. I'm really sorry about this, Ruby. I . . . I'll call you."

I nod and keep my smile in place until he turns and walks stiffly out of my kitchen, then out of my house. For a moment I just sit there, blinking rapidly, trying to make sense of what just happened. Then I glance at the corkboard on the wall, at the Josefsbergs' anniversary-party invitation, which I never took down. And suddenly, although I know I'm being ridiculous, I miss Walter so much I can hardly breathe.

23

Skimming the Cream, Churning the Butter

The Food Channel studios are located in Burbank, just over the hill from Los Angeles proper and about fifteen degrees hotter. Our two-car caravan pulls into the self-parking lot of the Marriott across the street and the kids and I climb out of the minivan. I sigh with relief that our fifty-mile—*three-hour*—journey on the 405 Freeway is over.

A sullen-looking Amy, an enthusiastic-looking Marcy, and an irate-looking Izzy alight from Izzy's Camry. (Izzy hates traffic and I can only imagine the constant stream of Spanish expletives she used on the way up.) As we head for the hotel, the sun beats down mercilessly upon us. I can feel Colleen's makeup sliding down my face.

The producers of *Cake-Off* are paying for rooms for me and my assistants, but I have secured an adjoining room for my kids, rationalizing that this is their big summer getaway. I offered to share my room with Izzy, but she declined, and I am secretly glad. I have enough trouble sleeping without her chain-saw/dying-walrus snoring routine.

After getting the kids and Izzy settled, Marcy, Amy, and I walk over to the Food Channel building to check in. I detect some tension between my two assistants, likely because they are such opposites. There were some conflicts earlier this week at the bakery, and I only hope they'll be able to put aside their differences and work together for the taping.

Since I woke up this morning, I've had a sense of fore-boding along the lines of a Stephen King novel, although I can't pinpoint its source.

Maybe it's because you're about to build a monolithic cake in only eight hours with a studio audience watching while being filmed for a national broadcast?

Yeah. That could be it.

The reception area is a wide, bright room done in the Food Channel's signature colors of lime green, lemon yellow, and tangerine orange. A television mounted high in the far corner airs an old episode of *Yum,* and on the screen, Morton Smythe, dressed as a mad scientist, gestures toward several beakers full of melted butter, vanilla, milk, and honey. Huge posters of celebrity chefs line the walls of the room. Andre Maroni, or "Macaroni," as he is known on his show, Lisa Winters, Joe Jenson, Patty Chambers, Devon "Fire It Up" Green, and Edna "Hot Potato" Gleeson all gaze down at us, their smiles wide. Of course they're smiling, I think ruefully. They have hit shows and make scads of money and don't have to worry about their bakeries closing or their homes being foreclosed upon.

And neither will you, after tomorrow, I tell myself, trying to bolster my confidence.

Unless your cake topples . . .

A reception counter runs along the back of the room, and behind it sits a young, smiling (of course) receptionist wearing a wireless headset over her sun-bleached mane. She looks up as we approach.

"Hi!" she says. "How can I help you?"

"Hello," I reply, stepping forward. "I'm Ruby McMillan. I'm here to check in for *Cake-Off.*"

"Oh, right, terrific," she says brightly. "Let me just see . . ." She taps pink-lacquered fingernails on her keyboard and fixes her attention on her monitor. A moment later, her brows furrow. "What did you say your name was?"

"Ruby." I swipe a bead of perspiration from my upper lip. "Ruby McMillan."

"Hmm." She types in another command, her frown deepening. "No Ruby McMillan."

"Um." I clear my throat and turn to Amy and Marcy, who are both watching Morton Smythe stir some kind of bubbling concoction while smiling diabolically at the camera.

"Just let me make a call," the receptionist says. She quickly dials a number on her phone, then cocks her head, listening. "Hi, this is Kimberly. I have a Ruby McMillan at reception. She says she's checking in for *Cake-Off*?"

I take a couple of deep breaths, then glance up at the gigantic face of Andre Macaroni. He seems to be mocking me.

"Oh, right. Sure." Kimberly nods to herself. "Okay, I'll tell her." She touches a button on the phone. "Madeleine Gingrich will be right down."

"Great, thanks," I say, then take a step away from the counter, wedging myself between Amy and Marcy.

"I just love this guy," Marcy says. "He is the cherry bomb, if I'm lying, I'm dying."

"He's not even a chef," Amy mumbles. "No credentials."

"He's got street cred," Marcy replies. "Or should I say, kitchen cred. Plus, he's a cutie patootey."

"Ugh! You think he's cute? He's a total nerd."

I can see where this is going, because aside from the fact that he's shorter, Marcy's boyfriend is the spitting image of Morton Smythe. I quickly interrupt.

"Okay, ladies, we have to make sure all of our stuff got here safe and sound. Check the cakes and prep the kitchen for tomorrow morning."

Last night, I loaded a pallet with all of the equipment and

prebaked cakes I'd need to create my masterpiece, and first thing this morning, a Food Channel van picked it up and brought it here. I used the previous evening's cake class to prep; had my students make buttercream, royal icing, chocolate plastic, and gum paste. They helped me wrap my two dozen yellow cakes in plastic and bubble wrap and inventory all of my food colors, tools, and equipment. And while I felt guilty using the class so selfishly, my students seemed to relish the tasks. They felt like they were participating in *Cake-Off* themselves, and Blanche even declared it the most instructive class to date.

"The better organized we are, the more smoothly the competition will go."

Amy and Marcy take a break from glaring at each other to nod in agreement.

"I have a list, which we'll go over back at the hotel—"

The door adjacent to the reception counter opens and a middle-aged woman with tortoiseshell glasses walks briskly into the room, holding her hand out to me. Her automatic smile doesn't reach her eyes and her manner is brisk.

"Ms. McMillan? Madeleine Gingrich." She grabs my hand and jerks it up and down a couple of times. Looking at her, I think of cherry compote, and not just because of her cherry-red hair. Cherry compote is a strong, capable dessert, but some people find it offensive. "Good to meet you. We're so glad you could fill in."

Fill in?

"These must be your assistants."

"Uh, yes. Marcy Kopeke and Amy Fine."

The producer takes a moment to pump each of their hands, then turns back to me. "I'll just show you to the studio where *Cake-Off* happens. Your equipment is already in your kitchen. Right this way."

She ushers me down a long hallway lined with action shots of various chefs in their TV kitchens, and I have to trot to keep up with her pace. Marcy and Amy follow us, with Marcy giving a running commentary on everything she sees, like the dressing rooms and the green room and each studio we pass, while Amy remains stoically silent.

"So," Madeleine says, "I really have to apologize. There was some kind of communication breakdown and only about half the staff was aware of the change. It's television, you know. These things happen. But it's no problem at all."

"I'm sorry, Ms. Gingrich—"

"Maddy, please."

"Maddy, I don't know what you're talking about."

She comes to a stop at the door to Studio 12. "Oh, well, I just assumed your partner told you. We originally had Ray Hartford slated to appear with Cody Armstrong and Thomas Bell, but Ray tore a ligament in his knee while doing the cupcake-skydiving stunt, so he had to pull out."

I blink a few times to keep my eyes from rolling back in my head.

"Cody Armstrong *and* Thomas Bell?" Thomas Bell is the *second* most winning competitor on *Cake-Off,* followed closely by—you guessed it—Ray Hartford.

"We were originally dubbing it the 'Heavyweight *Cake-Off,*'" she says, then seems to realize. "But don't worry. We pulled those commercials."

My mouth is suddenly dry. Parched. The Sahara has nothing on my mouth. Not only am I the only newbie, but I'm going against two chefs who have thirteen wins between them.

Rainbow tart with blueberries, kiwis, strawberries, tangerines, and star fruit with a cherimoya custard.

"I'm competing against Cody Armstrong *and* Thomas Bell?"

"That's right," she says, pushing through the studio door. "Initiation by fire, so to speak." She laughs shrilly. "Oh, you'll do fine, Ruby. Just fine." But I can tell by her expression that she doesn't expect me to do fine. She expects me to go down in flames.

I trail her on wooden legs through the vast studio. The back door is rolled up for loading and unloading, and a man in a gray work uniform stands in the bay next to a pallet, holding a clipboard. He looks up and gives Madeleine a curt wave as we enter. On the far side of the room are ascending rows of seating for the audience, and on the near side are three exhibition kitchens, their faux-granite countertops sparkling clean. Three show tables for the finished pieces stand in front of each kitchen, and although they are only four feet away, I know the short trip from kitchen to table, carrying an enormous and delicate cake, can feel like crossing the Atlantic. The judges' table is situated between the kitchens and the audience, and just the sight of it makes my heart skip a beat.

In the center of the studio, a huge tree of lights has been lowered to eye level, and another man, this one in jeans and a T-shirt with a tool belt around his waist, is perched on a stepladder, wielding a screwdriver.

"Hey, Ed," Madeleine calls to him as we pass. "So, Ruby, you'll be in Kitchen Three. Cody Armstrong is in One, of course, and Thomas is in Two."

She leads me to the last kitchen area and I swallow hard when I see the sign affixed to the counter, which reads: RAY HARTFORD, MAXIMUM CAKE. Madeleine follows my gaze. "That'll be changed by tomorrow," she assures me.

Behind the counters, ovens, and racks of Kitchen 3 sits the pallet we packed yesterday.

"Marcy, Amy," I say, my voice shaky. "Why don't you check our stuff?"

The girls head to the back of the kitchen and start tearing at the industrial cellophane wrapped around the pallet. The man in gray jogs over to Marcy and Amy, brandishing a box cutter, and slices through the wrapping with a resounding screech that echoes through my head. I realize that Madeleine is talking.

". . . of course, it can't be helped, but, you know, everything else will be ready for you."

"I'm a little confused," I sputter. "I signed the contract a week and a half ago. I mean, you've had my name for ten days."

"Oh, sweetie," she says, her tone now dripping with condescension as though I am a very small child. "*Cake-Off* isn't the only show we've got on the air, now, is it? Wires get crossed all the time, memos get lost, people just plain forget to communicate. It happens."

"Of course, I understand," I say, trying to sound conciliatory *and* intelligent.

"Like I said, everything will be taken care of by morning. And I am sorry about the coat, but I know you'll manage to soldier on."

"The coat?"

"Uh, Ruby?" Marcy calls from behind Kitchen 3, and I detect an uncharacteristic edge to her voice. "You might want to come take a look."

A pit the size of a football materializes in my stomach and I try not to panic. I hurry past the kitchen and see Marcy kneeling beside the pallet with Amy behind her, both of them staring down at the enormous box of cakes. I stop in my tracks and reach out to one of the metal racks for support.

I don't want to see, I don't want to see, I really don't want to . . .

"They're broken," Marcy says plainly.

"All of them?" I squeak.

"Well, I can't see the bottom ones, but the ones on top?" She glances at Amy. "Yeah."

Madeleine Gingrich walks into the kitchen. I can tell she is evaluating me, studying my reaction to this disaster. Although I've been letting down my guard lately, it dawns on me that this is not the time to exhibit my emotions. This is the time to bring out my game face, the calm facade, the mask. Luckily, I've had a lot of practice in the last few days, what with the Jacob disaster. I suck in a deep breath and blow it out on a sigh. Then I force a smile. "What are you going to do?" I say breezily, even though my heart is pounding. "That's life!"

"Oh, no, your cakes!" Madeleine exclaims, but her dismay rings false. "What a shame! That will certainly give you a disadvantage tomorrow, won't it?"

Aside from being a Cake-Off *virgin, pitted against the Goddess and God of the cake world?*

Keep smiling, Ruby.

"I've repaired worse," I say, even though I haven't yet laid eyes on my ruined cakes. "Buttercream's like glue."

"Well, you certainly are taking this like a pro," Madeleine says, impressed. She glances at her watch and her eyes go wide. "Gotta dash! I have a contract meeting with the Hot Potato." She leans in conspiratorially. "With what she's asking, you'd think she's bringing about world peace instead of whipping up spuds! All right, then. I'll leave you ladies to it. Be here promptly at eight o'clock for a nine o'clock go. Sound good?"

I nod. My lips are starting to twitch with the effort of retaining my smile. Madeleine whirls around and heads for the door to the studio. A thought occurs to me and I call after her.

"What were you saying about the coat?"

But she is already gone.

I turn to Marcy and Amy. I have a sudden urge to lower my guard, to allow myself to frown and moan and fall to the floor in a tantrum. But the two young woman are looking at me as though we're already dead in the water, so I hold on to my cheery attitude, if ever so tenuously.

"It's no big deal," I chirp, stepping closer, but still not looking in the box. "It'll be fine. I promise."

"Of course it will, Ruby Tuesday," Marcy says, trying to sound cheerful. I steel myself, then take another step forward and peer down into the cardboard box. The football that was in my stomach springs to my throat.

"Sure it will, it'll be just fine," I say through a rictus smile. Then again, maybe it won't.

At eight thirty the following morning, I stand in my assigned dressing room, staring into the mirror, horrified. Apparently, the wardrobe department didn't get the memo about the change in contestants, and there is not another *Cake-Off* chef coat to be had in the entire building. I am forced to wear Ray Hartford's royal-blue coat. Not to be cruel, but Ray Hartford is as wide as he is tall. I'm covered in yards of fabric that is so stiff and starched, it juts out like a pyramid instead of merely hanging on me.

"Couldn't I just use my own chef coat?" I feebly asked one of the production assistants when she'd come around to check me in. The girl, Samantha, who can't be more than eighteen, had looked at me like I was suggesting we slaughter a goat right there in the dressing room.

"Oh, you simply *can't*!" she shrieked. "It has to be a regulation *Cake-Off* coat. The rules are very clear."

"Cody Armstrong gets to wear her own coat," Colleen pointed out, ever my champion (not to mention that she was absolutely flabbergasted by my appearance).

"Cody has that right as *Cake-Off* champ! When you win more than her, then you can wear your own coat, too!" Samantha gave a dramatic eye roll, making me think of an Abba-Zaba, because I really wanted to tear her apart, even though I'm sure she's sweet as peanut butter on the inside.

"What about an assistant's coat?" I'd suggested.

"No, no, no!" Samantha cried. "I'm sorry, but it's stipulated in your contract that you must wear the chef coat provided. I apologize for the misunderstanding, but there's nothing we can do about it now."

So here I stand, thirty minutes to 'Go Time.' My face looks sallow despite Colleen's heavy layer of foundation, and I'm already sweating inside Ray Hartford's chef coat. Izzy paces the small room, crossing back and forth behind me, talking to herself in Spanish. Colleen is perched on the makeup counter, peering at me thoughtfully. My stomach is in knots and my nerves are buzzing. I am about to compete in my first *Cake-Off* looking like Violet Beauregarde in *Charlie and the Chocolate Factory* when she turns into a giant blueberry.

"*Bueno, bueno, está bien. Tu estás la mejor* cake designer *en todo el mundo.*"

"I think you might be stretching it a bit, Iz. I'm not the

best cake designer in the world. Pelican Point, maybe. If you don't count Adelle."

She stops and looks at me in the mirror, then quickly turns away, trying to hide her mirth.

"It's not funny," I snap. "I look ridiculous."

"Nah, not ridiculous. Just really, uh, *blue*. Anyway, the coat doesn't matter. You're going to do great, Ruby. You are. You practiced."

True, I had. Marcy, Amy, and I did a test run on Monday while Pam and Smiley held down the fort. In the end, we did manage to re-create my drawing. It only took us twelve hours.

Colleen shakes her head. "This is unacceptable," she says. "Totally unacceptable."

Just then, there is a knock on the dressing room door. We turn to see a head peek in. A beautifully coiffed, perfectly made-up, smiling blond head. A café au lait *pot de crème* with a scalloped rose of whipped cream and a dark-chocolate-covered espresso bean on top. Cody Armstrong, of course.

"Hi, hi!" she calls cheerfully. "I'm not disturbing y'all, am I?"

"No," I respond automatically. "Not at all."

She pushes farther into the room and we get a gander at her tailored, peach polka-dot chef coat. She is tall—not as tall as Izzy, but almost—and curvy in all the right places. I know she is in her forties—so said *Marie Claire*—but she looks much younger, and I can't tell whether or not she's been surgically enhanced.

She glances at my chef coat and does a double take, then puts her hand out to me. "Ruby, right?"

I shake her hand and nod. "That's right." I gesture toward Izzy, then Colleen. "This is my business partner, Isabelle Medina, and my daughter, Colleen."

Colleen smiles, wide-eyed, and I half expect her to ask

Cody Armstrong for an autograph. Or the name of the cosmetic line she uses.

"It's nice to meet y'all. I just wanted to wish you luck."

"Thank you."

"I remember my first time like it was yesterday. I was so nervous, I almost yakked all over m'kitchen."

What a happy thought, I muse, *especially in light of my recent stomach issues.*

You haven't thrown up in weeks, I remind myself. *Months, even.*

"Well, anyhow, I'll leave you to it. But, listen." She leans into me conspiratorially. "Just stay calm and get your work done. The first time's always vexing. But don't go and think about the judges or the cameras or all those people watching or the clock ticking down. And don't let ol' Tommy Bell intimidate you. He's a mean little thing, truth be told, but he's harmless. Just forget about all the other stuff, and do your work."

I nod wordlessly and she reaches over and squeezes my shoulder. "And remember to have fun!"

She breezes out in a flurry of peach polka dots, and I gaze after her long after the door closes.

"I'll be back in ten minutes," Colleen announces, and leaves.

"I'm gonna check on Marcy and Amy," Izzy tells me, following Colleen.

I wait until the door closes for the third time, then I rush to the little bathroom in the back corner of the dressing room and proceed to *yak* my guts out.

At eight forty-five, there is another knock at the door and a faceless, androgynous voice summons me to the studio. I scrub my teeth for the second time, then do my best to reapply my lipstick and head into the hall. Just as I reach the studio door, Colleen jogs up to me, breathless and flushed, with Kevin trailing her. Clasped in my daughter's hand is a beautiful scarf in shades of teal, lavender, and—yes—blueberry. Without a word, she wraps it around my waist like a sash and ties it in a knot behind my back. I step back for her approval, and although I can't see my reflection, I can tell from the triumphant look on her face that she has made a vast improvement on my appearance.

"Better," she announces. "Not great, but better."

"You're a genius, Col," I tell her.

She beams at me. "Shane's here," she says, "and he brought Annabelle. They left Pelican Point at five o'clock this morning. They've been sitting outside the studio since six, like groupies."

"Yeah, Mom. They made a sign and everything," Kevin adds. "It says 'The Cake Lady Rocks!' They're already in there with Izzy."

Although I know Jacob isn't coming, a part of me had hoped he would show up. But he hasn't called, hasn't reached out to me at all since Saturday, and his silence speaks volumes. For the past four days, I have been immersing myself in my preparation for *Cake-Off*, pretending not to care what happened between us, convincing everyone, including myself, that I am just fine. I've been trying not to think about Jacob's soft-shoe, or the look on his face when he toppled the roulette wheel, or the feel of his hands on my skin, or the amazing sex. I've been telling myself I don't have a broken heart—how could I, when there's no such thing as forever love or happily-ever-after or fairy tales? I've always known that. I just forgot for a little while. With each passing day,

I've put up another layer of bricks, and the walls I tore down just weeks ago are almost rebuilt. Jacob isn't coming. End of story.

But my kids are here. And that's the most important thing.

"Now don't be nervous," Kevin instructs, clutching my hand. "We're gonna be right in the front row. Clapping the loudest."

I smile, touched. "Thanks for everything, guys. I love you silly, you know?"

"We know, Mom," Colleen says.

"Good luck, Mom."

I air-kiss the tops of their heads, so as not to smear my lipstick, then release them and watch them walk down the hall toward the audience's entrance. I stand for a moment, trying to steady my nerves, breathing in and out. Finally, I push through the door of the studio and enter total chaos.

The stage lights are blinding, and I have to shield my eyes from their glare. Dozens of people sporting Food Channel IDs hustle to and fro, some carrying clipboards, others wielding equipment, all of them wearing headsets. A couple of guys are doing a final lighting check. A small battalion of cameramen is stationed around the studio, half with handhelds, half manning cameras on wheels.

Cody Armstrong is already in her kitchen, as is Thomas Bell, both of them being fitted with body mikes. Amy and Marcy are nowhere in sight, and I start to panic until I remember that the assistants stay in the green room until the last moment.

PAs and technicians and makeup personnel pass by, talking into their headsets, and I hear frantic snatches of conversations.

"Bell's mike is out?" says a PA. "Roger that. Joe, we got a problem with Bell's mike! Get a replacement in here, stat! We are at T-minus-twelve."

Another girl scurries by, an intern by the name of Betsy. "She says they're missing but no one knows where they are! No, I don't have any! We don't carry those in the vending machine! Roger. Claire, run to the 7-Eleven and get six PowerBars for Ms. Armstrong, the energy kind, no peanut butter! Me? Ms. Gingrich said? Yes, fine. Right away."

I'm tempted to ask Betsy to grab a few PowerBars for me, but I have lost the ability to speak. I stare around the studio in absolute shock and complete terror. My legs are shaking so badly I dare not move.

The studio is filled to capacity, though most of the assembled are still standing, waiting for instructions from the PA. I squint against the lights and can just make out my personal cheering section: Izzy, Kevin, Colleen, Shane, and Annabelle. They wave at me with maniacal glee, but I can't seem to lift my arm.

In front of the risers, Madeleine Gingrich is talking with the judges, three people I feel like I know for all of the *Cake-Off*s I've watched but never in a million years thought I'd meet in person. And I will meet them—in about eight and a half hours when they rip my cake (and my skills) apart. Candy Vansant, an older woman with impossibly black hair done in her traditional chignon, is laughing at something Madeleine says, while young, hip, celebrity cake maker Aaron Michaels tugs at his earring, looking bored. The third judge, Penelope Peters, wunderkind of the cupcake world, who started the national chain Sweetcakes! at the ripe old age of nineteen, sits on top of the judging table, swinging her shapely legs and making eyes at one of the lighting guys.

"There you are!" Samantha cries, rushing at me like a bull to a red cape. Even her nostrils are flared. "You have to get yourself miked!" She threads her hand though my arm and practically drags me to my kitchen.

We pass Cody, and I read the placard affixed to her counter: CODY ARMSTRONG, COWGIRL CAKES. She winks at me and I nod a response. Thomas Bell's sign says THOMAS BELL, BELL OF THE BALL BAKERY. Thomas, a wiry little man with a receding hairline and a perpetual frown, sniggers when I pass but tries to cover it with a wave.

When we reach Kitchen 3, I am relieved to see that my sign has replaced Ray Hartford's. RUBY McMILLAN, THE MUFFIN TIP.

Wait a minute. I stare at the sign and feel another wave of nausea wash over me. *The Muffin Tip?*

"Um, there's been a mistake," I say, but Samantha will not be stopped. She grasps at my elbow and yanks me along. "My sign. It's supposed to say 'Muffin *Top*.' Not 'Muffin Tip.' There's no such thing as a muffin tip."

"We are at T-minus-eight, Ms. McMillan. We don't have time to mess around."

"But my sign!"

A burly, bearded man by the name of Terry rumbles into the kitchen and sets about attaching a mike. "Wireless," he grunts, pinning it to my chest just above my right boob.

Meanwhile, Samantha rounds the counter and looks at my sign. She glances at her watch and frowns.

"I'm sorry. Nothing we can do now."

"Say something," Terry grumbles.

"What?"

"The camera hardly ever focuses on them anyway," Samantha assures me as she's swept away by another woman holding a clipboard.

"*Say* something. Into your mike," Terry repeats, aggravated.

I clear my throat. "Uh, hello. Hi. My name is—"

"Got it." Terry cuts me off, then abruptly leaves my kitchen.

Perspiration soaks my brow and we haven't even started yet. I reach into the pocket of my chef pants and withdraw a tissue to dab at my forehead. I stare helplessly out at the audience and motion to Izzy. She sees me and I jab a finger at the sign. Her expression goes from calm to irate in less than a second. She points to the PAs running around and I shake my head and hold up my watch. She immediately rises from her seat, scoots to the aisle, and steps onto the studio floor. A PA approaches her, but Izzy bats the girl away dismissively. She stomps toward my kitchen, and I swear I can feel each of her steps, like the impact tremors from a T. rex.

"What the fuck is this?" she demands.

"They don't have time to change it," I croak.

"How are people supposed to know to get a cake from the Muffin Top if it doesn't say 'the Muffin Top'? *Chingadera!*"

"Uh, excuse me, you're not allowed to be here." Samantha stares up at Izzy with her hands on her hips.

Izzy ignores the PA, just squints at the sign with a murderous look on her face. In the next instant, she shoves her hand into her bag and rummages around, producing a black Magic Marker. She kneels down and starts drawing on the sign, to Samantha's utter amazement.

"You can't do that!" Samantha shrieks, frantically looking around for help.

"The hell I can't!" Izzy fires back. After a moment she stands and smiles victoriously. "There. Good enough."

Samantha grabs the nearest man she can get hold of and pulls him to my kitchen. "Get her out of here."

The man looks up at Izzy—she's got at least four inches on him—and opens his mouth to say something.

"*No preocupes*, big guy," Izzy tells him. She heads back to the audience, sashaying her formidable hips. Luckily, she doesn't knock down a camera on her way.

I move around the kitchen and gaze at my sign. Izzy has made the I into a messy O, but it very clearly reads THE MUFFIN TOP.

Just then, Marcy and Amy make their way to the kitchen. Marcy is totally at ease, but Amy looks like a deer in headlights. The lemon-yellow chef coats flatter neither of them, but with me in my giant blueberry costume, who am I to talk?

"Hi, guys," I say, managing to sound cool and calm despite the fact that I am anything but. "You ready?"

They both nod, but only Marcy smiles. Amy's mouth is tight.

A voice sounds from the loudspeaker. "All right, everyone. Competitors, in your kitchens. We are T-minus-two minutes to go!"

A young kid, probably Shane's age, with a tattoo of a snake creeping up his neck and a shock of bleached, spiked hair, approaches my kitchen, carrying a handheld camera.

"Hi, ladies, I'm Carter," he says in a surprisingly cultured voice. "You're mine today. I'm going to be in your faces a lot, but I want you to try and relax and act natural, like I'm not even here. Okay?"

He hoists the camera onto his shoulder for a test shot. I almost pee in my pants right there and then.

"You okay, Ruby?" Marcy stations herself beside me while Amy moves as far back as the kitchen allows.

"Couldn't be better," I squeak. "You?"

"Well, I kinda wish my hair matched my chef coat," she jokes. "But other than that, I'm groovy."

I give her a sideways glance. "Aren't you nervous?"

"I was, but then I dropped some acid and now I'm tripping." I gasp and she giggles. "Kidding! I'd never do that kind of Shostakovich." (Marcy-speak for "shit.") "But this is the bee's knees, you know? Being on TV. Like, who'd ever thought? It's like a roller-coaster ride. Some people don't like 'em, but I do!"

"I don't like roller coasters," I say. "I can never catch my breath. Kind of like right now."

"Hey, Ruby-dooby-doo," Marcy says, pressing her hand against mine. "You know cake. That's what this is about. Making a cake. Simple. I know you're a good mom, and a good person, blah di blah di blah. But you're *great* at cake. It's your gift. You love cake. So just forget about all this other bull crap, and make a whama bama fantabulama cake."

I give her hand a squeeze. "Okay. Thanks, Marcy."

I glance back at Amy, who is pretending to arrange the tools we arranged yesterday.

"Is she okay?"

"She pukey-vanookied," Marcy whispers with a shrug. "You probably should have given her one of your Depends."

24

Spotted Dick

"Hi, everyone, I'm your host, Jaimie Hall. Welcome to *Cake-Off*."

The raven-haired beauty-queen-turned-chef walks along the perimeter of the studio, trailed by a camera. Blood rushes through my brain so loudly that I'm having trouble hearing.

Madeleine instructed me to hold still during the introductions, and I have to steel myself against the counter to keep from shaking. A drop of sweat falls from my forehead to my chin, but I don't dare swipe at it.

"Tonight we have three top cake designers competing for fifteen thousand dollars!" Jaimie Hall continues. "The theme? Fairy-Tale Romance Cakes! Let's meet our competitors!" She stops in front of Cody Armstrong. "In Kitchen One, we have the *Cake-Off* grand champion and owner of Cowgirl Cakes in Austin, Texas, Cody Armstrong!"

The crowd goes wild.

"In Kitchen Two," she says, making her way to Thomas Bell, "our second-most-winning competitor and owner of Bell of the Ball Cakes in Boca Raton, Florida, Thomas Bell."

The crowd goes wild.

She reaches my kitchen. "And, competing for the first time, owner of the Muffin Top Bakery in Pelican Point, California, Ruby McMillan."

My little section of the audience goes wild. I, however, do not go wild. I tinkle into my underwear.

Smile, Ruby. Wave. Do something!

Suddenly I raise my hand into the air and pump my fist.

Where the heck did that come from?

But the audience seems to love it and a new round of applause erupts. I can't help but smile.

Jaimie moves toward the judges' table, still talking.

"Our competitors have eight hours to create amazing cakes that will wow our judges. But we have a little surprise for them tonight."

My heart stops in my chest at Jaimie Hall's words. A surprise. Tonight. I'd been hoping there would be no surprises because they are *never* a good thing on *Cake-Off*. I'm going to have enough trouble getting through this *without* any surprises.

"But that's for later. For now, let's get started. Competitors, are you ready?"

I turn toward the other kitchens to see Cody Armstrong in One, smiling confidently and without a single bead of perspiration on her face. (Is she even human?) Thomas Bell is nodding like he's got this in the bag. Their eyes meet and each tips an imaginary hat to the other, as if to say, *It's on.* They don't even glance in my direction, which really pisses me off.

"I'm ready to kick some butt, Jaimie," I announce, surprised by the strength of my voice. Apparently, Cody and Thomas are surprised as well. They both glance over at me questioningly.

"You go, Ruby," I hear Marcy whisper behind me.

"Those're fighting words," Jaimie jokingly improvises. "I like that. May I have eight hours on the clock, please?"

All of us—designers, assistants, production staff, and

audience—look up at the enormous digital clock on the wall of the studio. It reads: 8:00.

"Your *Cake-Off* starts NOW!" Jaimie says.

With my heart pounding, I head for the back of the kitchen. As planned, Amy, Marcy, and I heft the base from the storage area to the workstation. The board is three feet square and has a forty-inch PVC pipe mounted in the middle. Glancing over at the other kitchens, I notice that both of my competitors have very complicated-looking bases, with pipes and armature cropping up from all over their boards.

Do not look at the other kitchens! I tell myself.

After positioning the base, the three of us powwow in the corner next to the fondant roller, and I look at my extremely detailed checklist, trying to ignore my shaking hand.

"You both know what you have to do?" I ask.

Marcy nods. Amy looks stricken.

"It's all here, if you forget," I say. "Marcy in red, Amy in blue, Ruby in black. Just like we worked out. Call for help if you need it. Mark off every task as you complete it. Okay?"

"Aye aye, Captain."

"Amy? You okay?"

Amy says nothing. Marcy slings an arm around her shoulder and squeezes her. "She'll be fine. She's a pro."

Amy gives Marcy a grateful look.

"I'm good," she says.

"I'm scared out of my wits," I confess. "But we're here for the Muffin Top. So let's make a great cake!"

The girls nod at me and each of us springs into action. Half an hour later, I lose my mind.

Which is a good thing, really. The first thirty minutes are hell, with Marcy and Amy and me trying to get into a groove, almost tripping over each other, and crashing into Carter, who is, as promised, in our faces with every move we make. But after a shaky start, as I begin to cut into my cakes and frost them, as my design starts to take shape, the cameras, the audience, the studio, my competitors, the judges . . . everything falls away and I enter my zone.

The broken cakes are not a problem today, since I've had to cut into them anyway. My design for Princess Mayblossom is a montage of the story. The tower is the central focus, climbing four feet into the air. The base of the tower leads down into several tiered layers, each of them representing another element of the story—Princess Mayblossom's adventures. The tiered cakes lead to the base, a sandy beach representing the island.

While Marcy works on the base—the island—and Amy colors white chocolate, I busily frost rounds, cover them with fondant, and stack them along the PVC pipe. Everything takes time, but we are on schedule. Though I have resolved not to look at the other kitchens, I can't help but glance at the clock every so often.

As Marcy finishes the island, I carry over the last of the tiered cakes and step onto the step stool to reach the top of the PVC pipe. Just as I am about to ease the pipe through the bottom of my cake, Candy Vansant appears at the counter. I jerk with surprise and my index finger tears through my beautiful fondant. Crap. The judges are sticklers for clean lines and castigate competitors if their work is less than pristine. Especially Candy Vansant. I'll have to re-cover this tier, I think, annoyed.

"That looks like it's going to be a tower," she says slowly, narrowing her eyes at the pipe. I freeze, not wanting her to see the tear.

"The top is," I say in a strangled whisper. This is the first time I've spoken to her, or any of the judges, for that matter.

"Might it be Rapunzel?"

"No," I answer, knowing the judges don't see the designs before the competition. "Not Rapunzel." The muscles in my arms start to spasm.

Go away!

"Hmm. Well, it's early yet, but so far your work looks fine." High praise from Candy Vansant. Thankfully, she strolls off toward Kitchen 2. I gulp some air and lower my arms, bringing the tiered cake with me. Then I head for the fondant machine to start over.

Television viewers don't know it, but every two hours, the producers stop the clock and the contestants are given a ten-minute break. Apparently, it's an insurance mandate, instigated during the first season of *Cake-Off* after one of the contestants fainted from exhaustion. When the first break comes, I practically fall to my knees with relief. I don't think I have ever worked so hard or with such intensity in my entire life.

A crewmember drags over three stools for us, and Marcy quickly grabs some of my special muffins and some water bottles from the fridge. Amy, who looks totally drained, flops down on one of the stools. I perch on mine, keeping my feet on the ground, afraid that if I relax too much, I'll never stand up again. Marcy stretches and does a set of jumping jacks and looks as fresh and energetic as when we started. Ah, youth.

As I nibble at my muffin, I glance at the cake. The tower isn't finished, the entire base is still uncovered, and we haven't even begun working on the finer details like Princess

Mayblossom, the Ambassador, the Prince, and all of the decorations that tell the story—the honeycomb, the rose, the oak tree, etc. I'd thought we were in good shape, but there is so much left to do, and only six hours left.

I allow myself a glimpse at my competitors' kitchens and am relieved to see that they are not much further along than me. Thomas Bell has constructed a staircase on his base, but the armature on either side is still bare. Cody Armstrong has erected what looks like a castle, but as of now, it is merely a large gray rectangle with no distinguishing features. A squat ball of cake sits on the front of the base, naked, and I have no idea what she intends it to be.

"How are you guys holding up?" I ask the girls.

Amy gives me a tentative thumbs-up. Marcy, who still hasn't sat down, smiles wide. "Okeydokey, artichokey."

The same crewmember appears in the kitchen and Amy and I stand, relinquishing our stools. He deftly whisks all three away. Five seconds later, the clock resumes.

And we're off!

I run my smoothing tool over the gray fondant that covers the tower when Jaimie Hall saunters into my kitchen, her cameraman in tow.

"Is it true that tomorrow's your birthday, Ruby?" she says into her mike. "Winning *Cake-Off* would be a great birthday present, wouldn't it?"

"It would," I reply absently as my fingers tuck a stray piece of fondant under the edge of the cake.

"I understand your bakery, the Muffin Top, has fallen on hard times lately."

I freeze, a grimace forming on my face, and I summon my internal grimace-smoother. "Um . . ."

"And you're here today to try and get your business back on track. Is that right?"

Gulp. I force myself to keep working and attempt a casual tone. "I'm here to make the best cake I can, Jaimie," I say evenly.

"Good for you," she returns, then flashes the camera a conspiratorial grin and slinks away.

Time elapsed: three hours fifty-nine minutes and fifty-eight seconds. Fifty-nine seconds. Four hours.

The buzzer sounds and I carefully lay the Princess Mayblossom figure I've been sculpting down on the counter. The stools reappear, but I bypass them and head for the bathroom in the back of the studio. My feet throb despite the sneakers Colleen begrudgingly allowed me to wear, and I have the beginnings of a headache right at the base of my skull. I would kill for an Advil. On top of everything, the Depends I'm wearing has started to chafe my upper thighs.

We're halfway through, and just about now I'm wondering how the heck I'm going to make it. I've pulled all-day jobs, even all-nighters, but never like this, with the cameras and the lights and the running commentary of a host who I have decided is a sadistic fruitcake despite her coquettish manner and two other cake designers who are so at ease that they actually joke with each other from their respective kitchens. I keep telling myself that I have nothing to prove to them, but the way they dismiss me, as though I'm not even here, makes me want to prove my worth, and the added pressure is getting to me.

At the bathroom sink, I take a moment to splash cold water on my face, unconcerned with what that will do to my makeup. At this point, my makeup is the least of my worries.

I gaze at myself in the mirror, and to my surprise, I don't look as bedraggled as I'd feared. Okay, so my mascara has run a bit and some strands of hair have come loose from my ponytail, but my eyes are bright and my cheeks arc flushed and I look truly alive and in the moment. Of course, another person might say I look like I'm on the verge of a coronary, but I'm trying to be positive.

I check my watch and quickly head for a stall, then set about the task of removing my chef pants. I cannot stay in these Depends a moment longer or my upper thighs will be rubbed raw. And since I have gotten somewhat used to the entire hubbub of the show, I am confident I no longer need them.

I make it back to my kitchen with just enough time to take a long swig of water. The buzzer sounds and Jaimie Hall takes her place in front of the judges' table. The clock remains frozen.

"All right, competitors. It's time for your surprise," Jaimie says dramatically. "Are you ready?"

I glance over at Thomas and Cody. Thomas looks bored. Cody looks excited. I am neither bored nor excited. I am numb.

"As you know, our theme for this *Cake-Off* is fairy-tale romance. And we've come up with the perfect way to inspire our designers to make the most romantic cakes they can. We're bringing in some very special people to help you finish—people in your lives who prove that true love really can be like a fairy tale."

What?

"May I have a spotlight, please?" Jaimie says, and a moment later a light shines down on the front center aisle of the audience. "To help Cody Armstrong, in kitchen number one, please welcome Cody's husband, Zachary Armstrong!"

I hear Cody squeal with delight as a trim, dark-haired man steps into the spotlight. The audience applauds for a moment, then he steps down onto the stage floor and heads for Cody's kitchen.

"And, for Thomas Bell, in Kitchen Two, his partner of eleven years, Christian Cole."

Another man, painfully thin and blushing from ear to ear, steps into the spotlight, waving shyly at the camera. Thomas Bell lets out a guffaw and crosses his arms over his chest as Christian Cole makes his way to Kitchen 2.

A lightbulb goes off in my head. It all makes sense now. Jacob *is* here! He's been here the whole time, waiting in the wings for his grand entrance. He probably hasn't been in touch because he was afraid he'd give away the surprise. I'll bet he and the producers and Izzy worked it all out. I smile in anticipation of seeing him, mentally forgiving him for his sudden disappearance now that I know the reason.

He's going to look so good on camera . . .

"And for Ruby McMillan, in Kitchen Three, please welcome Ruby's husband of eighteen years, Walter McMillan!"

My smile freezes on my face.

What the fuck?

After two and a half months of no communication, after dumping me and abandoning our family and sailing off around the world with *Cheryl,* Walter steps into the spotlight wearing a mauve polo shirt and grinning like an idiot. In the next second, Colleen and Kevin jump out of their seats and rush at him, hugging him tight. He laughs and embraces them and I suddenly feel like my heart is trapped in a vise grip. I glance at Izzy, who is gaping at Walter, just as surprised as I am. She turns to me, her eyes wide, and mouths the words *I'll kill him!*

"Wow!" Jaimie Hall cries. "That's a lot of love! You'd

think they hadn't seen each other in ages! Come on, kids, let him go. Your dad has work to do."

The kids release Walter and he steps down to the stage floor. As he heads toward my kitchen, I am surprised by how good he looks. He is tanned and trim and full of energy, the lines on his face somehow diminished. But more than that, he looks familiar to me, like an old pair of comfortable pajamas I'd forgotten I owned, but which I can't wait to try on again.

Remember what he did to you, Ruby, I warn myself.

"You okay, Ruby?" Marcy whispers from the back of the kitchen.

I don't answer because I'm not sure. Walter is four feet away, three feet, two. He stands on the other side of the counter, smiling at me. I am a mass of conflicting emotions, can't decide whether I want to clobber him to death with my rolling pin or throw my arms around him.

"Hi, Ruby."

"Hi, Walter."

"This is amazing," he says sincerely. "I'm so proud of you."

"How—how did they find you?" I ask, still in shock.

"Facebook," he replies.

"All right, competitors," Jaimie Hall says. "Your significant others will be in your kitchens helping you for the remainder of the competition, and that means that you will have to choose one of your assistants to stay, and one to go."

There are audible sighs throughout the studio. I tear my eyes off Walter and turn to Marcy and Amy. I shake my head despairingly. How am I supposed to choose? I mean, I know this doesn't have the gravity of, say, *Sophie's Choice,* but still. Marcy has been effective today, and she and I have a rhythm. At the same time I don't want to crush Amy, who has overcome her fear and worked so hard

After a brief hesitation, Amy steps forward. "It's okay, Ruby. I'll go. It's better if Marcy stays."

Marcy takes a step forward, too. "But Amy has more training than me. She should stay."

"But Marcy is better at working with you because she's your employee."

"But Amy wants to be a chef, and if you win, she can put this on her résumé."

"Competitors, we are thirty seconds to 'Go!' Please make your decisions."

"Seriously, Marcy. You're better at this. You stay."

Marcy looks at Amy, then shrugs. I reach out and grab Amy's hand and give it a squeeze. "I can't thank you enough for all you've done today."

"It's been an experience. But I think I'll leave the TV chefing to Mr. Macaroni." Amy smiles and walks out of the kitchen at the same time as the assistants from the other two kitchens leave their stations. The audience applauds them. Walter takes his cue from Carter the cameraman and steps into my kitchen. He looks around for a moment, then comes up beside me at the counter.

Marcy moves to my other side and plants her hands on her hips. She glares at Walter shamelessly.

"I can cut off his jewels with my carving knife," she hisses.

"What did you say?" Carter exclaims from behind his camera.

"I was asking about the princess's jewels," Marcy says sweetly. "We haven't gotten to them yet, but I can cut them out of fondant."

"Right," Carter says disbelievingly.

"Okay, Ruby," Walter says. "Where do you want me?"

This is more than I can wrap my mind around. It's too surreal. Walter. Here. Walter helping me. Walter working with me in my Food Channel kitchen. All the times I imagined my first post-*Cheryl* meeting with Walter—for which I had a very good speech planned—it never involved a nationally broadcast competition in which the odds against me are already stacked higher than a six-tiered wedding cake. This isn't like a fairy tale. This is like a nightmare. This is like *The Texas Chainsaw Massacre* in 3-D. A sheen of sweat covers my face.

I've got to get myself together. I glance around nervously, my mind blank. I notice that my competitors have already fallen back into a groove, likely because neither one of them has been estranged from their significant others for the past three months. Meanwhile, precious seconds are being swallowed up while I flounder. I grab my list and start scanning it, trying to figure out what Walter can do. I breathe in and out a few times, then turn to Marcy.

"You keep going with the tower. We've got to get that done, and I still have to finish the figures."

"What about me?" Walter asks. "Just tell me what to do. I'm all yours."

I flinch at his choice of words. "Since when?"

Walter's eyes dart to Carter, then back to me. "Look, I know we have a lot to discuss. But we'll have plenty of time for that later. Right now you have a cake to finish."

"Clock's ticking," Marcy says meaningfully.

Marcy is right and so is Walter (damn him). I don't have time for my personal issues. I have to push them aside. I have to remember everything that's brought me to this moment, and let it all go. Be present. Go with the flow. Roll with it. Paint on a smile and do what I do best.

"Okay, Walter. You process the wafers for the sand."

"I'm on it."

I thrust the checklist at him. "It's all there," I say. "Get going!"

For a while, everything is fine. Walter quickly falls in step with me, capably executing each task I bark at him. Despite our separation, we have a shorthand that comes in handy right now, and I am thankful for all the times he helped me in the kitchen. He creates vanilla-wafer sand and piles it in a stainless-steel bowl, then moves on to the fondant, kneading color into the dough. Marcy works like a madwoman, her focus laserlike, as she traces stone patterns on the tower, giving it definition and character. I work on the Ambassador, trying to get his uniform just right. Princess Mayblossom is finished and looks fantastic—if I do say so myself. She watches me from her perch on the counter.

Walter is the Ambassador, she tells me. *You know that, right?*

Uh-oh. My white chocolate figurine is talking to me. The pressure of the competition has finally gotten to me.

Jacob's your prince, she says.

"But Jacob's not here," I say aloud.

"You need something, Ruby?" Walter asks.

I shake my head and try to concentrate on the Ambassador.

Jacob's not here. Walter's here, I tell myself.

This isn't about Walter or Jacob. This is about saving the Muffin Top! Just keep working!

And I do. And slowly but surely, my cake comes to life. Then everything falls apart.

It happens so quickly, I think I'm hallucinating. We're in the middle of hour seven. My feet feel like two boats that have run aground. Every joint in my hands ache and I am having trouble holding my tools. The protein shake Marcy forced upon me during the last break is sloshing around in my stomach, making me nauseous. All in all, I feel like crap. But at least the cake looks great. The large elements are finished and we have moved into the final phase: the details.

Walter melts the isomalt, waiting for it to reach the proper temperature, when he will color it blue for the ocean. He stirs slowly and whistles a tune I recognize—"People"—which was the first song we danced to at our wedding. I glance at him sharply, certain he's trying to manipulate me, but he is completely oblivious to everything except the isomalt.

While Marcy carefully unmolds the brittle fairy bodies, made with poured sugar of various colors, I go to work on the spun sugar that will form their wings. As I swirl a fork of the hot liquid over a Silpat, creating little whorls of sugar threads, Penelope Peters bebops into my kitchen, her four-inch heels clacking against the floor.

"Those're pretty," she coos. She is in her midtwenties now, but she still seems like a teenager. "What're they gonna be, huh?"

"Fairy wings," I say.

Penelope has graced us with her presence three times during the competition. Candy Vansant, seven. Aaron Michaels, not at all, as he prefers to sit at the judges' table, covertly texting on his iPhone when the camera isn't focused on him.

"I just *love* your technique," Penelope says theatrically. "For a newbie, you totally do not suck."

This is the CEO of Sweetcakes!? Lord help us all.

She sashays out of the kitchen and I try not to roll my eyes.

I finish with the wings and drag them to the far side of the counter to cool, then grab a tub of piping gel and a brush.

"I'm going to pour the sand next," I tell Marcy.

"This is the last one," she says, indicating the mold.

I approach the cake and notice that the honeycomb on the second tier is pulling away from the fondant and is about to fall off. I climb the step stool to inspect it more closely. Gently, I press my index finger against it. Since Marcy is in the middle of the most delicate part of her task, I call Walter.

"Walter. Bring me the royal icing. Quick!"

He hurries over with the bag and watches as I make the repair. Holding the honeycomb in place, I sniff the air and detect a strong burning smell. I jerk my head toward the stove. Unattended, the isomalt bubbles over the side of the pan.

"Walter! The isomalt!" I shriek.

Suddenly everything switches to slow motion, and I become an inconsequential observer, an audience member watching the event unfold with no power to alter it. Walter rushes to the stove and grabs for the handle of the pan just as Marcy crosses with the tray of fairies. He swings around in a panic, bumping into Marcy, who goes flying, her tray hurtling through the air. And suddenly Walter realizes that the pan handle is hot, broiling hot, melt-your-skin hot, and he doesn't have a pot holder, and he reflexively drops the pan and the bubbling isomalt spills onto the floor. Marcy, who is trying to right herself, steps right in the gooey sugar, and her foot slip-slides out from under her. She crashes to the floor into a crumpled heap while Walter's howl of pain echoes through the studio.

Carter rushes around the counter, his camera recording every detail of the destruction in my kitchen. There is complete silence throughout the studio. I gape in horror, completely immobile, even as Carter swings the camera toward me and focuses on my face.

"Oh!" Marcy cries, and her single syllable jolts me into action. I climb down the step stool and kneel beside her, steering clear of the blazing trail of isomalt. I help her to her feet, supporting her with my arms. Walter hurries over, cradling his right hand, grasping Marcy's elbow with his left.

"Are you okay?" I ask her.

She smiles sheepishly. "Right as rain, kimosabe. No worries."

It's only after she puts weight on her ankle that we discover she is not, in fact, right as rain. She nearly collapses again, and we struggle to hold her up. Her face contorts with pain, and Carter moves in for a close-up.

"Back off!" I snap at him. I search the sea of faces surrounding my kitchen; the crewmembers, PAs, Jaimie Hall, Candy Vansant, and Penelope Peters. "Someone get her a stool!"

Walter's lips are white with tension. I glance at his hand.

"And a medic!" I add frantically.

I look toward Kitchens 1 and 2 and see that the other chefs have resumed their work. This is *Cake-Off,* after all. No points—or money—for second place.

Jaimie Hall turns to her camera and begins speaking in low tones as a crewmember hauls in a stool. "This is a disastrous turn of events for Ruby McMillan in Kitchen Three. If she loses both of her assistants, she'll have to finish her cake by herself. And with just over an hour left on the clock, that may prove impossible."

My heart pounds as I help Marcy to the stool. I bend down and tug at the hem of her jeans, lifting it to her calf. Her right ankle is swollen to the size of a grapefruit.

"Oh, Marcy," I exclaim, shaking my head. "That must hurt like hell." I stand and turn to Walter. "Let me see your hand."

"It's nothing," he says through gritted teeth. I grasp at his sleeve and pull his hand away from his chest, then carefully open his fingers to reveal bright pink blisters on his palm. He flinches at my touch.

"I'm sorry, Ruby," he says quietly.

"It's not your fault. I called you away from the stove—"

"It *is* my fault." He gives me a meaningful look and I realize his apology covers far more than the isomalt. "I'm so sorry."

Before I can respond, two medics hurry into the kitchen, one heading for Walter, the other for Marcy. I stand and step away, allowing them to work. A crewmember cautiously enters with rags and a scraping tool, gets down on his hands and knees, and begins to clean up the mess. The clock keeps ticking.

It's official. Both of my assistants are gone. And since the rules are clear about no substitutions, Amy can only watch worriedly from the wings. Marcy and Walter have been carted off to the local hospital for X-rays and burn assessment respectively, and I am in my kitchen, alone. Less than an hour is left in the competition.

The judges and Jaimie Hall and even Carter the cameraman are giving me a wide berth. I'd like to think they are being considerate, but more likely they are afraid of me. There are no mirrors in the kitchen, but I know how I look: like a Tasmanian devil on speed. Whatever remained of my makeup has been wiped clean by the waves of sweat gushing down my face. Half of my hair has come loose from my ponytail, and the strands that are not plastered to my cheeks stand straight out like I've been struck by lightning. But I don't have time, not to sip water, not to go over my checklist, not to take a breath, and certainly not to pull my hair back.

I no longer have illusions about winning. I just want to finish my cake. I work as quickly as I can, but the faster I go, the sloppier my work becomes, and I have to keep redoing things. My head is swimming. I want to throw up. My eyes are nearly crossed with fatigue. My hands shake. The wings break off the fairies; I have to reset them. The Ambassador falls into the sand as I place him on the rocky cliff. I have to carefully brush him off without marring his features. I put too much piping gel on the honeycomb and it drips on one of my tiers. One of the oak branches—the one offering the milk—bends backward when I bump into the counter. There isn't enough isomalt to cover the perimeter of my base. The graham-cracker crumbs are too dark. The Prince's hair is too light. The fondant on the bottom cake is cracking. Only two fairies survived impact, and the LED wires I inserted into them are showing. The coat of arms won't stay in place.

I cannot do this!

I stop suddenly and the bag of icing slips from my claw-like grasp. My throat constricts and my vision blurs and I'm afraid I am going to faint. Because the truth has just slammed into me like a Mack truck.

I have no business being here. I shouldn't have agreed to do this, not even for the sake of my precious shop. A sane person would never have done this. A sane person would have accepted her limitations, politely declined, and moved on. This show, this whole *Cake-Off* competition, is a dream, a fantasy, a golden rocket ship designed for those who dare to reach for the stars, not those who merely reach for recipes. I may be able to jump a handsome man in my kitchen when my kids are out of the house, but I am still, at heart, a middle-aged woman who only goes after achievable goals and doesn't dream at all. Who was I kidding thinking I could come here and take home the gold and save the Muffin Top? I'm not a superhero. Despite the past few months of shaking things up in my life, I am, at heart, Rational Ruby.

I think about walking away. It wouldn't be the first time a competitor has thrown in the towel. I've watched it happen.

My legs twitch with the anticipation of movement.

No one would blame me after having lost both my assistants. *Walk away,* I tell myself. *Be* rational. *You cannot finish this cake alone. Why kill yourself trying?*

I take a breath and push back from the counter, looking at the floor, at the lights, at the stove, at anything but my cake. I turn around and take a step. Another, and another. One more step and I'll be free.

Be strong, be smart, but try to believe. My mother's voice echoes through my head, clear as a bell. I vacillate at the back of my kitchen. I don't want to hear my mother's voice, her words. They make me feel small. How can I believe in everything, when I don't believe in myself?

Sure you do, Ruby. Especially when it comes to cakes.

Be strong, be smart, but try to believe.

Oh, Mom!

I want so badly to run for the exit, to step out into the muggy September day, to shuck this whole competition, categorize it as a mistake, and shelve it. But something keeps me frozen in place. A single thought. A simple question. *What then?*

I'm anticipating a stressipe, but none comes. And then, out of nowhere, as I stare at the stove of my kitchen, with my feet throbbing and my hands aching and every muscle from the base of my neck to my ankles crying out in pain, my mother's lovely soprano fills my head. And she's singing "Climb Every Mountain."

The absurdity of the made-for-cable-movie-moment strikes me and I can't help but burst out laughing. I double over as tears of hysteria stream down my face. My laughter is like a release of all the pent-up tension from the past few months and the past few years—perhaps from my whole life. I laugh until I'm gasping for air, until my stomach seizes, until my whole body quakes like an aftershock.

When at last I regain control of myself, I stand up straight and look around the studio. Carter kneels beside me, wide-eyed behind his camera. Cody Armstrong and Thomas Bell stare at me as though I've gone completely insane. Their assistants scurry around them, trying not to glance in my direction. The three judges gawk at me, along with the crew and the various PAs. Samantha has dropped her clipboard but seems not to notice. Jaimie Hall whispers into her microphone. "Ruby McMillan has finally broken under the pressure of *Cake-Off*. Let's see what happens now."

I wipe the tears from my cheeks and take a deep breath.

"Okay, Mom," I say. "I hear you."

I glance up at the clock. Twenty-nine minutes left. Without acknowledging anyone else in the room, I walk back to my cake and pick up the bag of royal icing. Two seconds later, I'm at work. Ten seconds later I'm immersed.

And quietly humming "My Favorite Things."

25

Icing on the Cake

I awaken Friday morning in my room at the Marriott and groan. I am officially forty-four. For the record, I don't feel forty-four. I feel a hundred and four. My kids, along with Izzy, Marcy, and Amy, surround the bed and sing "Happy Birthday" to me, then present me with a bran muffin with a candle in the center. I push myself up against the headrest and try to ignore the chain reaction of pain that burns through my entire body.

I haven't made a wish on a birthday candle since I was five. But this morning, it seems appropriate that I do. I close my eyes, muster up a wish, then blow out the candle. Colleen and Kevin sit beside me on the bed.

"What did you wish for?" Colleen asks.

"Painkillers," I tell her, and everyone laughs.

"You can borrow some of mine," Marcy says. She leans on her crutches and smiles. "They are abso-tively, poso-lutely the bomb."

"Thanks, Marcy, but I think I'll stick with Advil."

"You better get moving, Rube," Izzy says with a nudge. "Taping starts in half an hour."

I glance at the digital clock by the bed, which reads 9:30, and realize I've slept twelve hours. The last time I slept twelve straight hours was . . . never? I groan again. "The Food Channel is manned by a bunch of sadists."

"At least you get to be sitting down today."

"Do you think they could send a wheelchair over?" This gets another laugh.

"You did great yesterday, Mom," Colleen says, patting my leg over the bedcovers.

"I didn't win."

"Only because Cody Armstrong's pumpkin carriage spun around the castle," Kevin says. "Your cake rocked."

"You came in second," Colleen reminds me. "And the judges totally loved you."

I smile, thinking of Candy Vansant's rare praise: *Well, Ruby, I have to say that I have never seen a first-time competitor accomplish what you did, nor has any competitor overcome what you managed to overcome during this competition. You have proven yourself to be quite a contender.*

A contender. I like that.

"We're all going to head back," Izzy says. "But the kids and I will have pizza waiting for you for when you get home. Unless you'd rather go out?"

I shake my head. "Home sounds great."

She nods. "I'll make margaritas."

The kids get up as I push back the covers. I glance at Marcy, with her crutches and her cast. "Wait. How are all of you going to fit in the Camry?"

Colleen and Kevin exchange a worried glance. "Uh, Dad's going to give us a ride," Kevin says. "He's waiting in the lobby."

I feel a little stab at my heart.

"He wants to talk with us," Colleen adds. "Explain things, I guess."

I take a deep breath. "Okay." What else can I say?

Kevin shrugs and puts his hands in his pockets. "He's not with Cheryl anymore."

"I sort of figured that when he showed up yesterday."

"*Pinche chingadera,*" Izzy growls.

"Izzy!"

"What? They don't know what it means."

I laugh and push myself to my feet. "Go on. Get out of here. I'll see you guys later."

"What about your makeup?" Colleen asks.

"Your dad's waiting, honey. You go ahead. I'll be okay." She looks disappointed, so I give her hand a squeeze. "Just this time. Plus, they've got a makeup gal at the studio, in case I screw up."

I kiss the kids and they file out with Marcy and Amy. Izzy is the last to go.

"So, call us when you hit the off-ramp and I'll order the food."

"I will," I promise.

She glances at the bag of equipment by the closet. "What's that?"

"Food Channel can't deliver the pallet until Tuesday, what with the holiday. I took some things I need for the weekend."

"You want me to drop it at the Top?" she asks.

"I'll make a quick stop on my way home." I know that if I let Izzy put away my tools, I might never see any of them again. She nods and heads for the door.

"Hey, Iz," I call to her. "Sorry about the fifteen grand."

"Don't you worry about a thing, Ruby. Everything's gonna be fine."

"How do you know?"

"Mama told me. And you know Mama. She's got the eye."

I smile at my best friend. "Love you, Iz."

"Love you, too, Ruby. Happy birthday."

* * *

The *Cake-Off* postmortem goes off without a hitch. Cody Armstrong is my new BFF, having been properly impressed with my work. Her effusive praise during our breaks counterbalances Thomas Bell's decidedly chilly attitude toward me—apparently, he doesn't like coming in third. At the craft services table over coffee and sandwiches, Cody tells me all about her ranch in Texas, her six dogs, and her husband's secret dream of being a rodeo clown, and I tell her about Walter and Jacob and my trials and tribulations over the past three months. At the end of the day, we exchange e-mail addresses and phone numbers, and promise to keep in touch.

By five thirty, I'm back on the 405, dealing with the heavy Friday-afternoon traffic. Ordinarily, I would use the time to think, to analyze Walter's return, the Muffin Top's future, even the Jacob disaster. I would try to come up with practical game plans to deal with each situation. But not today. Instead, I crank up the Coldplay CD Colleen loaned me and let the music wash over me.

An hour later, I see the sign for the Pelican Point off-ramp, and although I've been in a mindless fugue state until now, I can't help but think of the last time I was on this stretch of freeway, with Jacob, on our way home from Santa Barbara. I quickly push the thought aside and reach for my cell phone.

"Happy birthday!" Izzy chirps by way of answering.

I laugh. "I'm about fifteen minutes out. Just a quick stop at the bakery and I'll be home."

"The margaritas are waiting," she says.

"You're the best."

"Don't I know it."

I disconnect, take the off-ramp, and slowly drive through

the center of town. Restaurants are bustling at the start of Labor Day weekend, their outdoor seating areas filled to bursting. Even from inside the van, I can tell that people are in a celebratory mood.

Minutes later, I ease to the curb in front of the darkened bakery. With my bag of tools in hand, I trudge to the entrance, my legs protesting painfully with each step. I turn my key in the lock and push through the front door, the jangling bells accosting my ears. But when I move to the keypad on the wall, I see that the alarm is still in disarm mode.

"Smiley!" I gripe, annoyed at his forgetfulness. I drop the bag at my feet.

"Did you call me?"

I nearly jump out of my skin as the lights in the Muffin Top go on.

"SURPRISE!!!"

Crowded into my exhibition kitchen stand at least thirty people holding drinks and noisemakers and sharing space with dozens of balloons, streamers, and a huge banner that reads HAPPY BIRTHDAY, CAKE LADY! Izzy and Colleen and Kevin stand in front, flanked by my staff: Marcy, Pam, and Smiley. Marcy is perched on a stool and looks a little buzzed. Also present are my students and Shane's niece Annabelle. Miriam and Ted are by the display case, Miriam looking absolutely breathtaking in a low-cut peasant dress. The kids' friends are here, too: Rachael and Zoe, Luke and Billy. Ida Sheerborne from next door beams at me, clapping her hands together. Even CeeCee Braddock-Jones has made an appearance, along with her husband, George. The counter is covered with brightly wrapped presents.

I am stunned and speechless. I smile and throw my arms wide. And as my children and Izzy come toward me for an embrace, the crowd shifts and I can just make out the familiar crown of brown hair, in the back of the kitchen, next to my convection ovens. As my children hug me tight, Walter's eyes meet mine. He lifts his bandaged hand in a wave and I give him a closemouthed smile.

"Happy birthday, Mom!" Colleen and Kevin chime in unison, hugging me.

"Thanks, guys," I say. "I can't believe you managed to pull this off."

"Everyone pitched in," Kevin tells me.

I run a hand through my hair, realizing the state it's in. "Oh God, Col. I must look a mess."

She eyes me critically for a brief second, then her face softens and she shakes her head. "No, Mom. You look great. I promise."

"Dad's here," Kevin says, a little too casually.

"So I see. I take it you guys had a good talk on your way home."

Colleen nods. "We yelled at him."

"A lot," Kevin agrees. "And he totally let us."

"He wants to talk to you, too," Colleen says.

"I'm sure he does."

Just then, Shane makes his way through the throng with Annabelle at his side. The young girl looks flushed and healthy and is actually smiling. Shane glances at Colleen and a meaningful look passes between the two of them which I pretend not to notice. Then he throws his arms around me and squeezes me tight.

"Happy birthday, Cake Lady," he says. He grabs my hand and pulls me toward the kitchen. "We made something for you. The class."

On the island, surrounded by Amy, Blanche, Carol, Stephanie, Calvin, Jessica, and Francie—all smiling proudly—sits a three-tiered, plum-colored cake, topped with a woman in an apron holding a clipboard and a whisk. The fondant is cracked in many places, the borders are uneven, and the woman looks a bit like a Cabbage Patch doll, but it is the most beautiful cake I've ever seen.

"I love it!" I exclaim, swallowing the lump in my throat. "It's wonderful! Thank you!"

"We won't be winning any *Cake-Offs*," Shane says.

"Join the club," I joke.

"It's a good thing we have two classes left," Blanche says with a cackle.

I look at my students, my children, Izzy, and my friends, and suddenly tears are streaming down my face. I feel the urge to fight them, then think better of it and let them flow.

"You need a drink, *chica*," Izzy announces.

Two minutes later, I have one of Izzy's trademark margaritas in my hand. Someone has put music on—Louis Prima and Keely Smith—and many of the revelers, the kids included, have moved into the seating area to get some pizza and salad.

"So? You like?" Izzy asks, raising her glass.

"You know how I feel about surprises," I say, trying to sound irritated.

"Yeah, I do." She grins.

"Thanks, Iz."

"Happy birthday, Ruby. You want some pizza?"

"Not yet," I tell her. "Soon."

As Izzy heads for the food, I catch sight of Walter, huddled next to the display case. He still hasn't approached me, but when he glances over and sees me looking at him, he immediately straightens and takes a step in my direction. My stomach clenches as he moves nearer.

"Happy birthday, Ruby," he says.

"Thanks, Walter," I return evenly.

"Can we talk for a minute, alone?" he asks. "I don't want to take you away from the party, but—"

"I think everybody will be okay without me for a minute," I say, putting on my brave face. I lead him to the back of the kitchen, down the hallway, and to my office. I turn on the lights and Walter follows me in. I head for the desk, wanting to put space between us. Walter stops in the middle of the room and looks at me.

"This is awkward, huh?" he says. "Kind of funny after eighteen years of marriage."

"'Funny' might not be the word I'd choose," I say. "How's your hand?" I ask.

"The Vicodin helps."

We stand in silence for a few moments and I gaze at my husband. He wears the blue button-down shirt I gave him for Christmas, which brings out the color of his eyes.

"I see you found your shirt."

"In a box in the garage," he says. "Along with the rest of my things."

"Are you surprised?" I ask, a bit defensively.

"I didn't expect you to excavate me from your life so soon. But I don't blame you. I deserve worse." He gives me a meaningful look. "You look good, Ruby. You're a sight for sore eyes."

"Walter—"

"You've been doing great without me."

I think of those first few weeks and how I'd felt like the sky was crashing down upon me. I think of *Cheryl* and my humiliation, of the kids and the mortgage, and the Muffin Top, of not knowing what the hell I was going to do. I think of all the things I wanted to scream at Walter, the accusations and insults born of my outrage. But my anger has suddenly abandoned me.

"I've been okay," I say simply.

"You've been better than okay. The kids told me about your cake class. And the *Cake-Off*? Who would have thought?"

"Certainly not you, Walter."

"Oh, I always knew you had it in you. *You* just didn't know it. I've always thought the world of you."

I can't help but laugh. "That's funny coming from the man who spent the last three months sailing around the world with *Cheryl*."

"It was a mistake, Ruby," he says. "A big mistake. The whole thing." He inspects his shoes. "Cheryl wasn't who I thought she was. And I wasn't who she wanted me to be. Or who *I* wanted to be. In the end, I was just me. By August, I wanted to throw myself overboard." He grins—the old familiar Walter grin. "I bet you wish I had."

"The though crossed my mind," I admit. "But I'm glad you didn't. The kids need you."

"What about you, Ruby? Do you need me?"

Do I? A week ago, I would have said *No way!* I would have told him to take a flying leap. But now, with him standing before me, full of regret, offering himself to me, I am conflicted.

Instead of answering his question, I ask, "Are you really filing for bankruptcy?"

Walter relaxes a fraction, then shakes his head. "No. It was Cheryl's idea to say that."

It figures.

"I got my job back, too. I didn't want to throw myself at your mercy empty-handed." He holds his bandaged hand out to me and looks at me imploringly, and I feel myself soften toward him. This is my husband, the man to whom I promised my life. The father of my children. How easy it would be to forgive him and go back to the way it was before that June morning. We could be a family again. My children would have both parents under the same roof. I wouldn't have to worry about the mortgage or the Muffin Top or adolescent crushes that only end up hurting me. It makes sense. It would be unerringly practical.

"What do you think, Ruby. Can we give it another go?"

Slowly, I wander around the desk. Just as I take a step toward Walter, Jacob Salt appears in the doorway and my breath catches in my throat. His hair is disheveled and there are dark circles under his eyes, and his posture is unusually slouched. His T-shirt hangs casually out of his jeans. But he is even more handsome than I remember.

"Ruby," he says.

My whole body tenses at that one word, not because I am angry with him (which I am) or because he has hurt me (which he has), but because until this moment I didn't realize just how much I missed him these past few days. I've known Jacob less than three months, and I missed him more than I've missed my husband of eighteen years.

"Ruby," Jacob says again, rushing across the worn rug. "I'm so sorry."

"And you are?" Walter asks, barely masking his annoyance.

"Jacob Salt," Jacob says awkwardly. "Ruby and I are—"

"Friends," I cut in. My heart pounds and I suddenly feel nauseous, but I can't decide whether it's the good kind or the bad kind.

"I'm sorry to come barging in like this," Jacob says.

"Izzy told me you were back here. I just had to talk to you. To explain everything. Happy birthday, by the way."

"Excuse me," Walter says peevishly. "We're kind of in the middle of something."

"Jacob, this is Walter."

Surprise registers on Jacob's face.

"Ruby's *husband*," Walter adds.

"Not for long," Jacob says.

"What did you just say?"

"After what you did to her, what do you expect?"

"Wait a minute, just who do you think you are?" Walter puffs up to his full height, but Jacob still towers over him. "For your information, we were just in the process of reconciling when you so rudely interrupted."

Jacob swings his gaze to me. "No. You're not serious. You can't." He puts his hands up in a conciliatory gesture. "I mean, you can do whatever you want, Ruby. You're a grown woman. But really. After what he put you through?"

"This is none of your business, buddy!" Walter says, jabbing at Jacob's arm with his good hand.

"Actually, it's Ruby's business," Jacob says calmly. "And do not poke me again."

Walter brushes past Jacob and grabs my hand with his left. "Please ask Mr. Salt to give us a few minutes alone."

I look at Walter, and at that moment I see it. It's so small, I might have missed it, am surprised I manage to catch sight of it without my reading glasses. A tiny hole in the fleshy lobe of Walter's ear. The stud is absent, but the evidence remains. Walter pierced his freaking ear, probably during some island ritual with *Cheryl*. And suddenly everything he did and all of the things he said to me come flooding back with vivid clarity. My hackles instantly rise.

"No." I shake my head and pull my hand away. "I'm not giving you a few minutes. Not even a few seconds. I've wasted enough time on you already."

"How can you say that?" Walter asks. "We have a life together."

"Which you gave up for *Cheryl.*"

"I told you it was a mistake. And I intend to make it up to you, Ruby."

"Ha!" I fire at him, savoring my renewed anger. "After all you put me through, it would take the whole of the Mesozoic to make it up to me!"

"Mesozoic?" he says confused.

"That period of time when dinosaurs roamed the earth? Sound familiar? Lasted almost two hundred million years?" I clench my fists. "Arg! You are so not shortbread."

"Shortbread? Dinosaurs? What are you going on about?" He waves his good hand dismissively. "I'm talking about *us.* Our marriage. Ruby, you are practical to a fault. You wouldn't throw away eighteen years of happiness—"

"Ha!"

"—for one tiny indiscretion. I know you wouldn't. The day I left, you were willing to take me back. You were willing to do anything to save our family."

I give Walter a cold stare. "That was a long time ago."

"It was not. It was two and a half months ago."

"I'm not the same person I was." I shake my head. "No, that's not true. I am the same person." I shake my head again. "I am and I'm not. The same and different."

"Are you schizophrenic?" he asks with a contemptuous grin.

"Yes. That's right. And neither of me would take you back for all the vanilla in Madagascar. You were right, Walter," I say, feeling my anger ebb once more. "We are not soul mates."

"But you don't even believe in soul mates!" he snaps.

"No, I never did. But I'm trying." I can't help but glance at Jacob. Walter follows my eyes.

"What, you think *he's* your soul mate?" His voice rises indignantly.

"I thought he might be," I reply calmly. "But I was mistaken."

"No," Jacob says quickly. "You weren't mistaken." He nudges Walter out of the way and faces me. "I'm so sorry for disappearing like I did, but my life got crazy complicated, like *Dallas, As the World Turns, All My Children* complicated. And I was so confused and conflicted and I didn't want to drag you into it, and I knew that if I told you what was going on, you wouldn't want any part of it. But I realized how important you've become to me and I knew I had to tell you and let you decide for yourself whether you still want to be a part of my life, or let me be a part of yours. I'm babbling, aren't I?"

"Yes!" Walter snaps.

"Jacob, tell me what's going on," I say.

"Kristen's baby is mine," he says.

"Who the hell is Kristen?" Walter asks.

"I thought she was gay," I say, utterly confused.

Jacob takes a deep breath. "She is. She used our fertilized eggs. From the clinic."

Oh, boy. Pear butter-stuffed pastry triangles topped with peach schnapps and lit on fire until they're nothing but ash.

"That night, when she called . . . Her hormones were going crazy, that much was true. She said she had to tell me the truth, that she hadn't been sleeping because of the guilt, that she couldn't wait one more minute. I felt so horrible leaving you like that, but I just had to process it."

I sigh as understanding washes over me. Jacob is going to be a father, but not in the way he planned. I can only imagine the conflicting emotions that have been plaguing him since Kristen's call.

"I didn't want to add more drama to your life," he says. "I thought it might be better to just let things end. But I couldn't stop thinking about you. I kept remembering that first night, when I told you about my dead wife."

"I don't know what the hell is going on here," Walter says miserably.

"When you touched my hand," Jacob continues, "I knew at that moment I wanted to be with you."

Regardless of the fact that this declaration has been made on the heels of a rather stunning revelation, I feel like my heart is going to burst through my rib cage.

"Oh my God," Walter exclaims, glaring at Jacob. "You're sleeping with my wife, aren't you?"

"So far, just the one time," Jacob says, totally unfazed. "But I plan to sleep with her a whole lot more. If she'll have me."

"This is outrageous!" Walter cries, turning to me. "This is perverse! You're casting me aside for some . . . some . . . what is it you do, anyway?"

"I work for Franchise Funding," Jacob answers smoothly, and Walter's eyes go wide.

"You're our mortgage broker!"

"No," Jacob says, kissing my hand. "I'm *Ruby's* mortgage broker."

"Ruby, seriously," Walter stammers. "Think about this. Think very hard. You don't even know this man. You know me. You know what you get with me."

Walter is right, of course. He's the safe bet and Jacob is the wild card, the unknown. If I choose Walter, I'll go back to the merry-go-round. With Jacob, and this new complication, I'll be on a roller coaster. Rational Ruby would have no problem with this decision—it would be a piece of cake for her. I wonder if I can possibly let go of her. Probably not. She comes in handy in emergencies. But perhaps I can live alongside her and call upon her as needed. It's certainly worth a try.

"You know what I think?" I say finally. "I think I need more Baked Alaska in my life."

Walter furrows his brow. "What does that even mean?"

"It means that you should go have some cake," I tell him. "And one of Izzy's margaritas. Or two."

Walter's mouth opens, then snaps shut. He stares at us, shaking his head, then finally stomps out of the office.

"I thought he'd never leave," Jacob says with a laugh.

"It didn't take him that long last time," I joke.

"Are you sure about this, Ruby? I'd understand if you wanted to call it quits. I'd be devastated, but I'd understand."

"I'm not sure about anything, Jacob. But you know what? I'm okay with that."

"Kristen wants me to be involved. She was never much for the great outdoors. She wants me to take her hiking, teach her to fish . . ."

"*Her?*"

"It's a girl."

"How wonderful," I tell him, thinking of Colleen. "Girls are tough, but worth it."

"I was hoping someday you might teach her to bake," he says, his green eyes shimmering.

I breathe deeply and sigh. "I'd be delighted."

He pulls me into his arms and presses his lips to mine. My body melts against him, and despite my aches and pain and fatigue, I don't think I've ever felt better. His kiss lingers, then he folds my head into the crook of his neck. We stay like that for a moment, breathing each other in.

Jacob pulls away slightly, cups my chin in his hand, and looks down at me.

"I felt really bad about missing *Cake-Off*. I wish I'd been there."

"Me, too," I say.

He kisses my forehead. "Izzy told me about it. I'm really sorry you didn't win."

"Oh, but I did, Jacob," I say. "I won."

Hot Buttered Rum

"Is that you?" my mother asks, pointing to the screen of my laptop.

We are seated on the patio of Casitas en la Mesa, under the shade of an umbrella. Mom giggles and beams at the photo of me from the Franchise celebration. I am relieved that she is so at ease with the computer. In her former life, Mom functioned quite well with technology, but to Maria von Trapp, a computer would be akin to a transporter from *Star Trek*. Still, she is taking my laptop in stride, even experimenting with the touch pad.

"You're quite the dish, aren't you?" she says.

I blush and shrug. "I guess so. Lately."

The late-October day is warm, but a breeze off the ocean cools our cheeks. My kids are back in school. Colleen has taken her senior year by storm. She has already heard from Stanford, and if she keeps her grades up ("No-brainer, Mom"), she will be living in Northern California in less than a year. Kevin is doing equally well, having been voted president of the surf club—an honor for a sophomore—and is busy organizing the Winter Beach Cleanup set for Christmas Eve.

Although I didn't win *Cake-Off,* the publicity from the show, coupled with our website, has turned our business around. For the first time the Muffin Top is thriving. We've added an online ordering system to the website, as well as a Stressipe Blog on which I not only give my recipe, but I describe the circumstances that inspired it. (Like when Walter showed up drunk for our first mediation and my lawyer had to wrestle him for his keys. A triple chocolate cinnamon schnapps brownie and a three-paragraph rant came out of that one.) I have been contacted by an editor from Harper-Collins about a cookbook, and the Food Channel has booked me for another show around the holidays. Unfortunately, with business booming, I was forced to give up my cake class, but my students come by regularly, often donning aprons and lending a hand when we're in the middle of a rush.

Shane and Colleen have begun a tentative relationship which, due to both of their schedules, is limited to nightly phone calls and the occasional weekend date. I don't know what will happen with them, but I'm trying not to worry about it. Colleen is almost an adult, and certainly thinks like one already, and I have to trust her to make her own decisions.

My divorce is not yet final, although it's only a matter of time now. Walter was contentious to start, but his lawyer, the inimitable Miss Stein, advised him not to rock the boat—so to speak—if he wanted me to play nice. He has taken an apartment in town, gone back to his old job, and has decided to try his luck on SoulMate.com. It's funny, but even though I was with him for almost half my life, I can hardly remember what it was like to *be* with him. Our time together has become like a movie I watched once, a pleasant movie—not an Oscar winner or a summer blockbuster—but one that I enjoyed; yet now I struggle to recall the name of it or exactly what the plot was about. But I only wish Walter well. Really, I do.

The patio door opens and Jacob emerges, carrying two glasses of lemonade. I am surprised by how my pulse still quickens at the sight of him. He sets the lemonades in front of Mom and me and sits on her other side.

"Thank you," she says, and rewards him with one of her dazzling smiles.

"My pleasure," he returns.

"You know, you remind me of my son Friedrich. Such a handsome boy. Just like his father."

"Well, thank you," Jacob says, winking at me.

Mom turns back to the laptop. "So, you make cakes," she says slowly.

"I do."

"Like this one?" She points to my Princess Mayblossom cake, which Jacob lifted from the Food Channel website.

"Yes. I made that."

"It's quite extraordinary, isn't it?"

"It's just sugar and flour," I say humbly.

"I daresay it's more than that," she says. "It's like a dream."

"I suppose it is," I agree.

"There's another one here, almost as spectacular," Jacob says proudly, clicking on another button.

"She's very good, isn't she?" she says.

Jacob looks past Mom and smiles warmly at me. "Yes, she's very special."

"Very special, yes. Just like my Brigitta," Mom says. She pats my hand and gives it a squeeze, then returns her attention to the monitor.

I sit back in my chair and watch my mother sip her lemonade while Jacob maneuvers through the website. What I told Walter was true. I am the same and different. I still think of myself as Rational Ruby, but also as Romantic Ruby and

Rock-'em Sock-'em Ruby and Roaring Ruby and occasion-ally Ribald Ruby. I am all of the colors of the rainbow now. Okay, maybe not *all*. But *more* of them. And I owe this to the two people across from me, one I've known my whole life, and the other only a short while. Mom may not remember and Jacob may not even be aware of it, but together they have taught me the most important lesson I have learned.

It's never too late to dream. It's never too late to believe.

READERS GUIDE

Sweet Nothings

QUESTIONS FOR DISCUSSION

1. Ruby has a clever, culinary way of characterizing all the people who come in and out of her life: her estranged husband, Walter, reminds her of shortbread; she refers to her mortgage broker, Jacob, as a baked Alaska. Her daughter, Colleen, is a seven-layer dream bar, who "can be any or all layers at a time." What sweet delicacy would you characterize yourself as and why? Discuss.

2. Ruby admits to feeling that Walter's departure was inevitable: "I never loved him the way he wanted me to." How do Walter and Ruby love differently? Discuss the concepts of comfortable love versus passionate love. What type of love is the best foundation for a long and fulfilling marriage? How do Ruby's and Walter's views on love influence their decisions in life? Is true love a license to love outside a marriage or a relationship?

3. Social media websites such as Facebook can be seen as a way to develop and maintain friendships. However, they can also be viewed as a voluntary forfeit of privacy and an invitation to investigation. Discuss the effect that social media has on the characters in this book. How has it changed the way they view relationships? How would Ruby's social life have

changed without the presence of Facebook? How does social media empower individuals in her community?

4. "I'm frightened of the unknowable future and angry that the past eighteen years feel remarkably like wasted time." What external factors and experiences have shaped Ruby's opinion of divorce and separation? Are failed marriages truly a waste of time? Why do some women see them this way while some see them as just another part of their history? How does Ruby's outlook on her situation change throughout the story? Describe how Ruby comes to terms with the breakdown of her marriage.

5. Issues of physical beauty, body image, and self-acceptance appear often in this story. What effect do clubs like Little Princesses have on the mothers and daughters who participate? What do organizations like this tell us about the values in our society? Which character do you feel is most conflicted with physical insecurities? How does this person combat this lack of confidence?

6. How do the characters in this book overcome their moments of anxiety? Does Ruby's recipe method actually help her during these incidents? How do her children handle their problems? Which character's pressure-management techniques do more damage than good, and why? Whose stress technique do you most identify with and why?

7. Ruby's inner monologue plays a very vocal role in her life. How often does she enjoy the moment rather than over-analyzing the situation? How do men and women differ in terms of rationalizing and living impulsively? Discuss how this outlook on life changes with age and experience. In what ways does this inner voice help or hinder Ruby from achieving her goals in life, love, and business?

8. Ruby's mother has always been an enormous source of inspiration and support to her. Unfortunately, Estelle Simmons's battle with Alzheimer's disease has drastically changed that role in recent years. How does caring for the person who once cared for her change Ruby? How do these visits with her mother help Ruby through difficult times? What part of Estelle's history plays a crucial part in guiding her daughter through an impending divorce?

9. Best friends. Loyal workers. Respectful students. Several strong female characters surround Ruby's life. How do these women help and support one another? Which of these women does Ruby learn the most from and why? What influence does Ruby have on the women around her? In addition to Ruby, which female character undergoes the biggest transformation of her own?

10. Ruby's ongoing struggle with confidence evolves while being a mother, a co-owner of a bakery, and a teacher. Which moments define the development of her newfound self-assurance? Do any experiences set her back momentarily? Which characters assist her and which ones threaten to stand in her way?

11. What does Ruby learn about herself and her emotions during her trip to Sunny Hills Bed and Breakfast with Jacob? How does her intimacy with him compare to the intimacy she shared with her husband of eighteen years? How does their failure to connect that night make Ruby feel?

12. Ruby is faced with the advances of a handsome young student named Shane. How does this make Ruby feel? Do you think her reaction would have been different if Jacob were not in the picture? How would she have responded if her daughter had not met and exhibited feelings for Shane?

What does this admirer mean to Ruby? How do Shane's actions change the way Ruby views herself?

13. What does the story of Princess Mayblossom represent to Ruby? How does this fairy tale echo her life? In the story, what do the attackers on the island symbolize, and why do you think the ambassador chooses to protect the princess from their assault? What major lesson can be learned from this book? What is more meaningful to her: the story itself or the passing down of the book from generation to generation?

14. The anticipation leading up to Ruby and Jacob's first time together is as intense as the lovemaking itself. However, Jacob is immediately pulled away from this romantic encounter by answering a phone call from his ex-wife. How could Jacob have better handled this situation? Where should Jacob's priorities have been after such an intimate encounter? Why do you think Ruby suddenly missed Walter after Jacob walked out?

15. Part of Ruby's journey focuses around making the right bet on a partner. Why do you think it took Ruby so long to realize what she really needed and deserved? Why is Walter so confident that Ruby will take him back after so much time has passed? What behavior does Walter reveal that makes it clear to Ruby that she has outgrown him? Do you think Ruby would have taken Walter back before Jacob entered into her life? Was there ever a point when you feel Walter could have successfully reconciled with Ruby?